All That We See Or Seem

Kristina Mahr

Uncommon Universes Press

Uncommon Universes Press LLC

621 N. Mulberry St.

Berwick, PA 18603

www.uncommonuniverses.com

This is a work of fiction. Names, characters, businesses, places, events, and incidents are either the products of the author's imagination or used in a fictitious manner. Any resemblance to actual persons, living or dead, or actual events is purely coincidental.

Content editing by Janeen Ippolito – www.janeenippolito.com

Line editing by Sophia Heotzler

Proofreading by Sarah Delena White – www.sarahdelenawhite.com

Cover Design by Seedlings Design Studio – http://www.seedlingsonline.com/

ISBN-10: 1-948896-07-9

ISBN-13: 978-1-948896-07-8

For my sister,
who dreamed the dream that inspired this story

Take this kiss upon the brow!
And, in parting from you now,
Thus much let me avow —
You are not wrong, who deem
That my days have been a dream;
Yet if hope has flown away
In a night, or in a day,
In a vision, or in none,
Is it therefore the less *gone*?
All that we see or seem
Is but a dream within a dream.
-Edgar Allan Poe, *"A Dream Within A Dream"*

PROLOGUE

There is a distinction to the sound of skin torn from bone.

There is no music in it, though music can be found almost anywhere. There is music in the breeze, in the trees, in the softly lapping waves. In the creak of the gallows, in the swing of a rope.

In a laugh, in a wail, in a shriek, in a scream.

There is a distinction to the sound of skin torn from bone, but there is no music in it.

The music comes after.

In a shriek, in a scream.

In the victory song before it's carried away on razored wings. Carried into the night, fading into nothing, a shadow of an echo.

The night is darkest in the silence that follows.

CHAPTER ONE

I wake up in the same place I always do, the same sense of dread in my stomach. I keep my eyes squeezed shut and wait. Listen.

The rope swings freely overhead, dancing on the breeze. No body. I open my eyes and am greeted by the full expanse of the night sky, by the stars and the moon and, when the wind sees fit to send it across my vision, the empty noose.

I roll to my feet and start walking all in the same motion. The streets are quiet tonight, but that doesn't mean they'll stay that way. I don't want to be around if something breaks the silence.

Still, I feign tranquility. I settle my features into a pleasant smile and swing my arms in a delicate pendulum motion while I walk. I even hum a light and airy tune, a remembered melody, off-key and quietly.

There is nobody to see my act. The narrow houses lining the street are shuttered, doors shut and curtains closed, and not so much as a sliver of light shines through the cracks. If there are people awake here, they are not making it known.

The act is all for myself. I have spent no small amount of time attempting to lessen the power this place has over me, to keep the dread from spreading from my stomach to my mind and my heart.

Some nights, I'm able to do so. I'm able to hum and swing my arms, sometimes even spin through the streets with my arms flung wide, and I'm able to forget for a few seconds at a time that this isn't a dream—this is a nightmare.

My steps don't falter until the first screech. My right foot forgets how to land properly, stuttering across the gravel in a way that would sting if any of this was real.

But none of this is real. I remind myself of it calmly first, sternly second, desperately third. The third reminder comes as the screams start.

The screeches are monster, piercing and harsh, but the screams are all human. They are frantic and wild, frenzied and terrified, hopeless and…doomed. They are doomed. I clamp my hands over my ears and start running.

I quickly realize that my flight won't matter. I can hear the screeches through my hands, more arriving to join the first, discordant and jarring until suddenly it occurs to my ears that the horrific sounds are parts of a whole. They overlap and blend in harmony with one another, intertwining into a beautiful, haunting song. It calms my heartbeat even though I am still running, even though I can still hear the very human wails beneath its sharp melody.

If I can still hear them now, both the song and the screams, I am too close. I am not nearly far enough. I am going to hear it.

I drop to my knees mid-stride and bury my face in my lap, digging the heels of my hands as deep into my ears as I can, screaming at the top of my lungs until I run out of air. And then I take a deep breath and start screaming again.

In that gap between one scream and the next, just as I inhale, I hear what I had been trying so hard to drown out. I hear the moment, the worst moment of them all, the very precise instant that the screams are cut short.

I fall silent, face still pressed against my nightgown and breaths coming out as gasps. The quiet echoes loudly around me as I repeat my tired litany in my head, over and over again, the same words that have played there every night of my life.

It's just a dream. It's just a dream. It's just a dream.

But it never feels like a dream.

I lift my face and drag my sleeve across my wet cheeks as I pull myself to my feet. I start walking again just as the song resumes, this time victorious and proud. It passes directly overhead, dragging shadows across my eyes. I look up just in time to see a dripping talon glint in the moonlight. I look quickly back down at my feet and curse this world.

My subconscious has never been kind to me. I have never known dreams of sunshine, dreams of laughter, dreams of love. All that exists for me when I close my eyes are nightmares, filled with monsters and bodies and relentless darkness. Glinting talons and killing songs. Tears dripping down my cheeks when—*none of this is real.*

I set my jaw and walk quickly to the wall now, the remembered tune of earlier forgotten, arms held rigidly at my sides, mouth set in a grim line. The victory song reverberates through my mind, settling into my spine and drawing it ramrod straight. I should've hurried in the first place. I shouldn't have pretended this place holds no power over me, when my damp sleeves so clearly make a liar of me. I should've hurried, and maybe I wouldn't have had to hear it.

When the wall finally looms before me, I don't even pause. I reach up to grab a twisting vine in each hand and pull myself up, toes digging into jutting stones and boosting my body higher. I climb quickly, hands and feet requiring no input from my brain to propel me to the top. They have been doing this for over a decade now, ever since I was big enough to do so.

The top of the wall is narrow, only a foot wide. I swing my feet up carefully to avoid kicking the towering monster seated there.

Not because it would feel it.

But because *I* would.

It picks sharply, ragefully, at its feathers. When I was a child, "monster" was the only label I could assign them, the word I would wake up wailing. Flurries of beaks and talons and every shade of blue under both the sun and the moon. Beautiful, almost. Deadly, always. Birds that should not exist. Birds that *do* not exist.

Because none of this is real.

I had found a picture once, in an old book in the library at home. A sketch of the exact thing that haunts my nights, with the word "falcon" assigned to it. The book had said they grow to be about the height of a man's shin bone, but the top of my head does not even reach the beak of the ones in this world. It had said they prey on birds smaller than them, on the occasional rodent, the even more occasional insect.

It had said nothing about humans.

I glare up at the one beside me as I pull myself to my feet atop the wall. I am no longer a child cowering in fear. As aware as I've always been of my invisibility, I used to feel certain that at any moment its eyes would focus on my face, and it would dive, and my skin would be torn from my bones.

It looks out into the city, scanning. The sharp intelligence of its burnished black eyes has always alarmed me even more than the curving beak or dagger-sharp talons of its kind. These are not mindless monsters, killing for sport. They are guards, dutiful and dangerous watchers, set on their task to shred anyone who sets foot outside their homes.

I often wonder what this place is during the day. If anyone is ever allowed to leave, or if the falcons keep the people locked inside, rats in a cage, filling each day with a little more desperation, a little more madness. If that is the case, it's little wonder that occasionally, one gets brave and takes to the streets at night.

Then there are the gallows.

The gallows were empty tonight, but they aren't always. Sometimes, a body swings heavily there. I can hear the difference in the weight of the rope against the wind even before I open my eyes. Sometimes the falcons get to the body before I arrive, and all that is left is an unrecognizable lump of torn flesh and dripping blood. Sometimes they're still there, mid-feast, shrieking joyfully. Sometimes they haven't yet arrived, and the body is swinging there, intact, waiting.

Each possibility is awful, none preferred, and so each night as I fall asleep, I pray that the gallows will be empty.

I stand beside the creature that haunts my every nightmare, looking out at the city. From up here, it looks like a maze, filled with winding alleyways that branch out from the main thoroughfare haphazardly and unevenly. Some of the alleys end abruptly, while others intersect and continue on in an endless loop. The houses are tightly bunched along the outskirts while the shops nestle within. I know these streets so intimately, I can point the individual shops out from here. The blacksmith, the cobbler. The butcher, the tailor. The baker with his collapsed roof, collapsed so many years ago and still not repaired. After rainy nights, I often wonder how much water he has to wade through in the morning to get to his oven.

In the far corner of the city, rising up against the night sky in sprawling splendor at odds with the cramped quarters of the city, lies the palace. It's nothing like the stately palace I call home. This one is sharp and deadly, haunting and dark. It gives no welcome, only warnings to stay away. I sometimes try to peel the night away from it, to picture it in the daylight. It does not lessen the edges of it. Vines crawl up the outer walls, threatening to swallow it whole. The few windows that remain visible through them never show any sign of light, of life. It is as though my subconscious took my beautiful home, with its air of lightness and splendor, and dipped it in darkness and hellfire.

I gladly turn away to face beyond the wall, away from the nightmare city. I'm able to breathe in fully for the first time since I arrived here tonight. The lake is waiting for me, calm and glistening, draped in the shadows of the forest which surrounds it. The moonlight is dazzling there, dancing across the trees and the water like a living thing. I'm more than ready to be on that side of the wall now.

I crouch down and shift backward, allowing my body to dangle from my fingertips for a moment. I let go without glancing down, landing on the same soft patch of moss that always cushions my falls. I lie there on my back and allow myself a moment to blink away the monster's eyes from my vision. I prefer to leave the falcons on their side of the wall, to give myself peace on this side whenever possible.

It isn't always possible, but I try.

I work my way over the slopes and divots in the grass, picking each step cautiously. With each step away from the wall, I remember a little more of the melody I had been humming earlier. The tune as a whole returns to me as I arrive at the lake, at my own mossy bed. Above me, the moonlight wars with the riot of starlight, and both remind me to be thankful that there is at least some light in this dark, dark world.

I sink onto the ground, eyes fixed on the water. This lake has been precious to me since I first discovered it years ago, and the comfort it provides has not lessened over time. It makes me think of home, of safety and of calm. The falcons keep their eyes to the city, leaving this place unwatched and free.

The feather-light tune lilting and weaving through my mind clashes with screams that cut suddenly short, over and over again in my memory. I start humming aloud again to drown out the latter, but when I realize that my tune has taken a turn, shifting into something dark and beautiful and vicious, I stop. There is no returning a nightmare to a dream.

Except for the nights, every now and then, when I see the boy.

I look over my shoulder, hoping, studying the shadows and seeking any sort of movement or sound, but none reach me. The boy doesn't come very often. I can't imagine how dangerous it must be for him to make it through the city each time, to climb that wall and sneak over to the lake, and then to repeat the whole process in reverse to make it home in one piece.

Still...I wish that he was here. I return my gaze to the lake and settle my arms over my bent knees, sighing over the loss of the melody and the loss of the life over the wall. I've heard too many screams cut short in my hundreds, thousands of nights here to count. I rest my chin on my arms and breathe in the night air.

It's been over a week since I've seen him, and I'm starting to get worried. I know that it's silly, to be worried about this figment of my subconscious, but the fear is there nonetheless. What if it was him tonight, frantically running away from the monsters? His blood I saw on the talons as they flew away? I abruptly stop that line of thought. It won't do me any good.

I settle a little deeper into my makeshift bed. I can't fall asleep in this world, although I often wonder what it would be like if I could. Would I dream within this dream? Would that dream be brighter and happier?

Just as I'm resigning myself to a long night of being alone with my thoughts, as though conjured by some combination of my wishes and the shadows of the trees, he appears. My eyes latch on to him, drinking in the cautious way that he moves, the gentle way that he lowers himself to the lake with just his feet touching the water, the wistful way he tilts his head to the sky.

Because the night is so clear, I can make out his features quite well from this distance. The dark hair falling across his forehead, the long lashes spiking shadows onto his cheeks, the slight crookedness in the line of his nose. The set of his shoulders, the curve of his spine. The rise and fall of his chest with every deep breath he takes, as though they're his first of the day, as though he's been starved for the night air. Oh, he is beautiful in the moonlight, as he always is. My subconscious may create some horrifying horrors, but it sure knew what it was doing when it created this boy. I am overwhelmed with relief that he's alive.

I pull myself to my feet and move to sit next to him. I leave a bigger space at first, glance at the side of his face, and then slide over to reduce the gap to a handful of inches. I feel overly desirous of his company just now, grateful for the peace his presence brings me in this nightmare.

He draws circles in the water with his fingertips, and I let myself imagine that he would see the ripples if I were to do the same. I don't try because I know he would not; the water here does not part for my fingers. Instead, I just sit there with him and wish, as I always do, to know what color his eyes are. But there is never enough light, and I never find out. I have to content myself with the shape of them. The depth of them. The steady way they look out over the water.

I can hear the echo of screeches in the distance, but I don't flinch. I feel safer when he is here. The first time I saw him was just a few months ago, but I've come to rely on him in a strangely powerful way. He is the first bit of brightness my dreams have ever held, and I live in fear that he will vanish as suddenly as he first appeared.

But for tonight, I push those fears aside and simply bask in his presence, aware that he will have to leave all too soon. He rarely stays more than an hour or two. Never long enough. The stars always dim when he leaves, but for now, they beam.

"Hello," I whisper, even though I could shout for all the impact it would have.

He continues drawing in the water, circles and swirls and shapes. I try to follow the patterns of his fingers, and I think I glimpse a few that could be letters. I wonder what he's writing. But it's dark, and I can't quite tell. So I pretend he's writing my name, over and over again.

I pretend he's writing it across my skin, that he's chasing goosebumps along my arms, that I can feel it. That I can feel the callouses of his fingertips, the warmth of his strong hands.

I pretend, and I pretend, and I pretend.

Time passes quietly as we sit side by side. Quietly and far too quickly, he suddenly leans back and sighs softly in what I know is his cue. He's about to leave. I get up as he does, standing with him as he takes one last long look at the water. My hand is just a shiver from his, and I wish I could entwine my fingers in his.

But this dream world is full of wishes that won't come true. Of screams that won't stop and boys I can't touch.

Just the one boy.

Just the one who I would give anything, I swear in that moment, *anything*, to touch.

He turns abruptly, shattering the moment. I follow him a few steps, but then I falter. As many times as I've seen him, I've never gathered up the nerve to follow him away from the lake. *Someday*, I promise myself. *There is no risk, nothing to lose from trying*, I tell myself.

This world can't hurt me. Physically, at least.

But my subconscious is not known for kindness, and I don't trust it not to have conjured a sweetheart, a lover, someone who fills the spot that I secretly want in his life.

In the life of this dream boy. I shudder and look down at my feet. I scare myself when I have these thoughts, these hopes in a world that does not exist.

And so I don't follow him. I let him leave. I watch him vanish into the shadows from which he appeared, and I let him remain my one bright spot in a world of darkness.

Chapter Two

The sky has painted itself up beautifully in the face of the setting sun, pinks and oranges and purples colliding along the horizon, reflecting upon the water. I drink in its beauty greedily, the myriad of shades that come between the light blue of the day and the dark blue of the night. I used to hate the sunset, the way it signaled night's approach. I would always plead with whomever controls such things to let the sun stay a little while longer.

It was always a futile wish. I stored it away when I got a little older and learned not to blame the sun for running away from the night. I would do the same if I could.

I tilt my face up into the breeze and let the rocking of my small boat lull my thoughts toward peace, or more directly, toward the memory of the boy in the moonlight. The memory shifts and turns, becoming a daydream. A familiar one. Him turning away from the water, toward me. Him *seeing* me. He reaches a hand out to touch me and I *feel* it. Down to my bones, I feel it. I reach back, and I brush the hair from his forehead, the way my fingers have always twitched to do. My hand lingers, drifts down to his cheek, and I can feel the warmth of his skin.

I want to stay there, in the picture I'm painting in my mind, but unfortunately neither my daydreams nor the rhythmic lapping of the waves on the wood of the boat can drown out Jax. His shouts are only getting louder and more insistent.

"Reeve!" he bellows. I wonder if the wind carried off the title that should come before my name or if he's so vexed that he forgot. I wave a dismissive hand in the air, not bothering to open my eyes.

"Get to rowing, or I'll come in after you!"

I tilt my head speculatively, weighing the sight of him wading into the water against the inevitable cost of his anger. Jax brokers in stony silences and scorching glares, and it usually takes some time for the debt to be paid in full.

With a sigh, I decide it isn't worth it.

I shoot a quelling look over my shoulder in his general direction, and the direction of the other three figures standing alongside him. I can tell them apart even from here, the way Jax stands rigid, nearest to the water, the way Tiven stands with his hands on his hips a step or two to the right of him, the easy way Percius leans against one of the jagged wood pillars on the dock as he runs one hand carefully through his hair, and Demes, of course, pretending to engage a nearby tree in a sword fight. My bodyguards, my keepers. My nursemaids, it sometimes feels like.

But also four of my dearest friends.

Setting my oars to the water, I give the colors of the sky a final few moments of notice while I row to shore, bracing myself for—

"Your father will have our heads if you're late," Jax bites out as soon as I reach the dock.

"No, he won't," I say sweetly in Tiven's direction as he helps me secure the boat, which he answers with only the barest hint of a smile. I can see sweat from the day's lingering warmth beading on his forehead and gleaming through the no-nonsense, closely-shorn hairstyle he insists upon. Though I tell him often that I think a longer style would suit him better, he never acknowledges my advice. "And anyway, I won't be late."

I say it with a confidence which falters when Jax lifts an eyebrow and jerks his head toward the horizon.

"Are you so sure about that?"

Only a sliver of the sun remains visible over the horizon now, dragging the pinks and oranges and purples with it. My stomach knots. It's later than I realized. My father won't have anyone's head, but he will be disappointed in me, and that is far worse.

I swallow my sudden burst of panic, attempting to maintain an air of assurance for Jax's benefit. If his stony silences and scorching glares are unpleasant, they are nothing compared to his smug smiles.

"Well then," I manage in a breezy tone, "if you're so worried, maybe you should stop standing there like a rooted birch and start moving!"

I spin around and take off toward the trees, though not quite fast enough to avoid hearing his answering growl. Demes races ahead of me to take his position on the front flank, and I try not to let it grate at me. He is my protector, sworn to give his life for my safety, and if that means I am never to lead my own way, so be it.

In my periphery, I see Percius take his place on my left and Jax mirror his position to my right. Without looking, I know that Tiv is behind me, no more than a handful of steps away. We run toward the palace as one compact unit, racing the night. Above the castle, a deep azure works to sweep away the lingering sunset hues. My jaw tightens. I push my legs harder, holding my skirts in my hands to keep them from tangling in my haste.

I imagine how we must look from afar, my pale gown at odds with the stark black of my guards' uniforms. They are night itself, cutting through the forest like silent shadows, while I am a darting beacon in their midst, running on similarly light feet but without a sword at my waist, without one hand braced on the hilt of that sword, with my eyes only focused ahead of me instead of scanning my surroundings for danger.

There is never any danger within the palace walls, but my guards scan anyway.

We cut through the informal gardens at the rear of the palace, tucked in the corner to grow wild in seclusion. While the formal gardens are orderly and segmented—roses over there, not crossing the boundary of gardenias over there, not to touch the orchids over there the informal gardens allow them all to blend together and mingle with one another. It is a riot of color, a stunning display even in the ever-dimming sunlight. I force myself to look away. There's no time to get lost in its beauty.

Demes swings open the door to the garden room and passes it off to Jax to hold for me. I point him toward a side staircase, wishing to avoid encountering my father on the main stairs. I make sure never to glance at Jax's face through the entire journey. I'm worried enough as it is without seeing the tension of every passing minute lining his face. Jax does not believe in tardiness, though I am ever proving to him its existence.

"Lord, Reeve," Guin mutters as I slide into my bedchamber. I wave a hand over my shoulder at my guards before closing the door on them, leaving them at their post in the hallway. Then I turn to raise an amused eyebrow at my lady's maid.

"I've asked you repeatedly to leave off the honorific, Guin, not switch my title from 'lady' to 'lord.'"

She rolls her light blue eyes at me good-naturedly and twirls a finger in the air. "Turn around so I can get started on those buttons, my lady. We don't have much time."

I give her my back, pulling my hair over one shoulder as I do so.

"There's no use standing on ceremony now with that 'my lady' business, Guin. You've already slipped up."

Her sigh rustles the hair at the nape of my neck. "You do try the patience, my lady."

"You and Jax should talk sometime. I believe you have some shared opinions."

This time her exhale is a laugh. "Get started on your hair, my lady. It looks in some disarray."

Looking down at where I have it bunched in my hand, I can appreciate her powers of understatement. I lean forward to grab a brush from my vanity and start working it through the snags. At the best of times, my hair is a thick, wavy mess of brown and gold. At the worst of times, it looks like something a bird could feasibly raise its family in.

The way it looks right now, I would not be surprised to see a sparrow eyeing it through the window.

I grit my teeth as I yank the brush hard, cursing the breeze I had been basking in not many minutes before. I should have known it was actively working to tie my hair in knots. I eye Guin's short auburn hair enviously. She keeps it pulled back with a few strategic pins, and it never looks anything but perfectly managed.

"Easy now," Guin cautions. "You'll make yourself bald."

I toss the brush back onto the table. My bedroom is sparsely furnished, with only my bed, a small window seat, my wardrobe, and this dainty dressing table and chair set beside the mirror. I love the openness of it, but right now, I wish I had a settee upon which I could dramatically collapse. "I give up. I need some Guin-magic."

She laughs and helps me step into my pale rose dinner gown. It shimmers in the candlelight of the room, a soft silk that I can't stop stroking with my fingertips. One of my favorite gowns. "I'll figure something out."

"Quickly?" I ask hopefully.

"What choice do I have?"

I toss my best smile over my shoulder to her in response.

She's good to her word, and in only a handful of minutes, she slides the final pin into place as my scalp's screams subside into whimpers and I vow for the several hundredth time to braid my hair more securely next time before I go outside and let the wind have its way with it.

"There," she says, stepping back. "Presentable."

"Such flattery."

She laughs. "You look beautiful, my lady, as usual. Go ahead, take a look."

I take one step toward the floor-length mirror in the corner of the room before pausing.

"Tiv?" I call out. "Time?"

"Two minutes, my lady," his muffled voice calls back through the door.

"All right, then. I suppose there's time to look." I take the final few steps to the mirror and turn to face it. The end result of Guin's labors adds a smile to my reflection. Nobody would know that my hair is a mess underneath her careful knot, and the few strands left free land lightly across my wind-blown cheeks. I suppose the wind did not entirely betray me, I think to myself, admiring the color on my normally pale complexion.

"Once again, you've worked wonders."

"Guin-magic?"

"Guin-magic!" I laugh, swishing my skirts from side to side, reveling in the feel of it against my legs.

Speaking of which. "Tiv?"

"We really should be going, my lady."

"Is Jax turning red yet?" I tilt a mischievous smile toward Guin.

"A very dark shade, my lady."

I think I hear a snarl from Jax.

I step into a pink pair of slippers that match my gown and toss a goodbye and a wave Guin's way before opening the door.

"You weren't kidding about the shade of red." I step into the hallway and study Jax's face as the four of them arrange themselves around me. "You really are going to give yourself a nervous breakdown with all of the worrying you do, Jax."

"*I'm* going to give myself a nervous breakdown?" he mutters under his breath.

I smile up at him before turning my smile on Percius. My heart forgets not to skip a beat. I really ought to be used to him by now.

"Shall we?" Perc brandishes an exaggerated hand forward, toward the main staircase. I drag my eyes away from the tousled dark hair, the deep-set dimple, the eyes that have no color, making them an unfathomable black. It's been some time now since my infatuation with him abated, but still, every now and then, my heart forgets.

"We shall." I echo his grand tone and settle a hand on my hip, taking a swaying step forward. Demes leads the way down the hallway with a little extra swagger, joining Perc and me in our fun. That is, until the first deep reverberation of the dinner gong crawls up the staircase toward us.

Blast.

I press a hand urgently against Demes's back, stopping just short of shoving him forward. He takes the hint. We descend the stairs at a near-gallop, skidding to a halt outside of the main dining room just as the final echo of the gong has made its way through the foyer, fading into silence. I let out a long breath and try hard to ignore Jax's smug smirk.

The dining room is occupied by one massive, endlessly long table, although tonight it is only set for six. It takes me a full minute to walk down the entire length of the table to get to my place, leaving my guards to settle into position amongst the other guards lining the walls.

My father and brother are already seated in their places at the end, identical in expression but nothing else.

I have our father's hair, unfortunately, a plain shade of brown about which nobody would be inclined to wax poetic, while Florien has our mother's beautiful shade of deep chestnut brown. Her hair and her grey eyes, the kind of grey that calls to mind the morning mist and storm clouds.

It's hard to see her in him, knowing that when I look for her in me, I will forever come up empty. Unbidden, a note of the song I'd been humming last night in my dream floats through my mind. I can't catch it, though. It goes as quickly as it comes, tugging at my heart in its wake. It's a song she hummed. A lullaby memory, accompanied by a soft hand on my cheek, the lilac scent of her perfume.

Her hand, her perfume, and always, always a bittersweet longing. A twinge of pain.

They stand when I approach. I slide into my seat beside Florien with a nod at my father.

"I'm happy to see you're on time," he says stiffly. Not unkindly, because my father is never unkind to me. He is unfailingly polite to me, always.

"Of course," I say, as though there was never any question that I would be.

Florien says nothing. I pretend that it doesn't bother me.

The dining room door opens once more, and the three of us stand as my uncle, King Carrick, and his wife, Queen Everly, enter. Along the walls where they stand, the guards bow in unison. I clasp my hands in front of me as my aunt and uncle approach, smiling a greeting at them that is infinitely less forced than the one I had offered my father and brother.

"Oh, do sit down," Everly says as Carrick escorts her to her chair beside his at the head of the table. "This is just a small family meal, no need to stand on ceremony."

Even so, we wait until both she and Carrick are seated before we retake our seats. They may be family, but they are still our nation's sovereigns, and some etiquette is too deeply engrained to be so easily discarded. Especially with my father here, watching. I know that my aunt and uncle would not have minded if I sat. They would not have even minded if I had been late. But my father cares for little else the way he cares for appearances, mine and Florien's as well as his own.

"Hello, dear," Everly says, leaning forward to touch my wrist with her small, warm hand. Although she is over a decade my senior, she appears my age or younger in both stature and openness of expression. Her blonde hair is sleekly secured in a low knot at the base of her neck, no strands falling forth to distract from her piercing aquamarine eyes. Every bit of her appears delicate and breakable, but those who know her know that she is neither of those things. No one would know that she carries the weight of her husband's worries so heavily across her slim shoulders.

I cover her hand with my own. "Good evening, Aunt Everly."

"I feel as though it's been ages since we talked." She leans back in her chair, letting her hand fall away. "How have you been?"

"Yes," Carrick interrupts, settling back in his own chair and draping one arm absentmindedly across his wife's shoulders as his grey eyes, those same grey eyes that Florien inherited, that same morning mist, those same storm clouds, crinkle at the corners. "Far too long."

It *has* been far too long. I had forgotten to look forward to tonight's dinner in the midst of my dread of being in my father's presence. Of having to be perfect, when I have a frustrating tendency to be so very far from that. When I am inevitably, it seems, doing or saying the wrong things. I feel some of that fear shrink away, though, in the face of my uncle's fond smile.

"I'd imagine running a kingdom keeps you rather busy." I smile at them both. "I've been quite well, thank you."

"Excited for tomorrow night?" Carrick nods at the footman hovering near his elbow as he directs the question my way. As he turns his attention back to me, he runs a hand over his dark, uneven beard as I've seen him do so many times since he let it grow out. It has not stepped up to the impressiveness of his father's beard as displayed on so many portraits throughout the palace, but it does lend him a certain youthful rakishness. I suspect that Everly appreciates it more than he does, the way I occasionally catch her stroking it fondly, and him often scratching at it with annoyance.

"Oh yes," I say, shifting forward eagerly. "Very much so."

"Eighteen." Carrick shakes his head in disbelief. "Can you credit it, greyham?"

My father clears his throat. "Time is a swift passerby, Your Highness."

Leave it to my father to remain strictly impersonal when discussing his daughter's impending entry into adulthood.

"Indeed, it is." Something like melancholy drifts across my uncle's face, but it doesn't settle there. I wonder if I imagined it.

Food begins to appear in front of us, carefully arranged on gold-rimmed plates. I have to hold on to my hands to keep them from instantly reaching for my fork. Small family meal though it may be, my father would not appreciate me diving into my food before the king and queen take a bite.

Though his displeasure would likely mean only the barest creasing of his brow, I would feel it as a dagger in my stomach. I keep my hands in my lap. Meanwhile, the footmen clear away the extra place setting, prompting me to turn a questioning glance my uncle's way.

"Were we expecting anyone else tonight?"

He sighs and shakes his head wryly. "I had hoped Thrall would be able to join us, but it seems he won't make it after all. He said that he was needed elsewhere."

I try to keep my relief from showing on my face. Our kingdom's wizard sets my nerves on edge, and I would not be able to enjoy this glorious spread half as much if he was sitting across from me. The salmon smells like heaven, there are generous helpings of cheese on every plate, and the bread is clearly fresh from the oven, warm enough to melt the butter as soon as it touches it. I manage to wait approximately three seconds after Everly takes a bite from her plate before diving into my own.

"I wondered, Reeve," my uncle continues, "what expectations do you have for tomorrow night's ball?"

I flick a glance at my father before returning my eyes to the king, quickly swallowing my bite of bread. "Expectations?"

"Well, you're a beautiful young woman. I'd imagine your dance card will be quite full!"

"I hope so, yes." I must be unsuccessful at keeping my uncertainty off of my face, because Everly swoops in to rescue me.

"What your uncle is trying to say, although not altogether clearly," she directs a fond smile his way, "is that we have rather high hopes of your making a match at the ball."

"Oh!" I say, my brow clearing. "Yes, I have the same hope myself."

I say it simply, honestly, but what I don't say is that it's one of my greatest hopes. It filters through my waking mind with increasing frequency and even follows me into my dream world, in certain moments when I'm sitting at the lake and I'm not alone. Of all of the adventures I envision for my life, none entice me so much as falling in love.

Everly beams at me. "Oh, Reeve, I'm sure it will be wonderful. Every man will be tripping over himself for a chance to dance with you."

I smile at the image and at Everly's enthusiasm.

"I'm glad to hear it, as well," Carrick adds. "Take careful notes on whomever captures your fancy at the ball. I'm sure we can come to an arrangement that will please all parties."

Something in the way he says it makes me feel as though we are agreeing to different things, but I don't have time to linger on the thought for long. This time when the melancholy passes over him, it stays there.

"Your mother would also be glad," he says quietly.

He does not mention my mother. Not ever. That he does so now sets me back into my chair and sends a memory through my mind, a perfumed memory of a lullaby being sung softly in my ear. The remembered tune whispers through my mind. I push it away, back to the corner in which I keep it locked. I only pull it out to study every now and then, always consciously, and I regret letting it slip out just now.

The melancholy doesn't leave Carrick. It lingers even as he turns the conversation to Florien and his lessons, remaining present in the creases at his forehead and the carved lines at the corners of his lips. He has been weighted lately, my normally jovial uncle, weighted and sad in a way I've never seen him. It worries me, and I wonder what, besides the usual hardships of ruling a kingdom, has settled so heavily across his shoulders.

I abruptly wish I knew more. More of what goes on beyond the palace walls, more of what my uncle faces. I live in my own world, here in the palace and in my own thoughts, which suited me as a child, but now I'm nearly grown. Very nearly eighteen. I should take more of an interest. I have always wanted an adventure, an adventure beyond these walls and beyond my own daydreams, so it would behoove me to ask more questions, to understand more of the world around me. Not here, with my father across from me and his ideas of what a woman should and should not involve herself with. He would disapprove of me asking, I'm sure, but Carrick would understand. He would welcome my curiosity.

I vow to ask him at the next opportunity, when he is less busy and his shoulders do not stoop so. The thought buoys me.

As the topic of Florien's lessons drones on around me, I make the appropriate sounds to feign interest before tuning out entirely and turning my mind resolutely toward tomorrow's ball. I envision the swishing of colorful gowns on the dance floor, the orchestra spinning music through the air, the man of my dreams bowing low over my hand before sweeping me out onto the floor.

The man of my dreams…what an apt turn of phrase, I think to myself wryly. I wonder if I will see him again tonight.

Oh, I hope the gallows will still be empty.

Chapter Three

I am not to be so lucky.

When I arrive in the square that night, my thoughts of love are quickly chased back into the waking world by the telltale groaning of the gallows above my head. I swallow hard and listen for the falcons, but I don't hear them. Either they haven't come yet or they've already taken their fill.

I roll onto my stomach and push myself off the ground without opening my eyes. I don't look up. I walk away as swiftly as I can manage, away from the sound of the body swaying in the wind.

Just as I'm about to round the corner and leave the town square behind me, I freeze. The figure swinging from the gallows—what if it's him? The worry whispers through me, then shouts, then wails. I can't stop my feet from turning back around.

I allow myself only the briefest glance, a blink, a darting look, but it's enough to determine that it isn't him—the shoulders are too narrow, the hair is too long, the fingers where they dangle are too short, too stubbed. I have studied the boy closely enough that I believe I could pick him out in a crowd.

The other key fact I determine in that quick look is that the monsters haven't come yet. Whoever it was is still whole, for now. As whole as a person can be when they have been hung by the neck until dead, which I suppose isn't very whole at all.

I wish I hadn't looked. No matter how many times I've awoken to a body swinging there above me in the square, I have yet to become immune to the sight. The unnatural tilt of the neck. The absence of color everywhere but the lips, which are dark in the glow of the moon. The way it still almost looks like a person, the way it *was* a person, just a little while ago.

My stomach performs a complicated roll, sending bile up the back of my throat. I swallow it back down and start walking.

My feet don't take me in the right direction. They carry me toward the wall, but in a meandering sort of way, through alleyways and side streets. I have not wandered in years, but I'm wandering now. I should have learned my lesson from last night, from the moment the screams were cut short by the falcons and the tears streamed down my face, but I continue on in this way. It is some time before I admit to myself what I'm doing.

I'm looking for the boy.

There's no reason for me to believe that he'll be out again tonight. He rarely comes to the lake two nights in a row. But still, I wander, veering down the paths he might take, those with the most shadows and the least space between buildings. The falcons wouldn't be able to track people as easily in these parts.

I hear voices occasionally from behind closed doors. I pause to listen once or twice, but I can never make out more than a word or two. I wish I could, to gain some understanding of the people who live here. When I was younger, I would make a game of it, each night pressing my ear to another row of doors, straining to hear anything at all. It was never fruitful. Either people slept, or they whispered their secrets to one another quietly in the dark.

I truly do not expect to see the boy, so when I do, I nearly walk right past him.

He's leaning against a building, in the shadows of an awning. Quietly alert, he scans the street and the sky over and over again before slipping away to the next covered spot. I shake myself out of my shock and follow him, cautious without needing to be. There is no risk to me out here, but so many risks for him.

"What are you doing?" I whisper to his back as he repeats his long study of his surroundings. "You'll get yourself killed, you know."

He probably does know. I exhale sharply and look down at my feet, frustrated by my inability to ask him why he does this. Why he risks his life by coming out here at night. I dart forward so that I'm standing slightly in front of him instead of behind him, hoping to better see his face. He looks right through me.

I've never cursed my invisibility here before, but I do now.

I jump out of the way as he takes a step forward, loathe to have him pass right through me as though I'm nothing but night air. As though I'm nothing at all. I fall into step beside him and join him in his journey through the streets. We don't stop again until we reach the wall, the stone and vines on it looming above us.

When we pause there—when he pauses there, and I wait alongside him to see what he does next—I turn to raise an eyebrow expectantly his way. This is the part I always wondered about the most. The falcons are spaced fairly evenly along the wall, leaving large gaps only where the wall is so straight that they can see down the length of it without difficulty.

They are not randomly placed. They have spaced themselves out so that nobody can slip past unseen, and the intelligence of this positioning, reflected in those liquid dark eyes, takes them beyond bloodthirsty monsters.

The boy reaches into his back pocket and pulls out a small object before repeating the motion with his front pocket. I crane my neck to see what he's holding. In his left hand sits a small stone; in his right, a slingshot.

He crouches in the shadows of the building opposite the wall, silent as the night. Well, silent as the night is right now. How quickly that can change. I crouch next to him, waiting. I can't help feeling as though we're part of a team, and I decide not to shake myself out of my delusion quite yet. For a little while, I'll allow myself to pretend. What harm can come of it?

The boy sets the stone against the elastic string of the slingshot and pulls it backward. He turns in his crouch to face the alley behind us, holding the small contraption up at eye level. I step to the side, out of his way, though I was never in it.

I catch the way he squeezes his eyes shut a moment longer than a usual blink. I see the way his chest fills with a little extra air, the slow way he releases it. I want to reach out my hand to lay it on top of his. In part to reassure him, and in part because it is what I always wish to do, to touch him in some way. The boy is so clearly aware of the danger in this, but he does it anyway. What is his life like, that he risks so much for an hour or two of sitting by the lake?

He releases the stone. It flies low and fast through the air before hitting the ground and skittering through the gravel. As one, the falcons take flight, falling into the formation in which they always chase their prey. The formation I've seen far too many times, a regimented *V* composed of talons made for shredding and beaks for gouging. They are a team as surely as my four guards are, as composed and intent on their purpose: not protection, but destruction.

The boy presses deep into the shadows and watches them pass.

He waits only as long as it takes the last falcon to disappear from view before spinning and launching himself at the wall. I dash after him, my eyes on his back and the way his thin shirt shows his muscles tense and stretch. He is no stranger to labor, that much is clear.

He has this path as committed to his memory as he had the one through the streets and alleys, feet and hands finding their places without pause or consideration. I watch as he disappears over the top of the wall while I am only a foot off the ground, still trying to shove my foot into the next loop of the thick green plant.

I'm thoroughly frustrated by the time I reach the top, jerking each foot free of the grasping vines and barely resisting the useless urge to call after him to wait for me. I remind myself that I have never had to exercise speed or caution, that my life has never been at risk when I have climbed, but it still nettles me to have fallen so far behind. I watch him vanish into the woods as I try to find a way down the other side that doesn't involve breaking my neck. The ground is nothing but a black sea of sliding shadows from up here, and I have no confidence in what lies beneath it. My moss is not promised here, at this particular stretch of the wall.

Although…the boy made it unscathed. I latch on to that knowledge and start to move, shifting onto my stomach and sliding inelegantly toward the edge just as the falcons return from their fool's errand. One settles uncomfortably near to my hand, its talons gleaming tauntingly. Still, their gleam is a dry one, a bloodless one, and I take comfort in the fact that their prey is on the other side of the wall, the side they do not face.

I drop down and am pleasantly surprised to land in a continuation of the vines from the wall, intertwining into nearly a crosshatch on the ground, catching my body neatly. I roll a little ways, coming to a stop on my back with my hair draped over my face and blotting out the stars. I swipe it away with an impatient hand, clambering to my feet and squinting in the direction I'd seen the boy disappear.

Luckily, I know his ultimate destination. I jog lightly through the trees, dodging between leaning trunks and over fallen logs, skidding to a halt only when I reach the very edge of the copse. I see him standing there, a shadow against the moon. He has fewer sharp edges out here, rounded at the shoulders and the top of his head and his eyelids when he slides them closed, tipping his head toward the sky. I can see the tension leave him.

I approach slowly, mesmerized by the shape of him. The boy lowers himself to the ground, settling an arm across his knees, and I do the same. If I leaned forward just a little bit, extended my hand a little upward, I could touch his face.

I don't lean forward, and I don't extend my hand. He stares out at the water, and I stare at him. This, I think to myself. This is what I wish for my future husband to be like. This is how he would move, how clever he would be, how he would look in the moonlight.

While he draws his shapes in the water, I lose myself in a daydream, one I haven't visited before. One that takes us away from here. I'm in a blue dress, the exact color of the sky just now, and he's approaching me with a curved smile cutting across his face. I have to pause here for a moment, to study his lips and think about how they might look as a smile. Like sunlight, I decide. Like brightness and gold and a new day dawning.

The boy reaches his hand out to me in my daydream, and I slide mine into his without hesitation. He tugs me toward the dance floor, where everyone else is frozen and the music is for us alone. We glide across the floor and past the frozen couples scattered throughout, his feet never faltering and his eyes never leaving mine.

I don't have to wonder what color his eyes are there. The lights are shining down on him, reflecting off of them, and they don't look past me or through me or around me. He sees me, watches me, studies me, the way I see him and watch him and study him now, under the moonlight, a nighttime away from that ballroom.

My hand is hovering suddenly in the air between us, reaching, a hair's breadth from his cheek. *It won't hurt*, I reason, to feel his skin under my hand and trace the curve of his jaw. *It won't hurt.*

I take a deep breath and start to lean forward the little bit necessary, but before my fingers so much as graze the stubble lining his face, I feel an abrupt tug from deep in my stomach, a calling I can't ignore, and with a gasp and a start, I'm sitting up in my bed.

CHAPTER FOUR

I press a hand to my chest and dart a quick look around my room, determining that it is still dark and that there is nothing and nobody in my room to have woken me. I am still trying to shake the feeling of almost touching the boy, the exhilaration mixed with fear, when a light illuminates my curtains and a rumble rattles my bedposts.

Ah. I lift my hand from my chest to my forehead, shoving my hair out of the way. A thunderstorm must account for my abrupt awakening. I fling back the covers and slide out of bed, my bare feet light across the smooth stone floor. I walk quickly over to the rug by the window, my toes curling into the warmth of it as I slide the curtains back silently.

Rain beads against the window as I catch a flash in the distance, immediately followed by another clap of thunder. I sit on the window seat, feet tucked under my nightgown, and lean my forehead against the cold pane.

I can't remember the last time we had a storm here, let alone one of this magnitude. The wizard Thrall is powerful in many things, but none more so than the weather. I'm convinced that no matter what he is doing, he keeps one eye turned toward the sky, studying the wind and the clouds and the sun, tempering and redirecting anything that threatens the order of things in Acarsaid.

We must have rain, so the farming families can raise their crops. We must also have sunshine, of course, and mild winters, and only the most occasional storm, though never powerful enough to do damage. Thrall keeps it all in order, and I wonder why he let this storm through. There must be a reason he didn't push the storm clouds back out to sea.

I trace a raindrop's path down the window, following its zig zags and the way it collects other droplets on its journey. I think about the boy and the way he had held me so surely in my daydream, the way he had smiled and spun me and tugged me in close. Lord, the way he had *seen* me.

I press my forehead harder into the glass and say thank you to the thunder.

It's a relief that my hand hadn't landed on his cheek. The inconsequence of my touch would have hurt, no matter that I had been so certain it wouldn't. My mind whispers that I might have known how his skin felt against mine, but I shake the thought away and tell myself more forcefully that no good would have come from it.

I spare my bed a glance, but I don't return to it. Even if I fell back asleep, I would only return to the square, to the body swinging in the gallows above. The boy would be gone from the lake by the time I made it back there. And anyway, I cannot trust my traitorous hand not to reach out to him just now.

So instead, I reach it over to the small shelf beside my seat and lift a book from the top of it. It is well-loved and coming apart at the seam, so I open it carefully, flipping to the first page and reading the familiar first line.

The worst thing that had ever happened to me in my short life took just three days to become the best thing that had ever happened to me in my short life.

That's all it takes—just the first line—for me to fall headlong into the story. I smile and snuggle down a little deeper into the cushions. It doesn't matter how many times I've read this book, nor how many times I tell myself to broaden my horizons and find something new to read; I always return to this one, to that first line.

It's a powerful thing, a book that reaches through your chest and grabs hold of your heart. It squeezes it, caresses it, whispers magic into it. I can never get enough of the feeling, and so I never get tired of this book.

The ship wrecks, as it always does. I get annoyed with the girl, as I always do. Her spoiled attitude, when all the boy is trying to do is help her. I get annoyed at him, too, for losing patience with her so quickly, when she is so clearly afraid and out of her element. They are the only two survivors of the wreck, after all. They need each other, though they don't see it at first. Anyone with two eyes and a beating heart can see that there is also want beneath that need, though it takes even longer for that to be acknowledged.

My eyelids grow heavy in the drowsy peace of the morning. My vision blurs as my eyes fly over the words, but the story is carved so deeply, so dearly into my mind that I miss none of it.

When the characters have had their adventure and found their love, I sigh and close the book gently. The storm has abated into a light rain, and even that looks unlikely to linger. White clouds chase the dark ones away as the sun stretches its rays and yawns its good morning to the world.

I put the book aside and stretch my own arms, anticipation for the day ahead chasing away the hushed stillness of my night of reading.

I have been looking forward to today since the morning, months ago, when Everly had breezed into the sitting room where I had been idly stitching and said, "Darling, how about a birthday ball this year?"

"Happy birthday, Reeve," I whisper to my reflection in the window.

⁓—✻—⁓

"My lady."

"I know, Tiven, I'm going."

"You said that five minutes ago."

I sigh. Guin has probably already paced a trench into my bedroom floor. Still, I lean back on my hands, burying my fingers in the coolness of the grass as I tilt my head as far back as it can go, squinting at Tiven's upside down figure looming above me, blotting out a portion of the sky.

"Come sit a moment, Tiv. All of you, come sit." When my guards grumble, I shoot them each a look in turn. "It's my birthday."

"Is it now?" Perc drops down beside me and stretches his long legs out in front of him. "We hadn't realized. I'm not sure you've mentioned its approach, oh, I don't know, once or twice a day for the past month."

I ignore his sarcasm and smile over at him before patting the grass on my other side in an insistent thud. "Come on, Tiv, Jax. Dem. It's such a small thing to request for my birthday, isn't it?" I insert every bit of saccharine sweetness I possess into the question. Dem sinks onto his knees in front of me readily enough while I hear Tiv's grumble drop closer to my ears as he sits behind me. I'm not surprised that the ground to my right remains unoccupied.

"Jax." I draw out his name into several more syllables than are strictly required.

"Somebody's got to keep a lookout," Jax mutters, shielding his eyes against the setting sun. "Bunch of lazy-bones."

"It's Lady Reeve's birthday." Demes mirrors my cajoling tone as his smile stretches to his ears. "You really gonna disappoint her, Jax?"

"Yeah, Jax," I ask, closing my eyes as the breeze tugs at my hair. The rain brought with it a chill in the late spring air, but rather than make me shiver, it refreshes me. "Are you really going to disappoint me?"

I open my eyes again not wanting to waste the view of the sunset. I know I have to go start readying for the ball, but I don't want to leave yet. Some combination of the wind, the sun, the rising stars, fills me with immeasurable hope. That things are changing. That something's coming. That adventure is on the horizon, at last, at last.

That my life will not always be precisely this. That I will not always be *hoping* for something better, something more. That I will actually *have* something better. Something more.

I climb to my feet and go to stand beside Jax as my other three guards talk quietly amongst themselves. Rather than look out at the painted horizon, Jax faces the palace, the whole of Acarsaid. It spreads out beneath our feet, a mix of trees and cobblestone roads and the small shadows of people going about their lives. I feel a fondness wash over me for all of them, for all of my country. Even draped in shadows, Acarsaid is a wonder to behold.

"Can you imagine anywhere more lovely?" I'm not sure I direct the question anywhere in particular, but as it is only spoken loud enough to reach Jax's ears, he's the one who answers. His dark hair is whipping around his face in the breeze, the very opposite of Tiven's no-nonsense hair. Jax lets his grow wild, like a pirate from a story book, fierce and untamable. It suits him well, especially when combined with the scar that slashes through his left eyebrow. If I didn't know him, I suspect that he would terrify me.

"From far away, anywhere can be lovely," he says in his deep timbre, always just this side of a growl.

"What do you mean?"

"It is only when you get closer, when you see the lines on a man's face or the callouses on his hands, that you see the true nature of the place in which he lives."

I squint up at him. "Do you think that up close, Acarsaid is a hard place to live?"

He sighs. "I think it is a fair place. King Carrick is a kind ruler and does his best by his people. But who's to say? We only see it from afar."

I look back out at my uncle's realm and think about Jax's words. He's right, of course. I do not truly know what it means to be an Acarsaidian, to be building and growing and holding the fortunes of the nation on my own back. I live behind palace walls, dreaming of balls and being spun across a dance floor.

Well, I amend, *not entirely*. I also dream of dark streets and the groan of the gallows under the weight of the dead. Of monsters who tear flesh from bone and drip blood from their beaks and talons as they leave the remains of what had once been a person, a life not fully lived, behind.

I shake my head to loosen the image from my mind. I will be back there soon enough. For now, it is time to immerse myself in those lighter dreams, the waking ones that feel as though they are shifting ever closer, nearly within my reach.

I turn away from Acarsaid and clap my hands at all my guards. "Come on then, lazy-bones. Really, you're going to make me hopelessly late for my own ball."

Perc swipes at the hem of my dress with one hand, sending me leaping to the side with a yelp and a laugh. They all stand up around me, and now I'm the one draped in shadows. They form a wall around me just like the one that circles the palace, keeping both dangers and the unknown at bay.

Looking around at them, I am filled with gratitude. Tiv and Jax were assigned to my protection when I was just five years old. They were fresh out of training at the time and likely chafing at the indignity of the assignment, but they never let it show. I was too young to question the need for guards, but I have since begun to suspect that my uncle was compensating for the loss of my mother, or attempting to honor her somehow.

Still, when Percius and Demes were added to my contingent the day I turned thirteen, I went to my father on a rare surge of bravery and complained to him about the excessiveness of four guards shadowing my every step. He had crossed his hands on his desk and said evenly, "It is your uncle's wish to see you well-protected. Do you want to go to him and make him think you are ungrateful?"

I had ducked my shoulders and bowed my head, summarily scolded. Nevertheless, I had resisted a little in the years that followed, enough so that one day, the evenness in his tone giving way to genuine impatience, my father had sighed and said, "Okay, then. Which two do you wish to see reassigned?"

I had opened my mouth, closed it, opened it again only to close it once more. In the end, I had no answer to give. I could no sooner select two guards to leave my service than select which two limbs I would most like severed. Though I must admit, on the days when he tries my patience the most, the limb that is Jax feels the least difficult to see severed.

They form a wall, yes, like that around the palace, but the palace wall does not laugh at the palace's jokes. It does not sit on the hard grassy ground at the palace's bequest, nor does it frown and offer comfort when the palace cries.

Still, as we make our way back to the palace, I wonder what it would be like to have nothing and nobody between me and the world.

CHAPTER FIVE

Probably because it is my birthday and for no other reason than that, Guin does not reprimand me for my late return. She merely offers me her warm smile and points me to the chair at my dressing table with the hairbrush in her hand. I groan when I realize what's coming.

She softens the blow of the impending torment by presenting a plate of my favorite raspberry cakes, a gift commissioned by her but prepared by her mother, our head chef. It is rare for the daughter of a chef to become a lady's maid, as family members almost never cross into different professions, but Guin had shown a remarkable lack of talent in the kitchen and an assured wealth of skill as a lady's maid, so Carrick had allowed the exception.

She's nearly through the torture of making my hair presentable - and I'm nearly through my cakes - when I'm surprised by the arrival of my aunt. She comes with her lady's maid, Marla, two footmen, and a beaming smile.

"Hi, dearest." She breezes into my room and wraps me in a hug. "Happy birthday!"

"Thank you!" I smile into her hair before pulling back.

"I thought it might be fun to get ready together." She gestures to the footmen standing slightly uncomfortably under the weight of her own dressing table and chair. "If you'd like."

"I'd love that!"

Her already luminous smile blooms. My aunt could never be described as anything less than beautiful, but when she smiles, I'm certain that there has never been anyone so lovely. She waves the footmen in and directs them to set up beside my table. Marla and Guin get to work on our hair as I fill Everly in on how I have spent my birthday thus far.

From my morning in the gardens to my evening on the hill, it has not differed greatly from the way I spend most days, really. Wandering, teasing my guards, and daydreaming of a future when every day is not the same. I don't tell her that, though. I don't tell her that I've grown restless with my life here in the palace. It would make me seem ungrateful for this privileged life I live, and I strive not to seem so. Undoubtedly there are some who would love the opportunity to spend their days so freely.

Free, so long as I'm within the palace walls.

I push my pensive thoughts aside, a shiver of anticipation running through me as the topic switches to the night ahead. Tonight, my guards will stay on the sides of the hall, at attention with the rest of the palace guards. They typically stay in formation for balls, surrounding me at all sides and effectively scaring off all but the bravest souls who desire a dance. Tonight, I have high hopes of spending the whole of the night being twirled and fawned over by handsome men.

I'm as mesmerized as ever by Guin's talent as she twists sections of my hair this way and that, loosely pinning up strands with what must be hundreds of pins. As a finishing touch, she plucks a midnight blue orchid from the vase on my dressing table and secures it at the back.

"There," she says with satisfaction, stepping back. "What do you think, my lady?"

I turn my head to one side and then the other as a smile spreads slowly across my face. "Guin-magic in its highest form. It's wonderful, Guin. Thank you."

She helps me remove my gown behind my dressing wall as Marla puts the finishing touches on Everly's hair. Everly's blonde hair is so straight and smooth, so easy to twist back in a beautiful knot at the nape of her neck. No strands escape, which is impossible to expect from my wavy masses.

"Do you have a preference in terms of suitors tonight, dear?" Everly calls over the wall as I step into my ball gown. "I'll need to know whom to introduce you to!"

I consider her question as Guin starts in on the tiny buttons along my spine.

"I suppose I most envision myself with a man not too much older than myself. And...dark-haired, I think. Taller than me, but not so much that he towers over my head. Lean, so I know he is not entirely idle. And kind. I'd hope for him to be kind."

I can hear Everly smile through her words. "Goodness, you do have a vision in mind! Kind, dark-haired young men, lean and not too tall. I shall be sending any I encounter your way."

I peek my head around the dressing wall. "Please do!"

We laugh together as Guin declares me fully dressed. I step around the corner and freeze as my reflection comes into view.

"Oh, Reeve," Everly sighs, clasping her hands under her chin as Marla finishes buttoning her sleek forest green gown. "You look radiant."

"You truly do, my lady." Guin walks around me in a slow circle, straightening the gown here and pinning back a strand of hair there, but my eyes do not leave my reflection.

I barely recognize myself. If I squint hard enough, I can see myself in the eyes, in the tilt of the chin, and the barest indentation of a dimple in one cheek, but if I unfocus slightly and don't seek out the pieces of me, it's as though I'm studying a stranger.

My dress is the very shade of the orchid in my hair, the blue of the night sky when there are no clouds to block the stars. The bodice dips lower than any dress I've worn before, although not so much as to completely throw modesty to the wind. The sleeves begin at the very edges of my shoulders and slip down only a few inches, and with my hair up, an expanse of skin is visible across my neck and collarbone.

"One final touch." Everly comes over to me as I shift lightly from side to side, watching the dress sway with my movements like a bell chiming out the hour. The candlelight in my room reflects off of an object glinting in her hands, and my breath catches in my throat as she places it gently around my neck.

"It belonged to your mother." She finishes clasping it and steps back so I can see the finished effect. I blink hard and try to mask a tremor, the past tense ringing in my ears. I have to swallow more than once to push aside the lump that has formed in the back of my throat.

The chain itself is simple, but at the end of it sits a diamond rimmed in garnets, shaped like a heart, and roughly the size of an acorn, dipping neatly into my collarbone. I can't take my eyes off of it. I feel for a moment that if I were to let my eyes travel up, to the wearer of the necklace, I would see her face there instead of mine. Her laughing eyes, her warm, close-lipped smile, the dimple in which

I used to rest my child-sized finger, just at the corner of her lips.

"Have you been up to see her yet?" She asks the question gently and unobtrusively, but I flinch anyway, eyes flicking down to the tips of my heeled shoes.

"No," I say quietly. "Not today."

"It might help," she offers.

It might, I think to myself, but it will also hurt.

It always hurts.

I shake off my melancholy and shift my gaze back up, to the dress that I envisioned wearing when the dream boy put his hand in mine. I start at the realization that I had not been describing a generic vision to Everly; I had been describing him. His lean form, his dark hair, the kindness I imagine in him as he traces letters in the water. I try to shake his face from my thoughts. He is making himself rather at home there these days.

But tonight is not for the dreams that can't come true, I remind myself. Tonight is for the ones that can.

CHAPTER SIX

I tug the bodice of my dress up yet again, although I know by now that it does not get any higher. What I had considered womanly and beautiful in my bedchambers has now become a display window through which men feel free to look their fill. Another man with a leer for a smile directs his introduction to my chest, perhaps forgetting that my response will not come from that region. I decide to wait until he remembers that I possess a face.

It takes him several seconds. Unfortunately, I had promised him the next dance, so once he looks up, I allow him to escort me to the dance floor. I plaster a smile on my face that shifts into something far more real as I lose myself in the simple melody of the orchestra. Thankfully, it's a fast-paced tune, and—I find myself subtly checking my dance card to remind myself of his name—the Earl of Pennick is not given the proximity necessary to continue his ogling on the dance floor.

When the song ends, I'm a trifle out of breath and silently apologizing to my feet as they scream in protest at my heeled shoes. I try to keep from limping as the earl escorts me back to the edge of the room where my father and brother stand. He bows over my hand

and looks up as though to say something, but his eyes get stuck some distance below my face once more. When he finally looks up the rest of the way, his eyes drift a little to the right, and he takes his leave of me quickly, to my relief and surprise. I glance over my shoulder in the direction his eyes had wandered.

Jax is wearing an impressive glower that follows the man as he scurries away. I smile at the reassurance he gives from his position there along the wall before allowing my eyes to roam in search of my other guards. Demes is easy to spot with his shock of red hair, standing near the ballroom entrance. When I catch his eye, he offers me his easy smile, a different form of reassurance than Jax's glare, but effective in its own way.

Tiven is also easy to spot for his size alone, taking up space near the terrace entry and towering above the guards on either side of him. If I'm not mistaken, he's also leveling Pennick a rather ferocious scowl of his own. Though they may not be by my side tonight, my guards are most certainly still *on* my side.

To find Percius, I need only look to where there is the largest group of women. Though he is a guard and supposed to blend into the background strictly by nature of his profession, he is too startlingly handsome to blend in anywhere at all. If I didn't know him so well, I'd think he was indifferent to the attention being paid to him by the ladies whispering behind their hands, but I can make out the barest smirk twisting his lips. He knows, and he enjoys it.

When he catches me looking, the smirk vanishes. He straightens and sends me a small nod of acknowledgement before looking forward stoically. I swallow a laugh at his expense. He tries so hard to hide from me the side of himself that is a young, handsome man, just under thirty and desirable to any woman in possession of eyes.

I don't bother telling him that I am also a woman with eyes, eyes which can see the way those women look at him and the way he sometimes looks back.

All guards accounted for, I turn back in the direction of the dance floor and am surprised to find my gaze level with a man's chest not three feet away. My eyes drift up, up, up and collide with a pair of green ones, dancing in the candlelight and seemingly aware that they are in the process of removing my breath from my lungs. The owner of the chest and the eyes bows deeply before me as Everly stands at his elbow with an irrepressible smile, her blue-green eyes clearly dancing to the same tune as those of the man beside her.

"Reeve, may I present Lord Arden Velasian, the Marques of Rynfall and future Duke of Baewar. Lord Velasian, my niece, Lady Reeve Lennox."

I try to regain my equilibrium as Lord Velasian lifts his head just the slightest bit, just enough so that his eyes are peering up at me through his long, gold-tipped lashes. He must practice that look in the mirror, because there is no way he can simply pause right there, the green of those eyes shining through the curve of those lashes, and not be aware of the effect.

When he straightens, I see the full extent to which Everly has failed her assignment.

Kind, dark-haired young men, lean and not too tall, I had said.

Even in my heels, the top of my head does not reach his chin. Although his hair is perhaps a dark shade of blond, it is not *dark*. His eyes don't shine with kindness, but with something dangerous and delicious and intriguing. He is at least lean, I allow, as my eyes wander down the length of him of their own volition. When they make their way back up to his face, he's smirking at me with an arrogance that can only come from a lifetime of female eyes wandering down him.

I sternly remind myself to blink.

And then his name sinks in.

Lord Arden Velasian. I shoot a startled look at my aunt, but her only response is a quick wink and a step backward before she turns deliberately to Florien, leaving us to our conversation. Lord Velasian's reputation precedes him. That she is introducing him to me, or that she is even allowing him within a hundred yards of me, quite surprises me.

As the man is standing before me, though, reputation and all, there is nothing for it but to curtsy and smile.

When his gaze tracks my curtsy by letting his eyes rest in the region just below the fall of my necklace, the swath of skin I had been trying and failing all night to shield from men's eyes, my smile falters and I can't help rolling my eyes. *Honestly.*

He catches my eye roll, and his own smile wavers for the barest moment before shifting into something that seems more genuine, less practiced. He appears amused by my annoyance.

"Lady Reeve, it is a pleasure to finally meet you." His voice is deep in a shivery way, with a handful of gravel thrown into its depths. I forget my annoyance in an instant. All I want is for him to keep speaking.

"And you as well, Lord Velasian. I've heard much about you."

"Have you now? All good things, I hope."

He steps forward with no small degree of smug swagger, forcing me to lift my chin up if I have any hope of keeping his face in my line of sight. He towers in a way I warned Everly was not my preference in men, but I decide that he warrants a chance through my aunt's recommendation, if not the recommendation of his face and his body and that smirk playing across his lips.

"Mm," I murmur noncommittally, enjoying the way his smile

slips a little again.

"Not wholly reassuring." His voice has not lost its smooth confidence, at least. "Tell me all about it over the next dance?"

I check the dance card at my wrist. "I'm afraid the next dance is promised to Lord Roneldon, my lord. And the ones after that are taken, as well." My regret is not feigned. I would not have minded more time spent with that face above mine, with that voice in my ear. However, the dance card is essentially sacred law at a ball. To renege on a promise to dance would be a grave insult.

He twists his mouth into a grimace, shuddering in mock horror.

"Come now, have you met Roneldon? He can't see his own toes to know to avoid treading on yours." He steps to my side and leans down conspiratorially, pointing toward a large man across the room. "I assure you, you won't leave the dance floor with fewer than three broken toes."

I smile a little at that even as my heart stutters through its next beat or two due to his proximity. I look at Lord Roneldon, glance down at his name on my dance card, and then I make the mistake of looking up at Lord Velasian. It's a mistake because as soon as I do so, I find myself caring less about what I should do and more about what I *want* to do. I want to dance with Lord Velasian. And so I find myself saying, "All right, then. You may have this dance."

My acquiescence really sets his eyes to dancing, the blazing candlelight of the ballroom reflecting off of them so that they look like dew-soaked grass, green and molten. I find myself mesmerized by the effect, by all of the pieces of him that form this unquestionably attractive whole. I'm not sure I've encountered a more handsome man.

And that's saying something, as I spend my days with Percius to my left.

My guard could not be further from my mind, though, as I slide my hand into the crook of Lord Velasian's proffered arm. All of my thoughts and attention are on the man whose body jostles lightly against my hip, who whispers in my ear as we approach the dance floor.

"I'm truly doing you a favor."

I shoot him an amused look. "Is that so?"

"It is, indeed. Your toes will thank you."

His breath tickles my ear, warm with a touch of whiskey. The man positively radiates charm; I think he must flirt as easily as he breathes. I look forward to this dance in a way I haven't since the beginning of the night. Before my first partner took me—or rather, my breasts, for all that he ignored the rest of me—on a spin around the dance floor. I wouldn't confess as much to Lord Velasian, but I had earlier watched as Lord Roneldon swung his partners around the dance floor as if they were wayward sacks of flour and had not been looking forward to the experience.

The orchestra slows into a waltz just as we reach the floor, and I say a silent thank you to the maestro for his timing. If ever there had been a moment for slowing the tempo, this dance, with this man's arms around me, was precisely the right moment.

Lord Velasian has a remarkable ability to make me feel as though I am the only woman in the room, regardless that his reputation informs me that there is no such thing as "the only woman" where he is concerned. His eyes stay locked on mine as his sure steps guide me in time with the melody, as though we are notes on the orchestra's sheet music. He does not falter, and so I don't either. We spend most of the dance in silence, his eyes locked on mine even as mine occasionally fluster and dart to his shoulder. The dance must be nearing its end when he finally speaks.

"Are you going to tell me what you heard about me?"

His question startles me out of the music. "I'm sure you've heard the rumors yourself."

A tilted smile. "I want to know what *you've* heard."

"Me, a perfect stranger?"

"You, a perfectly *beautiful* stranger."

Oh, he does it so well. The compliment, the smile.

My answering smile is pointed. "Very well then. I've heard that you devote your days to drinking and gambling and your nights to more of the same, although the latter also include seducing every wed and unwed woman of the court. It's said that your father alternates between despairing of you and bursting with pride."

He throws his head back in a bark of a laugh, drawing looks from around the dance floor and beyond. It takes me until then to realize that we have been the center of attention for some time now. "You don't mince words, do you?"

I sway slightly as he slows our steps, the violins drawing out the final handful of notes. I'm not sure how much of my imbalance is the punch I had sipped earlier and how much is that gleam in his eyes.

"I don't hear any denial. Are the rumors true, then?"

He pulls me closer even as we should be stepping apart, the song at an end. When he leans down to whisper in my ear, I'm very conscious of his hands at my waist.

"Every one of them."

He steps away and joins in the applause as the partners shuffle and the orchestra strikes up a livelier tune. I have to take a deep breath to clear my head from his words so close to my ear, shivering up my spine, before I allow him to escort me back to where my next dance partner will meet me.

"Lord Velasian," I begin to say as I let go and step back into my place beside Florien.

"Call me Arden," he says warmly, and I see it there plainly, the reason so many women have fallen at his feet.

"Arden," I start again, his name uncertain on my tongue. "Thank you for the dance. And I suppose my toes thank you as well."

His eyes crinkle at the corners as he bows over my hand. "I assure you that the pleasure was all mine. Happy birthday, my lady."

"Reeve," I call after him as he starts to walk away. "You may call me Reeve."

He turns just long enough to nod and wink before swinging back toward the crowd, disappearing in its midst. I have only seconds to regain my composure before my brother turns to me.

"No," Florien begins, instantly setting my jaw to tightening. "Poor choice, Reeve."

"Hello, Florien," I say grandly, tilting my chin into the air. "Why yes, I am having a splendid birthday, thank you for inquiring."

His shoulders slump a little. "Apologies. Happy birthday."

"Thank you."

He promptly resets his shoulders. "But honestly, Reeve, Velasian is bad news. You ought to avoid him."

"Oh, calm yourself, Florien. It was just a dance."

"I saw the way you were looking at him."

I feel my cheeks flush. "Did you now? I would have thought you had more important things to occupy your time these days than taking note of how I may or may not be looking at someone."

Once upon a time, I would have listened. There is nobody I would have listened to more attentively. I would have believed that he genuinely cared for and worried over my well-being, and I would have taken that concern into consideration.

But that time has long since passed. Now he is my father's miniature, and I am certain that his only concern for me is for my reputation, and how my association with Lord Velasian reflects upon our family.

He has the gall to huff in annoyance. "He drinks, Reeve, and gambles, and leaves a trail of broken hearts in his wake. He's trouble."

"He was nothing but nice to me." For the most part. "I've heard the rumors as well, Florien, but I prefer not to judge him on hearsay." Never mind that the man in question confirmed the rumors to be true. "And anyway, it's no concern of yours."

Florien opens his mouth, more protests forming on the tip of his tongue, but I'm already turning away and wiping the glare from my face before it can entrench itself there. My next dance partner is approaching, and it's my birthday—there is no room in this night for the stranger my brother has become.

CHAPTER SEVEN

Several dances later, I'm seriously considering whether anyone would notice if I went the rest of the night barefoot when Everly approaches with another man in tow. This one does not have the instant appeal of Arden, but he does have darker hair and less of a towering stature. Furthermore, as he gets closer, I note that his brown eyes are soft and warm—I might even say kind. They also hold a hint of nerves that further softens my opinion.

I smile reassuringly at him before looking to Everly for introductions.

"Reeve, dearest, I believe Lord Delavar has your next dance, but as you haven't been introduced yet, I thought I might do the honors. Lord Delavar, this is my niece, Lady Reeve Lennox. Reeve, this is Lord Willis Rowe, Duke of Delavar."

Delavar. The name sounds familiar, but I can't quite place it. I watch carefully as he bows, and as I drop in an answering curtsy, but his eyes do not once stray below mine. Impressive. I give Everly a mental nod of approval even as my eyes drift over Lord Delavar's left shoulder, and then his right, seeking someone whose eyes *did* wander, and glitter, and unleash butterflies in my stomach.

I find him easily, in the midst of the only circle of women in the room larger than the one by Percius. I sigh and refocus on the man in front of me.

"Lord Delavar, a pleasure. This dance is indeed yours."

"I have been looking forward to it, my lady. Please, allow me to escort you."

He holds a very proper arm aloft, keeping a very proper distance, and I remind myself that this is how dances are supposed to be. This is propriety as it's been ingrained in me since childhood, and the way Arden had held me, the way he had leaned down to whisper in my ear, had been highly improper.

Our dance is a jig, sufficiently fast-paced to make my feet resume their protests. The nature of the dance is such that Lord Delavar and I are rarely next to each other, only clapping one another's hands occasionally to then spring back amidst the rest of the dancers. Still, at every meeting, he offers me a sincere smile, and I decide that he certainly isn't an unattractive man. His face is a bit round, and his hair flops about quite a bit with his movements, but the kindness in his eyes reminds me of dipping my toes in a calm lake. Not at all the headfirst tumble into a raging monsoon that Arden had inspired.

And really, isn't the calm lake preferable to the raging monsoon?

I have a flash of a memory of a different calm lake, one that *is* preferable. One that would be preferable for the company it provides. If it was real.

If *he* was real.

I resolutely pull my mind back to the present, to reality.

As the dance finishes and he escorts me back to my place, I wait patiently for him to say something. When it's clear that words are not forthcoming, I pull a handful out of my ever-full cache of small talk.

"You're a splendid dancer, my lord. I hope you've enjoyed your evening thus far."

He clears his throat. "I have greatly, my lady, thank you. I hope that you in turn are having a wonderful birthday."

"I am, thank you. It's everything I dreamed of."

This is how conversations should be, I remind myself. They are supposed to be trivial and light. If I am a trifle bored, it is only because Arden shook me a bit to the side, just outside of my normal expectations. I need to readjust back to the norm, to where Lord Delavar is a perfectly nice man who did indeed dance well and is perhaps only a bit too shy to continue on in our conversation.

He takes his leave of me so quickly that I have to decide whether or not to be offended.

I decide not to. He really did seem quite shy. And Jax is still over my shoulder, with lord knows what expression directed this way.

I turn to make my way over to the punch table, the effects of my earlier glass worn off and my throat positively parched from dancing, but before I reach my destination, I catch a glimpse of Lord Roneldon barreling toward me. His weight shifts from side to side with every step, and he doesn't even attempt to circumvent others who might be standing in his path; his stomach proudly parts the crowd for him.

My mind races, considering and discarding ideas of what to do, what to say when he reaches me. I owe the man a dance, and if he comes to collect, my feet will never forgive me. In the end, my instincts take over—I turn to make a run for it. In so doing, I collide headlong into a hard, male chest, which would have seen me careening backward and landing unceremoniously on my rear had a hand not shot out to grab my arm. I take a moment to steady myself, still feeling a strong instinct toward flight, before glancing up at my rescuer.

Arden has one eyebrow lifted while his free hand, the hand not radiating warmth through my dress and my skin and possibly my very bones, lifts a glass to his lips.

I shoot a look over my shoulder at where Lord Roneldon is getting ever closer before looking back up at Arden frantically. He flicks his quizzical gaze over my shoulder and spots my predicament instantly. Shifting his hold from my upper arm to my elbow, he turns me toward the terrace doors.

"Come now, let's get you some fresh air."

He escorts me quickly through the crowd while I wave away any concerned inquiries along the way with smooth words and reassuring gestures. I tell them all that I have a headache from so much dancing, and I ignore the way their eyes turn knowing when they see Arden beside me.

I know them all, I suppose, but I also don't know any of them. Everly used to try, on my behalf. She would invite girls of around my age over for tea or some such trivial thing, and I would try, really I would, but I would also be making faces at my guards to try to get them to laugh, and looking longingly out the window, and...my mind would wander. I would always want to be somewhere else, talking about something other than dress styles and flower arranging. Looking back on it, I wish I'd tried harder to get along with them. I'm sure there were some I could have truly been friends with. Now it feels too late. Now they all have their small groups, and they all know one another, and I am on the outside looking in.

So I pretend I cannot hear the way they whisper as I pass them by.

Tiven catches my eye just as we reach the doors. He seems reluctant to swing them open for us to pass, but I try to convey with my eyes that I am quite all right and that he needn't worry. I add a reassuring nod and smile to the message, and he opens the door as slowly as he can possibly manage.

I don't miss the way he keeps the door partially ajar instead of closing it behind us. Rather than be annoyed, I appreciate his ever-present concern for me.

The terrace is bordered by luminous lanterns every few feet, spreading a warm glow that is far less forceful than the light of the hundreds of candles in the ballroom. If I lean over the terrace railing far enough, I can see the fireflies flickering greetings to one another in the garden below. I smile a little in a greeting of my own and tilt my head back, into the delicate evening breeze.

The dark of the night pulls my thoughts back to the place I'm trying to avoid. I want to stay here, and now, but my subconscious calls to me. It reminds me of someone else. Someone I wish I was standing on this terrace with, but someone who is not flesh and blood. He is beautiful, whoever, wherever he is, in different ways than the man beside me. He steadies the roar inside of me instead of shaking it up. He is—

Not real.

Lord, Reeve, I chide myself. *Stay here. Stay now.*

"Aren't you going to thank me?" Arden leans back against the railing beside me and takes another generous sip of his drink, his proximity grounding me in reality.

I suppose I must. "Thank you."

"I daresay 'rescuer of damsels in distress' was not one of the rumors you heard about me," he muses.

"It most certainly was not," I laugh. "'Creator of the distress damsels find themselves in,' more accurately."

"Ah well," he sighs dramatically. "Can't win 'em all."

I turn to squint up at him, but the glow of the lanterns flickers in the breeze, sending shadows across his face so that I cannot fully read his features. Still, I hear in his tone and see in his stance enough to realize something.

"You like your reputation, don't you? You actually like it."

He shrugs carelessly. "I live my life for one purpose: to enjoy it. To hell with what anyone else thinks of it."

I shake my head in amazement, and he shakes his head right back in mock seriousness.

"What about your father? I assume he has opinions on it."

"He believes I should get my wild ways out of my system now, so that once he passes on and the dukedom settles on me, I can hunch over my desk and crease my forehead worriedly and spend the remainder of my life immersed in responsibility and tedium."

"You sound thoroughly enthused by the prospect."

Another unconcerned shrug. "When it comes, I will meet it. For now, I'm living as I wish."

"And what of marriage?"

Arden flicks a glance down at me, and I'm not sure if I imagine it or if he's moved a little closer. He takes another sip.

"When it comes, I will meet it. For now, I'm living as I wish."

I shake my head wryly at him. "Even more enthused."

I'm beginning to think his most natural facial expression, the one he falls into when nobody is looking, is a smirk. "I make no secret of the fact that I should like to avoid that particular circumstance for as long as possible."

"Spoken like a true romantic."

"Romance has no place in marriage."

I laugh out a scoff. "There is no better place for romance than marriage!"

Arden's smirk softens at the edges. "Ah, so *you're* a romantic."

I straighten my shoulders and lift my chin against his scrutiny.

"You're young yet," he continues softly. "Full of fairy tales and optimism, no doubt. I'm sorry to tell you, my lady, that in real life, love is not what you've been promised."

"I've seen it." I think of Carrick's arm across Everly's shoulder, her hand lifting to stroke his cheek. "I know that it's possible."

He reaches out to lightly brush a strand of hair from my face, letting his hand linger there. His smile is surprisingly gentle, without its usual trace of arrogance. "You're very beautiful, you know."

I swallow hard. I feel utterly young and out of my element with his hand on my cheek, my own hands twisted in the fabric of my gown.

"Thank you," I whisper.

I'm sure then that Arden is going to kiss me. He leans forward an inch or two, his hand still touching my face lightly. I feel his breath land hot across my lips, and then, at the last second, I turn my face away. His lips land on my cheek. They linger there for a second, and then he steps back with a short exhalation of a laugh. I look down at where the toes of my slippers peek out from under my dress and wonder what just happened. I hadn't meant to turn my head.

"Smart girl," Arden says quietly. I look up at him through my lashes as he stares at me with an inscrutable expression. The night breeze ruffles his hair and makes him seem younger somehow, for just a moment. Then he silently offers his elbow, and after only the slightest hesitation, I loop my arm through his. He walks me back into the bustle of the ballroom and bows over my hand briefly before disappearing into the crowd. I think about calling after him, but I don't. I don't know what I would say.

Later that night, when the palace is quiet and I'm alone with my thoughts in the comfort of my bed, I replay those moments in my mind over and over again. Him, leaning down to kiss me. Me, turning away. Him, disappearing into the crowd. Me, left standing alone in the middle of it all.

CHAPTER EIGHT

Memories of the evening follow me into my dreams. I open my eyes to the empty rope, but for a moment, all I see is Arden. I can feel his hand on my cheek. In the wind, I hear the soft way he'd called me beautiful. But when I blink, all I see is him walking away.

Why had I turned my head from his kiss? I search my memory as I climb to my feet, reaching deep into my thoughts to find whichever one had compelled me to turn away. I can't find a conscious thought from that moment, and so I think it must have been instinct. What instinct, though? And why? That would have been my first kiss, and I can think of worst first kisses to be had than one from Lord Arden Velasian.

I am surrounded on all sides by shuttered windows and winding alleys, as I always am, but I have no desire to wander tonight. Not even to try to find the boy. I trudge to the shadows, away from the square and toward the alley which will take me most directly to the wall. My mind is too full of churning memories, too full of Arden's face near mine and a litany of recriminations, to hear the footsteps until I'm nearly upon them. I freeze mid-step and listen. They must be just on the other side of this row of shops, intersecting this street only a few yards away.

Whoever is there is making far too much noise. I can hear each footstep crunching against the gravel, and if I can hear it, so can the monsters. The footsteps are unsteady and slow, too slow. They have no hope of getting away.

I know all of this. I know it from years of experience on these streets, from a lifetime of listening to people get torn to shreds here. I tell my feet to turn away, to run, but then I hear a sound, no more than an inhalation, sharp and laced with pain, carried over delicately and carefully by the wind and tilted into my ears as though addressed to me directly. It should never have been able to reach me, but it has, and I cannot unhear it.

Instead of turning, instead of finding another way to the wall, one that will take me far away from the sounds of this person's death, I take a step forward. And then, I take another.

There is nothing I can do, I tell myself sternly. *There is no reason to look.*

I look anyway. I reach the intersection and look to my left, and there she is, haltingly making her way down the alley. She drags one leg behind her, leaving a dark trail of blood in its wake. The moonlight glints off of the blood in the same way it sparkles over the lake on the other side of the wall, but it glistens ominously instead of reassuringly. From the looks of that stream, she's been losing blood for some time now.

I shouldn't have looked. Now I will know whose screams are cut short, whose blood will drip from the monsters' talons, in whose death the monsters will triumphantly rejoice. It did neither of us any good for me to have looked. I cannot change what's about to happen.

I take a small step to the side, trying to convince my feet to take me away from here, somewhere I won't be able to hear it happen. My bare feet crunch softly against the gravel.

My steps are never careful here. They have never needed to be careful here because I have only ever been invisible here.

So it does not make sense when her eyes shoot up to collide with mine. To meet mine. When I stagger to the left, back toward the shadows, they follow me. They track my movements. As she gets ever closer to where I now stand frozen, they do not leave mine.

"You need to get out of here," she mutters through gritted teeth as she passes right by me. She shoots a glare over her shoulder at me when I don't move. "Go, now."

I take a stuttered step in her direction, and then several more as I fall into step with her.

"You can see me?"

Her forehead is creased in some combination of the frustration and pain reflected in her eyes. I look for fear there, too, but I can't find it. "Yeah, I see you, and the falcons are going to in a few minutes, too."

Falcons. I look anxiously toward the sky. I turn off the part of my brain screaming questions and shift my focus back to the wounded girl. Her short mess of hair is matted at her forehead, and I see blood there, as well.

"You need to get inside, too."

"I'm working on it."

"I can help you." I lift her arm across my shoulder and wrap one of my arms around her waist.

She briefly struggles against my hold. "You'll get there faster without me."

"Well, yes," I concede. "But you won't get anywhere at all without me."

She reluctantly allows my assistance, and together, we start to move a little more quickly through the streets. I wince at every crunch of gravel under her dragging leg, certain that we're on borrowed time. There's no way the falcons haven't heard us.

"Come on, come on, come on," I mumble under my breath. Her weight at my side grows heavier until I'm nearly supporting the entirety of her body. When I glance at her face, I can tell even in the dark that it's turned an ashen white. I know what's about to happen a second before it does.

"No!" I whisper. The girl slides to the ground at my feet, her eyes rolling back into her head. I stand there for the span of several heartbeats. My mind frantically works through the realization that I'm visible, the certainty that the falcons will be here soon, and the fact that there is an unconscious girl at my feet. It requires a force of will to shove these thoughts into the back of my mind and focus.

I grab her under the arms and start backing down the alley, my only goal now to get her away from the shops and to the row of houses. If we can get to where there are other people, maybe someone will rescue us. At least we have a better chance there.

I clench my jaw hard at the sound of the girl's body dragging across the stones, even louder than her footsteps had been. It echoes through the night air tauntingly, and there's nothing I can do about it. My own feet scream in pain at my brisk pace across the sharp gravel, an entirely different kind of pain than my heels had provided at the ball. The memory of Arden walking away is a distant thing.

I bite back a gasping sob at the first sound of flapping wings above us. We're so near to the houses now. I keep dragging her, trying to ignore the shadows converging overhead and blocking out the moonlight. I have heard their voices a thousand nights before, the way they lift and converge and harmonize against each other. I know what it means for their terrible shrieks to transform into a hauntingly beautiful song. For now, they remain shrieks–horrible, grating screeches that make my ears ring, but they mean that I have a little more time.

I yank the girl the final stretch of the way into the narrow alley, where at least the falcons cannot all descend at once. I want to both laugh and cry at what small reassurance that provides. One alone could tear us to shreds; it would just be quicker if the rest joined in.

My arms are shaking badly from the weight of her. I can't go any farther, and anyway, it wouldn't make a difference. If I'm going to do something to stop this, I have to do it now, before the killing song starts.

I drop her and shove her quickly against the seam where the building meets the ground, as far into the shadows as possible. Then, I sprint forward a ways, trying to draw the falcons with me. I'm still not sure if they can see me, or whether it was just this one girl, this one random girl gifting the whole of her blood to the streets of this nightmare world, to whom I was somehow visible.

I start screaming. With every ounce of strength and volume I possess, I scream at the top of my lungs there in the middle of the alley. I scream for help, for mercy, for somebody to save us. Not a single window flickers, not a single door opens. It could be that I'm invisible after all, except...

Except that half of the falcons follow me.

The other half stay where they are, circling the area where I left the girl, while three of them come after me. They are so organized that I suspect somewhere in their shrieks they've signaled to one another who should stay and who should go. The most dangerous of monsters, the kind with intelligence and the ability to plan. Once I see that they're coming for me, I revise my course of action.

I won't let them have us both.

I run back over to her, my own private squadron of falcons following closely, and I fling my body in front of hers, back to her, arms spread wide, face tilted up toward the sky, toward *them*, just as they begin their killing song.

I have heard it so many times, the beautiful melody so haunting and vicious, but never this close. I have never been directly below it, a front row seat to their performance, as they sang it out, as they prepared for their dive. It would not have been out of place at a ball. A different sort of ball than any I have ever attended. A ball without any candlelight, set beneath the full moon, and nobody is smiling, nobody is laughing. I hear in the melody a waltz, three-quarter time, sharp and scandalous with a splash of blood beneath each step. Figures spinning faster and faster and there is no chance that anybody will leave that ballroom alive.

I close my eyes and wait, shielding the girl as well as I can manage.

If I die in a dream, do I die in my real life?

I will find out soon.

I hear the whoosh of wings underneath the song, both growing nearer, but at the same time, I hear something else. Something almost like words, carried on the back of the wind, although I can't make any of them out. They're coming from one end of a long tunnel, and I'm on the other end. I squeeze my eyes shut more tightly, not wanting the last thing I see to be beaks and talons and the promise of death in their eyes, but the words are starting to overpower the falcons' song, growing louder and louder until they're being shouted in my ear.

"Move!"

The word jolts me into motion, my eyes flying open just as the song breaks into a series of disjointed squawks, rage playing through the sounds. Their wings take them back a few feet, beating against the wind and reevaluating, as a figure in front of me wields a sharp object that glints in the moonlight.

I don't wait to see more. I snatch the girl up under her arms and continue down the alley, jogging backward with renewed strength. I glance over my shoulder and see a door left ajar a few houses away. The shadow of our rescuer looms large as he keeps himself between us and the falcons. I watch that shadow beat them back with an impressive ferocity and an almost inhuman snarl, so distracted that the open door is suddenly beside me.

I lurch to the left and yank the dead weight of the girl over the threshold with me, falling backward in a heap with her draped across my legs. Seconds later, our rescuer dives in after us, slamming the door shut behind himself. He releases a colorful string of curses under his breath as the falcons fling themselves at the closed door. Leaning forward with his palms pressed to it, he absorbs each jarring blow.

The closed door plunges the room into darkness. There is one small window, but it's narrow and pushed high against the ceiling, allowing very little of the moonlight to enter. I blink rapidly, impatiently waiting for my eyes to adjust. While they decide about obeying, I rely on my ears.

The falcons are angry. It's difficult to remember their song, the way their voices collided so beautifully, the lift and fall of the notes and harmonies. Now there is only rage. The room echoes with the evidence of this rage—their discordant screeches, their bodies thudding against the door. I stare hard in the direction of the sounds, waiting for the wood to splinter but praying that it won't.

The last of the screeches dies off at the same time the thuds halt. I can hear my own heart beating, my ragged breaths, those of our rescuer. They feel like silence. Like a reprieve, like peace, like we beat the unbeatable.

But then the scratches start, the long, low sound of talons dragging against wood, and I remember why no one rescues people here.

There had been a woman once, when I was too small to know to run. I had followed the sound of her footsteps eagerly, hoping to get a good look at one of the residents of my dream world. I hadn't known yet that her footsteps, and that my hearing of her footsteps, meant she was as good as dead.

I caught up with her just as the first falcon appeared overhead. She started yelling for help when the second joined, screaming for it when the third came, wailing for it when the fourth, the fifth, the sixth came. I had stood frozen just a handful of yards away, mesmerized by the killing song and the way the talons—so many talons—glinted under the night sky. Everything about them, from their beaks to their razor-feathered wings to those talons, portended death, but I had been unable to look away.

Until the wails stopped. A door behind her had opened abruptly, a hand reaching out to yank her through it, and then it had slammed shut just before the first falcon had completed its dive. One after the other had slammed into that door in an endless loop, and only then, only for their angry screeches, did I think to cover my ears. I had blocked my ears but not my eyes, and so I witnessed what happened when they finally conceded their prey for the night. I saw them drag their talons down the door, each one in turn, until the door was clearly marked.

The next night, when I had walked past that same house, there had been no door. Just a gaping hole into an empty room, an empty home, covered in broken plates and overturned furniture and, lord, so much blood. I had turned and run away, and I had never seen anyone rescued since.

Until now.

It feels like hours pass as talon after talon carves into the door. I use that time to calm my breathing, to shove the fact of my visibility as deep into the back of my mind as I can manage. There is a bleeding girl across my legs, and the falcons have marked our rescuer's door. Everything else can keep.

We do not move until the last whoosh of flapping wings carries them away. Once it is truly silent, the moment in the room comes unfrozen, unrooted. I feel our rescuer drop to the ground beside me, watch the shadows of him feel his way to the girl's neck, where her pulse resides. Where I hope it still resides. I can hear his sigh of relief clearly enough in the fresh silence.

He gets back to his feet and walks away. I try to follow the movement of his shadow, but I lose him until he steps through the slight beam of moonlight. He's in the corner opposite the door, rummaging, looking for something. I wait, unsure what else to do.

The crisp echo of a match being struck. My eyes instantly go to the tiny flare of light before it goes out. The next time it strikes, my eyes shift just above the light, to the face above it. I barely have time to see anything before it flickers out again. He curses quietly, or I assume he does as I can only make out the tone and not the word, and then, on the third try, the flame finally holds. It bursts into life, illuminating the space immediately around it. My eyes are already above it from before, already resting on the face there.

Still, it takes a moment for the realization to sink in. For the way the hair falls across his forehead, the sharp angle to his chin, the long lashes of his eyes to fully hit me. Conflicting emotions slam into me: the relief that this specific face has always brought me and the dawning horror of what that face, being here with us right now, means.

There are scratches on his door.

Oh lord, I've doomed my dream boy.

Chapter Nine

I barely have time to process the realization before his eyes lock onto mine. Before I see him see me for the first time. He doesn't look through me or past me. His eyes land on mine and stay there, and I feel a shiver all the way down to my toes. It is just a look, nothing more, but it makes my cheeks turn red and my heart stutter through its next several beats. He can *see* me.

He breaks the eye contact, which is good because there is no way I would have been able to. I find time to breathe again while he circles the room, lighting candles here and there, bringing two of them back with him to set beside us. The candlelight serves me two purposes: to illuminate how much blood the girl has lost and to remind me that the boy beside me is beauty in a nightmare world. I try hard to focus on the first and not the second.

This time when he curses, I hear it.

"Hell."

He jumps back to his feet and takes three long strides back to the far corner of the room. This time, there's enough light for my eyes to follow his progress. They also manage to take in the rest of the room, as it is exceptionally small and apparently all there is of this place.

Of his home. It is one room, a narrow bed shoved against the wall, a small sink, a cabinet without a door, a meager pile of clothes, and stacks of books. My eyes linger longest on the books, where they lean against the wall beside his bed, before sliding back to the boy.

He reads. Or at least, he has books. He appears to have so few things, but he has three full, leaning, stacks of books. They do not look haphazardly piled. They look...treasured. I turn this fresh piece of knowledge over in my mind more times than I should just now, but I can't help it. I have imagined so many details of his life, of who he might be and what he might be like, and here is one detail I do not have to imagine. One I never could have imagined.

He is a person who treasures his books.

He returns with a pitcher, a bottle, and a handful of rags. He sits back beside me and takes a deep breath.

"Can you hold the candle over her?"

It takes me a moment to conclude that he is speaking to me. A jolt runs through my body. I followed him through the streets, I sat beside him and reached out to touch him, and now suddenly here I am, being looked at by him and spoken to by him, and I don't know what to do with any of it. It pounds against the door in my brain when I shove it back there.

One thing I cannot shove aside, though, is the way his voice pulses through me. He isn't a boy at all. His voice is low and miles deep and there is no longer any way that I can call him anything but a man, fully grown. Older than me, I think. In both years and life experience, based on the way he so carefully runs his hands over her wound, the way he does not flinch at the sight of the blood.

I take the candle and hold it above her leg, careful not to drip any of the hot wax. I watch as he picks up the jug and tilts it over her wound, sucking in my breath as it cascades down into the blood. The blood runs a paler shade for a moment before returning to its darkness. Pink into red, my brain fills in, though the shadows hide the color.

He continues to pour, wiping away the blood with one of the rags as he does so. The blood keeps coming, and he starts shaking his head.

"It's too deep," he mutters. "Needs stitches."

I lean forward to study the wound, but I trust his verdict more than anything my untrained eyes can see. In a world like this, he surely knows about this sort of thing.

"Hold this." He shoves the rag into my hand. "Against her wound."

He pulls my hand over to cover her wound, to press the rag against it, his long fingers circling my wrist and setting my nerve endings aflame over the feeling of his calloused fingers against the soft skin.

Back of my brain, I remind myself. Lock it behind the door. You can examine this moment later.

I maintain the pressure on her leg as he walks away once more. This time my eyes don't follow him. They stay locked on the girl, on the blood pooled around her. She can't have much left in her, running through her veins and keeping her heart pumping. I worry that I didn't do enough to save her life.

He comes back and trades my hand for his. I absentmindedly wipe the blood onto my already bloody nightgown. Dark streaks on bright white. He unscrews the cap of the bottle with one hand and pours it generously into the wound, the air between us mingling the sharp smell of the bottle's contents with the sickly-sweet scent of her blood.

When I look down at my hand in my lap, I'm surprised to see a small box dropped into it. I stare stupidly at it for a moment before looking up at him.

"What is this?" My voice comes out like the gravel still haunting my cut-up feet. I had shouted a lot, and screamed even more, and my vocal cords are feeling the strain.

"You'll find fishing line inside." His eyes are trained on mine again, but this time they spark uneasiness in me. "And a needle."

"Fishing line and a needle," I repeat, nodding, still not understanding.

"I can't do stitches. My hands are too clumsy for such fine work."

"Your hands…" I start to repeat again, but I catch on abruptly, rearing backward. "I can't do it either!"

"You've got the hands for it." He stays so calm, his words smooth and even and lacking any special emphasis. I suppose that makes sense, though, as he's not asking himself to stitch up a gaping wound. "I can tell."

I glance down at the hands in question, where the box still sits in one palm, my fingers unwilling to curl around it. All I can decipher from them is that they are small and bloody. I look back up at him.

"I can't." It comes out a whisper.

"You can." It comes out with force.

I flip open the lid of the box. Sure enough, fishing line and a needle. I humor him, reaching for each item. I put the box beside me and hold the end of the line up in one hand and the needle up in the other. Both hands are shaking so badly that the line misses the eye of the needle by a good inch on my first try. On my second, it misses by two.

"I *can't*," I say again, misery lining my tone.

He keeps one hand pressed to the cloth on her leg, but he uses the other to grab the bottle. He lifts it up to my mouth, just below where my nose shudders over its smell. I go nearly cross-eyed looking at it.

"What is that?"

"It'll help steady your nerves."

I continue staring at it warily, but I open my mouth a little bit. He pushes the bottle against my lips and tilts it upward.

I swallow before I process that it has set my tongue on fire. My gums, the roof of my mouth, my throat as it travels downward, all up in flames. I sputter and wrench my face to the side, away from the bottle of liquid fire, coughing. I turn on him with a blistering glare.

"That's supposed to help?"

I think that if circumstances weren't as they are, he'd be laughing right now. As it is, worry lines his face a little less.

"Try again."

At first, I think he means the liquor, and I open my mouth to shoot some choice words his way, but he flicks a telling glance down at where my hands still grip the fishing line and needle. I reluctantly hold them back up in the air and do as he asks—*asks?* Orders.

I thread it on the first try. His worry fades a little more, smugness playing across his lips. It vanishes, though, and the worry returns in full force when we look back down at the wound.

"I really don't think I can do this."

"You don't have a choice."

I feel my chin start to work itself into a petulant jut at his tone, but then I look away from the wound and back at his eyes, where they're locked on mine. It is still too dark to see their color, but I can see their plea. He isn't ordering me to do this; he's begging me. I set the needle to her skin and count each inhale and exhale until I get to ten. I nod at him, and he lifts the cloth away.

Still, the actual pushing of the needle through her flesh draws me up short. I sit there for a long minute as the head of the needle indents her skin just outside of the still-oozing slash. I tell my hand to push, to break the skin. My hand ignores me entirely, frozen in place and useless.

I look helplessly up at him, at where he's staring at my hand and perhaps also ordering it to push. His command holds no more weight than mine, though, and so he looks up at me.

I steady myself in his eyes. I remember the nights by the lake, the way he would look through me, and draw strength from the way he now looks *at* me. Into me. His eyes ask questions of me now, and I can't find it in me to resent those questions because it is infinitely better than the silence they used to give me. I take a deep breath, and I push the needle.

I pretend I'm in my sitting room. I pretend I'm working on a new handkerchief for Carrick, embroidering the hem of it with small masculine leaves because once I gave him one stitched with red flowers and had seen the way his face had tried to swallow a grimace. He had still made a big show about appreciating it and had worn it half out of his pocket the next several times I'd seen him. Still, the one I'm pretending to stitch now will have a rather more masculine motif. Leaves and branches and blood—*no*. Not blood. I blink to clear the blood from the vision.

When the wound is closed and the fishing line is knotted, I allow myself to return to this small room. To the knowledge that there was blood, a lot of it, no leaves, just blood, and skin, and my needle stabbing through the skin. I sit back heavily, falling off of my knees. My fingers release the needle of their own accord, letting it fall silently onto the dirt floor.

He picks it carefully back up as he leans over to check my handiwork, while I use the hem of my gown to scrub the added blood from my fingers. It's hopeless, already half-dried under my fingernails. I tuck my hands into my nightgown in an attempt to hide them from myself.

When he looks back up at me, he's smiling. It's a tilted smile, tinged in cautious relief and abated anxiety, pulling wide enough that it shows a small dimple set in his cheek. Pulling wide enough that it flips my heart once, twice. His teeth are straight and even, but there is nothing straight or even about the line of his smile. It is endearingly slanted and nothing at all like I imagined all of those nights sitting beside him by the lake. I could not have imagined the pull of it, the way I wish it would never fade.

It makes me smile in return. I don't even know what I'm smiling about, with blood caked under my nails and in the creases of my wrists and the girl still not stirring between us, but the sight of his smile makes it impossible to hold mine back. He checks her pulse once again, exhales another relieved sigh, and settles back himself, plopping onto the dirt.

"Okay, then. Tell me what happened."

CHAPTER TEN

What happened? Lord, where to begin…I think quickly and decide to start at the truth.

"I was walking—"

"Why? After the sun had set? Wearing that?"

I pause with my mouth open, mid-sentence, fingers drifting over the cloth at my sides before looking down at the garment in question. I realize then that I'm sitting in a room alone with a man to whom I have not been introduced—well, alone in that he's the only other conscious person present—wearing my nightgown. I feel my face flush and hope that the shadows of the room hide my discomfort.

And then I think about how to answer. The truth seems a less sure path.

"I…got lost?" It comes out far too close to a question, not nearly a definitive answer. "I got lost." There, that's better.

"You got lost." His is more question than statement, too, except it has a layer of skepticism worked into it.

"While sleep-walking." There, that's believable. Or at least I think it is, though his left eyebrow climbs in a way that indicates his disagreement. "I must have wandered right out of my house, and when

I heard this girl walking through the street, it startled me awake."

"Where do you live?"

"I…A few streets over."

"How old are you?"

"Eighteen." That one's easy. I beam a smile at him, relieved at the opportunity for complete honesty.

He blinks and stares at me for a long moment before shaking his head and pressing his lips firmly together.

"Why aren't you training then? I've never seen you in training."

I open my mouth to answer before realizing I have no answer. I'm not sure what he means by training.

"I'm…busy?" Not my finest attempt.

"You're…busy."

His habit of handing my own answers back to me after painting them in disbelief is really getting annoying. I feel as though I'm in the midst of an inquisition, one for which I am ill-prepared. I cross my arms defensively across my chest and square my shoulders. If I'm going to lie, I should at least pretend as though I believe my own lies.

"Yes," I declare with false certainty. "My father has been sick, and I've been staying home to care for him."

"If he's sick, they would have taken him." Something in his tone flattens. I want to ask who "they" are, where they take the sick, why his jaw is suddenly set in that way. But I'm trying hard to cling to a story that won't have him questioning my sanity.

"They don't know he's sick."

He stares hard at me for a moment before his eyes wander back down my body. It's nothing like Arden's appreciative scan or the lewd stare of the other men at the ball. It's really no more than a matter-of-fact appraisal. And yet…

I fervently hope that it's too dark for him to see my blush.

His gaze softens abruptly. I'm watching him closely enough to see the shift, the way his skepticism falls away and is replaced by…pity? Is that pity? I decide that it is, and I decide that I don't like it.

"It's okay," he says soothingly. "I'll make sure you get back in the morning."

"Get back?" I lean away from him warily even though he makes no move toward me. "Where?"

"To the asylum." He says it with such kindness, such gentleness, that I almost don't get outraged.

Almost.

"The asylum?!" It comes out a bit like a parrot's squawk. I jump to my feet. "I'm not insane!" It would probably help my case if I had not just squawked.

"I know." Every movement is as slow and careful as his tone as he climbs to his own feet. "Everything's going to be all right."

I run an agitated hand over my hair and realize that it is once again hopelessly knotted. Somewhere in the run through the streets, it must have come loose from its braid. I have a mental picture of what it must look like, and when I combine it with the nightgown—the *bloody* nightgown—I can reluctantly see why he has come to his exceptionally unflattering conclusion about me.

So much for devising a story that won't make him think I'm crazy.

"Look." I hold up a placating hand. "I can understand why you are making such an assumption, really I can, but I am truly not insane. I'm not an asylum escapee." Good lord, the insult. "I…haven't been entirely honest about why I was on the street tonight."

My brain works frantically at a more plausible story while his pity falters. I latch onto that falter, certain that any emotion at all would be preferable to pity.

"I'm asleep."

Evidently, I have opted for the truth. Once the words erupt from my mouth, I realize that they are the right ones. I don't wish to lie to him. I want him to know the truth of who I am, of where I come from.

Still, there is a lengthy silence following my blurted proclamation. I start to second-guess myself even as I continue in a rush.

"I dream this place every night. Always this place, always these streets. I've only ever been invisible here, though, until tonight, when I am somehow, quite unexpectedly, visible."

His head tilts slowly to the side. He's looking at me like I'm something entirely new, something he has not yet encountered in his life. A creature from another planet. From another world. I am that, I suppose, although I am also a girl, in a nightgown, trembling from head to toe as everything I have shoved to the back of my mind tonight threatens to spill over. I had pulled out just the one thought to give him, the one fact that I am suddenly visible here, and now I try desperately to cram it back in so I can close the door back up.

I twist my hands into my nightgown, bunching the fabric in my fists, waiting for the pity and the offer of an asylum return to resurface. Honestly, if he thought I was mad before...

"You're asleep...currently." Not a question. A dry, emotionless statement. Still, I answer.

"Yes. At home, in Acarsaid."

"Acarsaid." The word trips off of his tongue, unfamiliar.

I nod a confirmation, and he shakes his head in return. He lifts his hand up to the back of his neck, rubbing it back and forth, over and over again. I wouldn't be surprised if he's rubbing the skin raw.

"This doesn't make any sense."

"I know," I say, not without sympathy. "It is nonetheless the truth. When the sun rises, I wake up in my own bed at home. When the sun is down and I am asleep, this is where I come."

He exhales long and slow through his nose, hand still at the back of his neck, head still shaking slowly from side to side. My nightgown crunches slightly in my hands, an unfamiliar feeling that takes me a moment to understand.

Dried blood.

I glance back down at the girl at the same time he does. There is blood on my hands, on my nightgown. On his hands, on the floor all around us. Her clothes are covered in it. It is a river outside that someone will find in the morning and be able to follow to this door. This marked door.

And she has still not woken up.

What if she never wakes up?

He sighs again, even more slowly, even more drawn out. I wonder if his thoughts are running similarly to mine. If he, too, is scared. If he is, he is hiding it well.

"Okay, let's set that aside for now. Tell me the rest. How did you find her?"

"I heard her. I don't usually look anymore when I hear someone out, because I know that if I've heard them, the falcons soon will too, but I looked. And she was there, dragging her leg—"

"Dragging it?"

"Limping. Loudly. I tried to help her get back home, but she fainted before we could get too far, and then the falcons came, and, well…you know the rest."

Our eyes have been fixed on her this whole time.

"Will she be all right?" My question is a whisper, a worry.

"She'll be fine. She's a tough one."

I look sharply back up at him.

"You know her?"

His eyes stay on her. "She's a friend."

I take the opportunity presented by his averted gaze to let my eyes linger on him. His shirt hikes up slightly due to his lifted arm, revealing a thin strip of skin. In terms of skin usually hidden from my gaze, it's a very small thing, but it makes my stomach flip anyway. It makes my fingers twitch as though they want to reach, when of course they cannot. I cannot. I swallow hard and return my eyes up to his face.

Where he is now looking back at me.

"What's your name?"

"Reeve." I leave off my title without thinking. Once I do consider it, I'm glad for my decision. Here, in this world, I am just Reeve.

"Reeve." The simple way his mouth forms it, the echo of it in the air, in his voice, calms my shaking. I take my next few breaths more easily. "I'm Bran."

Bran. I hold the word aloft beside his face and feel that it fits, that it is a natural piece of the mystery he has been to me all of these months.

"Brannen, really," he adds with a bit of a self-conscious shrug.

He's changing, right before my eyes. He's no longer my dream boy by the lake. He has self-conscious shrugs and tilting smiles and a nervous motion of his hand at the back of his neck. His voice is deep and smooth and soothing, the calm lake the day after a storm, the sky without any clouds. I feel my suppositions start to fall away and this fresh knowledge slide into place, forming a more real and clear vision of him. Of him as a man.

"It's nice to meet you." I don't even have to fight the instinct to drop into a curtsy. Here, I am just Reeve, I am a girl who doesn't curtsy. I nod instead, and he nods back.

"I still don't buy your story," he warns, finally dropping his hand to his side.

I can't help a small laugh. "I suppose I can't blame you."

In the subsequent moment of peace, my trembling calmed and his hand no longer at the back of his neck, my immediate worries ease enough to feel the throbbing pain in my feet. I feel the dirt in each small cut, a stinging sensation that layers over them like another skin. I slowly lower myself to the ground to avoid the embarrassment of crying.

I lean back against the wall and let my head thunk against the knotted wood of it, closing my eyes. I hear him sit, too, a distance away. I wish that he was closer. I wish that we were at the lake, side by side, barely any space between his shoulder and mine. A lean away. I wish that he was drawing in the water and I was watching the way his hands move. That we were there, but that he could still see me.

But we are here, and he is far away from me, and I can feel his wary eyes upon me. The world is a different place than it was by the lake.

CHAPTER ELEVEN

"They marked your door," I whisper into the darkness behind my eyelids.

"They did." He suddenly sounds exhausted. Weighted. The smooth edges of his voice turn rough.

"What will you do?"

"I'll leave at first light."

I open my eyes to look at him. He's tracing shapes upon his floor with one finger, circles and swirls just like by the water. Through the candlelight, I can see the clenched line of his jaw. I wonder what emotion he is keeping at bay.

"Where will you go?"

"Cecily and her brother live a couple streets over. I'll bring her home in the morning and stay there."

Bran's eyes refocus on the girl, and I assign another name to another face. Cecily.

"I'm sorry."

He looks up at me, and once again, it takes my breath away. Seeing him see me has not yet ceased to stagger me. The directness of his gaze. The depth of it. It is such a far cry from being looked through. I feel the impact of that look down to the marrow of my bones, and I don't blink. I don't look away.

"Why?"

"Because you have to leave your home."

He studies me. I sit still under his scrutiny, steadied by it. By the tilt of his head, the slight arch of one eyebrow. His eyes are narrowed slightly, but it does not lessen the effect of having them on me. "It's just four walls and a roof. I couldn't very well let them get Cec. Or you."

The corners of my mouth curl a bit around the way he says "you." He couldn't let them get me. Whatever I built him to be all of those nights by the lake is nothing in the face of who he is now that he is looking at me, now that he is speaking to me. He is *real*.

"Thank you."

He shrugs and faces the room once more. I follow the path of his eyes as they touch on his bed, his books, the clothes sitting there, the meager contents of his cupboard, the table with a single chair. I follow as they return to his books.

"What will you bring with you?"

"What I need. As much food as I can carry, my clothes."

"Your books?"

His eyes still linger there.

"No."

His answer is curt and guarded. I tell myself not to pry and almost disobey my own orders immediately before consciously swallowing the words. It is difficult for him to leave the books behind, that much is clear.

"When will you go?"

"First light. After the falcons return to their cage and before the guards take to the street."

"They won't hunt you down?"

Bran's shrug is careless, nonchalant, not the self-consciousness of earlier. "Too much effort. The guards'll take whatever I leave behind and keep it for themselves, but they won't go out of their way to figure out whose home this is. Was."

He swipes a hand across his eyes, abruptly young again.

"You can come along to Cecily's if you need to. There's space enough."

I smile at his offer. "I won't need to, but thank you."

He sighs. "Because you won't be here in the morning."

"Right."

We sit in silence a little longer, time marked only by my heartbeat and the shifting of the moonlight as the earth turns.

"You can take the bed." He makes the offer so abruptly, just when I had been settling into the silence, that I jump a little.

"Oh. No, you take it. I can't sleep here."

He lifts an eyebrow. "Here as in…"

"In this world. I'm already asleep in mine, so…I can't sleep here."

He shakes his head slowly. "Something tells me I should stop trying to make sense of this."

I nod empathetically. "So you can go ahead and get to sleep. I'll be fine here."

I shift and lower myself onto the ground on my side, curling my arm beneath my head in a poor approximation of a pillow.

He squints down at me skeptically. "Yeah, you look like you're on a regular pile of feathers there. Go on, take the bed."

I furrow my brow. "No. I don't sleep. I don't need it."

"Do you also not feel discomfort in this dream of yours?"

I try hard to ignore the sarcasm layered into his tone.

"Don't be ridiculous. It's your bed, and your last night in your home. You should get to sleep in your own bed one more time."

He appears to give the matter a moment's thought before abruptly lying down on his back, fingers laced behind his head. I stare at the side of his face, brow furrowing more and more deeply until it's a fully formed glare.

"What are you doing?"

"Getting some sleep." He closes his eyes.

I make a sound which, when I consider it in hindsight, can only be described as a growl.

He lifts his eyebrows but doesn't open his eyes.

"This is silly."

Even in his prone position, he manages a nonchalant shrug.

I consider a variety of curse words, most collected in moments when Jax had not been aware I was listening, before biting my lip hard.

"Well, if neither of us is going to take the bed, we should at least put the girl—Cecily—in it."

He opens his mouth too quickly for his next words to be anything but an argument, but then he pauses, considers.

"That's actually a good idea."

I huff and sit up, my arms flailing a little in my pique.

"'Actually,'" I mutter.

He rolls to his feet easily while I clamber slowly to mine, trying and failing to contain a wince as each throbbing foot is forced to bear my weight.

Unfortunately, Bran notices. He squints down at my feet and then points to the bed.

"Sit."

I set my jaw. "I thought we just settled this."

He scowls. "You're bleeding all over my floor. Just sit so I can take a look."

"I am not," I say quickly, looking back down, but there is no denying it. I had felt the gravel do its damage outside, and I can see the bloody footprints I've been leaving on his floor. I am inclined to blame most of it on the girl, but I know that I have contributed some small part. I shoot him a disgruntled glare before gingerly stepping over to the bed and perching on the corner.

He comes over and squats in front of me. He picks up my left foot first, carefully, as though it's far more fragile than bone covered in skin, and turns it so that he can see the bottom of it. He *tsks* softly before setting it down and repeating the process with the other. I can't stop looking at the contrast of his fingers against my skin where they wrap around each ankle in turn.

Yes, I believe I *have* lost some blood. That would account for my sudden lightheadedness.

He stands back up and retrieves the bottle of liquid fire and a few more clean rags from the pile. I start shaking my head as soon as he turns back to me.

"Really, you don't have to. They'll be fine, good as new, when I wake up in the morning."

He tilts a quelling look up at me before reaching for my left foot again. I quickly pull it out of his reach, crossing it with the other under his bed. He looks up at me with an exasperated sigh.

"Are you so sure? You said you weren't visible before tonight, so how do you know your cuts will be healed in the morning?" He has the look of someone being forced to use irrational logic to attempt to reason with an irrational person, and he doesn't appear to be enjoying it. If he clenches his jaw any harder, I expect it would shatter.

"I just…it wouldn't make any sense, to wake up in my bed and have my feet suddenly covered in cuts."

"Because everything else about this makes total sense."

He reaches again, and I slide my feet even deeper under the bed, eyes fixed on the bottle in his hand.

When I look back to his face, I see the way the shadows slant over his tensing jaw. I also see exhaustion there, which is far more effective in convincing me. So when he looks back up at me and says, "Humor me," I sigh and reluctantly slide my feet out. He did save my life earlier, after all. The least I can do is let him take care of my feet.

Another illogical thought in a thoroughly illogical evening. I bite my lip to keep from smiling.

As he upends the bottle's contents over my foot, though, any urge to smile vanishes, my bite now at my cheek to hold my tears in check. The liquid was fire down my throat, and it's fire on my feet. It takes a good deal of restraint to neither yank my foot out of his grasp nor kick him in the face with it. He quickly sets to work wrapping it in the cloths, dousing the burning feel in soft cotton and light touches.

"Couldn't put shoes on in your dream?"

He surprises a laugh out of me, distracting me from the pain. He smiles up at me through his lashes as he reaches for my other foot.

"I would have to wear them to sleep at night, and it's dreadfully uncomfortable to sleep with shoes on."

He huffs out a chuckle of his own, the sound coming just as he pours the liquid fire onto my other foot, just in time for my eyes to forget to tear up because my ears are so wrapped up in the sound of his laugh. It isn't even much of one, in duration or volume. But it is a whole lot of one in what it does to my skipping heart. I made him laugh.

He bandages that foot, too, the callouses of his hands only occasionally brushing my skin, sparking flames of a far more pleasant sort than the bottle's contents. I start to wonder if I'm possibly drunk from the earlier sip of the stuff. My thoughts and my body are tingling in a tipsy, pleasant way.

He sets the freshly bundled foot beside the other and pushes back onto the balls of his feet.

"Thank you, again."

He meets my smile with his own, and *lord*, it's a nice smile. One side always seems to climb higher than the other, lending it a crooked quality, an imperfection that does the opposite of lessen its appeal. My next exhale is dangerously near to a sigh.

I really must be drunk.

"Yeah, well, couldn't have you bleeding all over my floors."

And then his smile falters and falls, leaving no trace of it behind. He looks over his shoulder, and I realize what he has surely just realized.

These won't be his floors much longer.

I start to apologize again, but I pull the words back before they reach his ears. He already brushed my apologies away once, and anyway, they won't do him any good.

He goes to pick up the girl, Cecily, and I stand on my freshly pillowed feet to move out of the way. They feel infinitely better, cushioned and clean and touched by his hands. He lowers her to the bed with the same gentleness he just showed my feet, the same kindness I'd always imagined him to have.

I return to the hard lumps of the dirt floor while he goes back to his own spot, across the room, where he is more shadow than man in the light of the lone candle. Still, he makes for a very tired shadow. I expect him to lay back down, as he had mockingly done so earlier, but he stays sitting.

And he keeps looking at me.

"You can go to sleep," I say when the silence stretches uncomfortably. Uncomfortably for me, at least. He seems content to let it continue on.

"I'm not tired." I'd imagine it's very inconvenient for him that it comes out accompanied by a yawn.

Since he has already negated his own words, all I do is lift an eyebrow in response. He's not the only one capable of that particular trick.

Once again, he seems in no rush to break the silence. He lets his blatant lie hover in the air between us, leaning back against the wall on the other side of the room and stretching his legs out in front of him. When he crosses them at the ankles and folds his hands in his lap, I consider whether it would be unladylike to throw something at him.

I suppose it would be.

Also, the only thing within my reach is that damnable bottle of alcohol. And though he is exasperating, I don't wish to give him a concussion or cover him in cuts.

Exasperating. I add that to the list of qualities I can now tie to his face. Bran, an exasperating man—not boy—who has a voice made for soothing and keeps his books in careful stacks.

His books.

I glance back over at them.

"Do you like to read?"

He lifts one shoulder in a shrug, and I reconsider the bottle. I clench my hands into my nightgown to keep them from reaching for it.

Fine.

"I love to read. Novels, especially. There's one I reread to death about a shipwreck and the two people who survive it and end up on a deserted island together. They're utter opposites, but they end up falling in love, of course. It wouldn't be much of a story without a happy ending, and falling in love is about as happy an ending as one can hope for."

Am I speaking loudly? I feel like my voice is echoing in the silence of the room. And he is staring at me as though I have grown an additional head or limb or possibly just as though I am prattling on about a book and love to a complete stranger.

In contrast, the return to silence is even more deafening. I open my mouth to fill it once more, but, mercifully, he cuts me off.

"Do they get off the island?"

He sounds only reluctantly interested, but I grab hold of his question with both hands.

"The book ends with them finally catching the attention of a ship in the distance, so though it doesn't show them actually leaving, it's strongly implied that they do so."

He tilts his head to one side, his eyes narrowing.

"Hm."

In any other scenario, I might be impressed by how much skepticism he is able to inject in that one short syllable. However, in this specific scenario, I am too busy getting annoyed to feel impressed.

"What's that supposed to mean?"

"What's what supposed to mean?"

"You said 'hm.'"

"Well, then, I meant exactly that."

I've changed my mind. I want him to go back to being my boy at the lake, not this stubbornly infuriating man sitting across from me.

"You obviously meant something more by it," I bite out.

He studies me for a long moment. I wonder if the shadows are hiding as much of me as they are of him. For as long as he stares at me, I wish I could know what he sees.

"Okay," he says, leaning forward a bit. "What I meant by it is, that that's not much of an ending. It's great that they fell in love and all that. But anyone can fall in love on a deserted island when it's only the two of you there. You said that they're complete opposites.

So, how's that going to hold up once they get back to the real world?"

I certainly hope that he can't see me clearly through the shadows, because it takes me several seconds to close my mouth. It dropped open at some point there, when he called into question my favorite book, one of the formative love stories of my life.

"I…" I stammer before clearing my throat. Honestly, I cannot believe he is making me defend the love of Charlotte and Tristan. He doesn't even know them. Their story, I mean. He doesn't even know their story. "They *love* each other. That doesn't go away just because they change locations."

He is quiet for the span of three or four heartbeats, and then— "Hm."

I lean forward as far as I can, resting my palms on the floor. If he couldn't see me clearly before, he certainly can now. I am firmly in the glow of the candle.

"If you say 'hm' once more, I will not be responsible for my actions."

Leaning forward, I can see him better, too. So I can see the shift, the lift, the way his skepticism gives way to a full-fledged smile. The tilted one, the one that melts my insides like butter on a hot roll. The one that, apparently, pokes holes in my annoyance and deflates my outrage in two seconds flat.

Lord, it's a nice smile.

"Did you just threaten me?"

I scoot forward, so that I am more firmly set in the candlelight's reach.

"I may have," I admit. It seems ridiculous now, in the face of his smile. Okay, I suppose he can stay this version of him, this real-life man version of him, infuriating as he may be, if he just keeps smiling at me like that.

"The thanks I get for saving your life," he says, his smile settling in rather than fading.

"I had it covered," I say with false bravado and a roll of my shoulders. And then, because I know how ridiculous of a boast it is, I let my shoulders drop back down and offer him my own smile, as bright as I can make it. "But thank you all the same."

It may just be a trick of the shadows or a false sense of vanity, but something in him seems to falter when I smile at him. His eyes shift down to my lips before flickering back up to my eyes and then looking away entirely. I blink, and his smile is gone again, to wherever it goes when he is discomfited.

"It's a nice idea," he says at last, amusement also vanished from his voice. "Thinking they would've stayed in love after the story ended. Just not a very realistic one."

And my smile is gone, too, and I am reminded abruptly of my annoyance.

"A cynic," I mutter. First Arden, now Bran. Why does everyone seem to think I am naïve to believe so strongly in love? "Haven't you ever seen it in your life? Someone you know, in love? In *that* kind of love, the kind that lasts? I have. I know it exists."

"I'm not a cynic," he counters. "I'm a realist. I don't know what things are like in Ac—wherever it is you're from, but here, the last thing on anyone's mind is love. It's surviving another day. It's getting food on the table. It's training and keeping your mouth shut so you don't end up swinging from a rope as dinner for Rancore's pets."

I want to pull each sentence apart and study the pieces, these glimpses at what life is like in this place every day. I also want for his jaw not to be clenched so tightly, for his hands not to be braced on the floor like that, for his smile not to have become such a distant memory so quickly.

I pick one piece.

"Rancore?"

He stills and steadies, emptied of his outburst, folding his arms across his chest and becoming a statue of a man. The change is a marked one, a worrying one. I wonder if I picked the wrong piece.

"You don't know him?" He sounds guarded. Like he has weighed and measured those four words and will do so with all of the ones he will utter henceforth.

"I don't know anything about this place," I admit. "Like I said, I have only ever been invisible here, and only ever here at night. The only people I have seen are either already hanging from the gallows or about to be torn to shreds."

And you, I don't add. *I have seen you.*

What would he think of it? Nothing good, I imagine. And he is guarded as it is right now. No, I will leave that unsaid.

As I sort through my thoughts, he says nothing. Obviously mention of this Rancore has wrought the change in him, and I wish I had known. I wish I had picked a different piece. A piece that would bring the smile back.

But I chose my piece, and it cannot be undone.

"I assume his pets are the falcons?"

Still and still and still silence. I sigh and drop my chin, watching the small flickering flame instead of him. Even the fire gives me more to go off of than he does just now.

"Acarsaid doesn't have falcons," I whisper to the flame. "It's very different from here. This has always been a nightmare world to me. So, I suppose if here, people don't believe in love, I cannot fault them. But where I come from, it's very real."

What if this is it? Some fluke of magic, some hole in my subconscious, the only night in which I am to be visible in this place? The only night in which I am seen by the boy at the lake, who has become so much more than that in such a short span of time? Who has become *real*?

What if this is the only night that I can talk to him?

I don't want this to be how it ends.

I look up at him and let myself feel the force of my eyes colliding with his. I let myself absorb it, just in case this is it. Just in case I will never feel it again.

"How old are you?"

He visibly starts at the shift, either in the conversation or in my tone. I have lightened it considerably, determined to lighten the heaviness before it fully settles between us. I can see him weighing his answer to this, as well, but he must decide it will do no harm, because he answers.

"Twenty."

I smile encouragingly in response, pleased to have gotten an answer.

"I'm eighteen. Just eighteen, actually. Today, or yesterday I suppose, if it's after midnight, was my birthday."

Something loosens a little bit in him. One corner of his mouth twitches upward in what cannot yet be considered a smile, but it's close. Closer, at least. I take it gladly.

"Happy birthday."

My own smile cannot get any brighter.

"Thank you." I look around the small room. "Do you live here alone then? At twenty I suppose you're fully grown."

When I look back over at him, he has stiffened again, even that hint of a smile once more gone. Damnation. I feel as though the room is lined in landmines and that I keep stepping on them unwittingly.

"I'm sorry," I say in a rush, wanting to smooth over whatever insult I had obviously inflicted. "I didn't mean to pry."

Not entirely the truth. I am hungry for details, for more information about this world, and, most especially, more information about him. I want to layer in as many facts of him as I can, form as full a picture of him as I can to carry with me in case this is the only chance I get.

I hear his sigh.

"I used to live here with my mother. She's gone now." He says it quietly. Flatly. An emotionless statement of fact. He does not say where it is she's gone, but he doesn't need to. It's there, in the flatness.

I swallow hard.

"My mother is gone, too," I say without meaning to. Because it isn't something I say. They aren't words I utter. But they are out now, in the air now, and I don't try to pull them back. After all, from the way that his eyes soften in the candlelight and the way he leans just a little bit forward, I can see that he understands. And it feels nice, a soft edge to the sadness of the words between us, to be understood.

"You'll be gone in the morning?" He asks it reluctantly, still only half or maybe not even half believing.

"When the sun rises, unless I'm awoken at home before then."

"Just like that? Here and then gone?"

"I don't know. I've never seen it from this side before, but I think so."

Another lapse into silence.

"Do you expect you'll be visible tomorrow night?"

I swallow hard. "I'm not sure."

"And if you are?"

"I'm not sure about that either," I admit. It seems like too large of a thing to consider right now, after the chaos of the night. What I will do if I am still visible, what I will do if I'm not.

He sighs and rubs at the back of his neck with one hand in what is becoming a familiar gesture. One that says he doesn't know quite what to do or what to make of things.

"You're a whole lot of trouble, is what you are," he mutters. It seems to be more to himself than to me, but I hear it and take offense regardless.

"I am not." Each word comes out clipped. "I didn't ask for any of this. To dream myself here every night, and then to suddenly be seen."

Didn't I? Didn't I ask to be seen, by him? Didn't I wish for it so many nights out by the lake?

I did. But he doesn't need to know that.

A whole lot of trouble, indeed.

He settles back against the wall. I wish he would move closer instead, but there is a wall somewhere between us, invisible and unmovable, and he will not take it down. I suppose I can't blame him. I feel as though I know him, or at least as though he isn't a stranger, from all of those nights by the lake, but to him, I am entirely a stranger. The strangest of strangers, a girl who claims to be from another world. Honestly, I suppose I should count my blessings that he has not yet shoved me outside his door.

There is a soft sound from the bed, and we turn our heads simultaneously to look toward it. The girl. I had almost entirely forgotten about her. She shifts slightly, another slight moan of pain escaping as she does so, but she does not awaken.

We look back at each other.

"You saved her," he says quietly. And that, I realize, is probably why I am still in here. Why he has not escorted me to the door and given me up to the night. "If you hadn't been…visible, or whatever, tonight, she wouldn't have had a chance."

I hadn't thought of that. Whatever it is about tonight that has allowed me to be visible…I send it a silent thought of thanks. That I was close enough to save her. That Bran heard my screams and came to our rescue. That we all survived to be here right now.

"I'm glad." I mirror the quiet of his tone. "I'm glad I was there."

And I don't know if I imagine it, but the shadows fall off of his face. I see him a little more clearly right then, and my eyes trace the angle of his cheekbones and the line of his jaw greedily. The details of him. The beauty of him.

I didn't imagine it, I realize at once. It's a little brighter in here, and the candle is not to blame.

I glance quickly up at the one small window in the room, and it only confirms what I already feel. The sun is rising, and here it is. The familiar tug from deep in my stomach. It comes on so suddenly that there is little I can do but look away from the window and stare frantically at him for one, for two, for no more than three seconds, wishing in those seconds that I had had more time, that I could have asked more questions, that I could have heard him speak just once more.

Wishing, as I am yanked back into my bed, into my real world, my head buried in my feather pillow and my feet unwrapped and pressed into silken sheets, that I could have seen or asked or known the color of his eyes.

CHAPTER TWELVE

I plead a headache, which is a far simpler excuse for why I don't leave my bedroom all morning than the truth would be: "Ah, Guin, I think I'll stay abed this morning as I am suddenly visible in my dreams and have rather many thoughts to sort through regarding these new circumstances." No, Bran's skepticism with regard to my sanity has put me off telling the truth to anyone else at present.

Bran. Having a name to put to the face that has haunted so many waking and dreaming moments these past few months sends a thrill through me. I envision that it is *Bran* coming to sweep me off my feet at the ball, that it is *Bran* twirling me across the dance floor.

Although to be honest, the Bran I began to know last night does not much seem the dancing sort. I continue the work I had begun last night, the work of layering the truth of him through the daydreams I've built of him, relishing rather than resenting this shift. As stubbornly exasperating as he had been at times, it had made him real to me. He was never real before. I find that the truth of him as a fully formed man is far more intriguing to me than the picture I'd been spending so much time painting in my head.

Paintings are beautiful to look at, but they are frozen and untouchable, whether seen from afar or up close. Last night, for the first time, he was not untouchable. The door sits ajar now, and so I carefully select the memory of his hand grazing the inside of my wrist, the gentle way his fingers had encircled my ankle. I sigh and nestle deeper into my pillows at the memory of his smile.

Not all memories are so carefully pulled forth. Some tumble free, shoving aside his smile and his hands, replacing them with gleaming talons in the moonlight, a killing song floating so close to my ears, a river of blood through the gravel. I can't look at my nightgown, so crisply white and soft, without remembering it caked and dark with the girl's dried blood.

Will I always be visible now?

I think of the falcons and hope that I won't be, and then I think of Bran and pray that I will.

I am a mess of contradictions for the duration of my morning, left alone to my musings and my worries and all of the unanswered questions that may never be anything more. I hope that he made it to Cecily's home this morning. I hope that he's safe. I hope that last night is not all there is.

I'm not sure how much of the day has passed when a knock sounds at my door. A glance at the window confirms only that the sun is shining cheerfully on the other side of it, drawing forth longing from my chest. I should at least carry my musings outside, perhaps to my garden. My guards are always good about leaving me to my thoughts.

I assume that it's Guin at the door with my lunch tray, but she arrives empty-handed and with a beaming smile on her face determined to put the sun to shame, enough degrees brighter than her usual smile for me to deem it suspicious.

"Is your headache any better, my lady?"

I'm certain I could spend the remainder of the day, and possibly the next several as well, circling over and through and around my thoughts from last night, but her grin has me intrigued.

"It is, thank you. Why do you ask? You look as though you might imminently explode, Guin. Out with it!"

"You have a visitor, my lady." She does a little bop on the balls of her feet, her excitement positively contagious. I fling my covers back without even pausing to consider her words.

Once my feet have transferred from the warmth of my sheets to the cold stone of the floor, I pause and look over at my lady's maid speculatively.

"Who is it?" I suddenly remember what I had forgotten in the midst of the upheaval of my night: a blond head disappearing into the crowd. Me, left alone. Anticipation seizes my stomach.

"A Lord Delavar, my lady." I can see the sparkle in her eyes from here as she leans forward a little. "And he's quite handsome!"

The blond head transforms into a brunet one, not disappearing into the crowd but coming toward me, outfitted with kind brown eyes and a patient smile. I can't help deflating a little, the butterflies settling back down in my stomach to return to their rest, even as I sternly remind myself that Lord Arden Velasian is trouble. Far from marriage material. Not at all right for me.

It does not matter that he made my heart forget its rhythm.

Really, it doesn't.

It should not be so difficult to convince my heart of things my head knows to be true. As they have resided in the same body for eighteen years now, they really should have reached an accord by this point.

Guin's glee falters in the face of my deflation. I muster up a smile for her benefit, darting over to the rug near my dressing room. The cold floor reminds me that my feet are bare, which in turn forces me to note that they are utterly uncut. I forget my wish that Arden be my visitor. I make a dangerous wish that my feet be cut and bandaged and that Bran be at my door instead, dangerous in its impossibility and in the fact that I would even think to wish it. My real life has no place for dream-world wishes.

"Do you know why he's here?" I ask before splashing water on my face. I pat it dry with a towel as I stare at my reflection in the mirror, wondering for a flash of a moment why my hair is so calm after my run through the streets.

But that was all a dream, of course. There were no streets, no bleeding girl, no Bran. My subconscious delights in torment and has likely only shifted its course to amuse itself, making me visible in the nightmare world it built for me.

It's the darkest of the considerations I've held this morning, the one I would push aside the moment it passed through. It feels impossible that last night was any less real than this morning, that the world that holds Bran and Cecily and the taloned monsters is any less real than Acarsaid, than this room and this palace, especially when last night I could reach out and touch it.

I should wish for it not to be real. For there to be no falcons, no hanging rope so often occupied. But that would be the same as to wish that Bran was not real, that he was merely a figment of my subconscious, and I cannot find it within me to hope for such a thing. I hope for the very opposite, that he's real and alive and that he's at my door.

Lord Delavar is at my door, I remind myself sternly. *Focus, Reeve.*

I realize then that I had asked a question, and that Guin must surely have answered it by now, but I was too busy turning worries about in my mind to pay any attention.

"I'm sorry, Guin, my mind wandered. Did you say you do know why he's here?"

She comes over to touch my forehead lightly with the back of her hand. "He's hoping to take you on a picnic. Are you sure your headache is better?"

I manage a smile and gently remove her hand from my head, clutching it between my fingers for a moment. "I'm sure. Thank you, Guin. Will you help me get ready quickly?"

She sets to work on my hair, and I try hard to shove every worry and question the dream world gave me back behind the door in my mind. I regretfully shove Bran back there, too.

*

"Lord Delavar," I exclaim, sweeping into the entry room less than thirty minutes later, outfitted in a smart plum walking gown with my hair tucked neatly under a matching sunhat. "It's a pleasure to see you again, and so soon after our last meeting!"

"My lady," he bows deeply. "I hope you don't think it forward of me to call so soon, but I did so enjoy our time together last night and was eager to further make your acquaintance."

I wonder briefly whether I was remembering our brief conversation last night differently, with its stilted politeness and awkward silences, but I brush the thought aside. His eyes are as soft and warm as chocolate that has been sitting out in the sun, as quiet and kind as I remember. I drop into an answering curtsy and force my smile a few degrees higher.

"Of course. I enjoyed our dance and conversation as well. My lady's maid mentioned a picnic. Is that our plan for this afternoon?"

"Yes, my lady, if it's amenable to you. I brought a basket prepared by my kitchen staff."

"That sounds lovely." I lean back toward the doorway and catch Tiven's eye. "Tiv, we're going to have a picnic. Feel free to notify the kitchen if you four would like a basket prepared for your lunch, as well."

He nods and flags down a passing footman as I turn back to Lord Delavar. I'm surprised to see a crease in his forehead that had not been there a second before.

"Is something the matter?"

"It's just that…" He shakes his head and looks down at his shoes uncomfortably. "It's just that I hoped we might have some time alone to get to know one another."

I stare at him blankly. "Yes, I believe this picnic will accomplish that goal nicely."

He clears his throat. "Is it absolutely necessary that your guards be present? We will be just outside in the gardens, I'd imagine, and it's difficult to truly get to know someone while a handful of guards are watching."

My eyebrows inch higher and higher as he speaks, as I realize what he's asking.

"I assure you, my lord, my guards are very circumspect. They will stay a small distance away and allow us to chat privately."

"Still…" He clears his throat again, the sound stiffening my spine. "It's not quite what I had envisioned."

"I apologize for the fact that you had other expectations, Lord Delavar, but my guards *will* be accompanying us, by order of the king."

He seems to realize that my tone has been growing colder and colder until it's frigid, and he deflates before my eyes.

"I'm terribly sorry, my lady, of course you're right. I should never have suggested…My sincerest apologies." I watch his Adam's apple bob as he swallows hard. "I only wished to spend some time with you and did not intend to overstep in so doing, but clearly I have. I hope you will accept my apologies."

I can practically hear the four men behind me bristling at the turn in this conversation. Still, the man before me looks frantic to smooth over his insult, and his apologies ring true. I remember now that he came into his title when he was quite young, possibly not even completed with his schooling, and perhaps this accounts for his lapse in etiquette. I feel myself softening toward him, my spine slackening a bit.

"Of course, my lord, I understand. Your apologies are accepted."

"Thank you, my lady." He trips over his words and nearly reaches out for my hand before catching himself. "Thank you," he says again.

"You're welcome." I am officially looking forward to this afternoon even less than I had been when Guin had first announced Lord Delavar's arrival. Still, my guards will be with me, and the sun continues to beckon me outside. I'm sure it won't be as awful as my mind has convinced itself it will be.

CHAPTER THIRTEEN

It's worse.

I shoot a glare over at my guards, wishing that we had worked out some sort of signal for when I'm in need of rescue. Not life-or-death rescue, but social rescue. Instead, they blithely tuck into their lunches, only glancing up to ensure that I am of a piece and that a safe distance exists between Lord Delavar and myself before returning to their sandwiches.

A safe distance exists, yes, but I would not mind adding another few feet or yards or miles to it.

It isn't that Lord Delavar has been untoward. Far from it. Rather, he's been so utterly *boring*. He spent the duration of the walk through the gardens extolling over the blue of the sky—exceptionally blue today! —before moving on to the red of the roses—such a stunning shade of red! —and the green of the grass under our feet—like glistening emeralds!

After that riveting garden color discourse, we had the topic of our lunch to fill the next few minutes of conversation. The sandwiches are delicious, so well-assembled! The apples are so sweet and crisp! The cheese is so well-aged and yellow! He really is inordinately preoccupied with color.

Normally I am well-versed in small talk and able to hold up my end of any conversation, but today I am struggling. The night before weighs heavily on my mind, and exhaustion had settled in by the time we got to the topic of the roses' red. Everything that followed has only served to further convince me that I should have remained in bed today.

Not that bed was much better. I had wanted a distraction from those thoughts, from worry over what last night meant, whether I'll ever be visible there again, what it even *means* to be visible there. What it means to be tying very real traits to a man who may only exist in my subconscious.

If I spend too much longer circling those thoughts, I'll go mad. Especially because I will find no answers here, in the sunlight, night still many hours away.

I force myself back into the present and try for one more surreptitious glare at my guards while Lord Delavar examines the layers of the trifle. I'm waiting for him to begin waxing poetic on the translucency of the jelly, the sweetness of the cake, the *orange* of the custard.

Demes appears to meet my eyes, and I assign a ferociousness to my scowl that hopefully travels across the dozen or so yards to reach him. Either it doesn't, or he utterly misinterprets it, because he turns away cheerfully to dig another apple from their basket.

I turn back to find Lord Delavar looking at me. I realize a second too late that I had forgotten to erase the scowl before turning away from the guards. I hastily do so, but first I watch the corners of Lord Delavar's mouth droop.

I sigh long and slow.

"I'm sorry, my lord. I was in bed with a headache for much of the morning and thought it had abated sufficiently to join you on this picnic, but I'm afraid it has only worsened. I apologize for not being the most pleasant and conversational of picnic companions."

His mouth instantly curves back upward. "No need to apologize, my lady. I'm sorry to hear your head is paining you. Perhaps we should wrap up our outing so you can return to your bed and get some rest?"

I eagerly bound to my feet before remembering that my head is supposed to ache. I force myself to slow down, to press my hand against my forehead and arrange my face into less eagerness, more regret.

"Yes, I think that would be best."

I help him clean up the remains of the picnic and fold the blanket as my guards catch our movements and do the same. The six of us begin to make our way back to the palace, my hand tucked in the crook of Lord Delavar's arm.

He clears his throat.

I brace myself. We have not yet discussed the purple of my gown.

"My lady, if you'd like, you may call me Del. My closest friends do so, and I'd be honored to consider you such."

I'm touched in spite of myself. "Thank you, my lord—Del. And you may call me Reeve."

He beams a smile down at me. Maybe I've been a trifle harsh toward him, my melancholy thoughts borne from the night before bleeding into the picnic and making it seem more unpleasant than it had actually been.

"My lady…that is, Reeve, I wondered if I might ask you something a bit personal."

My curiosity piqued, I tilt my face up to him.

"Go on."

"Now that you're of an age, I'd imagine your mind is turning toward your future. And, of course, marriage to an eligible gentleman."

It's not a question, but I nod anyway. "Yes, it is a thought that is crossing my mind with increasing frequency."

Emboldened, he begins to speak more quickly. "It's a thought often on my mind, as well. And as I'm convinced that there is no woman more beautiful, and none more perfectly befitting the role of duchess, I hoped that you might consider becoming my wife."

I trip over the hem of my dress. Percius makes a snorting sound that can only be a laugh, but he tries to cover it with a cough. I look up at Del's expectant face, his brown eyes soft and inquiring, and I wonder if I've just been proposed to.

I start walking at a brisker pace as I search for a response.

"That is the kindest offer anyone's ever made me, Del, thank you. And while marriage is a thought I've been entertaining of late, I'm afraid it's still far too soon for me to make such a decision."

There. I feel rather pleased with my response. It puts him off without issuing an outright dismissal. I glance up to see how it's being absorbed and am surprised by the taut edge to his jaw and the sudden hardness in his eyes.

"Of course," he says stiffly. "I understand."

I wrack my already overwrought brain for a way to smooth over the perceived insult.

"It's truly not personal. I'm not prepared to marry anyone just yet. But any woman would be lucky to be your wife, Del."

He smiles tightly down at me, but I can still feel the tension in his arm as he escorts me back to the palace. It feels rather like Arden's arm under my hand last night, after the rejected kiss. And I imagine if I had been close enough to touch Bran last night, when I asked questions he clearly had not wished to answer, his muscles would have been just as tense. Will I never do the right thing, or say the right thing, where men are concerned?

He takes his leave almost immediately after dropping me off back in the palace foyer, as though he can't be rid of me quickly enough. I stare after him as he practically gallops down the front steps and into his waiting carriage. I feel entirely caught off guard by his reaction.

"Did I handle that completely wrong?" I ask dejectedly, still staring out the front door.

"That depends," Jax responds. "Did you never want to see the man again?"

I sigh and droop my shoulders, pulling my sunhat off my head. "I thought I was being polite. I did tell him it wasn't personal."

"No man can help but take rejection personally, my lady."

I spin back around to face my guards. "We could have avoided this whole fiasco had you all rescued me when I clearly indicated that I needed an exit strategy."

"We were eating our lunch," Percius says a bit defensively. "We didn't notice anything amiss."

"He didn't make any improper advances," Tiv adds. "We were keeping a close eye on him, and he kept a proper distance between the two of you."

"There is such a thing as social rescue," I mutter, crossing my arms.

The four of them blink back at me.

"He was going on and on about the food!" I exclaim, throwing my hands in the air in exasperation. "It appeared to be all he was capable of talking about. The color of it, the way it tasted…"

"So, he appreciates a finely prepared meal," Jax says.

"Don't seem like a crime," Dem shrugs.

"I'll pass the message along to Cook," Tiv nods.

"Oh, good idea," Perc says, leaning against the wall to my right.

"She'll appreciate the compliment."

"For the love of…I was *glaring* at you! To get your attention!"

Again, I get a long stare and a slow blink from all four sides of me.

"Ahhh," they say collectively.

"I thought you just had the sun in your eyes," Demes offers. "Making them go all squinty."

"I thought you were just batting your lashes at your gentleman caller," Perc says with his most winning smile, all blinding white teeth and unreasonably deep dimples. My heartrate is already accelerated from my annoyance, though, so his smile holds no power over it.

"I do not bat my lashes," I bite out. "Ever."

"I beg to differ, my lady," Tiv says with a shake of his head. "You were causing a right windstorm with them last night with that gent you accompanied to the terrace."

"Borderline scandalous," Demes says, his voice dropping to a stage whisper.

"I had half a mind to follow you out there," Jax growls.

"Oh, I had an eye on it the whole time," Tiv says with a dismissive wave of a hand.

"You…" I sputter. "You were *watching*?"

"It's my job, my lady."

"Oh, *then*, it's your job. When I'm in no need of rescuing!"

I throw my hands up in the air and spin toward the stairs just as Florien reaches the bottom step. I pull up short, startled.

"Was that Lord Delavar?"

"It was." I allow those two words readily enough but halt any further explanation before it crosses my tongue. My brother has not earned my explanations.

"Did you accept, then?"

"Did I…" I trail off, and then my mouth drops open. "Wait, you were aware that he planned to propose?"

"Yes. I encouraged him to do so."

I gape at him for the passing of several seconds, unsure whether I'd heard him correctly.

"You…you encouraged him to do so? Are you mad? I met the man last night, we spoke for less than ten minutes, we—Florien, I met him last night! Why would you encourage him to propose?!"

He sets his jaw. "I had good reason."

"Would you care to share that reason with me?" My shock is rapidly morphing into outright anger.

He opens his mouth, closes it, looks behind him up the stairs. He takes the last step down and grabs my wrist, hauling me into the sitting room just off the foyer and closing the door behind us. I'm too surprised to put up any protest, this action so out of character for the person my brother has become.

"Look, Reeve…" He pauses, looking toward the ceiling as though carefully plucking from the air just the right words. "There's a dossier."

I stare blankly at him and wait for him to pick more words. Better words. More helpful words. Florien takes a deep breath.

"Carrick and Father compiled a list of suitable husbands for you. I caught a glimpse of it in Father's study just before the ball, and I just…I was trying to help by directing Delavar your way. Believe me when I say that he is the best of the three options presented."

My mind remains stuck at the words "list of suitable husbands" until he finishes speaking, only galloping forward to catch up in the quiet that follows his pronouncement. I'm abruptly reminded of that moment at dinner the night before my birthday, the fleeting feeling that I was agreeing to something I did not understand. The words, "I'm sure we can come to an agreement that pleases all parties." Carrick and Everly's relief that I was so enthusiastic about finding a husband.

About finding *love*, though, is what I had meant.

I should have known. I am the niece to the king, and it had been naïve of me to think that I would be in control of choosing my own husband.

"Who else is on the list?" The question comes out strained, bowing a bit in the middle under the sudden weight of the pit in my stomach.

"Lord Roneldon."

"Lord...Lord Roneldon?! He's old enough to be our father!"

Florien nods seriously. "And he has both the appearance and the personality of a toad."

I might laugh at the accuracy of the comparison if I wasn't so busy drowning in affront. *Lord Roneldon!*

"You can see why I encouraged Delavar," he continues.

"Who is the third?" I persist.

He sighs and scratches at his chin.

"Velasian."

The face that matches the name appears in my mind instantly, wiping away all visions of toads.

"Velasian," I repeat in a considering tone.

"No. Don't go all dreamy-eyed, Reeve. Velasian is bad news, a hundred times less suitable for you than Delavar. He'd pull your heart out and rip it into rose petals to hand out to other women."

I wrinkle my nose at the vivid image. "I suspect you judge him too harshly."

"I don't. *You* judge him too lightly, just because he has a nice face."

And a nice voice. And a nice figure. And a way of making my skin shiver.

I manage not to say any of that aloud.

"You should have given me the option, Florien, and informed me of the list right away, rather than leading poor Lord Delavar to believe that I would welcome his proposal."

"Why *didn't* you accept? He seems perfectly pleasant, and his reputation is spotless."

"He has the personality of an end table!" I throw my arms in the air. "Truly, I had no idea that a person could spend so much time talking while saying absolutely nothing at the same time."

Florien shakes his head, his lips twisting to one side. "He's the best of your options, Reeve."

"I will decide the course of my own life, thank you very much."

I turn toward the door, my mind raging with a fresh batch of anxieties. I twist the knob slowly, tilting my head slightly down and to the right, so I can still see my brother in my periphery. He opens his mouth as though he is about to say something, as though he wants to stop me from leaving.

But he is the son of a duke, and he has not been a friend or a confidant or even a brother to me since that day four years ago when our father had arrived at our schoolroom door, framed uncomfortably in the opening, and declared that it was time for my brother to begin his private lessons. When Florien had left that day, he had left behind our days together, spent running through the forest and swimming in the lake, reading aloud in the playroom, laughing as though the world was ours for the taking.

He had left behind *me*.

I let myself out, and this time, I'm the one who doesn't look back.

CHAPTER FOURTEEN

I don't know how I fall asleep that night, how my churning thoughts slow enough to allow sleep to creep in, but one moment I'm staring at my bedroom ceiling, and the next I'm staring at the stars.

I thank them for joining me here, for bringing their particular brand of comfort, and then I climb to my feet, away from the gallows, and dart for the shadows. I hear the heavy pull on the rope of another body, the second in two nights. There is no peace to be found here. My back digs into the wall. The shadows fully engulf me, but I can't get deep enough.

Taking a deep breath, I reach for the gravel.

My fingers pull a handful up easily. I let them roll across my palm, touching them lightly with my other hand.

If I was still invisible, I would not be able to move them. My touch had held no meaning in this world before last night, before I was seen. I feel relief mingle with terror at the confirmation that I am still visible.

I still feel a tiny edge of uneasiness which I'm not sure will fully abate until I'm acknowledged in this world, whether it be by human or by falcon. I'd prefer the former, if I'm being honest. One human in particular, if I'm being even more so. I regret more than ever not asking Bran where Cecily's home is. I'll never find him in this maze of alleys, especially not without being caught.

The creak of the gallows draws my attention. I don't want to look. I never want to look. But I have to know. I have to make sure it isn't him.

I look over only long enough to determine that it isn't him. That it was a woman, and that she's still whole.

There is barely time for relief to spread through me before that observation truly sinks in.

She's still whole.

My eyes dart toward the sky, but it remains still, quiet. It won't be for much longer, though. The falcons always come to pick at the bodies.

I have to go. But where? My heart starts thudding hard against my ribcage, trying to make a run for it on its own since my feet are glued to the street. I wrestle my fear into one corner of my mind so I can focus on a plan. A half-formed plan, one that I had danced around this morning when I had been uncertain of everything, from whether I'd still be visible to whether I *wanted* to still be visible.

I tell my feet to turn, and they reluctantly obey. They carry me away from the square, keeping to the shadows, only risking me to the view of the sky to dart into the winding alleyways. I find the path, the one on which I encountered Bran a couple nights earlier, and I mirror his footsteps from that night. I pretend that he is in front of me, that I'm following him, and that he is guiding me to safety.

When the wall is suddenly looming before me, I'm startled out of my imaginings. I can't believe that I've made it this far, that I haven't yet been caught. Now only six feet of ground, a stone wall, and a row of sharp-beaked falcons stand in my way.

The word "only" has no place in that thought.

I still have the stones I picked up earlier clenched in my fist. I uncurl my fingers now and study them, selecting the biggest of the bunch before crouching down to let the others fall silently to the ground. Standing back upright, tucked in the murky dark of the shadows, I consider the stone in my hand.

I don't have a slingshot like Bran had. I have only my arm, and however far my arm can fling the rock. It won't go as far, but will it go far enough for me to get to, up, and over the wall before the falcons return?

There is only one way to find out.

I angle my body toward the alley I had just taken, pulling my arm back as far as it can go. Just before I unleash it, though, I hear a sound from a few streets over, a light, skittering sound that echoes through the still night air. I'm not the only one who hears it. As one, the falcons rise up off of the wall, soaring in the direction of the noise.

I don't pause. I launch myself at the wall, clawing my way through the vines with frantic hands, propelling myself up with speed of which I had not known myself to be capable. I'm to the top and dropping down the other side before I even hear the first flap of returning wings, giving silent thanks to the adrenaline coursing through my veins.

I don't land in the right spot. I land hard to one side of the viney bed, my right elbow and knee bearing the brunt of the landing. They skid across the dry dirt as I attempt to stop my tumbling, but the ground is slanted here, curving downhill toward the woods. It's some time before I'm still, lying flat on my back with no air to be found in my searching lungs.

Tears of pain rise up in the backs of my eyes, no matter how I try to blink them away. My knee bellows in protest, refusing to carry its share of my weight. My other one attempts to compensate, but the going is slow. I feel certain that at any moment, an enterprising falcon will glance over to this side of the wall and spot me here, in plain sight, dragging my wounded body and spirit toward the cover of the trees.

Is this going to be every night for the rest of my life? A desperate dash to safety, a scramble over the wall, my body flung into the dirt? This line of thought does nothing to chase the tears from the pools they have created.

It's a small relief when I reach the woods. I don't stop, though. I continue pulling myself deeper and deeper inside of it, until the trees are so thick that they blot out the moonlight entirely. I listen for the gentle lapping of the water at the lake and walk toward it, tripping over roots and trying to ignore the blood running warm down my arm.

Finally, the trees thin. I come out the other side of the forest and am once more greeted by the moon. It's waning now, just under half present, but its light blinds me momentarily anyway. I'm so relieved to see it, to have the whole copse of trees between the falcons and me. I take a few more steps forward so that my toes touch the water.

A sigh slips out at the feel of the cool lake water lapping at my toes. My heartbeat calms. I think that I feel prepared, and so I turn my head a little to the right, along the waterline, to where my mossy bed lies empty. He isn't there. I tell myself that I hadn't truly expected him to be there anyway, that it was unlikely that he would risk the journey a night after losing his home, but disappointment floods my veins nonetheless. I may not have truly expected him, but I very much hoped.

My knee throbs in time with my heart. I'm afraid to look down at the damage, both there and at my elbow, so I keep looking out at the water instead. At the horizon. Straight ahead, and not to the right, not toward the empty spot where he isn't.

A tingle starts at the base of my spine, traveling up and up, tickling at the back of my neck. I feel suddenly exposed, standing out by the water with the trees several paces behind me. I should err on the side of caution and return to the woods, find a place to sit and wait for the sunrise to call me back home.

I swing back around toward the trees and pull up short.

He's there.

He's watching me.

"Hey there, Trouble," he whispers, so softly that the words barely reach my ears intact.

I limp the handful of steps to where he is and fling my arms around his neck.

CHAPTER FIFTEEN

"Oof."

He staggers back a step under my weight before catching both himself and me, his arms coming up around me in what is likely just instinct but feels like a hug. I hold tight to his back, my fingers clenching and creasing his thin shirt, my face buried in his neck.

"You're here," I mumble into the warmth of his skin. I had lied to myself all morning when I had thought myself uncertain as to whether I wished to still be visible. The truth of it is here, in the tumbling, breathtaking relief of him seeing me.

It takes me a moment, therefore, to realize that his arms have dropped back to his sides, while I am clinging to him in a rather unladylike way.

I step quickly back, away, smoothing out my nightgown to hide my sudden discomfiture. I may feel like I've known him a long time, but I am still more stranger than anything else to him. I should have tempered my reaction and not run forward on instinct alone, relieved to see him, to be seen by him, or not.

"So are you," he says. My eyes follow the lift of his arm, his hand landing at the back of his neck.

"I am, and mostly whole, too." I wince down at my bloodied elbow.

He shakes his head and touches my arm lightly, turning it into the light of the moon so he can see it. I don't look down at it, this time not because I don't want to see how bad the wound is, but because I can't drag my eyes away from him just yet.

"You really threw yourself off that wall, didn't you?" The scolding in his voice is gentle and gruff. His hand is still on my arm, a fact which is impossible to forget. The feel of it there occupies the majority of my thoughts for a moment, refusing to be shoved aside.

"You saw me?"

He drops his hand, eyes flicking up to meet mine, a smile, *that* smile, flickering across his lips.

"I was about twenty yards behind you for half of your walk through the city. You were moving fast, and I couldn't get your attention, so I followed you."

"You were there? I can't believe I didn't notice you."

"Yeah, well, you seemed pretty focused. And you did well, sticking to the shadows. You actually took almost exactly the route I usually take to the wall."

My heart stutters a bit, hitching my next breath in my throat, so I shift my focus back to my elbow to change the subject. I lift it back into the light and study it critically.

"Here," I hear him say. "Let me take care of that."

I look back up in time to see him begin to unbutton his shirt.

"You…how do you intend to do that?" Every bit of fluster I feel makes itself present in my tone.

He flashes me a quick smile. "What would the hero in that book of yours do? I'm obviously going to seduce away the pain. That oughta help, don't you think?"

If the blood from my elbow looks nearly black in the night, I wonder what color my face is right now. Darkened, certainly. All of the blood that hasn't exited my knee or my elbow is now present in my face, warm and simmering. My eyes can't help but follow the path of his hands, the expanding flash of skin visible as each button is undone. The way his chest looks carved out of stone, and the way my whole body feels like it is about to lean. Like I won't be able to stop it. Like it will lean, and lean, until I am close enough to reach out and touch his chest and confirm whether it feels as hard as it appears to be. Whether the skin feels as smooth as it looks.

"I just…I don't see how taking off your shirt is going to help my elbow."

"I'm going to tear off a strip of my shirt to wrap it." He says it simply, pragmatically, possibly to my face, but my eyes are still too busy watching his fingers to know for sure where his eyes are directed. "And *then* I'm going to seduce away the pain."

I tear my gaze back up to meet his lightly mocking one.

"That isn't necessary. Uh, the tearing of the shirt, not the seducing. Not that the seducing *is* necessary, I…" I take a deep breath. "What I'm trying to say is that I can tear a piece of my nightgown. It will be fine and whole when I wake up in the morning, and the same can't be said for your shirt."

"Ah, the nightgown." He glares down at the offending garment. "Yes, I see you went with the same look as last night."

"It's what I *sleep* in."

Bran sighs. "So you've said. And no, we're not tearing a piece from it. It's short enough as it is." He throws my bare legs a dark look before shrugging off his shirt and using his teeth to rip it. I don't even take a moment to appreciate the sight of the first shirtless man I've ever been this near to—outside of my brother, swimming in the lake with me before he'd left me, and even then, he'd been more boy than man. No, I'm too busy with that look he'd just given my legs.

I look down at them now, too, confirming as I'd suspected that my nightgown covers all the way down to my knees. Just past them, in fact. For a warm night, with the rapid approach of summer, it's an entirely appropriate nightgown. He hadn't needed to *glare* at my legs.

By the time he looks back up at me from his shirt, my pique has reached an impressive height. It does not help when another quick flash of a smile appears on his face, the corner of his mouth lifting high as his eyes dance.

"Are you riled again?"

"I am not *riled*."

"Are you going to growl again?"

"I don't growl!"

"Hm, if you say so."

"My nightgown is not *short*," I...well, I growl. It does not help with my annoyance. "It's completely appropriate."

"Appropriate? I can practically see through it!"

"Well nobody says you have to look!" I step forward to rip the piece of shirt from his hands and start toward the forest, barely resisting the urge to look back down at my nightgown. I'm suddenly filled with worry that it is, in fact, transparent, but I refuse to give him the satisfaction of seeing my worry.

As I reach the forest, a branch snaps loudly under my careless steps. I freeze as the sound reverberates through the trees. I'm abruptly reminded where I am, that every step here is a risk, that I've been foolish and thoughtless and may have risked not just my life, but Bran's.

I look back over my shoulder at him helplessly, but he's already on his way, almost already to me, reaching for the strip of cloth held tightly between my whitening knuckles. He tugs it gently loose.

"Come here."

I come. I follow him quietly where he leads, placing my feet with the utmost of care, silent as the night now is. The falcons don't seem to have taken any interest in a cracking branch on the outside of the wall. Still, I struggle to take my next breath smoothly.

"Sit." He points to the stump of a tree a yard or two away from the forest's edge, far enough to feel hidden but close enough to still benefit from the offer of light from the sky.

Bran starts wrapping my elbow, silently at first, eyes on the task at hand, before pausing in the middle of his work to look up at me.

"You can breathe, you know. It's all right."

I want to believe him.

"I forgot where we are. I forgot how dangerous it is to be out here, not just for me, but for you. And after you followed me all the way out here to rescue me."

"I didn't rescue you." I think that if his hands weren't busy at my elbow, one of them would have lifted to the back of his neck just now. "I just…helped." He finishes his wrapping and settles back on his heels with a sigh. "And then I insulted you. Sorry, Trouble."

I should take umbrage at the nickname he seems to have assigned me, but it warms my insides pleasantly, lights a comforting fire across my skin and around my body that makes me feel safe. Incongruously, unaccountably, safe.

"It's okay," I say quietly, because it is. Because everything is, for just a moment, all because he's here with me. Whatever reliance I came to feel toward him those nights by the lake has grown tenfold, a hundredfold, in these past two nights of visibility. I shy away from the intensity of it even as I lean another inch toward the warmth of his bare skin.

"It…distracts me. You wearing that." The words sound as though they are wrenched from somewhere deep within, somewhere he had intended to leave them, but somehow they came to be on his tongue, and then out in the air between us. This time his hands are free, and one reaches up to the back of his neck as though of its own volition. I can see how uncomfortable his admission makes him, how much he wishes it unsaid.

And then I process the meaning behind his words and feel the safe fire glow that simmers over my skin swell into a raging inferno.

It distracts *me,* his words and the fact that his shirt is off and the top half of his body is right there in front of me, and lord it is a nice half of a body. There is nothing in excess there. He is all lean muscle, all evidence that he does not lead an idle life. All traceable lines and edges made for fingertips and moonlight.

I look down, away, and silently lift my bloody knee out to him. He seems grateful for the task, as grateful as I am for a distraction from my wayward thoughts, and sets to work tearing another strip from his shirt with which to wrap it. There will be very little of his shirt remaining once he gets through with tending to my wounds. I think of the meager pile of clothing I'd seen in his room and feel gratitude mingled with remorse.

"Thank you."

He doesn't look up from his wrapping. "Do you think this will be a nightly thing, or are you going to try not to shed blood tomorrow night?"

I smile at the top of his head, a giddy smile at the thought of seeing him nightly. I try to keep it out of my voice when I answer. "I shall endeavor to contain my blood."

He looks up to meet my smile with his own, his fingers tying off the makeshift bandage. He touches it lightly when he finishes, and I store this memory somewhere easy to reach so I can pull it out in the morning: the smile in his eyes and his fingertips on my leg.

I have so many questions I want to ask him. They had been circling and ricocheting inside of my head all day, and now I have my opportunity to ask. I refuse to wait another interminable day, another day without knowing if I'll still be visible to ask the next night. I open my mouth to ask the first, the most important.

"What color are your eyes?"

It isn't what I intended to ask. Certainly not the most important, in the grand scheme of things. But I find that it's the most insistent, the first in line on the tip of my tongue.

He squints up at me through the very tips of his hair where they just barely touch his eyelashes, just enough so that I don't know where his hair ends, and his lashes begin. The look he gives me is steady and considering. I knot my hands in my lap and wait.

"Why?"

I feel the aggravation from earlier start to rise back up in my chest, a tangle of it sliding its way toward my throat. I acknowledge that my question was perhaps unexpected, perhaps unnecessary, but it's a straightforward one. It can be answered in a word, maybe two if he feels the need to include a qualifier such as "light" or "dark." But really, the asking of why…it makes me uncomfortable, on edge, uncertain. Self-conscious.

I stand abruptly, and it isn't until he stands, too, until his collarbone is six inches from my face and his bare chest is the slightest of reaches from my hands—*do not reach, do not reach*—that I realize just how close he is. He doesn't tower over me, but I have to tilt my chin an inch to meet his eyes.

His indeterminately colored eyes.

"It's a simple question."

"But a strange one."

The aggravation climbs a little higher. I swallow it down. I feel his nearness acutely.

"It's just something I've wondered." *Since the first day I saw you by the lake. Every time thereafter when I sat next to you and watched you draw pictures, shapes, letters in the water. Last night, this morning, each time I see you, I resent that there is never enough light to tell the color of your eyes.*

I'm not quite ready to tell him about those nights, not quite sure how to do so. The more I think about it, the more certain I am that it won't go well. To reveal that in those moments when he'd thought himself alone, just him and the moon, I'd been sitting beside him, thinking about touching him.

No, I will definitely not be telling him that anytime soon.

"Hm." He's staring down at me as though I'm a puzzle shy a piece, shy a handful of pieces, and he's trying to find what fits there. Testing and trying for the proper shape, the proper fit, but he can't quite get it. He can't quite get me.

If he'd just answered the question the first time, I think peevishly. If he'd just answered it, lightly, easily, we could have moved on and the air could be moving freely between and around us again. Instead, the air is frozen, and we are frozen, and I can't pluck my question back and have it forgotten.

"Never mind," I mutter, attempting to step to the side and put some space between us. I will be able to think more clearly and to ask the questions that need asking, not just the questions that *want* asking, if I have some space from him and his bare chest and his careful hands.

He stops me with one of those hands, at my chin, keeping my face and therefore my body in place. He appears to want to keep studying me, to not give up his puzzle, to find the pieces.

"Blue."

That one word which should have come so easily does not. It comes out like sandpaper, like he pulled it from the same place he pulled from earlier, the deep place where words must be pulled by the roots, not plucked from the stem. He steps abruptly away, and my lungs are grateful when the air starts moving again.

I stay in place as he returns to the water. He settles his hands on his hips and looks out toward the horizon while I note the tension in the muscles of his back. I wonder why that one question had such an effect on him. I don't ask this question. I force it to the back of the line, far from my tongue's edge.

Once it becomes clear that he intends to stay out there, I follow him. I stand beside him and look out at the water, up at the moon, into the stars. He doesn't say anything, and I sort through the remaining questions in my mind for the ones that matter most.

He has blue eyes.

Chapter Sixteen

"What happened this morning?" I keep my tone a whisper, no louder than the lake lightly lapping at our feet. "Was I there and then just...gone?"

"You were," he says slowly. "You were there and then just gone."

I wring my hands. I can't imagine it. Vanishing into thin air like that. It makes me seem less than real, and I don't like the thought of him seeing me that way. I don't like the thought of *being* that way.

I want so badly to be real somewhere. Anywhere.

Here.

With him.

"I blinked," he continues, reluctantly, like he doesn't believe the words even as he says them, "and it was like I had something in my eyes. You were blurry. I blinked to clear it, and that time, when I opened my eyes, you were gone."

"So...you're not going to try to drag me to an asylum then?" I try for a light tone, but I'm not sure I manage it. I'm still trying to shake the feeling that I'm the one who is a piece of a dream.

He turns his head only enough to glance at me out of the corner of his eye before facing the water once more.

"No asylum," he says. "Unless I'm the one who needs to be checking in."

I reach out to touch his arm, but this time, I manage to stop myself. My fingers flutter in the air for a second, thwarted, before I drop my hand to my side. My touch would not reassure him.

"You aren't crazy. This is just…" What is it? I should have planned an end to that sentence before I began it.

Instead, he finishes it for me.

"Dark magic." He turns to fully face me. "It feels like dark magic."

I take a step back, away from the fierce look spreading down his face from his furrowed brow to his pressed lips.

"I've often wondered if there is a magic component in these dreams," I whisper. "But why would you assume dark?"

"Because dark is the only magic Rancore practices. There is no other kind."

There's that name again. Spit out into the air as though he hates the very taste of it.

"I still don't know who that is."

He stares at me so hard I wouldn't be surprised if he was seeing clear through me. Through my pounding heart and racing thoughts to the forest behind me.

"I want to believe you," he says at last.

"Good," I start to say, almost stepping forward. Almost, but then he keeps talking.

"Wanting to isn't the same as actually believing you."

My feet replant themselves where they are. I had been so happy to see him. He had followed me all the way out here, he had wrapped my elbow and knee so gently, he had told me his eyes were blue.

How can there be all of that, when he does not believe me?

"Why did you follow me out here, then?" I try not to let my hurt feelings bleed into my tone, but I do a poor job. I sound miserable even to my own ears. "Why bother if you think I'm a product of dark magic?"

The moonlight caresses his throat, and I see him swallow hard.

"In case you aren't," he says, an undertone, just shy of a whisper. "I came in case you aren't."

I am asleep, at home, but here, I am suddenly exhausted. I lower myself to the ground, turning deliberately toward the water and not him. The water is soothing. It laps at my toes gently.

I can feel his stare burning a hole in the top of my head, but I don't look back up. As badly as I want to be seen by him, I don't want to be seen like this, through distrustful eyes, however blue they may be.

Slowly, slowly, slowly, he sits down beside me.

No, not beside me. He leaves enough space between us to fit two people, should they come upon us and wish to sit in the simmering pool of tension that now lives between us.

"You saved Cecily," he says, but not to me. To himself, I suppose. To the water, to the stars, to whomever he keeps council with out here. It certainly isn't me. "I saw you there, shielding her body with yours when the falcons started their dive. And you stitched her up. You didn't have to do that either."

I wonder if, in the silence after he speaks, he is listening for an answer. From the water, from the stars.

Certainly not from me.

"Unless it was all to gain my trust," he mutters.

"For the love of…" I throw my hands in the air and swivel to face him. "Why? Why would this Rancore have sent me out into the night in an attempt to gain your trust? Are you so special, then? Do you hold information that he wishes to procure? If so, keep it! I don't want it! Don't tell me anything of any substance that you believe could be used against you. I don't care. I am not here for any purpose other than to pass the night until I wake up, at home, in my own bed, where people trust me and don't question my motives and don't *insult my nightgown.*"

His eyebrows have climbed so high that they've disappeared into his hair by the time I've finished speaking. I had at least managed to keep my torrent of words to a whisper, but even so, the silence after that last word, bitten off and bitter, echoes.

He opens his mouth, and his expression turns so thoughtful that I hope for something kind. Something gentle.

"I said I was sorry about the nightgown."

I swear, I have never growled in my life and now here I am, making a sound that can be called no other thing for the second night in a row.

And he *smiles.* He smiles, and it should not have the ability it has to so thoroughly deflate my ire, but it does. It does because it slants, because it shines, because it puts the moon to shame. I'm sure it would put the sun to shame, if there was ever a sun by which to see him.

His smile pulls on a string that lifts the corners of my own lips, and I let him off the hook too easily, far too easily, smiling back at him like this, but I don't know how to help it.

"You're right," he says. "I'm not that special."

Was that what I had said? It cannot possibly be what I had said.

He leans back onto his hands, the tension flooding from his shoulders as he rolls his head from side to side.

"This isn't a world built for trusting strangers."

"I can see that," I say. "Do you require a reintroduction? We aren't strangers anymore once we've been introduced."

He tilts his head my way, flashing a deep, shadow-filled dimple. He moves a little closer. Just a little, but it feels as though we've jumped a ravine. Closer and not farther. Progress.

He sticks a hand out, and I stare at it.

"Bran," he says, the slightest note of teasing in his tone. "And remind me, you are…"

I roll my eyes, but I don't think it matters. My smile only grows as I take his hand. I've never shaken a hand before. Are all men's hands this warm, this strong? His palms are work-roughened against my own unmarred ones, but rather than scratch, they reassure. My hand feels safe in his.

"Reeve." I say it as slowly as I can say a one-syllable name, as though he is hard of hearing or slow of learning or both.

"Nah," he says, squeezing my hand hard enough for my fingers to feel it and think about protesting. And yet, and yet, incongruously, I wish he'd hold on more tightly. "Trouble."

My head falls back as I laugh, and I imagine the notes of it dancing up into the sky. I've never laughed beneath this particular set of stars. I've never held a man's hand under *any* set of stars. I wonder how long a hand shake is supposed to last. I don't think it's supposed to be this long.

I hope it's supposed to be all night.

But we are still some distance apart, and our arms are fully stretched between us, and eventually, he lets go.

I clench my hand into a fist to try to keep some of the warmth of his locked within.

He reroutes his own hand to the water, using one finger of it to start drawing shapes and swirls as he has done so many nights before.

"You made it to Cecily's house this morning?"

"If I hadn't, I wouldn't be here."

The chills that race across my skin have nothing to do with the nighttime air.

"Is she okay?"

"She's fine. She'll have a limp for a little while, and she woke up with a raging headache from that knock on the head, but she'll be all right. Stitches held well."

I feel a small swell of pride. "I'm glad to hear it. Did she tell you what happened to her?"

His finger in the water stops swirling, prompting me to look over at him. His jaw has tightened noticeably, the sharp edge of it pale in the moonlight.

"She's been attracting trouble for a while now. She's got a face on her, and a mouth on her, and the combination...It was bound to come to a head."

"You mean it wasn't an accident? Someone did that to her?"

The smirk he tilts my way has no humor behind it. "Yeah, Trouble. Someone did that to her."

"What kind of world is this?" I whisper it to him, to the water, to the very world I question. He sighs long and low.

"A dark one. Even in the daytime, when the sun is up and shining, it's a dark world." He goes back to his drawing. "What's it like where you're from?"

I think of Acarsaid from the hill, Jax beside me, his caution that we only know it from afar. "I think it's a fair land. Our king is kind, and he genuinely does his best by his people." I know this much to be true, at least. Whatever occurs beyond the palace walls that I may not know, Carrick feels the weight of it, and he does what he can.

Bran scoffs beside me. "I'm not sure Siber even knows that there are people in Tenebris beyond his court."

I start at the unfamiliar names. "Is Siber your king? Is this place called Tenebris?"

The humor returns softly to his lips, the smirk loosening into a smile. "Sorry. Yes, King Siber of Tenebris. Our leader, our sovereign, our indifferent liege."

My thoughts pull to the gallows. The sway of the rope, the particular sound it makes when it's weighted by a body. The savage delight of the falcons feasting on it above my head. "He leads by cruelty?"

"He doesn't *lead* at all. He allows Rancore to do so for him."

I don't want to ask. I don't want to break this peace between us again by asking. But at the same time, I have a hard time *not* asking. Rancore of the dark magic. The name that tastes like dirt upon Bran's tongue.

He takes pity on me.

"Wizard. Rancore is the wizard of Tenebris. The falcons are his particular pets."

"His *pets?*"

"They're dark magic. Maybe they were ordinary birds once, but he changed them. Made them the monsters they are, guarding the streets at night and slaughtering anyone who sets foot outside."

I swallow hard. Dark magic. I've never heard of it being used in Acarsaid, certainly not where Thrall is concerned. I can't imagine our principled old wizard holding any credence in such a thing. He uses his magic to gentle the weather, not to manifest cruelty in the form of winged creatures.

"Why are you outside, Bran? At night, with those monsters— those falcons—portending death. Why risk it?"

He shrugs, his finger pausing for just the barest of moments, so brief that I would've missed it had my eyes not been following each sweep, each swirl of his fingertip in the water, before resuming. "I thought you might be out tonight, getting into all sorts of trouble. I figured, after Cecily...I owed you."

I feel a strange sense of disappointment settle inside of me, draping itself loosely over my heart and coiling into the pit of my stomach. I stop watching his finger and instead dip my own hand into the water, using it not to draw, but to scoop, to hold the water in my curled fingers and let it stream lightly out, down back into its source, over and over again. I feel its coolness, its fathomless weight, its resilience. I wish I could be as cool, as fathomless, as resilient. Instead, I listen to the echo of his words in my head.

"I think you can consider us even now." My voice sounds soft, dismal, even to my own ears. I think about delivering it unto his ears just like that, unadorned and honest, but I force a smile at the last second to sharpen its soft edges.

He lifts his finger from the water and shakes it lightly, droplets skittering noiselessly across the air, across my vision. I try to focus on my own hand, on my own patch of water, even as my periphery strains to watch him shift, to watch as he turns to face me more fully.

"Where will you go tomorrow night?"

I scoop up another handful of water. "Here, I'd imagine."

"Every night?"

The thought of it tightens the covering on my heart until it threatens to suffocate me, hardens the coil in my stomach into a stone. I think of the desperate scramble over the wall, the handful of heartbeats between landing on the other side and the falcons' return. It will be a near thing.

Every night.

"Every night that I am visible." Still dismal, still soft. I don't have a smile to offer with it this time.

I reach for the water once more, my movements automatic now, no conscious link between my brain and my hand. I'm only stopped by his hand, only stopped by it touching my knee, only stopped by his eyes on mine when I look up at him.

"You can stay at Cecily's. They have room, even with me there. I'll explain to them your…situation…and I'm sure they'll be fine with it."

I offer what would be a smile, an unforced smile, except I feel the sadness in it. Can a smile be a smile if it's layered in sadness? I offer it anyway.

"You don't owe me anymore, Bran. You never owed me. You saved us last night, and you saved me tonight."

His hand is still on my knee, warm, resting solidly. It tells me to keep relying on him, to keep needing him, even as I shake my head at his offer. I should push it off, to stop the swelling need, but my strength only extends to the shake of my head. I used so much of it to get to the wall and over it, to drag my body through the trees and to this lake, and I find that it's in short supply just now, with his hand on my knee.

"I'm not offering because I owe you," he says with quiet solemnity. His eyes glint, and I wonder if they're so dark, so unknowable, because they blend in with the deep, deep blue of the night sky. I wonder if, away from the night, I could see the color for itself. I wonder if there will ever be an "away from the night" for he and I.

"Then why?" My head no longer shakes, but it doesn't nod either. Not yet. He considers his answer for long enough that I wonder if he even knows himself why he's offering.

"I'm trying to save the falcons from you," he says finally, his tone lightened. "You'll scare them half to death with that growl of yours."

I think about glaring, but I surprise myself with a quirk of a smile instead. My lips twitch entirely of their own volition, and they shift even more fully upward at an answering quirk from his lips.

"Or maybe I'm too much of a gentleman to leave a girl from another world wandering the streets in a scrap of a nightgown."

I'm fully grinning now, no tangle of annoyance even at the mention of my nightgown, because he is fully grinning now, too. The reflection of the moon on the lake shimmers toward us, its beam a path running directly between us, through the gap which I thought could hold another person but now somehow couldn't even hold half of one. Somewhere in our shifting, in our turning to face one another, in our grinning, my knee is just a lean and a tilt from his. His hand has fallen off of it, but I can still feel the warmth embedded in my skin. I hope that I can bring it with me when I awaken, the outline of his hand against me. I hope that I can bring this one thing with me.

But if I can only choose one thing, maybe it would be his lips, the way they tilt, the way they lift. Maybe it would be his eyelashes, the way they slope, the way they tangle.

No, it would be his eyes, the way they flicker, the way they shine. It would be his eyes, the way they see me.

"Okay, then." I nod easily now. "If you're sure it's all right, I'll stay there."

"I'm sure. Where do you..." Bran clears his throat. "Where do you arrive when you...get here?"

My smile shifts into wicked delight at his discomfiture. "I float in on a cloud, and it drops me where it sees fit."

It's amazing how easily his smile can transform itself into a scowl.

The tilt is already there, the angle of his lips, so it's really just a tightening deep in the corners, accompanied by a creasing between his eyebrows. It delights me even more. My laugh threatens to be buoyant, but I dampen it to the night. He shakes his head at me in mock censure.

"Are you always going to be this difficult?"

"Me? Difficult?" I flatten a hand against my chest.

"You. Difficult." He jabs a finger into that hand. I try to grab at it with my other, but he moves too quickly, and instead his hand is the one capturing mine. He holds the fingers of it securely, immovably, and I think about struggling against his grip but don't. I don't struggle because he is holding my hand, and I want for him not to stop.

But the sky is shifting around us, the darkness changing. I don't pull my fingers from his grasp, but I answer his question seriously this time, aware of the passing minutes.

"I arrive in the middle of the city square every night, beneath the gallows."

"Hell." He shakes his head. "Not the most subtle of places."

I grimace a little, thinking of the nights when I arrive right in the midst of the falcons' feast. "Not at all. It's never mattered before."

He nods thoughtfully, looking back out toward the water, seemingly unaware that his hand is still holding on to mine. I'm aware, though. Even with the image of waking up beneath falcons rending skin from bone, beneath falcons who can *see* me, dancing across my mind, I'm aware.

"I'll meet you there. Make for the shadows as soon as you get there, and I'll be there. I'll lead you to Cecily's."

Will I never stop owing this man? Gratitude swims through my veins, glowing and warm and soaked in the moonlight. Before I can put it into words, before I can find the words to encompass the magnitude of it, he sighs softly in what I know is his cue. It's time for him to leave.

And so I have to settle for the simplicity of, "Thank you."

He squeezes my fingers once before letting go, and I realize then that he *was* aware. He was aware, and he held on to them anyway. I tell myself to wonder about it later, because right now, he's pulling himself to his feet.

"How will you get back to the other side?"

He is towering now, his shadow blotting out a swath of stars, but I find that I don't miss their light. I would rather look up and see him than look up and see a whole world of constellations. He is the beauty of the starlight, the beauty of the moon, the beauty of the whole night sky. I would rather look up and see him than look up and see anything else.

"There's a tree a little ways down with a branch that dips near the wall. I stand there and shoot a rock over the wall, down the street, and the falcons chase after the sound of it. It gives me enough time to jump from the branch, to the wall, and down onto the other side."

I smile up at the shadow of him, remembering a nighttime wish that feels forever ago but was really just yesterday, or the day before, or the day before that. I remember thinking that this is what I wish for my future husband to be like. This is how he would move, how clever he would be, how he would look in the moonlight.

This, this, this.

He starts to back away. "You'll be all right?"

"I'll just stay here until I wake up."

A tilted smile in response. I work hard to memorize it, to embed it in my memory just in case. Just in case this is the last night.

"See you tomorrow," I call after him.

The shadows steal the sight of his smile from me, but I hear it in his voice as he answers. "'Night, Trouble."

The forest swallows Bran whole, and the night collapses into silence around me. I use one finger to draw shapes and swirls in the water, and it parts for me, as it's never done before. It lets my touch change it, shift it. It lets my touch matter.

I spell out his name, over and over again.

CHAPTER SEVENTEEN

"Are you sure you're all right?"

"Mm," I murmur noncommittally in response to Tiv, trailing my fingers lightly along a hallway table as I walk. I tap a finger against the side of a golden vase as I pass it, and I think of Bran's hand on my knee.

"She's smiling an awful lot," I hear Demes say in his version of a discreet tone.

I turn my head to look at a painting, but instead of seeing my grandfather, King Draegen, I see Bran. Instead of King Draegen's full, grey beard, I see the sharp line of Bran's jaw. Instead of King Draegen's stoic face, I see Bran's grin. I feel the way it made me feel last night to look at it. I keep walking, each exhale halfway to humming until they fully form a tune, a melody, a happy little song.

"Do you have any actual *plans* for the day?" Jax cuts in finally. "Or are you just going to wander the hallways?"

I beam my smile up to the right, to my most taciturn guard. He answers it with a look that implies I've taken leave of my senses. Perhaps I have.

"I thought that we could go out to the gardens for a while. Would that make you happier, Jax?"

"Only if it would make you a little *less* happy," he grumbles. I laugh outright, and he circles his eyes all the way up to the ceiling with a shake of his head.

"Ah Jax," Perc contributes from my left. "Let her be happy."

"She's always happy. This is something else altogether."

He's right. I *am* almost always happy. This is…something else, yes. This is joy. This is promise. This is a vision for a future without an empty space beside me. With a face there…a *dreamt* face there. The tune drops abruptly off, away, forgotten. My smile does, too. Reality likes to keep to the shadows of my mind sometimes, but it's always there. It's always known. It makes sure to remind me of its presence in fits and starts, leaps out of corners at just the right moment. Just the *wrong* moment.

My subconscious taunts me in uncountable, immeasurable ways. It creates horror, it creates beauty, and then it strips away the beauty to leave just horror. Just uncertainty, just sadness.

"Hey now." Jax peers down at me. "You know I didn't mean anything by it."

"I know." I'm saved from having to think up an explanation, for both my exultant happiness and its abrupt disappearance, by a heavy thumping approaching from just around the corner. As it gets nearer and nearer, my hands shoot up to my head to make sure my hair is in place, or as in place as it will allow, before darting down to smooth my dress.

His cane rounds the corner before the rest of him. I have a moment to take in the heavy wood of it, the carved head clenched beneath a withered, stubby-fingered hand. And then Thrall steps out behind it.

My spine snaps ramrod straight from my neck to my bottom, my chin frozen in a sharp tilt, a pleasant smile glued to my lips. This is my uniform, my armor, whenever I encounter Thrall. Eighteen years under the same roof as the wizard, and my trepidation toward him has not yet lessened.

He looks like he's of a mind to walk right past me without acknowledgement, but between my guards and I, we take up too much of the hallway for him to pass by easily. He thumps one more time, one more step, and then pulls up short a few feet away.

I drop into the deepest curtsy I can manage—not an easy feat with an unbending spine.

"Thrall, sir. Good morning."

"Yes." His voice is booming, entirely at odds with his diminutive stature. If we were standing side by side, he would come only to my shoulder. As it is, from a few feet away, he looks liable to be stepped on by Tiven without my tallest guard even noticing.

He always looks in some state of disarray, and today is no different. The tufts of white hair that remain on his head stick out at all angles as though drawn toward the walls, the ceiling, everywhere but the floor. He has lines inside of lines inside of lines creasing his face, showing every bit of the century and a half he is purported to have lived through. I don't suppose any of them are laugh lines, though. I have never even seen Thrall smile, let alone make a sound that could even marginally be interpreted as a chuckle.

He bows his head an inch. No more, possibly less. And that is all. A booming "Yes," followed by the barest show of respect he can muster, and then he steps around us to continue on his way. My guards bow deeply as he passes, awe showing plainly on each and every one of their faces. Even dour Jax can't hide his veneration for the old wizard.

We stay in place until the thumping cane and its cantankerous wielder turn another corner and leave our sight. I slump back into my natural posture, still proper from years of etiquette training, but not as though I'm strapped to a tree trunk.

"Lord, he's terrifying," I mutter.

Demes barks out a laugh, Perc chokes on a snicker of his own, and Tiven and Jax offer me a matched set of disapproving head shakes.

"You should respect him, my lady. He does immeasurable good for this kingdom," Tiven chides.

"Yes, I know," I sigh. "And I *do* respect him. But that doesn't mean he doesn't terrify me."

We turn to make our way toward the garden room, but we don't make it more than a few steps before Aunt Everly sweeps out of a room and intercepts us, a giant bouquet of flowers held aloft before her face. She tilts it to one side so she can see me.

"I thought I heard you! Look what arrived for you, dear!"

My mouth drops open at the festoon of peonies, orchids, roses, and lilacs. They form a pastel rainbow, pale and lovely and deliciously fragrant.

"For *me?*"

"There's a card!" She sets the vase carefully on a side table and reaches into its bowels to pull forth a small envelope. I take it from her and slide the card gently from its casing.

> *A belated thank you for the dance.*
> *From my toes.*
> *– A.V.*

The corners of my lips stretch upward as I read, as I reread, as I reread once more. Three short lines, but I spend enough time scanning them that they may as well be a novel set there on the bit of vellum.

Once my eyes finally flick away from the words, I see that Everly has her hands clasped in one another, pressed to her chest. My smile grows as I take in her obvious excitement.

"I have no wish to invade your privacy, but I fear that I will perish from curiosity if you don't tell me who they're from."

I laugh and tuck the card back into its envelope. "They're from Lord Velasian."

The squeal she lets out is so girlish, so unqueenly, that I can't help laughing.

"Oh, *Reeve*, I knew that the two of you would hit it off! I'm always sure that there is no man more handsome than your uncle, but when Lord Velasian's in the room, I forget my certainty."

I wipe tears of laughter from my eyes, my shoulders still shaking in my amusement. "I'll try not to tell Uncle Carrick."

"Oh, please don't. It would take weeks to soothe his ego, and I find I'm rather busy these days."

I rest a hand lightly on her arm. "Your secret is safe with me."

She looks down at my hand for a long moment, and I can hear the long, deep breath she takes, just long enough and just deep enough to pull the lightness from the moment.

"Are you all right?" I ask quietly.

She looks as though she's about to wave my concern aside, but she can't quite manage it. Instead, she lifts one shoulder helplessly.

"In all seriousness, I worry about him. He always carries more than his share of worries—Acarsaid's share, really, as it should be with the king—but lately, it's more. I can see the stress eating away at him. It's a difficult thing for me to witness when there is so little I can do to help him."

I had seen it myself at dinner the other night. The weighted look to him. The smile that didn't fully curve, that struggled to reach his eyes. I had known something was amiss, but for Everly to confide in me like this…it must be worse than I suspected.

"I'm sure just being there for him is of help," I say, my hand sliding down to hers and squeezing it hard. "I can see it in how he looks at you, that your very presence makes the load a little lighter on him."

Her answering smile seems to be more gratitude than anything else. "Thank you, Reeve. You always know just what to say."

She leaves me to attend to her duties, and I slide the card back out of its envelope to reread a handful more times. I don't know what I search for between those few short words, but I search anyway. Hidden meaning, perhaps. I think of that moment on the terrace and hope that these flowers mean that Arden is not mad at me for turning away.

Florien finds me there, still in the hallway with the card in my hands, my guards shifting their weight from one leg to the other in their impatience to get moving. I look over my shoulder at the sound of the approaching footsteps, but turn away without comment when I see that they belong to him.

"Reeve," he greets me, either unaware of or unconcerned by my reluctance to speak with him.

"Florien." I keep my tone free of inflection or encouragement. Hopefully he will be like Thrall, just passing through and content with the barest of greetings.

I am not to be so lucky, though.

"Have you given any further thought to Lord Delavar's proposal?"

I turn to face him more fully, the hand grasping the card dropping to my side. "I have not given it a moment's more consideration. I gave him my answer."

His jaw clenches so tightly that I'd imagine the slightest of taps to it would cause it to shatter. "Did you even *listen* to a word I said yesterday? You have to marry, and he is your best option."

"In *your* opinion, he is my best option," I bite out. "And as I made clear to you yesterday, your opinion carries no weight with me."

His jaw clenches, and I abruptly wish it hadn't, because what clenches it is hurt. I see it plainly in his eyes, a passing ache there in their grey. The same deep grey our mother's held. That hurt in that grey builds a tangle of regret in the pit of my stomach for my words and their bite.

I see him visibly shake it off, shoving aside the hurt until stubbornness resumes its place there. It loosens the tangle in my stomach so that I can remember why I put the bite into my words. It was not unearned.

"Life is not a fairy tale, Reeve." He sounds unaccountably tired beneath the iron tone. "There is no knight coming to sweep you off your feet. Delavar will be kind to you, and he will ensure that you want for nothing. What more could you possibly be hoping for?"

Love, I want to tell him, but in his words, I hear the echo of Arden's on the terrace. More than that, I see the dancing green of his eyes, I feel his hand at my elbow, the tickle of his breath in my ear. I feel his arms around me on the dance floor, and I see his head leaning closer and closer to mine.

My fingers clutch his card, the belated thank you from his toes.

I blink, and I see myself on his arm out in the village, envious eyes on us.

In the next blink, I see Arden lowering his head to listen to whatever I whisper in his ear, I see his eyes sparking in response, his lips curving dangerously, his arm tightening around my waist.

I see myself outside of these palace walls.

No guards, nobody but me to lead my own way. To lead my own way, but with someone by my side. With a companion, a Tristan to my Charlotte.

I see an *adventure*, an adventure that isn't a dream, an adventure that isn't a story, an adventure that is more than Lord Delavar ensuring I want for nothing.

Nothing but love.

I see all of those things, and I feel all of those things, and so I speak rashly.

I want desperately, in that moment, to prove to Florien that I control my own destiny.

"I have already made my decision, Florien. I am going to marry Lord Velasian."

The final word drops from my lips at the same moment his eyes flick just above my shoulder. At the same moment I process that there have been footsteps growing ever closer, footsteps whose echo had been lost to my self-righteous proclamation. There could be any number of people behind me in that moment, any number of people who had been walking down this hallway and stumbled upon us standing here, but the voice that floats up from behind me is the worst of all possibilities.

"Wonderful, Reeve. I'm pleased to hear you came to a decision so swiftly. I will inform His Majesty at once."

As though in slow motion, I turn. I catch the deepened lines at the sides of my father's face, the faint smile there in a place where smiles are scarce. I watch as he turns to start back down the hallway, toward the east wing of the palace. Toward my uncle's study. Toward *the king's* study.

I think that I had been about to flounce back down the hall. I think that I was going to head toward the gardens with my guards and gloat at the look of shock on my brother's face, to revel in how my bluff had jolted him. Instead, I stand frozen and watch my father walk away.

As he walks, he carries with him every hope and every dream I had held for my future.

CHAPTER EIGHTEEN

The grandfather clock ticks away the seconds that pass as I stand frozen in place. My father has long since rounded the corner, long since disappeared from view. Florien is still somewhere behind me, and my guards form a scattered diamond figure nearby. None of us move so much as a muscle as the clock continues to count out every moment that passes since my reckless declaration.

I have declared my intention to marry a man I only just met. A man with dancing eyes, yes, but also glinting eyes, dangerous eyes. Dangerous in their ability to make my heart move in unexpected ways. A mercurial man who does not believe in marriage, in faithfulness, in romance.

I have to stop this from happening.

I pull my feet from the ground as though pulling up rooted trees. They resist heavily for a moment before coming unglued and propelling me forward, along the same path my father had just taken. I hear rather than see my guards fall into formation, my mind replaying over and over again my father's voice and the smile on his face.

The journey is quick with my mind in upheaval. I'm in front of the king's study door before I even realize it, my hand poised to knock. It takes three attempts, three times of my hand resting lightly, soundlessly there, before I manage to truly knock. My uncle calls out that he is in a meeting, but I knock again, more insistently, even my years of etiquette bowing to my desperation.

He finally bids me enter, and I swing open the door to find him leaning forward at his desk while my father sits on its other side, also leaning forward. A swath of papers rests between them, and I wonder if it's the dossier of which Florien had spoken.

"Reeve!" My uncle's tone is jubilant, harkening back to years before when the weight across his shoulders was lesser. Back when this tone was commonplace, and his smile came easily. Something in me pulls at it, at hearing it there laced behind my own name. "Your father and I were just discussing the good news. I cannot tell you how pleased this makes me."

I smile uncertainly, a faltering smile, just because it feels expected from me. I don't know how to respond, and I'm saved from having to do so by my father.

"Yes, I am as well. I'm proud of your selection. It's a very responsible one, aligned with the interests of the kingdom."

My smile shifts into brilliance, desperation leaking away in the face of his words. My father, proud of me! I have never heard him profess such, and I am sure then that I will do anything, marry anyone, to keep that look in his eyes, to keep it directed at me. It takes me several seconds, of standing in that doorway and grinning like an idiot, for the words following "proud" to make their way into my mind.

My resultant confusion must shine through on my face, for my uncle laughs and leans forward to clap my father on his shoulder.

"Ah, greyham, I doubt she even knows of our interests! You saw the way they danced at the ball, obviously the beginnings of young love." He turns to me, his gentle smile heavily painted with relief.

"Reeve, I'm pleased for the match for the kingdom's sake, but I'm even more pleased for your sake. It was one of your mother's greatest wishes to see you married well, and this...this is a very good marriage."

I swallow hard and try to find words. Not just any words, but the right ones. "I wasn't sure how you would feel," I say slowly, carefully. "His reputation..."

"Ah." Carrick waves a careless hand. "All young men go through a wild time. He will settle down into marriage, I'm sure. I saw the way he looked at you. For you, he will settle."

"What," I clear my throat through my doubt, through the uncertainty his words unleash inside of me when I can still remember Arden turning to walk away from me, "what is the benefit of the match to the kingdom?"

"You needn't concern yourself..." my father starts to say, but Carrick steps in.

"If she wants to know, greyham, I see no reason not to tell her." He turns his attention back to me. "Arden's father, Lord Baewar, is a valuable member of my council. He has always been so, even before I took the throne. He is a traditionalist, though, and for the measures I wish to pass...I would like to ensure as much as is possible that he will be on my side."

He is carefully vague, stepping cautiously around details which he cannot share with me, and so I don't push him on the specifics. Instead, I study the slope of his shoulders and know beyond a doubt that they stoop less than they did the last time I'd seen them. They combine with the jubilance and the relief in his smile and eyes into something too big, too marked, for me to take away. I remember well the melancholy passing over him at dinner a couple nights before, and I would give anything not to see it there again.

I would give my future. The vision I had for it. I realize then that I will give that and more, whatever they ask of me, for my uncle's relief and my father's pride.

I excuse myself quietly as they return to their papers and their discussion. I retreat back into the hallway and allow the memory of their faces to follow me for the whole of the quiet walk to the gardens. I allow only them, only the reasons behind what is to come, to circle my thoughts. Only once I reach the informal gardens and lower myself to a bench do I allow myself to think on what *is* to come.

I am to marry Lord Arden Velasian.

The card from his flowers is crumpled now, balled tightly in one fist. I put it on my lap and try to straighten it out with my shaking hands, seeing the words there but no longer absorbing them. I am to marry him, and he doesn't know. He sent me flowers, and I trapped him in marriage. I hardly know him, but I know enough of him to know that he will not take kindly to it. He had called marriage shackles, and he had hoped to avoid it as long as possible. I had allowed him two days from the night we met to avoid them, and then I had slapped them onto his wrists myself.

I shudder at the thought of his reaction. It will be an inauspicious beginning to our union. To our *marriage*.

The word dances across my thoughts and down to my pounding heart. I have a faint, distant memory of Bran standing above me and blocking out the stars, a memory of his hand on my knee, but both feel like they were pulled from my imagination. They feel like dreams, just dreams, in the face of my new reality.

"I am getting married." I try the words out loud. Dem, Perc, and Tiv have taken their usual places on the benches around me, while Jax has taken his usual place hovering on the edge of the garden, constantly vigilant. The others are vigilant, too, but they don't have the same rigidity that Jax applies to his watchfulness.

"So we heard," Tiv answers, slowly.

"You fairly shouted it at your brother," Dem adds. He tilts his face into the sun, his skin already matching the red of his hair after mere minutes outside. I realize that I have forgotten my sunhat, and that my face will be hopelessly freckled in short notice, but my worry fades quickly into the background of my thoughts.

"And then you chased down your father." Perc leans back onto his hands, his long legs sprawled out in front of him and crossed at the ankles. His curls are plastered to his forehead, his tanned skin glistening. The sweltering heat of approaching summer is unpleasant for me, and I'm not dressed head to toe in black and armor. I feel abruptly sorry for my guards and stand, rerouting our small party to the shade of the forest.

"Yes, thank you for the summary," I mutter tartly as we walk. "I did notice both of those things."

"Did you intend to say it?" I look up to meet Jax's inscrutable gaze.

"It was a bluff," I admit. "To wipe the superiority off of Florien's face. I meant to take it back, but the way my father and uncle reacted...I couldn't do it."

"And now you're getting married." Jax's face is somber, his tone set to match.

"Lord, Jax, it's not like a death sentence. The king wouldn't marry her off to someone if he wasn't a good'un." Dem jogs on lightly ahead of us, spinning briefly to direct his words to Jax before turning to face forward again.

"No, he wouldn't," I agree musingly. He had sounded so thoroughly unconcerned by Arden's reputation, so certain that marriage would change him. Settle him. That *I* would settle him. I think of what he said about the way Arden looked at me and wonder if it was any different than the way he looks at other women.

I feel suddenly, overwhelmingly, that I must warn him. That I must explain before he finds out from the king or his father. If I am going to spend the remainder of my life with him—the thought stutters my heart sideways, unmoors it, sends it down to the pit of my stomach—I would like to start it with honesty. Consideration. Understanding.

I need to talk to him.

I pause mid-step, Tiven nearly barreling me over from the suddenness. Demes continues several paces before he realizes that the rest of us have stopped, and then he joins the others in directing a questioning glance my way.

"I need to go back."

They don't ask for an explanation, only turning in place to prepare to start back the other way. Gratitude washes over me as we return to the palace, for their presence, even if it is their job, and for their support, though it is not their job. My guards are nowhere to be found on the family tree on the giant tapestry in the palace library, but I imagine them there anyway. I imagine that they are just above me, sheltering me from the storms.

As I return to my bedroom, to Guin's warm smile, I imagine that she is just beneath me on that tree, bolstering me, pushing me upward into the sunlight. I return her smile with as much of one as I can manage. She sees my preoccupation and excuses herself quietly, leaving me alone to my thoughts.

Alone to my parchment paper, seated at my desk.

I let my pen hover over the paper for a moment before deciding on the words.

And then I crumple that sheet up, start again, decide on new words. It takes some time to perfect, but I end up with a few short sentences, requesting that Arden call on me at his earliest convenience and making sure to emphasize the urgency of the matter. I hand the note off to Demes to bring to our swiftest footman for delivery, asking Dem to impress upon the footman the importance of waiting for a response to bring back to me, and then I pace my bedroom like a wild animal, locked in a cage of my own making. I close the door and rip the envelope open, scanning it with the same hunger I had devoured his earlier card with. This one is even shorter.

Regretfully indisposed.
Will call in the morning.
– A.V.

I throw my head back and stifle a growl. I had underlined the word "urgent" *three times*. Surely that had warranted at least a little more concern than this handful of words.

Darting back out into the hallway, I ask Dem to fetch the footman. I wait impatiently in the hallway for them to return while my remaining three guards do not even attempt to be subtle in their exchanged glances.

Once the footman is standing uneasily before me, I hold the note from Arden aloft.

"Did you see Lord Velasian write this?"

"I did, my lady." He glances uneasily from me to the guards in a semi-circle behind me.

"How did he look when he wrote it?"

"Look, my lady?"

"Did he look as though he was about to go out, or like he was ill, or…?"

"He looked normal, I suppose. Didn't appear ill. I overheard him say to his housekeeper that he would be staying in for the evening."

Staying in, is he? I fight to keep my impatience and frustration from my face as I thank the footman and dismiss him. As he practically sprints down the stairs, I turn to face my guards.

"I would like to take the carriage."

Their eyebrows collectively inch upward. I almost never leave the palace grounds. Carrick has always insisted upon tripling my guard when I leave the walls, and truly, rolling through the village in a palace carriage surrounded by twelve guards is like being a reluctant member of an entirely unexciting parade. One time I had gone out to buy myself a new hat, but because of the way it had stopped traffic and set everyone to staring, I have sent for the milliner to come to me ever since.

"I have an errand," I continue, attempting to insert certainty into my tone when in truth all I feel is an absence of it. "A small errand. I won't be needing the full contingent of guards."

I try to use my most authoritative tone, but all four of them shake their heads before I even finish speaking.

"We follow the king's orders," Tiven says firmly. "Only if we receive orders from him to lessen our ranks will we do so."

I bite the inside of my cheek, hard. I can't show up at Arden's home with twelve guards surrounding a palace carriage. I can't have the whole of Acarsaid watching me walk up to the bachelor lodgings of Lord Arden Velasian. The talk it would produce…No, it's impossible.

I begin to formulate a new plan, a reckless plan. I back slowly into my bedroom to feel it out in its entirety, shaking my head at my guards as I do so.

"Never mind, then."

I close the door behind myself and settle onto the window seat, looking out at the brightness of the day and thinking. I focus entirely on my plan, not allowing my thoughts to wander. There are far too many places they could go, to steady blue eyes or glittering green eyes, to a lake at my feet or a terrace at night. I keep them steadfastly on the task at hand, and I plan.

If Arden will not come to me…well, then, I will have to go to him.

CHAPTER NINETEEN

Some time later, under the cover of night, I order my hand to knock.

But it is as though I'm outside my uncle's study once more, once more at odds within myself, and my hand steadfastly refuses.

Truly, the hard part is done. I had lied to my dearest friends, to Guin and my guards, and convinced them all that I had a pounding headache and would be resting for the duration of the night. I told them that I was not to be disturbed, and under the weight of their concerned expressions, I had nearly called off the entirety of the plan.

Instead, I had taken a deep breath, plastered a reassuring smile on my face for Guin's benefit, and clung to my need to warn Arden, to explain.

I had let the lie stand.

From there, the plan had involved my window, the giant oak outside of it, a quick dart through the informal gardens. A little used forest path Florien and I had discovered on one of our childhood jaunts, the collapsed portion of earth beneath the wall there. A hurried walk past the village shops now shuttered to the night, and the finding of Arden's home.

I've never seen the village like this. On my own. In the dark. I am not nearly as familiar with these streets as I am with the ones I wander every night while I sleep. Those are crammed and crooked, full of sharply winding alleyways that may lead somewhere or may lead nowhere. I used to constantly wind up at dead ends there as a child, having to turn back and retrace my steps. The buildings on either side always loom there, close together, tall, narrow.

The streets of Acarsaid are nothing like those nightmare streets. There is one main thoroughfare, and at one end of it sits the palace. Beyond the palace, there is a long stretch of road that runs through the forest, and then suddenly, the village appears. There are small branches of roads running off the main road once you reach the village, but they don't wind. They are all straight, direct, easy to navigate. The buildings are short and wide, welcoming even in the dark.

The forest route I took allowed me to avoid the long main road and the giant gate where guards would surely have stopped me from leaving the grounds without my own guards, let alone the whole contingent. By the time I got under the wall and through the last little stretch of woods, the village was already in sight.

And now I'm standing before the door, and my hand is poised to knock, and it steadfastly refuses.

"You're being ridiculous," I mutter to myself.

I knock purposefully three times.

The door opens so swiftly that I feel abruptly, self-consciously certain that the butler had been watching me through a window, observing my faltering knock and flagging courage. I take solace in the fact that the hood of my cloak pulls down low, the shadows of it hiding most of my face.

"Can I help you?" He inserts an impressive degree of ice into the question, standing so rigidly and properly that I wonder if he has suffered some form of spinal injury. He looks down his stub nose at me as though he has mistaken me for a rodent. His nose is the only part of him given to roundness. Everything else I see, from the high cheekbones to his jutting chin to his wrists where they peer out from his gloves, seems as though it would be more at home on a skeleton than on a living human being.

"I'm here to see Lord Velasian." I keep my voice low, although I'm fairly certain that nobody around would recognize me purely by my voice.

He looks as though he would like to close the door in my face, but instead he simply narrows his already narrow eyes even further and steps back, allowing me to enter. He escorts me three steps to the left into a sitting room and gestures imperiously within.

"I will fetch His Lordship. You may have a seat."

He leaves hastily, closing the door behind himself, leaving me to wonder why he hadn't asked for my name, why he hadn't offered me a refreshment or a cup of tea, why he had acted as though it wasn't entirely out of the ordinary for a young woman to show up alone, on the cusp of night, unannounced, draped in a cloak.

Then I realize what it means. Perhaps it *isn't* out of the ordinary. Arden had made no secret of the fact that his reputation is an earned one.

I wander the cavernous sitting room slowly, taking in the sparse decor. It's clearly the sitting room of a bachelor, one who does not host proper parties or teas, one who has no need for any furniture beyond a small curved loveseat, a long, narrow table beside the door, a single straight-backed chair. There are no paintings on the wall, only an antique-looking sword beside a dull, rusting battle axe, above a row of old, evidently used, shields.

I spend some time studying them, as they are by far the most interesting part of the room. I wonder at the battle axe, especially.

Is that long-dried blood on its blade? I shudder at the thought. Acarsaid has not seen war in over a century now. There had been an uprising under King Draegen's reign, and the country had divided into civil war. The wealthy versus the poorer class. From what little I remember having read in history books on the topic, the poor had not stood much of a chance. They'd had the element of surprise in their favor, and once that had expired, it was largely over.

But the death toll had been high.

It makes me think of Bran. Of the world he lives in, with its brutality and rule by terror. I had said Acarsaid was not like that. And it isn't. But perhaps it had been.

I didn't know my grandfather, King Draegen, but I have rarely heard a bad word spoken against him in the palace. For all intents and purposes, it sounds as though he was a kind ruler, as Carrick is. But if that was the case, why had there been an uprising?

I wish I had paid more attention to my history lessons.

These thoughts distract me for a little while, but eventually, there is no hiding from the knowledge that I am standing in Lord Arden Velasian's sitting room. Alone. Unchaperoned. At night.

I whirl around instantly to face the door at the sound of it opening.

Against the glaring lights of the foyer, he is little more than a shadow at first. He enters slowly, each step smooth and slow, a glass in one hand. I get the unwelcome impression of a predator stalking his prey, and as he shifts from shadow to man, I find myself having difficulty drawing a full breath.

"What have we here?" His voice is a drawl, almost a purr. It does not help in my search for breath. "I wasn't expecting anyone tonight."

He is as lean and towering as the buildings of my nightmare world I had been pondering earlier, and, right now, I am just as uncertain of what I will find within him as I am of what I would find in those buildings. Though he had said he wasn't expecting anyone tonight, his expression can only be described as expectant. As though he is only feigning surprise. As though nothing in this world holds any sort of true surprise for him.

I push back the hood of my cloak, and he staggers sideways. Not backward, but slightly to the left, as though he has been knocked off kilter. I wonder if that is not his first drink of the night. He rights himself quickly, though, and I remember that he is as practiced in drinking as he is in flirting.

"I'm sorry," I say through a quiver in my throat. "But it really was urgent that I speak with you. It couldn't wait until the morning."

I watch his face transform into something different. His lips curve into a smile, but it stops short of his eyes. His eyes glitter with something harder than mirth. They dance with something far more dangerous. I take a step back as he takes one forward, but the room has suddenly shrunk, and I feel as though the wall is at my back, and at my sides, and that there is no escape from the coldness radiating from him.

He holds his glass without gripping it. It seems as though his hand is simply curved, and the glass simply rests there. He tosses back the remainder of the liquid carelessly and steps to the side, away, to the decanter that sits on the table by the door. The movement gives me a second to breathe.

I open my mouth to continue, to provide a further explanation for my presence, but he halts my words with a cut of his eyes toward me as he pours himself another glass. That look slashes through the air that had been about to be filled with my words, my excuses, my apologies. I close my mouth.

"Such reckless behavior," he sighs, and tsks, and smiles in that same humorless way. "You're lucky I'm not the caging sort, or I'd have no choice but to put a stop to it once we're wed."

I bite the inside of my cheek hard. "Lord Velasian…"

"Now, now," he interrupts, turning with his freshly filled glass to resume his slow stalk in my direction. "I believe I told you to call me Arden. And in light of recent circumstances, you may even soften it to 'dear,' or 'sweetheart,' or 'darling.'"

I swallow hard, my gulp audible to my own ears and hopefully not to his, though he grows ever nearer. I want badly to step back again, again and again until my back hits the wall, but I hold my ground. I tell myself that his blatant, simmering rage doesn't scare me, and then I tell myself to forget that that's a lie.

"Arden, I came to explain. There was a misunderstanding—"

"So I supposed," he interrupts again, swinging his glass-bearing arm grandly in a sideways arc while somehow managing not to spill a drop, "when the flowers I sent to you somehow became a proposal of marriage." He bites that last word out hard, dropping the layer of false velvet around his words.

He only pauses in his approach when he's an arm's length away. Far too near for propriety, and far too near for my already-pounding heart. I am a coward for a long moment, keeping my eyes straight ahead at his chest instead of looking up, willing my heart to steady itself. Willing my breaths to come out more evenly. Slowly, slowly, I tilt my head back to meet his eyes. And instantly, I wish I hadn't. His chest had borne no recrimination, while his eyes bear it in spades.

"Arden," I continue resolutely, but then he reaches a finger out. Just the one, on the hand not pouring whiskey down his throat, and just far enough to barely graze the side of my neck. He drags it slowly, lightly, down the line of my throat, his fingertip leaving a dizzying mix of chills and fire in its wake. The fire travels up to my cheeks while the chills work their way down my spine. I don't remember the words I had been about to say. They are chased away by the realization that anger isn't the only thing I see when I look up at him now.

"It was very unwise of you to come here alone, at night." He has wrapped these words in an extra casing of velvet, perhaps a scrap of silk. My stomach forgets its anchor and flips once, twice.

"You're drunk." My voice is uneven, not wholly recognizable as he leans closer. No. *He* hasn't leaned closer. I recoil when I realize that *I* am the one who moved.

"Generally," he says agreeably, his finger falling harmlessly away in the wake of my recoil. "Something you'll grow accustomed to, I'd imagine."

The bite is back in his words then, but it feels far less dangerous than what had been there seconds ago. I straighten my shoulders, shifting my gaze slightly to the right of his so I won't forget myself again so easily, and I say what I came here to say.

"The flowers were beautiful." I cut his inevitable interruption off with a raised finger and a pleading look. He closes his mouth. "I had your card in my hand, and I had my brother pushing me to marry Lord Delavar, who is as fascinating as a throw pillow, and I just…I said I had chosen you. I had your card in my hand, and I blurted it out. It was a bluff, just to get him to stop *pushing* me, but then my father overheard, and he went to the king. I wanted to take it back, but…they were so proud. And Carrick was so relieved. And they had narrowed the list of my potentials down to you, Delavar, and Roneldon, and I didn't know how to take it back, how to take away their pride and relief, and I didn't know how to agree to marry Delavar or Roneldon."

I feel his stare leveled on me, and I force myself to be brave. I shift my eyes back to meet his. They are filled with speculation, with a spark of wildness and at least a little less anger than had been there before.

"I'm sorry. I'm sorry that I trapped you in it, that I didn't give you a choice."

The anger flares a little at the word "trap," but it fades quickly, drowning in the other emotions there. He takes a slow sip from the glass in his hand, but he doesn't drop his eyes from mine.

"You didn't know how to agree to marry Delavar or Roneldon," he says, softly. "But you knew how to agree to marry me."

I swallow hard, unsure what to say. I don't even understand it myself, the way my staggering unwillingness to marry Del or Roneldon lessens into something manageable, something almost intriguing, when shifted into the possibility of marrying Arden.

He drops his head a little, a concession of an inch or two, which brings his face an inch or two nearer to mine. His artfully rumpled blond hair is less artful today, a little more savage, and I wonder how many hours he has had to turn the news of our betrothal over in his mind.

His finger lifts back slowly into the air, seemingly of its own volition, his eyes not leaving mine to track its progress. I hold my breath as the back of it touches lightly at my cheek, runs tenderly along the curve of my jaw, retraces its earlier path down my neck.

"Roneldon is a toad," he says finally. "And I hated the sight of you dancing with Delavar."

My heart skips, skips again, forgets its normal rhythm.

"I will make a terrible husband." I hear the note of true, unvarnished certainty in his words. I wonder if he merely believes it to be true or if it *is* true. "I don't believe in fairy tales or love."

I swallow and think about stepping back, out of reach, just as he steps forward, closer, his hand now at the back of my neck, touching lightly at the base of it. It is far too warm in here to pretend my shiver is anything but a response to his touch. Anything but attraction. Anything but *oh, lord,* I should step back, I need to step back, but I don't want him to stop touching me.

"You shouldn't have come here," he says finally into the taut silence between us. His voice is gruff, an irreverent mix of gravel and smoke and temptation. I can smell the liquor in the air, can taste it on my tongue. I'm back on the terrace, and his head is lowering toward mine, and I'm wondering what my instinct will be this time. I'm there, but I'm here, and I'm too uncertain, too on edge, too lost in the wilderness in his eyes, for any of it.

I step back. He drops his hand easily, only following my movement with his eyes, simply watching my retreat.

"I should go," I say into the echoing silence. The room is cavernous again, gaping, no longer closing in around me.

"Yes," he agrees, quietly. He throws back the rest of his drink, once again left with an empty glass in his hand. I'm not sure he will be standing much longer. I'm not sure how this man will be my husband.

"Arden," I begin, then stop. I think about what I want to say next. I think about what is most important to say next. "Can you forgive me?"

His face settles into its default, into the smirk that his lips produce most naturally, except he leaves it a little softer at the edges. He leaves it gentler than I deserve.

"I'd imagine this marriage will be more of a hardship for you than it will be for me."

His words ease one worry and add thorns to another. A romantic marrying a cynic. What hope is there for us? But he looks soft in the candlelight, with his disheveled hair and his lightened smirk, and I almost see it. I almost see the hope lying there, in spite of his words.

I decide to leave before I lose sight of it.

"Goodnight, Arden."

I let myself out of the room and out of the house, the icy butler nowhere to be found. Perhaps dismissed when Arden was informed he had a female visitor. I make my way down the steps and all the way back onto the walkway before he comes after me. A glow appears around me as the door suddenly swings back open, as the candlelight of the foyer bleeds out into the night, and then there is his shadow, blocking out pieces of the light.

"You *walked* here?" He sounds suddenly, remarkably sober. For once, his hand is without a glass. It looks startlingly empty, hanging there at his side while the other holds the door open.

"I didn't think it was a good idea to show up with the full contingent," I say defensively. "People would talk."

"And you thought it was a good idea to *walk*? Have you no self-preservation?" He starts shaking his head before I even have a chance to answer. "Wait here. You're taking my carriage back."

I mirror his head shake with one of my own, although mine is far more frantic. "If I show up at the palace gates in your carriage, that will be even worse!"

I discover then that beneath the swagger, beneath the smirk and the eyes and the velvet-wrapped words, Arden possesses iron. I hadn't expected it, which is perhaps why it takes me another moment, long enough for him to lean into his house and call out behind him for the carriage to be readied, to continue my protestations.

"Arden, really, I'll be fine."

The iron is most present in his jaw, in the stark lines of it, as he comes down the stairs to stand beside me. "Don't care. I cannot believe that you *walked* here."

"I walked through the village and down your street! There is nothing unsafe in either of those places."

"Says the girl who lives behind palace walls with her head in fairy tales," he mutters. We both turn to watch the carriage rumble over to us. "I'll tell the driver to drop you off around the corner from the gates and to watch for you to enter. That way my carriage won't be seen at the gate."

My instinct is to continue arguing, but I pause and consider. I can wait just around the corner until the carriage leaves, and then I can circle around back to the forest, returning to the palace the same way I'd left it. It will work. And anyway, I'm fairly certain that nothing I could say just now would sway Arden.

"Okay," I say quietly as he beats the carriage driver to opening the door for me. "Thank you."

He smirks as I take his hand and allow him to help me up onto the velvet seat. "I'm glad to see that you can occasionally be made to see reason."

I answer his smirk with a scowl as I settle back into the shadows of the carriage. He starts to close the door, but at the last possible second, my hand darts out to stop it. He looks down at my hand, then up at me.

"I…was wondering something. One more thing."

It had just occurred to me, just now in the moment before the door closed, but it blooms quickly, growing into something large and demanding. I swallow hard and blurt it out.

"Would it be possible for you to court me before the engagement is announced? I've never been courted, and it's just occurred to me that I never will be now, unless you would be willing to do so. And… it would be nice to have a chance to get more used to one another."

His lips curl into something that stops just short of disdain. "What would this entail?"

"Oh, flowers. A picnic, maybe. A walk through the palace gardens." I smile hopefully. "Poetry?"

He actually, visibly, shudders. "Haven't I been punished enough?"

I slump back into the shadows, my hopes deflating as suddenly as they had blossomed. He sees it, though, even through the shadows, and he sighs long and low.

"Fine. One day. One picnic, one walk. I'll check my schedule and inform you of my next available day."

Just like that, I reinflate. I nod eagerly, reaching out to grab hold of his hand and squeeze it in both of mine. "Thank you!"

Arden squeezes my hands once, hard, before handing them back into the carriage with the rest of me. He starts to close the door once more, but this time he is the one who stops it at the very last second. He leans in a little, his face filling the gap and blocking out the glow still spilling over from his entryway.

"And Reeve?" I lean forward, and there it is, the dancing in his eyes. The iron has receded, and the anger has faded, and they are dancing. "There will be no poetry." He closes the door firmly, knocks on the roof of the carriage, and sends us bustling along on our way.

CHAPTER TWENTY

In the comfort of Arden's carriage, the ride back to the palace takes no time at all. I'm so lost in my thoughts that I feel as though I have only blinked and then the carriage is rumbling to a halt. I glance out the window and am relieved to confirm that we are just around the corner from the gates.

The driver helps me out onto the pavement, and I think I catch a hint of a knowing smile as he bids me goodnight. I sigh a little at the realization of what he must think of me. Still, I can imagine that Arden's servants are a very discreet lot. They rather have to be, with the lifestyle he lives. Lived? I sigh again. Lives.

I round the corner and press up against the shadows, waiting for the telltale grating of the tires as the carriage gets back underway. Once it has faded off into the distance, I poke my head back around the corner, note the emptiness of the street, and cut over to the other side of the palace drive, the entryway to the forest. It is fully dark out now, and I stumble over many roots and fallen branches on my way to the wall. It reminds me so strongly of my dreams that my thoughts shift away from Arden, to Bran. I will see him soon. Anticipation starts to build within me as I start to push the events of the day aside, back, behind the door in my mind.

I make it to the wall, under the wall, back through the forest on the other side without incident. Once I reach the gardens, though, one shadow peels away from the rest, a lantern lifting high up into the air to illuminate a familiar face.

"Reeve," Percius exhales, and I am close enough to know that the honorific did not vanish in the breeze, but merely in his abject relief. "Are you all right?"

I hurry over to him, tripping over myself at the deep creases in his usually smooth brow. "I'm fine, Perc, really. Oh, don't look like that!"

He takes one second to drag his eyes from my head down to my toes, to reassure himself that I truly am fine, and then he turns away, lifting two fingers to his mouth to give a low whistle. It's answered by one to the north, another to the west. A shadow appears from each direction, and once they are close enough, I make them out to be Tiven and Demes.

"You're all right?" Tiven's eyes perform the same perfunctory scan that Perc's just had. Even Demes has no smile to be found on his usually bright face. I feel the full weight of the worry my absence caused them.

"I'm fine, Tiv! I'm so sorry I worried you all. You weren't even supposed to know I was gone!" I start to say more, but I pause, realize. I'm one guard short. "Where's Jax?"

"He's upstairs, with Guin. She's the one who noticed you missing, nearly an hour ago." I've never heard Tiv's voice so taut, a wire wound tight and moments away from snapping.

"Oh, Guin." We start toward the palace doors, nearly reaching them before I freeze. "My father..."

"We didn't tell anyone," Perc says as he moves around me to

glance through the doorway, to check in the windows if anyone is present. "We were doing a thorough sweep first, just to make sure."

"Another quarter hour and we would've had no choice but to go to your father and the king," Tiven adds soberly as we pass through the empty garden room.

We make our way up the side staircase, quietly and carefully. Their normal formation is gone just now, a triangle rather than a diamond, loose and unstructured. My absence had shaken them. I feel guilt and shame surging and tangling in my stomach as we reach the hallway of my bedroom and round the last corner. Jax leans there, outside of the door, and in the moment before he sees us, the distress etched into his face threatens to bring me to my knees. It staggers me.

He catches sight of us, though, and the worry vanishes beneath a flash of relief, his eyes performing the same scan as the others had done, before the look in his pale, piercing blue eyes settles onto anger. I open my mouth to speak, but he flicks his chin toward my bedroom. I close my mouth and follow him in. The others file in after us, closing the door behind them. The first thing I see is Guin, standing by the window, tears dripping down her cheeks.

She turns at our entry, gasps at the sight of me, and I'm already on my way, already rushing over to throw my arms around her shoulders. I hold her tightly, and she squeezes me in return. For once, I let go before she does. I hold her at arm's length, allowing her to reassure herself, as the others had done, that I am okay.

"What happened?" She asks through sniffles, swiping at the tears with the back of one hand. "I thought you were kidnapped!"

The tangle grows until it threatens to strangle me, until it's nearly impossible to speak through. I'm drowning in my own guilt and shame.

"Oh, Guin, no. I wasn't taken, I had to leave. I had to go speak with Arden, to explain to him, and I knew that if I told any of you, you would feel obligated by your positions to stop me or tell my father. I didn't want to put any of you in that position."

I scan their faces, the faces of my five oldest, dearest friends, and I see the emptiness of my excuses reflecting back at me. They don't just look angry; they look disappointed, and that disappointment, from the people who know me and love me best, hurts more than any disapproval I have ever felt from my own father.

"I'm sorry," I whisper miserably. "I truly didn't think any of you would notice. I thought that I'd be back before you ever knew I was gone."

"I brought you soup," Guin says, her voice hardening into a tone I rarely hear from her. "I was worried that your headache would only worsen without food in your belly. And when you weren't here…"

"She told us," Tiven finished for her. "And we split up and searched the palace and the grounds."

"We're glad you're all right," Demes offers, his face the least disappointed, his voice the least hard. He tries to smile at me reassuringly, but I think it's too soon for that, because it falters. I scared them all badly.

Jax still has not spoken to me.

"What can I do?" I ask. "How can I make this right? I truly am so sorry for scaring you."

I'm met by silence. I almost fold beneath the weight of it before Tiven speaks up.

"It's late," he says. "We should all get some sleep."

The others evidently agree, because they follow him silently from my room. Only Dem looks back over his shoulder at me. Whatever he sees there enables him to muster that reassuring smile, to keep it from faltering this time. He nods at me, a goodnight nod, but also maybe a forgiving nod, and then he is gone with the others, the door closed behind them. I am left with my unanswered question echoing in my ears, with the sight of Guin's tears and the creases in Perc's face and the heavy silence of Jax's anger.

I slide silently out of my dress and into my nightgown. Climbing into my bed and sinking into the sheets, the edges of my day start to close in on me. I am engaged to be married, and I have let down my dearest friends. I can barely remember this morning, the buoyancy of it, the way I had carried it over from my dreams before reality had washed it away.

It requires a monumental act of will to shove the entirety of the day behind the door in my brain, but I manage it. I manage it because I know that once I close my eyes, once the dream world comes to fetch me, I will open my eyes in the square and Bran will be there.

CHAPTER TWENTY-ONE

I no longer have the luxury of listening for the gallows. Instead, the moment I feel myself arrive, I roll to my feet and sprint for the shadows. Only as I run, as I'm halfway to the nearest alcove, do I allow myself to glance over my shoulder at the swinging rope.

It's empty. For tonight, it's empty, there are no falcons, and I am safe.

Safe as my own silence. Safe as my ability to blend into the darkness, to hide in the shadows, to quiet my own breathing. For so many years, I have taken it for granted that I would survive the night. They had been strange nightmares, but they had been just that: nightmares. Nothing had been able to touch me here. Now...I am seen, and I am vulnerable, and my footsteps matter.

Safety is a relative thing here, but at least, for this moment, there are no falcons.

Instead, there is Bran.

In the moment between looking back at the gallows and swinging back to face the shadows, he appears in front of me, stepping out of the blanket of darkness, shedding it like a cloak, all of him suddenly bathed in moonlight before me. All of his dark hair and hard lines and gleaming skin where his sleeves are rolled up. Gleaming skin where the collar of his shirt ends. Where I know, where I cannot forget, what lies beneath the rest of that shirt.

Where I seriously consider, for half of a second, that it might be worth another wound so that he has to divest himself of this shirt, too.

He startles me, but my body doesn't think to skid to a halt. My body thinks to keep running to him.

He places his own steadying hands out to catch me before I can collide into him, my heartbeat pounding from some combination of the fear of this place and the sight of him there. My body curves into his hands, or perhaps his hands curve around it, but either way the whole of it sighs in remembrance of the warmth of his touch. It leaks out from behind the door in my mind and reminds me that last night, before the day had come and turned utterly upon its head, I had been happy.

I smile giddily up at him. His lips twitch an answer, but he also lifts his finger to his lips, as though I had been about to shout a greeting. I scowl an "of course" in response, and he fully smiles. Every other smile he has ever bestowed upon me pushes out from behind the door to join it. I let them come. The door is now there to hold the daytime—to hold Arden, Guin, my guards...my father's pride, my uncle's relief. I lock them all inside and welcome the nighttime memories.

I fall into step behind Bran as he starts forth, mirroring each footfall, each surveying look, each lingering pause. I remember a different walk, another time I had kept a few steps behind, a time when he hadn't looked back to make sure I was still there. I answer each look with a smile because I may never get used to the feeling of being seen by him.

The streets stay quiet for us. We make no sounds as we walk, not even the slightest shifting of gravel under our practiced feet.

Nobody else decides to get brave tonight, at least not anybody with unpracticed feet. We wind our way through the narrowest of alleys without difficulty until Bran suddenly stops, reaches for a doorknob, and turns it lightly. He steps inside and bids me to follow with a meaningful lift of his eyebrows. I dart in after him, and he closes the door silently behind us, locking out the night.

It's possible I haven't exhaled since arriving here tonight, because now, in the safety of this house, I breathe out long and slow. As the breath escapes, my eyes slowly scan the room in which we stand.

It's no bigger than Bran's home had been, but unlike Bran's, this room is clearly intended only as a common area, not a bedroom. There's a staircase tucked into one corner, a tower of wooden crates stacked in another. Each crate overflows with dishes, cups, tools. Odds and ends. There are wooden crates on the opposite end of the room, as well, but these are overturned, set in a semi-circle around the fire.

The fire…my body sways toward it, drawn to the dancing flames and the beckoning warmth. Summer is approaching at a rapid clip, with the solstice nearly upon us, but the nights have insisted upon clinging to a small bite of a chill to their winds, and beneath my nightgown, my skin is a torrent of goosebumps. I leave off the rest of my study of the room and allow myself to drift toward the heat, a moth to a quite literal flame.

I stand before it, my feet nearly in the ashes, and close my eyes, my hands splayed before me, absorbing the radiating heat. It takes the span of several seconds, however long it takes for the heat to travel up through my fingers, over my arms, across my body, for me to remember Bran.

My eyes fly open, and I whirl around to face him.

He's leaning with his back against the door, watching me.

More than just watching me.

Seeing me.

His eyes travel slowly down the length of my body before traveling just as slowly back up to my face. There is just enough light in the room for me to see it when he swallows hard.

I suddenly have no need for the fire. I take a step forward, away from it. I'm several degrees warmer than the fire ever could have managed because his lips are curled upward, and his eyes are on me, and while I still cannot see the color of them, I see that they are unwavering and ponderous. I wonder what he ponders, and if he finds answers in me.

"Are you warmed up?" Ah yes, his voice. That memory is there, too, another escapee. It is not gravel or smoke or temptation, but it is steadying and vital, the lake after a storm, eight miles deep and worth drowning in. I push the counterpart of the comparison back where it belongs, behind the sturdiest part of the door. I bolt it.

And I smile.

"Yes." I don't tell him that the fire was not entirely responsible.

He reaches his hand up and up, behind his neck, and I tense a little at whatever he is about to say next. His head tilts down, but his eyes are still on mine.

"So, Cecily wants to talk to you."

Those words alone would not worry me, but the tone in which they're delivered does. Still steady, but careful.

"What about?"

"I told her...some of what you told me. Some of what I know about you. She doesn't wholly believe it."

I smile reassuringly at him. "Well, it isn't a wholly believable thing, I realize."

He scrunches his face up a little, halfway to a grimace. "She thinks you belong in an asylum."

My chin drops to my chest as I stifle a groan. It appears as though, in this world, my sanity is to ever be in question. I look back up at him pleadingly.

"But you told her I don't, right? You told her that I explained it, and that you saw it, and..."

"Yeah, she wants to hear it from you, though. I think she thinks you put some kind of spell on me, to be honest."

"Now I'm a wizard on top of an asylum escapee? Bran..."

"I know. Look, all she remembers from that night is that a girl in a nightgown rescued her, and she vaguely remembers a lot of screaming."

I flash back to that night, to trying to draw the falcons away, and, yes, to screaming at the top of my lungs. I hang my head and shake it slowly at the memory of how I could hardly even fault Bran when he thought I belonged in an asylum. I had managed to fault him, certainly, but it had been difficult given the circumstances.

"Tomorrow night, I'm going to start wearing normal clothes to bed," I mutter.

I hear him chuckle somewhere above my bowed head, somewhere nearer and then nearer still until it's just above me. I look up to meet his eyes, to see that he's less than a foot away.

"Come on. Cec is all bark, no bite. I'm sure that if you explain it to her like you explained it to me, she'll believe you."

"You didn't believe me until you saw it with your own eyes," I say a trifle miserably. I reach up to try to straighten my windswept braid, pulling out the tie at the end and working my fingers through it. I'm suddenly very conscious of my appearance and of how near to an asylum resident I truly must look.

He opens his mouth to answer, but he seems to get distracted by my lifted arm. He touches my elbow lightly, pushes it a little bit to the side, studies it. I wonder how many touches I will gather each night to store away and study later. I hope that there are many, infinite, endless touches. They always steal away my worries, or at least lighten them into something more manageable. This one is no different.

"Completely healed," he says, more to himself than to me. "Not even a scrape."

I twist to look at it myself, even though I know, of course, that he's right. I smile up at him, no trace of misery to be found. "Told you."

He shakes his head and answers my smile, taking a step toward the stairs. When he sees that I stay rooted in place, he reaches back, palm up, the perfect place for me to slide my own hand. I do so without reluctance, and he rewards me with a light squeeze and a tug toward the stairs.

Everything feels more manageable with my hand in his. As though I could face far worse than whatever I'm about to. I feel as though I've needed his hand in mine for far more than just this. As though I could have used it all day, with the impromptu engagement, with Arden's dizzying fingertips, with my guards' and Guin's disappointment. I needed to be steadied, and nothing seems to steady me better than Bran's presence.

"You'll stay with me when I tell her?"

"Have I abandoned you yet?" His voice travels over his shoulder, down the steps between us.

"No, but I worry anyway."

"I noticed," he says wryly, and any response I might have made has to be swallowed when we reach the top of the stairs and turn into the first doorway on the right.

There is only one candle lit, and it works hard to spread its light beyond the corner it occupies. A boy sits in the chair beside it and tilts a book into the glow, squinting, but he looks grateful to give up and set it aside upon our entry. A few feet away, I recognize Cecily, stretched out on her side taking up nearly the full length of the bed. One arm is curled beneath her head while the other hand traces the lines of her threadbare blanket. She looks up at the sound of the boy's book snapping closed, only then noticing Bran in her doorway, my face hovering above his shoulder behind him. She shifts upward until she is sitting with her back against the wall. If the motion pains her, she gives no sign of it.

"Hey, Nor," Bran says easily, stepping forward to swipe at the top of the boy's thick brown hair. The boy who must be Nor ducks a little, swipes right back at Bran, but Bran dodges with a short laugh. It is such a small interaction, but it makes me happy to witness it. To see the ease with which Bran laughs here. I'd always wondered, out by the lake before he could see me, if he had happiness in his life, and here it is.

He shifts into something else for Cecily. His smile softens, loosens, and he perches on the side of her bed carefully.

"How're you doing, Cec?"

She had hardened her face for our entry, and I think she would like to keep it that way, but she seems unable to manage in the face of him. In the face of his soft smile.

"Since you asked thirty minutes ago? Still fine, Bran."

He grins a little sheepishly, a different smile than he's ever offered me, and touches her bandaged leg lightly. "I'm just making sure."

"I know," she says fondly, but with something else, too, something more than fondness. She leans forward to brush Bran's hair from his forehead, and I'm sure then, at that swipe of her hand, that she is in love with him. The knowledge of it drops like a stone into the pit of my stomach, drops my gaze down to my toes. I'm suddenly too much of a coward to search within his eyes and his tone for how he feels about her.

I always did worry that my subconscious would be cruel in this regard—that it would have conjured a wife, a lover, someone to adore him and to be adored by him above all others. It would not surprise me to discover that it had done so.

But it would hurt me. It would hurt me far more than it should, says the stone in my stomach and the next stuttering thump of my heart. So I keep my eyes on my toes, coward that I am.

"Cec, Nor, this is Reeve."

I look up then because I have to, because he said my name, and also because he's returned to stand beside me.

He touches my back lightly, reassuringly. It makes the stone in my stomach think about dissolving.

"Ah yes, the girl from another world." Her voice is instantly different, colder and sharper and more considering. Her eyes mirror it, studying me. The candlelight does its best, but it keeps most of her in the shadows, only telling me that her eyes are on me and that they're steel.

Nor does me the favor of picking up the candle and carrying it over to our small tableau, to put on a narrow table beside Cecily's bed, and then I can see the whole of her face.

I had not realized that night I had dragged her unconscious body through the streets, nor as I'd stitched up her bleeding leg. I remember that Bran had said she has a face on her, and I see now that she does. She is beautiful.

Her hair is utterly out of fashion, cropped abruptly at her chin, but it falls in abstract abandon, in thick, pitch black pieces. The pieces across her forehead are shorter, messily shoved out of her face in a way that should not be pretty but is. Her features are petite, her nose pert and tilted up the slightest bit at the end while her eyes have the gentle curve of a cat's.

I make sure to keep my sigh silent and internal at the realization that I look like an asylum escapee while she looks like a delicate fairy princess. I sneak a glance up at Bran through my lashes, wondering what he thinks of the comparison.

He seems oblivious, his attention on Cecily.

"The girl who *saved your life*."

She does not keep her sigh silent and internal. "Yes, I know." She shifts her expression into something less hard. "Thank you, Reeve. I truly appreciate all you did to save me."

"Including stitching your leg up."

"Yes, Bran," she says with blatant exasperation. "I'm including that in the saving."

His hand presses a little more firmly into my back. I see the moment she realizes that it's there, and I know then that I have an uphill battle ahead of me to convince her of my story. She seemed already settled in her dislike of me, and now, with Bran's hand on my back, she seems inclined toward hatred. Her eyes shoot sparks, of the cold and icy variety.

"You can go get some sleep, Bran. You've had a few late nights in a row, and Nor says you were sloppy in training today."

My hand that is farthest away from Cecily's observant eyes creeps up behind my back to grab tightly to his. I keep it in a death grip while he answers casually, "I'll stay and listen. I'm awake. I'll be fine."

"Fine," she says, and the ice has made its way to her voice, too, as she focuses on me. "Tell me your story then."

I take a deep breath. I drop my hand back to my side, letting the heat from Bran's hand at my back thaw the sting of her tone, and I begin.

CHAPTER TWENTY-TWO

"I have dreamt this place every night for my whole life."

I quickly realize that I will have to look away, away from her glare and her blatant skepticism, if I am to tell this story. I look for somewhere else to focus. Nor has taken Bran's earlier place, perched beside his sister on the edge of the bed, and his face is inscrutable. It isn't cold or skeptical, but it also gives no quarter. It waits.

I want to turn to face Bran, to direct my story toward his steady gaze, but that won't do me any favors where Cecily's concerned. So I choose the safety of the candle, the very edge of it, just where it begins to fade from fire to glow, and I focus there while I let the words come.

"I have only ever been invisible here, unable to affect any changes. I could reach out and touch things right there before me, but if they were to move, they would pass through me as though I was nothing but air. I couldn't pass through walls, but nor could I open doors. I've always just been like a strange sort of ghost, passing through each night to witness the horrors here without ever really being a part of them.

"But then, the night I turned eighteen, I was suddenly visible. That was the night I saw you on the street. I was so shocked that you could see me, I didn't know what to do. So I focused on getting you to safety. But that was the first night I was visible, and I've been visible every night since. Still, when the sun comes up, I always return home, and I wake up in my bed in Acarsaid."

Silence meets the end of my story. I think about adding more, explaining more, but what explanation could I give? It's something I don't understand myself. So I wait, and I reluctantly shift my gaze back to the girl and her brother. Cecily's face is still frozen in its cold, mistrustful mask, but her brother's...I do a double-take when I see the grin spreading across his face.

"That's about the coolest damn thing I've ever heard."

"Nor, don't swear," his sister says automatically, looking away from me to glare at him.

Bran laughs, and I think there's a hint of gratitude in it. In me, there is a whole swell of it. Even to my own ears, my story had sounded farfetched. For him to simply believe me, let alone to consider it impressive, goes a long way to easing some of the tension from my shoulders.

"Leave it to you, Nor," Bran says.

"Seriously, you're from another *world?* Acarsaid, you called it?" He shakes his head, and I'm not sure how his mouth could stretch more, but it does. His smile traverses the whole of his face, and I feel my own stretch to match. "It sounds like magic."

"Dark magic," Cecily cuts in.

"I've often wondered if there's a magical component," I muse, my smile fading a little.

"You never thought to ask anyone?" The derision in her tone tenses my spine, and beside me, I feel Bran tense, too.

"I didn't realize that my dreams were different from everyone else's until I was seven or eight years old. My brother mentioned a dream he'd had the night before, a happy dream about our mother, and I was surprised to hear it. I told him that my dreams are filled with monsters, always the same monsters, and always the same world, and I wander the streets of it every single night.

I kept talking, kept describing my dreams, how I wake up beneath the gallows to the monsters tearing apart the body above, until he begged me to stop. He looked…frightened. And I realized that my dreams were not normal. I wanted to tell someone, to ask why this was happening, but I kept remembering the look on his face.

One night, I woke up screaming, and my nurse came rushing in, thinking I was being murdered, and when she heard that I was in such a state all because of a dream, she was annoyed and dismissive. She told me that I mustn't get so worked up over a pretend thing. And I just…bottled it all up. I found a spot to go each night and hide until the morning, away from the horrors of the city, and it became a less terrible place."

They are all staring at me, all intently, but the weight of Bran's stare is the heaviest. I glance over to meet it, and I'm surprised at its intensity. He looks grim, a little sad, ponderous once more. He looks as though he wants to say something to me, but instead, he turns resolutely to Cecily.

"I saw it, Cec, the other night. One moment she was there, and the next, the sun was up and she was gone. And I saw it today, in the square. It was empty, and then I blinked, and she was lying there, smack in the middle of it, right under the rope. It's the damnedest thing, but she's telling the truth."

"I believe you," Nor says, his grin faded but replaced with an openness, an acceptance, that warms me in a different way than Bran's hand at my back does. "I'm sorry that you don't know what it is to have a good dream."

I smile gently back. "They're getting better now."

Bran's hand shifts slightly, settling a little more firmly in the small of my back, its every movement tracked by a part of my brain which cannot keep itself in this conversation for as long as his hand is there.

Meanwhile, Cecily shakes her head slowly. Some of the hardness there leaks away, leaving confusion in its stead.

"It doesn't make any sense."

"I know," Bran says, not without sympathy. "But it's happening anyway."

"I'll need to see it," she says firmly. "I'll need to see it with my own eyes."

I bristle a little at the command in her voice, but I nod. If she is to provide me shelter for however many nights I will be visible, I want to have her on my side, not against me. I want her to believe me, and I want her to accept me.

I want Bran to not be in love with her.

It's a selfish, cruel thought in the face of her love for him and of her hospitality. I think it anyway. I think it more than once.

"She can have the room at the end. It's a little musty, but it's a safe place to pass the night." She nods decisively. "I'll meet you downstairs before the sun rises, then, to see it happen."

Summarily dismissed, we start to leave the room.

"Reeve," Nor exclaims from behind me. I turn back to him, finding that his contagious grin has swept back into place. "I've got about a million questions for you."

"Tomorrow," Bran says from the doorway. "I'm not the only one who was sloppy today, kid. Go to bed."

Nor rolls his eyes good-naturedly. "I'm just three years younger than you, you know. Not a kid."

I look back at Bran in time to catch his shrug, as good-natured as Nor's smile. "Go to bed anyway."

Smiling at Nor, who abruptly reminds me so much of Demes in his ability to set me at ease, I wave a cheerful goodnight to him and one slightly more stilted to his sister. "I'll see you before sunrise."

She nods, and I follow Bran into the hallway.

He leads me to the end of it, to a narrow wooden door that sticks when he tries to shove it open. It finally gives way with a creak and a jolt, nearly propelling him headlong into the room.

The word "room" perhaps gives it too much credit. As I lean around him to study it, I think that perhaps "cell" is a more fitting term. It's half the size of my dressing room at home, perhaps a foot or two longer than I am if I were to lie down and stretch across it. It has no windows, which likely accounts for the stale air that greets us. A pile of cushions is shoved to one side of it to form a sort of bed, but everything else in it is wooden. Wooden walls, a wooden ceiling, a wooden floor. I study it for far longer than its square footage requires and tell myself that it's silly to suddenly want to cry.

"This will do nicely." It comes out a whisper, a trifle forlorn. I swallow and summon a smile to offer him, although it arrives somewhere near his collarbone. I can't bring myself to meet his eyes. "Thank you."

I feel him study me, then see him shift to look at the cell. "I'm sure you're used to better."

I tilt my head a little at that. "What do you mean?"

"That's a fine nightgown you have on. Finer than any clothes I've seen."

I touch the nightgown in question gently, my fingertips so familiar with the feel of it, and so unfamiliar with the feel of anything that might not feel this way, that I don't even know how to answer him. He's right. I'm not accustomed to small rooms and cushion beds and that musty odor in the air. But that is not the cause of my sudden melancholy. It's something else entirely, though with him right here, I can't sort it out.

"No, really, Bran. This room is quite fine. I appreciate it."

"I know it isn't much, but I can promise you it's safe."

I step inside and force myself to meet his gaze, to remove the layer of unaccountable sadness from my tone and inject some gratitude. "It's more than enough. Really, it's perfect."

The last word sticks a little on my tongue, but it must convince him, because he nods once before backing out through the doorway. I keep my smile in place as he swings around to disappear into the shadows of the hallway, and then, I close the door behind him so that I can let the smile drop.

It drops fully. All the way, the corners collapsing into themselves as melancholy rises up and sends tears to my eyes. I fall back onto the cushions and allow them to come. I feel them slide silently down my cheeks and try to sort through my thoughts enough to determine why I am suddenly so dismal.

I don't have enough time to figure it out. There is a short knock on the door, and then another jolt of it as Bran reenters. He has a blanket tucked under one arm, a lit candle in one hand and a book in the other. He tosses the blanket onto my lap as he sets the book beside us. He starts to put the candle on top of it, but the light of it catches my face, and then his eyes catch my face, and the room is so small that the one candle does enough. I can see the small crease appear between his eyebrows, the furrow of it.

He crouches down in front of me, setting the candle beside us, and swipes lightly at my damp cheeks.

"Ah, Trouble. Why are you crying?" He asks it quietly, with unbearable kindness.

"I'm not crying," I lie, reaching up to wipe away what his hands had missed. "My eyes are just…leaking."

He looks skeptical. "Does that happen often where you're from?"

"When we're sad," I admit.

"Why are you sad?" He drops down to the ground, cross-legged, his elbows propped on his knees while he leans toward me. I look down at him sitting there, the lone candle chasing shadows across his face as it sways with the air coming in through the open door, and I understand my sudden sadness.

"I'm being silly." I understand it, but I also understand its foolishness.

"Tell me anyways."

"I'm really very grateful," I say, leaning forward a little to touch his arm earnestly. "Really. It's safe, and these cushions are fairly comfortable, and I appreciate everything that you and Cecily and Nor are doing for me more than I could ever say. And now you can stop chasing me around at night, and you can actually *sleep*, and that's a good thing! I can come here to this…to this cell each night and hide out until the morning, and you can sleep, and you can return to your normal life, and I won't disrupt it anymore. You won't even know that I'm here."

It is supposed to be reassuring, grateful, and it starts out that way before shifting back toward whispered misery. I hear it well enough that I try to counteract it with a smile, but it wobbles, and it falters, and it's gone before it ever fully settles. For two nights, I have had him as a companion, and now I feel it ending. I feel it slipping away.

I will come here each night, and it will be safe, but I will be here. In this room. While he is in his own, sleeping or whatever it is he did with his nights before I wholly disrupted them.

My nights of sitting beside him at the lake are over, and now, too, are my nights of talking to him, laughing with him, feeling the weight of his eyes on me.

I knot my hands into each other and twist them as I listen to the echo of my ingratitude. The echo is loud enough that only a couple of heartbeats pass before I open my mouth to apologize.

I don't get a chance. Because first, the corners of his mouth twitch. The left, a little upward. The right, a little upward. I tilt my head at the sight of it and hold my apologies, confused.

I'm even more confused when they twitch up into a fully-borne smile. It stretches out to show his dimples, set shallowly into his cheeks, only visible because the candlelight turns them to shadows. He smiles up at me, and then, after another heartbeat, he laughs.

His laugh pours over me like honeyed sunshine, like cascading raindrops and a summer night's breeze off of the lake. It's warm and effortless and makes my heartbeat an unreliable measure of time. It bounces off of the wooden walls and back to my ears, and back to my ears, and back to my ears again. I smile, too, even though I remember that I was sad just seconds before.

I poke him in the knee with one finger. "What are you laughing at?"

"You," he says, the word still a laugh. "I'm laughing at you."

I try for a glare, but I'm not sure it succeeds in the face of that laugh. Nobody can even pretend anger in the face of that laugh.

"That's very rude, you know," I tell him.

"I know." His laugh quiets, but I can feel it lingering in the room. It isn't a cell right now, with him in it. It's just the right size, just the right warmth. "We aren't locking you in this—what'd you call it?—this *cell* every night. It's just so you have a space of your own. And I won't be able to forget you're here. Just so you know."

Maybe not *just* the right warmth. Maybe a trifle too warm.

"I'm sorry."

He shrugs, an easy motion. "You don't have to be. The fire's still lit downstairs. Want to escape the cell for a little while?" He can't seem to help smiling at the word "cell."

He was sloppy in training, Cecily had said, and helping me has kept him awake far too late these past two nights. But there isn't a chance of me saying no, not with him looking at me expectantly and the promise of the warm fire downstairs and the way his laugh still lingers in my ears, so I nod and follow him down the stairs.

CHAPTER TWENTY-THREE

We ignore the overturned crates and sit side by side before the fire. I sit with my legs bent up under my nightgown, the blanket he'd given me upstairs wrapped around my shoulders and my arms draped across my knees, while he leans back onto his arms and stretches his legs nearly into the flames themselves. He pushes at the embers with the heels of his shoes. The fire is in its dying stages, but it's still warm, still allowing me to see his face through the darkness, still a reason to be sitting here beside him instead of alone in my cell.

"You train every day?" I feel for once that we have time, that I can ask him some questions from the endless list in my mind.

"Every day but Sunday."

"What do you train for?"

I rest my chin on my shoulder to see his face and watch it shift into grim lines.

"War." That one word is as grim as his face, low and cold.

"Against whom?"

Bran kicks at the ashes again. "Don't know. All we know is that war is coming, and that we must be prepared."

I am so used to the evenness of his tone that the chill there now shoots shivers down my spine. "They won't tell you more?"

"No. I get the feeling that when the time comes, they'll point us in the right direction and say, 'Kill.'"

I look back toward the flames, burying my chin deeply into my crossed arms.

"And then you'll kill?"

His sigh is deep and long. It takes him a long time to answer. "I don't know."

"Does everyone train?"

"Once they reach thirteen. Until then, they help the rest of us. Apprentice in one of the trades, like smithing, sewing, cooking... And once we're too old to fight, or if we get hurt or sick, we go back into the trades, too. Everyone pulls their weight."

"What if you're too sick or hurt or old for the trades?"

"Then you're no good to anyone."

I want his voice back. His warm, steady voice. This one sounds twice, three times, ten times his age, and hard. Unyielding. I feel young and naive in the face of it.

He's been training for war since he was thirteen years old, and here I am, eighteen and still as soft as the day I was born. As sheltered, as unprepared for anything but picnics and balls.

Useless.

We spend some time in silence, broken only by the crackling of the fire and the light swirl of ashes under his feet. I feel lulled by it, by the feel of sitting beside him and the music of the flames, more at peace than I've ever felt in this world despite the lingering ghost of the chill in his voice, the way he had said, "War."

"Where did you go to hide here?" Bran asks eventually. The quiet of his voice only adds to the peace of the moment, doesn't break it.

"Hm?"

"You said you found a place to hide from the horrors of the city, to make it less of a nightmare world for you?"

I remember saying so, remember the story I'd told him and Cecily and Nor, and in the next blink, the peace is gone. Tension floods me from head to toe as I realize what he is asking, what my answer will be. *Where did I go to hide? Beside you. Next to you. I reached out to touch you and only stopped because of the thunder. I thanked the thunder.*

I hid beside you when you thought you were alone.

The urge to lie flits through me briefly, but I don't let it linger. I can't lie to him. After all that he's done for me, I can't. Instead, I shift, turning away from the flames to face him, and I wonder to what degree everything is about to be ruined.

He has his head tilted into the lengthy silence following his question, studying me as I turn toward him. He straightens a bit, still leaning back on his hands but more alert, no longer paying the ashes any mind.

"When I was big enough," I start slowly, carefully, "I learned to climb the wall."

He smiles a little. "I wouldn't have known it, the way you flung yourself over it last night."

I am too worried to smile back. Too worried for the moment when his smile will fade, because it *will* fade, and I won't be able to blame him when it does.

"I sat at the lake. Every night since I was big enough to climb the wall, I went and sat beside the lake." I finish it in a rush, eager to blurt the words out even as I wish them unsaid.

He looks confused by my blatant uneasiness at first, but then— and I see the instant it happens, because it is the same instant my heart falls to my feet—his face freezes. His whole body freezes, even though it hadn't been moving.

"You sat by the lake?"

I nod, miserably.

"I sit by the lake," he says slowly, leaning further and further away from me with each word. "Every few nights, when I can manage it, I go and sit by the lake."

I nod again, this time haltingly. This time, it isn't confirming something I've said, but confirming something he's realized. Confirming a betrayal of sorts, an invasion of his privacy, something that, at the time, I cannot imagine handling differently. Seventeen and a half years of being alone in this world, save for the bodies in the gallows and the people in the streets about to be torn to shreds before my eyes, and suddenly, there he had been. Beauty in the moonlight. Solace. A respite from the horrors. Was I supposed to have turned away from it? From him? When all this was to me was a dream?

"You saw me."

It is razor-edged, dripping in accusation. It isn't a question.

I nod anyway. My head is attached to a string, being slowly lifted and dropped, mechanically. There is no way out of this, no way for any of this to be undone.

"You saw me...once? Twice?"

"I always sat in the same spot," I whisper. "And one night, a few months ago, you started coming there. And I saw you every time you came."

"Every time? You...watched me?"

He sounds utterly aghast, horrified, and it isn't even the worst of it. I swallow hard against the rest of it. The next handful of words that will change things irrevocably. I want so badly to shove them back down, to hide them away, to pretend it didn't happen.

But I cannot lie to him. I have to tell him all of it.

"I just wanted to not feel alone for a while. You showed up one night, like a dream within a nightmare, one of the first people I've ever seen here who didn't get torn apart within minutes. You'd sit there, and I'd want to not feel alone for a little while, so I'd go, and... I'd sit by you."

"You *sat* by me? Next to me?" Bran draws his legs up, stops propping himself on his arms so that he can lift one of them and rub at the back of his neck in agitation. "Hell."

"I realize now that it was wrong of me to do, an invasion of your privacy, but...I didn't think of it at the time. I was just so happy to see you there, to watch you draw in the water and pretend that I wasn't alone."

"So that was it? You'd just sit by me when I was at the lake, and then...what about when I went home? Did you ever follow me?" His lips twist to the side, a sudden flare of anger crossing his face. "You knew the route I took to the wall. You took the exact same one." The accusation is hard in his voice, blistering. It batters against the heart at my feet and fills me with shame and guilt even though I know, *I know*, that at the time, in those moments, his presence had saved me. It *had* made them dreams. After a lifetime of nightmares, his arrival had made them dreams.

But I had stolen his privacy. He'd thought himself entirely alone, and I had been there watching him, studying him, thinking about reaching out to touch him. It's a hideous violation, one which I cannot imagine reacting differently to. I cannot fault him for his anger.

"I followed you one night." There is nothing for it but to tell the rest of the miserable truth. "I was curious how it was that you made it over the wall each night, and so I found you, and I followed you."

He pulls himself to his feet and starts to pace, his hand still kneading the nape of his neck raw.

"It saved my life," I add, standing up myself. "Following you that night saved my life the second night I was visible, when I had to get to that wall. I'm sorry that I did it. I truly am. But it did save my life, following you, and it did make my nights less of a nightmare, sitting beside you."

I leave him to his pacing. I walk quietly up the stairs, into the stale air of my small cell, now bereft of the echo of his laughter because all I hear is the accusation in his tone. All I see is the way his face froze when he realized that I'd sat beside him. I close the door firmly behind me and flop onto the cushions, leaning my back against the wall and replaying the scene over and over again.

I was right to tell him the truth. I know that I was, even though I wish I could have hidden it. I wish to go back to the blissful drowse of the moments before I told him, of sitting beside him and listening to the fire. Just between the coldness of his tone when he talked of war and the heat of it when he found out about those nights.

The rest of the night passes slowly in the wake of my regrets. At some point, when my thoughts get too loud and tangled, I reach absentmindedly for the book he had placed beside my cushions earlier. It's a small, thin volume, worn heavily at the edges, clearly well-read and well-loved. The cover is too marked and faded to make out the title, but as I start flipping through the pages, I discover that it is a book of poems.

And so, to distract myself, I lose myself in the book. I blot out the memory of his face and the memory of his tone and instead put images to the words on the pages, whisper the words out loud when I need to drown out his voice. They are soft, rumbling poems, ebbing and flowing like rivers streaming across the pages, beautiful and mesmerizing, and each one makes me think of Bran in some abstract way. I don't think it consciously, but he's there, between the lines. In the spaces between words. In the lift of each syllable.

Eventually, footsteps sound in the hallway outside of my door, and I realize that morning must be near. The sun will rise soon and call me home. I promised Cecily and Nor that they could see me return. I wish that I could continue hiding here in my cell, with my book of poems and my shame, until Acarsaid summons me back, but I tell myself to be brave. I set the book gently aside and make my way downstairs.

They're standing in a tight circle beside the now-dormant fireplace, the three of them. Cecily is leaning heavily on a makeshift cane, but even so, she comes nearly to Bran's height. Nor is the shortest of the three, but even he is taller than me. I stand on the bottom step and simply study them, the way their heads lean together and the specific smiles each one offers the other—Bran's is different for Cecily, different for Nor, just as each of theirs is different depending on whom they address—until finally, Bran notices me standing there.

His expression is carefully blank. I hate it. I would rather there be anger still shining there, accusation still etched there, anything but that careful blankness. I walk over to the wall opposite the three of them and slide down it, to the floor, wrapping my arms around my legs to wait. The sky outside of the small windows is already a lighter, more relenting shade of blue, a tinge to it that promises orange to come. It won't be long now.

Bran comes to squat in front of me. I don't want to meet his blank gaze, but I force myself. They aren't even his eyes now. His eyes are ocean deep, and these lie flat. These are shuttered, emptied of anything that I seek within them. Emptied of solace. Of forgiveness.

"Do you want me to meet you tomorrow night?" He asks it quietly, only for my ears.

"No, I can find my way here." If you want me to come here, I think I should add. I don't, though, because I'm afraid that if given the out, he will say no, that he'd rather I did not.

He studies me, and I study him right back, still wondering at that look in his eyes. "Are you sure?"

I nod.

He pushes back onto his feet and goes back to join the others. The three of them stare hard at me, each with something different. Bran carries nothing, less than nothing, completely indecipherable to me, Nor carries anticipation, and Cecily carries so much skepticism that I imagine the weight of it will buckle her knees. They wait, and they stare, and I feel myself growing nearer and nearer to annoyance.

"It isn't a precise science," I say finally.

"The sun is up," Cecily points out, the beginning of a gloat in her tone.

"It isn't *exactly* at sunrise. Sunrise or a couple minutes before, a couple minutes after."

"Mmhm." She does impressive work layering so much doubt into such a small, short sound.

I'm about to open my mouth to retort when I feel it begin. The rope connected at my stomach pulls taut, and I only have enough time to shift my eyes back to Bran, to get one more look at the flatness in his eyes, before the rope yanks me back into my bed, back to Acarsaid, back to my real life.

CHAPTER TWENTY-FOUR

For the first time I can remember, Guin does not greet me with a smile. Her lips are pressed tightly together as she comes in with my breakfast tray, as she slides the drapes open and fills the water basin. My mind is still in my dream, still lingering on Bran, so all I do is watch in silence as she goes about her morning tasks.

It's getting harder every day to open the door and shift things around. To shove the nighttime back behind it and pull forth my waking world. I don't even remember at first why Guin might not be smiling. I wrack my brain, to dig through the pile behind the door for a minute before I find the right memory. When I find it, my shoulders droop. Guin, my guards, even Arden…they're all angry with me. How could I forget?

I could forget because of Bran. Because Bran is angry with me, too, and his anger is freshest in my mind. But I have to push it aside. I can do nothing with it today.

Instead, I focus on what I *can* do. What I *can* fix. I can fix this.

I slide out of bed and block the door before Guin can leave. She sets her lips even more firmly against one another, leaking them of their color.

"I'm so terribly sorry, Guin." My hand thinks about reaching out to touch her arm, but I keep it in place. She is uncomfortable with my overt affection on a good day, and today is not a good day. "Tell me what I can do."

She sighs and tugs lightly at the ends of her hair, where they just barely brush against her shoulders. She seems to be engaged in an internal struggle, and I hope that the side of it that wants to forgive me wins out.

"Promise me you won't do something like that again," she says finally. "Promise me you won't lie, and sneak out, and scare me half to death."

"I promise, Guin. Truly. It won't happen again."

She finally releases her tense hold on her lips and allows them to curve a little, a shadow of her usual warm smile but a step in the right direction. I feel a small swell of relief even though I know my work is far from done.

<hr>

I offer my guards a formal apology in the hallway outside of my room, sincere and heartfelt, and I give them the same promise I had given to Guin. Demes had already started to forgive me last night, so his smile is easily come by. Percius looks to be at the beginning of forgiveness but not yet there. Tiven and Jax appear unmoved.

With guilt swimming unpleasantly through my veins, I spend much of the day in the kitchens. I cajole Chef Margorie into helping my cause, and then I pretend that I am any help at all as she sets about the tasks I had begged of her. We bake peach tarts for Dem, apple pie for Perc, warm bread for Tiv. All of their favorites. Jax takes some pondering as he has never shown preference of one dessert over another, but I settle on the one for which Chef Margorie is most renowned throughout the palace: her chocolate chip cookies.

Though they are upset with me, they are still respectful and thus each insist upon carrying the basket full of the treats up to the hilltop I point to as our destination, the sunniest hilltop, the best spot for picnics. Each except for Jax, who does not speak. Who does not acknowledge that there is even a basket. Or that there is even me.

I insist harder than the three who do offer and drag the basket up myself, arms straining and breath coming out in pants by the time we reach the top. Once there, I take a moment to wipe the sweat surreptitiously from my brow before offering each guard their respective treats with a bowed head and my most pleading smile. Demes accepts his eagerly, Percius with a knowing smirk. Tiven holds out, but when I show him the freshly whipped butter to lather onto the bread, he concedes with a sigh.

Jax looks through me.

He doesn't reach for the cookies.

He takes a step back, away, and he crosses his arms as he turns to face the sea.

My shoulders slump.

"These tarts are delicious," Demes tries.

"I'm going to gain ten pounds from this pie, but I don't even care," Percius adds as he shoves a full quarter of it into his mouth.

"He'll just need a little time," Tiven says quietly. "He'll come around."

I nod down at the untouched plate, then up at the sky. The sun makes it a brilliant blue directly overhead, a midday sea kind of blue, a clear and cloudless splendor, but I turn instead to look where Jax looks, toward the approaching clouds. Heavy grey clouds, coming to hang over us. To hang over me.

There is a note waiting for me in the foyer when I return to the palace. I recognize the stationary at once, and I wonder how many times I will reread this note, this inevitably sparse handful of words, searching for hidden meaning. I tear it carefully open and find that I don't have to read—I only have to look. One look, for one word, for one promise.

There is also no need to search for hidden meaning. The one word is laden with it, full to the brim, overflowing even.

Tomorrow.

—A.V.

CHAPTER TWENTY-FIVE

The rain clouds of Acarsaid follow me into Tenebris. I am soaked to the bone within seconds of arriving, the driving rain and the dark of the night making it difficult to see anything when I first open my eyes. I hear it first, then. I hear the heavy swing of the rope, the creaking of the gallows. There was a hanging today, and I am lying under the body.

When my next blink clears my vision, I see that the body is whole.

I roll to my feet and sprint, skidding into the shadows as I hear the first flap of wings. The first shriek, although it is quickly joined by more. They appear through the rain like phantoms, gliding through the downpour and landing on the scaffolding, clinging to the rope, their talons digging into the body. I press deeply into the shadows and hold my breath, wishing I was anywhere but here. With nowhere to go, and nothing to do but watch and listen as they tear the skin from the bones. My nightgown clings to my skin, but I don't entirely blame the rain or the cold for the way my body violently shakes as I push my shoulder blades into the wall.

I can't look away, I can't look away, I can't look away.

A hand clamps abruptly over my mouth, and my whole body

stiffens. I think about biting it, about screaming through it, but my eyes are still locked on the falcons. A scream would mean death. I strain my eyes to the left and follow the hand to an arm, the arm up to a face. To Bran's face.

He lifts a finger to his lips with his free hand and waits for my answering nod before lowering his hand. We stand shoulder to shoulder under the alcove until the body is barely recognizable as such and the falcons have started their victorious song. I shiver from the rain, from the song, from the nearness of those talons. From the warmth of Bran beside me, although that shiver comes for a different reason. That shiver runs down my spine and curls all the way to my toes.

Once they are gone, dragging the echo of their song behind them, Bran's hand finds mine and tugs me on our way. Even though the falcons took the echo with them, I feel it ringing in my ears as we walk. It was so near. The sound that flesh makes when it is separated from bone is so marked, so distinctive. It twists and combines with the song and savagely dances through my mind. I am numb to the feel of the rain pouring down onto me as we make our way to Cecily's.

He pulls me through the door after him and closes it behind me, shaking his head like a wet dog as he does so. Water droplets spray from his hair onto me, but there would be no way to know which water is from him and which came straight from the sky. I am soaked from head to toe, and I am still numb. His hand stays wrapped warmly around mine for a moment or two longer, and I am grateful for it. I want for it to erase the ringing in my ears.

He takes one look at me and pulls me over to the fire. I stand shivering before it and strain my ears toward the crackle of it, the snaps. I think about protesting when he lets go of my hand, but instead, I wrap both arms around myself and try to quiet my shaking on my own. I hear his footsteps up the stairs at the same time two other sets come down them, but I don't look over my shoulder. I focus on the flames and try to let them erase everything else.

"Are you okay?" Nor's voice is tentative and solemn over my shoulder. I force a smile and a nod as I turn reluctantly away from the fire. He looks as though he is about to say more, but he suddenly freezes, becomes a statue made of stone, and he remains that way for a handful of seconds before he is abruptly propelled out of the way by Bran, blanket spread wide between his hands, diving to wrap it around my shoulders.

"You're freezing," he mutters as he tucks it securely in place so it covers me from neck to knees. He leans a little closer and says only for my ears, "And now I can *really* see through that nightgown."

I snap my head down to look at myself, though the blanket hides everything that may have been transparent. I take hold of the blanket's edges myself and make sure that they are fully secured, all the while hoping that the firelight isn't strong enough for them to see my blush.

"Ah, Bran, you ruin everything," Nor says from behind us, less solemnity now and more cheer. Bran shoots him an impressive scowl.

I clench my jaw against the chattering of my teeth, and Bran's scowl becomes a less frightful thing, more of a concerned expression, as he drags his hands up and down my arms rapidly, spreading warmth. He also shoves me a little nearer to the jumping flames.

"Are you going to push her *into* the fire, Bran?" Cecily takes a seat on one of the overturned crates beside us, leaning forward to stoke the flames with a sharp-ended metal poker before glancing up at me. "What happens if you die here?"

The speculative way she says it renews the chills down my spine. She has danger spelled out in her eyes, in her eyes that watch Bran's hands on me. I drop down onto a crate of my own to give her less cause to speculate, carefully tucking the bottom of the blanket under my feet. Bran sits on the crate beside me, and Nor stretches out on the ground, between Cec and Bran. He seems at home there, a cheerful puppy lounging at the hearth.

"I've wondered that," I admit. "Until a few nights ago, it was never a concern, but now…I don't know. I can't carry injuries home with me, but I'd imagine death is something altogether different."

"No way to find out, is there," Nor muses.

"Well, there is the one way." Cecily tries for innocence in her tone and expression, but she can't quite manage it.

"No, we're not killing her to test it out," Bran contributes mildly. "We'll just have to make sure there's no dying while she's here." I glance to my right to smile at him, and I discover that his crate is quite close to mine. If I were to lean just an inch to my right, maybe even less, my shoulder would brush his.

But the way we left things last night lingers in my memory. He has not forgiven me yet. He came out into the rain tonight to escort me here because he is kind and chivalrous. I should not read more into it than that.

"So you believe me, then?" I ask Cecily. "About this being a dream?"

She shrugs a little helplessly, reminding me that she can't be much older than me, regardless that she acts it. "Either that or you put some sort of spell on all of us. You were there, and then you weren't."

"I promise you that if I was capable of magic, I would be using it to try to *avoid* the gallows and the falcons, not wake up beneath them each night."

"That was a near thing tonight," Bran says, his voice low. I feel his shoulder touch mine, and I reprimand myself for leaning into him until I realize that I have not moved. That *he* is leaning into *me*. I wonder if he realizes it. I sit frozen in place and hope that he doesn't shift away as the nerve endings where our bodies meet roar to life and my body finally stops shaking.

"What were you doing out there? It was dangerous for you to come. I told you I could manage it."

The shoulder touching mine lifts in a shrug, but it doesn't pull away. "I knew there was a hanging tonight, and I knew that would draw out the falcons. I thought you might need some help out there."

I turn to smile at him again, my softest smile, filling it with all the gratitude it can hold. I don't think I imagine it when he leans more deeply into me. My whole right side is flooded with warmth now.

"But you managed without me," he finishes, meeting my smile with the tilt of his. "Again."

Cecily jabs the fire extra hard, the poker driving deep within the flames and knocking a piece of wood from the pile. A small billow of ashes rises up, and we all turn to face it.

And then, I turn to look at her. Her expression is half grimace and half rage, but then she tempers it, rearranges it, makes it blank and careful. She does not want him to know that she's in love with him. Which makes me wonder if maybe, just maybe, he's not in love with her.

"How was training today?" she asks, her tone as tempered as her expression.

"Hard," Nor says, as somber as I've ever heard him. "They're pushing us harder every day."

"Us too," she mutters. "I think it's coming."

"The war?" I ask.

"Mm," she answers noncommittally. "Whatever war it is."

"They'll have to tell us soon," Nor says, and I can tell from the look that Bran and Cecily exchange that this is a frequent topic of conversation. A frequent assertion from Nor.

"They don't *have* to tell us anything." Bran's tone is even, matter-of-fact. "You saw what happened to Rafferty today when he spoke up."

"What happened?" I ask, although their expressions tell me I probably don't want to know.

"The body in the gallows," he says, grim and quiet.

Their expressions were right. Putting a name with the body, with the rope's heavy swing and the talons tearing...my chin droops. I don't even know him. *They* know him. Knew him. The three of them are bound for war, and I spend my days on hilltops, in my quiet boat, in my peaceful palace. One night I might arrive and they might all simply be gone.

"I'm going to get some sleep," Nor says. When I look over at him, I find that his eyes are on my shoulder, on Bran's shoulder, on the place where they touch. Nor looks over at Cecily with sympathy, with gentleness, and I know that he knows that she's in love with Bran. "Come on, Cec. That leg needs a rest."

"Have you been able to train on it?" I ask.

"No," she mutters. "I'm on sewing detail until it heals."

"And Cec's stitches are awful," Bran adds, kicking lightly at the side of her good leg. "Not like yours, Trouble."

Cecily's face is a flinch, a mask, hurt. Bran looks up too quickly for her to hide it, and his whole face falls. "Hey, I'm just kidding, Cec."

"No, you're right," she says breezily, her face changing into one that can allow for breeziness. "They're awful. Luckily, I should be back to training in another day or two. Come on, Nor. Goodnight, Bran. Reeve."

She retreats quickly upstairs, Nor trailing behind her. He turns back before the first step and calls over to me. "I still have a million questions. Tomorrow?"

"Tomorrow," I agree, even that one word unaccountably fragile.

Chapter Twenty-Six

When they're both gone and in their rooms, no sound but silence traveling down the stairs to reach us, Bran finally swings back to the fire. "Hell. I hurt her feelings."

I reach out to touch his leg reassuringly. "She knows it was a joke. When she has a moment to think on it, she'll realize it."

He picks up my hand where it rests, and instead of handing it back to me, he studies it. He turns it over and traces a light line down the palm. I flinch and laugh, trying to pull it away.

"That tickles."

He tilts his head a little, peering up at me through his lashes with a taunting quirk of his lips, and he does it again. I laugh and try harder to escape, shoving at him with my free hand. He dodges my attempts and does it again, and again, drawing shapes and figures lightly across my palm like he draws them in the water, until I've dissolved into laughter beside him, too weak from it to even fight him off anymore.

"You're horrible," I say through my laughter.

"I know," he says, finally ceasing his torment and rubbing at my palm as though to erase whatever he'd drawn. Perhaps it won't come out, though. Perhaps it is etched there now. Perhaps this is one thing I can carry with me when I awaken.

My laughter dies in my throat at the feel of his steady strokes across my palm.

"I'm sorry," I say. "About last night."

He's quiet, still focused on my hand. I wonder what answer he seeks in it, what answer my small hand can possibly provide.

"No," he says at last. "No, I'm the one who's sorry." He looks away from my hand with just his eyes, his head still tilted down though he looks back up to me. "This place is hellish. I'm glad you weren't always alone. I'm glad that I could make your nights a little less of a nightmare, even if I wish that I'd known you were there. I wish I could've seen you."

I swallow hard. "I always used to wish for that, too."

"But now I can." His voice is always steadying, except right now it isn't. Right now it unmoors my heart and flips it, turns it, sends it sideways. His voice incites a riot in my body. An uprising. Breath that comes too fast and a heart that wants out of the containment of my ribcage. I'm not sure it belongs to me anymore.

"Now you can."

He gives my hand carefully back to me as though it is glass and he does not trust himself with breakable things. I'm not sure that *this* belongs to me anymore, this hand, the palm of it still full of things he'd tried to erase.

"I should head up," he says, more to the dying flames than to me.

"Yes," I agree, reluctantly. "Nor says you've been sloppy in training," I add with a smirk for him.

He swipes out at me, grabbing my hand back up where it belongs—in his—and pulling me to my feet. "Come on, Trouble."

I follow him up the stairs, and he escorts me to my door. He helps me unstick it, to shove it open, and I realize that the memory of its cell-like qualities was not exaggerated in my mind. Still, his comments from the night before, about how I must be used to better, stick in my mind and have me swallowing any dejected comment I might have made. Instead, I ask, "Where's your room?"

He leans just a little to the left and pushes the door there open. It swings quietly and easily, unlike mine. I lean around him to glance inside at the low cot, the scattered unlit candles, the window where it pulls in the moonlight. There is a pile of books in one corner, from which he must have pulled the book of poems, and I'm so grateful that he saved them. That he didn't abandon them in the home with the marked door, the home which is no longer his.

I feel him studying me as I study his room. "Right next door?"

"Right next door." Deep, low, right in my ear. It sends flutters through my blood, flutters and heat.

I lean back toward my cell, away from him, and I curse my inability to be brave. My inability to say what I want to say, what clamors to be said, words that want to come out even though I don't know what they'd be. How they'd sound. What they'd mean.

"Well, then," I say instead, lamely. "Goodnight, Bran."

He's still studying me. I look up to meet his eyes, the open door to his room allowing moonlight into the hallway with us, allowing me to see the depth of his eyes and the way they are a sea of drops. They carry something deep, something enticing, something that calls to the unsaid words inside of me.

He settles one arm above me, resting on the doorframe of my cell, and he leans a little closer. I find that air is suddenly hard to come by.

"Is that what you wanted to say?" Flutters and heat, spreading and spreading. His voice is the very opposite of steadying.

I shake my head slowly.

"What did you want to say?" His face is a little nearer to mine now, the sea of his eyes so close that I feel like I could dive right in. I *want* to dive right in. I want to drown in them.

"Stay," I exhale, no more than a breath, a weightless word. A plea, the most pressing of the unsaid words.

He tangles his hand in mine and tugs me with him, through his doorway, into the glow of the moon that fights through the ebbing drizzle of rain. I hear it lightly now, tapping a soft rhythm against the window's glass, and I can't remember the sound of the falcons' song. I can't remember the glint of their talons. It's all muffled now.

Bran closes the door quietly behind him and comes to stand in front of me in the room's center. Both of my hands weave within both of his, and he leans down just the slightest bit, just enough to touch his lips to my forehead. I press into it, into the simple affection of it, rising a little to the tips of my toes, and I close my eyes. This, my heart agrees. This, this, this. This is what I've always wanted.

"Are you spoken for at home?" His voice is muffled against my skin, his lips still pressed there warmly.

I start to shake my head, because there is a door in my mind, and the door is closed, and there is only Bran on this side of it. There is only Bran as I tip my face up, as his lips leave my forehead and dance across my eyelids, my cheeks, the tip of my nose. They are traveling lower, and they are traveling closer, and then the door creaks open and I remember.

My eyes fly open, and his lips stop traveling. They hover in the air just a breath away from mine, but whatever he sees in my wide eyes has him leaning away instead of forward. He is mostly in shadows, no candles lit and only the unreliable moon to light him, but I can see the question in the squint of his eyes.

"I am," I whisper to answer it. "I am spoken for at home."

We stay frozen there with his hands in mine and mine in his, my words sitting in the air with no breeze to carry them on and away, and then he steps away. He untangles my hands from his and leaves both them and my forehead cold.

"Okay then," he says quietly. "Okay."

He starts to turn, but I reach out and grab hold of his wrist. It is such a small motion, but he lets it halt him. He stands still and waits.

"It only just came about, a couple days ago. It's…it isn't a love match."

"Then what is it?" Everything about him is quiet and careful in the moonlight.

I'm not sure how to describe it. I'm especially not sure how to describe it in such a way as to prevent Bran from walking away.

"It will benefit the kingdom," I say slowly. "And my uncle most of all."

"In what way?"

"The father of the man I am to marry is very influential within the king's cabinet. And…" I swallow, knowing that things will change with these next words though not knowing how. "My uncle is the king."

He remains quiet and still for only a heartbeat longer before his wrist is abruptly gone from my hand, his body somehow across the room. "Your uncle is a king. You're a princess?"

"No," I shake my head frantically. "No, my mother is. I'm not royalty. I'm just a lady of the court."

A lady of the court with four guards. Dwelling in a palace. Spending her days uselessly wandering, meandering.

"*Just* a …Hell." His hand is at the back of his neck again, just before he begins pacing. I sigh and lower myself to the edge of the cot, watching him as he paces back and forth, around and back again. His steps are long, nearly a prowl. His back is rigid. I can't stop shaking from the echo of his lips against my skin, from the cold left in their wake. From the fact that every time we get closer, I have words that I must say which send us backward. Away from one another.

"Why are you so agitated?"

He frowns. "I'm not agitated."

"Your pacing implies otherwise," I retort.

"I'm not *pacing*."

"I don't suppose one of those books in your possession is a dictionary."

He scowls and swings around, pausing in his pacing—or whatever it was he was doing that looked an awful lot like pacing—to face me.

"You should've told me."

"That I'm spoken for?"

"That you're related to *royalty*."

"Why does it matter?"

He drags both hands down his face, and when they drop, the moonlight shows me the toll so many late nights have taken on him. It shows me the droop of his shoulders and the lines of his face.

"I don't know. I just…I knew we were from different worlds. I just hadn't realized *how* different."

"I'm still who you know me to be. Still Reeve."

"*Lady* Reeve." My title sounds foreign on his tongue, and it does not sound gentle. It slides out sharply, razor-edged. My spine stiffens against the bite in it. "I should've known. Your nightgown. Hell, I should've *known*."

"It doesn't change anything."

"You should've told me."

I blink back my rising tears. "I'm not her here. I'm not Lady Reeve. I'm just Reeve. I didn't want my title to matter here."

Bran shakes his head slowly, eyes drifting away from me and toward the window. He cuts a stark figure, tired and somber.

"You should go."

There is no room for me to argue in those three words. He leaves no gaps in them, no place to fill them with pleas. My hands and my forehead are no longer cold; they're numb. My body is numb in all of the places he touched it.

I let myself out.

The rest of the night passes uneasily as I lie in my cell, counting the cracks in the walls to try to forget the lines of his face. I wish for my mossy bed, for the cool breeze of the lake and the riot of starlight beaming their reassurances. I wish that I had said no when he had asked if I was spoken for, if only so I could know what would have come next. If only so that my body would not be numb.

But I was right to tell him, I remind myself. I was right not to lie to him.

War is coming, though. I don't know how many more nights I have with him. It could all be gone so suddenly, and I have so many things waiting impatiently on my tongue to be carried to his ears, to be met with his smile, with his laugh.

I swallow them all. I swallow the memory of his hands and his lips. I push it all behind the door with my waking life, and I read poetry until the sun rises to call me home.

CHAPTER TWENTY-SEVEN

I take extra care getting ready in the morning. Even though I know precisely what Arden's note said—it would be impossible to forget—I reread it anyway. "Tomorrow," he promised. I don't know when, or what to expect of it, but I know that today I am to be courted. I use both hands to shove Bran and the night behind the door, lean the full weight of my body against it to seal it shut. There is so much behind it that I don't trust it not to tumble open at the most inopportune moment, so I focus on picking out a dress, on letting Guin work her magic on my hair, on looking my very best for the man who is to be my husband.

I try to make space behind the door by dragging out every memory of Arden I possess while Guin braids my hair. The gravel of his voice comes easily to me, as does his smirk, the tantalizing dance of his eyes, the way he set his arm above my head and leaned into me—

No. *Bran* set his arm above my head and leaned into me. That was Bran, not Arden. I force the image back behind the door and straighten my shoulders. I fight against the feeling that this is all becoming too much for me, that I am being split into two. Day Reeve and Night Reeve. I'm not sure they are one and the same anymore.

I stare at my reflection, wondering if Night Reeve looks different. I suppose she must, with her nightgown and wild hair. Day Reeve, meanwhile, has hair that is swept up off her neck and into an artful bun near the top of her head. Day Reeve looks put-together and dignified. Day Reeve looks ready to be courted by a near stranger with dazzling green eyes who is soon to be her husband.

"Is it all right, my lady? I can do something different if…"

I cut her off before she can finish. "It's perfect, Guin, thank you."

"Are *you* all right then? You look troubled."

I smile into the mirror at her reflection over my shoulder. "It's been a long few days is all. I'm engaged to be married now, Guin, did you hear?"

She straightens the sleeves of my pale green gown. "There has been talk of it downstairs, yes. I was waiting for you to tell me yourself before offering my congratulations, though."

I turn to face her, the real her, the warm and alive version of her rather than the flat reflection. "I meant to tell you earlier, I've just been…sorting it in my head."

She waves off my excuse. "No need to explain. I could see that you hadn't wholly wrapped your mind around it yet. And after the other night…"

I slump my shoulders a little, remembering. "Yes, those go hand in hand, I'm afraid. I rather trapped him in the marriage, and I wanted to explain to him."

"Trapped, my lady?"

It's too early in the day, and he's too near to coming, for me to tell her the whole of it. I shake my head and twist my lips into a wry smile. "Suffice it to say, this betrothal is not according to his wishes."

She scoffs, and the sound is so informal and familiar that the wryness leaks from my smile and leaves fondness in its place. Leave it to Guin.

"He's lucky to have you, my lady. Any man would be."

"Proceed with caution, Guin, or I'm going to be forced to hug you."

She laughs and backs away, waving me off. I leave with a wistful wish that I could tell her the other half of my worries, the ones that I carry with me from the night. But I still find myself reticent to share with anyone the places I travel in my dreams. The person I am in my dreams.

~*~

I spend an hour perched in the sitting room, pretending to myself and to my guards that I'm doing anything other than staring out the window, and then, utterly fed up with myself, I lead the way to the pier. I tell a footman to direct Arden there whenever he sees fit to arrive.

I sit on the dock alone with my guards standing watch at the entry to the pier, my shoes tossed beside me, and I draw shapes in the water with my bare toes. The water is a balm to my soul, cool and quiet. It ripples lightly as my toes pass through, and in the ripples, I see Bran's fingers, trailing along and carving their own shapes there. Swirls and letters, circles and hopes, or fears. Maybe a mix of them both.

I don't know what to expect tonight.

In my next blink, his fingers are in my palm instead of the water. I clench my fists against the feel of it, the phantom drag of his fingertips across my skin. This is all supposed to be behind the door. It sprang free of its own volition, even after I'd bolted it, and I wonder how it will ever hold a lifetime of nights when it can barely hold these past few.

I swish my feet side to side in the water to erase where I have drawn a B, an R, an A, an N.

As it turns out, Arden has no stealth. I hear every snapping twig under his feet as he approaches, every muttered curse word. I twist to face the direction of his approach, peering through my guards' stiff backs. All four of them have their hands on their swords, but they relax their hold when Arden finally appears through the trees.

Well, three of them do. Jax's hand stays on the hilt, even though he still has not spoken to me.

"There are at least seven thousand species of insect in that forest," Arden says by way of greeting.

I tilt my head back, catching my hat just before it slides off and squinting through the sunshine at him. "Hello to you, too."

His face is a grimace, a squint against the blinding light of the sun. Last night's rainstorm is a distant memory today, every trace of dampness dried up by the warmth. He sighs and lowers himself carefully to the pier beside me. He looks ill at ease here in a way I have yet to see him, and it rather delights me.

He settles his back uncomfortably against a short wooden stump at the corner of the pier in his nice white shirt and tan trousers, still struggling to open his eyes to more than a squint.

"Hello, wife." Even with squinted eyes, his smile is wolfish and razor-sharp. A smirk lined in daggers.

I shake my head, though my stomach flips. "Not yet."

He finally concedes to the sun and lifts a hand to shield his face, to block out the insistent glare. He opens his eyes more fully, and I see them for the first time in the daylight. The green of them had been captivating in the candlelight of the ballroom, the lanterns of the terrace, the glow of his sitting room, but in the sunlight...they don't just dance, they whirl. They soar. They pirouette. I hadn't realized that the candlelight was such a poor imitation of their orchestra.

"You know," he muses, distracting me from his eyes, "you are alarmingly beautiful in the sunlight."

I laugh abruptly in response, an uncomfortable and jarring sound, trying to hide the fact that his words make my blood rush at twice its standard pace. He does nothing to change or lessen my discomfiture, merely tilting his head and watching as I sputter.

"You're clearly blinded by the sun," I say self-consciously.

"No, just blinded by your beauty," he says, but I hear the note behind it this time that makes me know it's practiced. I am far from the first woman to whom he has directed those words.

"Are you trying to seduce me?"

His smirk leaves behind its daggers and draws forth honey. "Is it working?"

I shake my head and roll my eyes.

"Ah, there she is."

"There who is?"

"The girl in the ballroom who told me my father despairs of me."

I laugh fully at that. "Did I say that?"

"It's an impossible thing to forget."

"Did you think then that you'd be stuck with me forever?"

He rubs his chin thoughtfully. "I hoped I'd be stuck with you for a little while at least. Preferably in my bedroom."

My mouth drops open, tries to close, drops back to open. I probably most closely resemble a fish. He leans forward to lessen the space between us to a handful of inches. "Am I doing this courting thing correctly?"

"You most certainly are not! You are supposed to spout *poetry*, not…not…whatever you call that!"

"Seductions," he fills in pleasantly. "Temptations, allurements…

Take your pick. And anyway, I'm fairly certain I said no to poetry."

"Yes, well," I mutter. "There was no need to go to the far opposite extreme."

We spend some time looking down at where my feet still brush against the water. Birds call languidly overhead, and my guards stay just out of earshot. It feels a little like we're alone out here, beside a lake, like I've been dozens of times before with someone else in a different world entirely. Someone behind a door in my mind who is trying his hardest to escape.

"Incidentally, you forgot to return the compliment," he muses.

I look back up at him quizzically. "What do you mean?"

"I told you that I find you alarmingly beautiful. You have yet to tell me how you find me."

I shake my head wryly. "Would you like a fishing pole? It might help you."

He laughs a little, his gravel laugh, and I'm happy to hear it. I'm happy that *I* have made him laugh. Maybe there's hope for us yet.

"I'm waiting."

I make sure he sees the full roll of my eyes. "Why, Arden, you look dreadfully dashing this morning. So handsome in the sunlight, a blessing for my eyes."

He leans forward a little more, only stopping to dart a glance my guards' way. Jax's hand is still on his sword. Arden smiles dangerously, a different sort of danger than Jax guards against. The kind that is dangerous to my equilibrium, to the anchor in my stomach and the one that holds my body still, that stops it from leaning into his.

"Why thank you. We can work on it more once we're married. Over the course of many, many nights."

I scowl through my reddening cheeks, redirecting my focus to the water. "Must you insist on shocking me?"

I catch his careless shrug in my periphery. "You wanted the day to get used to me. I'm allowing you to do so."

I concede the point with a sigh. And then I ask, with no small degree of discomfort but a burning need to know, "Will I be fighting any others for space in your bed?"

The silence that meets my question eventually requires me to look away from the water and back at him. He's watching me steadily, the earth turning enough so that the sun no longer bothers his eyes.

"You will have first rights to it," he says quietly. "But I can't promise the space to you alone."

I needn't have worried about the anchor in my stomach, after all. It does its work well, better than well, dragging my stomach down to my feet, meeting my heart there. I have to swallow several times through a tangle in my throat, a tangle that feels like the possibility of tears, before I'm able to speak.

"So it won't be a true marriage."

"Oh, it will be a true marriage," he says, a little of his smile's danger now in his tone. "As I said, I plan on many, many nights of improving upon your compliments."

"I don't want a husband I have to share." It is the very opposite of what I want. It may be common amongst the upper-class in our society, and maybe I would even be more accepting of it as a result, but I know that there is nobody for Carrick but Everly, nobody for Everly but Carrick. Theirs is my favorite fairy tale, the most true of them.

He sighs, a frustrated exhale. "Reeve..." I think it's the first time he's said my name. No endearment, nothing soft wrapped around it. "I won't make you promises that I can't keep."

"Why can't you even try to keep them?" He is not the only one frustrated, even though I know, *I know*, that I am to blame for all of this. That I trapped him in this.

"Because I don't believe in them," he says evenly. His smirk is gone. What's more, my guards are gone, the lake is gone, the sun is gone. Even the door is gone. There is nothing but this moment, him sitting in front of me, setting out the shards for my heart to step on.

"What if—" The next words get stuck for a moment, caught in the tangle. I force them out. "What if you fall in love with me?"

He angles his head, almost a pitying angle but stopping just short. Not pity, but sympathy. A wish that his next words would be different.

But they aren't.

"I won't."

It isn't that I love Arden. It isn't even that I can imagine loving him, this mercurial man who breathes fire and flattery the way other people breathe air. It's the certainty behind those two words. The complete and utter conviction that no, he will not fall in love with me. The muscles in my face are not nearly strong enough to keep it from falling.

He reaches out to touch them, the muscles of my face, the skin of my face, and maybe the guards had vanished for him, too, under the weight of this moment. Jax clears his throat, though, low and warning, and his hand falls away.

"I don't believe in it," he says. "You are beautiful, and you do make me laugh. I don't believe it will be a hardship to have you for my wife. But I won't fall in love with you. I don't want you to go into this believing that I will."

He has laid out a shattered glass menagerie's worth of shards. An entire roomful of broken figures, placed just under my heart so that each beat sees it pricked. The wounds are not fatal, but I feel the stings over and over again, sharp and morose.

"Why?" I push. "It isn't a myth. I've seen it with my own eyes. How can you simply not *believe* in it?"

"Because I used to believe," he snaps. "And I was cured of it."

My guards reappear, the lake reappears, the sun reappears. The roaring in my ears recedes so that I can hear the lake again, its gentle sway, the birds in the trees. Everything around me is gentle, and I gentle too. I gentle because his snapped words are pained, hurt, "cured of the belief in love."

He believed in it once.

I stand up, dragging my damp feet carefully across the wooden planks to dry them without inheriting slivers. I slide them into my walking shoes and hold my hand down to Arden. He regards it with suspicion, still somewhere under the weight of the moment, but then he smirks, and the world rights itself. I answer his with one of my own as he takes my hand and lets me pull him to his feet.

He doesn't release my hand, instead drags it lazily to his lips and kisses the back of it. I am more flooded with relief than I would have expected by the return of this Arden, the charmer, the one who sets me off kilter. I wonder which is his truer face, this one or the one from just before, the one who used to believe but was cured of it.

I tuck my hand into his arm and gesture forward, down the path. "Walk with me?"

"To the ends of the earth."

I laugh at him, and then with him, and we walk.

Chapter Twenty-Eight

"I've never gambled," I muse as we wander through the forest, bound for my favorite hilltop under the careful watch of my guards. "Is it fun?"

"I'm not sure 'fun' is the right word. It's a high, an addiction. When you're winning, there's nothing better, and when you're losing, there's nothing worse."

"High highs and low lows. Why not moderate those into constant contentedness and avoid it entirely?" Even as I say it, I wonder what life would be without its high highs. Without joy, without elation. Even at the expense of sorrow, of grief.

Unbidden, I think of my mother. No, perhaps I could sacrifice some joy so as not to endure such loss again.

He laughs. "How boring that would be. I'll take you, once we're married. Show you the allure."

I beam a smile up at him, delighted by the idea of getting to go somewhere. Getting to experience something new. Something *outside* of these grounds. "Would you really? That would be marvelous!"

He smiles back, the softest version of his smirk. Maybe not even a smirk anymore, but a real and true smile. "I'll take you wherever you want to go."

One sentence, one true smile, and he sweeps aside the shards. Now my heartbeats are anticipation, excitement, a vision of a grand adventure. I will be like the heroine in my favorite book, and he will be the hero, and we will lead a life of laughter and adventure side by side.

When his side is free to me. When there is not someone else there, someone else holding his arm, someone else in his bed.

"I've never played before, though. Will you teach me?"

His dangerous grin reappears. He shifts his arm, my hand falling away as he reaches into the inside of his jacket to pull forth a deck of cards.

"How about now?"

I squeal and grab his empty hand in both of mine, dragging him the last handful of steps to the hilltop. Arden follows me easily, laughingly, sitting where I point while I carelessly plop a few feet before him, only arranging my skirts around me as an afterthought.

I watch mesmerized as he shuffles the deck, not caring that he laughs at my avid gaze. There are no weights in this moment, nothing bowing my shoulders or tugging at the back of my mind, and I savor the feel of the freedom.

"My game of choice is twenty-one. It's very simple in concept, but it can steal the whole of your fortune in the span of one evening if you aren't careful."

He explains the rules to me quickly. It really is simple: whoever's hand is nearest to twenty-one without going over wins. I hurry him along in his shuffling, eager to try my hand at it. Florien and I used to play games, and in the years since our relationship has been strained, I have occasionally tried to drag my guards into games to varying degrees of success. To have such a willing opponent, and such a handsome one, fills me with a lightness I've missed of late.

He plays as dealer, setting one card face up and one face down before him while giving me two face up. I stare at the face of the spades' king and the five of diamonds, and then I look up at Arden. The smile playing on his lips could mean *anything*. He looks confident, but doesn't he always? I squint, trying with all of my might to delve into his mind and read his hidden card.

"What'll it be, sweet? Stay or another?"

I shrug helplessly. "Another?"

"Such confidence," he teases. "Such certainty."

"Such a chatty dealer," I retort. "Are they like this in the gambling halls?"

"They're largely silent, actually. Dull."

"And far be it for you to be either silent or dull."

"Careful, there. That was almost an unprovoked compliment."

I laugh and wave at him impatiently. "The card, Arden."

He flips it over. A ten of diamonds. I know without needing to add them that I've gone over, thanks to Arden's smug smile. He reshuffles the deck, deals them again. I tell myself to play more carefully, more wisely.

I lose the next six hands.

"You're positively abysmal!" he crows after the sixth. "I should have wagered on these games."

"I don't understand how I can lose every single time," I mutter, slumping a little into the grass. "What are the odds?"

"The odds are high when you're greedy. You always ask for another card, every single time."

I do. I don't know when to stop, it seems. Not when there's a chance that the next card will make the difference. The risk to me always feels worth the reward, although, thus far, I have yet to win any sort of reward.

"Well, you'd think just once it would work in my favor."

"One more hand?" He waves the deck tauntingly under my chin. "Surely you can't lose eight in a row."

"I dislike you at present."

He smiles, leans a little forward, tips my chin up with the cards. Dangerous. "You don't."

He's right, of course. I don't. I'm not sure I've ever liked him more, actually.

He settles back to keep shuffling. "How about we make this winner takes all? Place a wager on this one?"

"What do you have in mind?" I ask warily.

I'm right to be wary, based on the look on his face. "If I win, I get a favor."

"What kind of favor?"

Arden shrugs, feigning an innocence I'm not sure he's ever actually possessed. "To be determined by the victor."

I furrow my brow, tilt my head, bite my lip. "I don't trust you with that much power."

He laughs. "Nor should you. How about I promise it'll be a small favor. One which needn't occur in a bedroom."

I roll my eyes, then check to make sure my guards remain out of earshot. I wouldn't be able to face them for a month if they overheard.

"All right," I concede. "But if I win, I get a favor of my own choosing."

"Hm," he says, speculation gleaming in the waltz of his eyes. "Deal. I won't put any locational limitations on it, though."

I bare my teeth in a gritted smile. "Just deal the cards."

He keeps his eyes on me as he does so. It doesn't flip my heart, though, or flood color to my cheeks, and I wonder if my body's getting used to him finally.

I flick my eyes down to my cards. A two and a seven. I feel confident enough in it to ask for another. He flips it over for me, eyes still on me instead of the cards. A seven. I'm less sure now. Sixteen is a solid count. I should stop here. But I can't shake the feeling that he has a seventeen, an eighteen, a nineteen, a twenty… And really, what are the odds of losing an eighth hand in a row?

Very high, as it turns out. I ask for another, he tosses me an eight, and then he laughs until he nearly cries. I glare at him the entire time.

"Eight hands in a row! Eight hands in a row you busted. I never even had to beat you with my own cards, because you busted all on your own. I'm going to have to bar you from the tables when you come with me to the hall, otherwise you'll beggar me."

He keeps right on laughing through his words, gravel and glee.

"Are you almost finished?" I ask archly.

"Almost," he says, his buoyant laughter fading into a chuckle, which fades into a smile, which sits there on his face so naturally and so unpracticed that I feel as though I'm witnessing an eclipse or a thunderstorm, something rare and almost magical. My pique fades, vanishes completely. I'm glad of anything that put that smile there, even if it means my loss.

My loss.

Which means…

Lord, I owe him a favor.

He sees me realize it. I can tell by the shift in his demeanor, the return of the danger. He slides the deck of cards back into his pocket without breaking eye contact. His eyes make a lot of promises, but I know that none of those promises are love.

"Okay," I sigh. "Tell me."

"Tell you what, sweet?"

"Tell me what I owe," I say through gritted teeth.

"Hm, not yet," he says mildly, standing and offering me his hand. I slide mine into his and let him pull me to my feet. He pulls a little harder than he needs to, though, and my body sways close to his. Dangerously close. The whole afternoon has shifted into danger suddenly, and not even the sunshine can abate it.

We start walking back down the hillside, toward the forest path that will lead us back to the palace.

"What would your favor have been, had you won?" He has a genuine note of curiosity in his voice.

"I was going to ask you a question."

"Dare I ask?"

I look up at the side of his face. He's so much taller than me, but he cranes his neck a little, lowers himself toward me. I will spend the rest of my life on his arm, this arm, looking up at him. I don't know what to make of it.

"I was going to ask how you were cured of it," I say seriously. "How you were cured of your belief in love."

His head moves a little lower, but I don't think it's for my benefit. I think it's just…drooping. I wonder if it's the weight of the memory, the weight of the cure. Anyway, I lost. He doesn't need to answer my question.

I'm surprised when he does.

"There was a girl," he says quietly. "Of course. That's the beginning of a hundred thousand stories. It always starts with a girl."

My eyes aren't on the path in front of us at all. He could lead us right into a tree or into a ditch and I would never see it coming. All of my attention is glued up and to the right, on him.

"I thought I loved her. I thought she loved me. I was young, and stupid, and she was entirely unsuitable. There was never any chance of it working, but I convinced myself that there was. When my father refused to listen, I told him to give the title to my brother. I told him I didn't want it anymore. And then I told her what I'd done."

I watch his throat move as he swallows.

"She got married a week later, the day before we were supposed to run away together. I had some half-formed plan to live in the countryside and raise sheep—can you even imagine, *me* raising sheep?—and I was just trying to sell enough of my belongings to have the coin to get us out there, and in the meantime, she went and got herself married. To a man who wasn't getting disinherited, and who didn't have plans involving sheep."

Arden shrugs, though it is far from careless. "Anyway, I was cured of it."

I don't know when we stopped walking, but we're just on the edge of the forest, just outside of the reach of the sun, frozen in place. My guards surround us, but they maintain their distance. They are careful to preserve my privacy, even Jax, with his hand apparently glued to his sword.

"Did you talk to her afterward?"

"There wasn't much to say. She was married."

"But maybe she was forced into it. Maybe it wasn't her choice at all. Maybe—"

"Maybe I was about to be disinherited and she found me decidedly less appealing without my title and my fortune." His voice brokers no argument. He wants to be done with this story, and anyway, he didn't even need to tell it. I'd lost.

"I'm sorry," I say quietly. He hadn't looked at me during the story, but he looks at me now. His eyes are unfathomable. Still. The same stillness of the forest. There is no breeze here, so the trees don't dance.

His eyes don't dance. "I'm sorry she broke your heart."

He lifts his hand to my face to push a collapsing strand of hair back into place, to tuck it back under the pin from which it had escaped. There are shadows on his face. All around him. Covering him. He is the Arden he was at the pier, but he is also the charming one with his finger gliding down my temple. I wonder if this, too, is practiced.

"Sweet girl," he murmurs. "Will your guards cut off my head if I try to kiss you?"

I lift my shoulders helplessly, firmly back on shaky ground. "Only if it appears unwelcome."

His hand stops its glide at my chin, which he tilts upward. Up, up, and up. He is standing close enough that I have to tilt it forever backward to see him. "Would it be unwelcome?"

Yes. No. My mind and my body have different answers. "Is this your favor then?"

Both sides of his lips quirk up, a quiet sort of curve. "Yes. Let's say yes."

And then he kisses me.

My thoughts race madly ahead as his lips press gently to mine. Maybe this is the moment, the moment everything will change. Maybe this is when he starts to rethink his certainty that he will not fall in love with me. Maybe this is the beginning.

I don't know what to do with my hands, so I clench them deep into the folds of my dress. I focus on how soft his lips are, on how nice it feels for his hand to be at my chin and for the other one to be at my waist. It shouldn't feel so nice, the way he radiates heat on an already hot day.

It's over before my thoughts have a chance to quiet themselves. I blink up at him, dazed and wondering if I should have done something different with my hands. Wondering if I'll be able to tell if anything has changed, if he's beginning to love me.

But his smile shifts into the smirk I know. The smirk I recognize. He is only the charmer as he drops his hand from my face and leans down to whisper wickedly in my ear, "The beginning of the favor, let's call it. Part one."

He escorts me back to the palace at a rapid clip. If I'm being entirely honest, *I'm* the one who sets the rapid clip. I'm practically dragging him along with me. I don't make eye contact with Demes as he holds the door open for us, because I'm sure that my face is already red enough without that embarrassment. Lord, all four of my guards had witnessed my first kiss.

When we reach the entryway, Arden hands me a bouquet of flowers that had been left on the foyer table. They're orchids, midnight blue, precisely the same as that which had been tucked into my hair the night of my birthday ball. I wonder if he remembers or if it was just a coincidence.

"I believe flowers were part of the agreement."

"Thank you. They're lovely."

"You're welcome." He kisses the back of my hand lightly, so lightly that I shouldn't be able to read anything into it, but I do. I read promises into it. The continuation of part one. I'm about to back away, possibly to sprint away, when Carrick comes around the corner.

"Oh. Hello, Reeve. Velasian."

I curtsy, my scattered mind settling a little thanks to my uncle's presence. Arden bows, and when he straightens, he's taller than he's been all day. His back is straight, his chin up. He looks dignified and proper. I arch my eyebrow a little at the transformation.

My greeting overlaps Arden's. Mine is a smile and a cheerful,

"Uncle Carrick," while his is a nod and a stiff, "Your Highness." It's wrong of me to take so much pleasure in Arden's unease, but as a man who seems to fit within his skin with utter contentment, it's refreshing to see that even he gets nervous.

"Did you have a nice outing?" Carrick's words are directed toward us, but I can't help but feel that his thoughts are a hundred miles elsewhere. My betrothal may have lessened the weight on his shoulders, but it has not taken it entirely away.

"We did, yes." I'm extremely surprised that Arden inserts no innuendo at all into his words. I wonder if I should ask Carrick along to chaperone all of our conversations.

"Did you get a chance to discuss the engagement ball?"

I look at him quizzically while Arden clears his throat. "I'd forgotten, actually."

Carrick laughs. "That's what we get for tasking a man with delivering news of a ball." He turns to me. "Everly's throwing together a small celebration in honor of your betrothal, in three days' time. Nothing too grand, but she wanted to mark the occasion."

In three days? It had taken months to plan my birthday ball. I can't imagine how this one will be managed in so little time. But the idea of another ball, of another night of dancing and music, fills me with anticipation. I smile at Carrick and tell him that I'll look forward to it. He excuses himself, leaving the foyer once more to me, Arden, and my guards.

"When did you two have the chance to discuss a ball?" I ask.

"I met with the king and my father before I came to find you outside. We went over some terms of the engagement, and Queen Everly stopped in to propose the idea of the ball."

"Terms of the engagement? Why wasn't I included in the discussion?"

He waves a dismissive hand. "Trust me, it was boring. All paperwork and numbers. Be glad you weren't subjected to it."

"It does involve me, you know," I grumble. "Just the slightest bit."

The tension had left his body as soon as Carrick left the foyer, and he is entirely himself when he leans back against the door to answer me, all drowsy indolence on top, coiled predator beneath. "I'll tell you about it later. Maybe if you can't sleep one night, I'll go through it all with you. You'll be out in no time." He can't resist adding a wicked smile, dropping his tone for my ears alone. "Although, I can think of better ways to pass the time if you can't sleep."

"Well, I should be going," I say, entirely too loudly. It echoes through the entryway, bouncing off the walls, off the chandelier, flinching against the ears of Arden and my guards. I start backing away. "Thank you for the outing, Arden. I'm sure we'll be in touch."

I'm sure we'll be in touch? I frantically feel my way up the staircase backward, all the while pleading with myself to get a grip.

"I'm sure we will be." Laughter is laced through his words, and though I can't see his eyes well enough to be sure, I would wager that they are far from still. It's a far safer bet than any I had placed in twenty-one. "Until next time, wife."

"Not yet," I call back, swinging around to bolt up the rest of the stairs, the sound of his chuckle following close on my heels.

CHAPTER TWENTY-NINE

I fully intend to return to my room and replay the events of the day, but instead of turning left at the top of the stairs, I turn right. I walk to the very end of the hallway, to the narrow door there, and I open it. I walk up the small flight of stairs, my guards traipsing behind me. They don't ask where I'm going; there's only one room up this way. Only one place I could possibly be going.

My mother's room.

I knock softly at the door at the top of the stairs before swinging it open on silent hinges. The nurse leaps out of her chair, her knitting falling to her feet at the floor.

"My lady. I didn't know to expect you."

She never knows to expect me. I never know to expect myself here. I don't come often anymore, and I never plan on it in advance. I suspect that my arrival here is always a result of my heart conspiring with my feet, letting them know that this is where I need to be. There is no consultation from my mind.

"I'm sorry, Lydia. I'll try to give you some warning next time."

She curtsies and ducks quietly out of the room, closing it behind her. My guards remain in the hallway, so it is just me in here.

Just me and my mother.

I take a deep breath and look over at her. I stand still and watch as her chest rises and falls evenly, gently. There is no hitch, no pause, no change. Her breaths come as easily as they have come for the past fourteen years. I walk quietly to her bedside, my feet silent on the floor, even though it does not matter.

My mother fell asleep one night when I was four years old, and she never woke up. As far as the doctors can tell, there is nothing wrong with her. Nothing to prevent her from opening her eyes, from reentering the world she had abruptly abandoned. From reuniting with the children she had abruptly abandoned.

Florien and I used to play in this room all the time. We used to drag our puzzles and blocks all the way up here, laughing as loudly as possible as we played. We'd yell and shout and chase each other around, and every now and then, we'd pause and look at our mother. We'd cross our fingers and hope that our noise had disturbed her, that she'd open her eyes and admonish us for shouting so loudly.

But her breaths would stay even and gentle, and her eyes would stay closed.

Not even Thrall could help her. For all of his magic and his century of knowledge, all that he had been able to do was ensure that she stayed alive. Tubes run down from the ceiling and disappear under her blankets, filling her with nutrients, with sustenance. I try not to look at them while I'm in here, because they serve as a reminder that this is not an ordinary sleep.

As though I need a reminder. As though my mother's absence from the past fourteen years of my life has not sufficiently informed me that this is not an ordinary sleep. If it was, she would have woken up. She would have held me when I cried, she would have kissed my scraped knees, she would have helped me get ready for my eighteenth birthday ball. She would know just the right words to say to me right now, while I sit beside her, engaged to a near-stranger and sinking deeper and deeper into a world that only lives in my dreams. She would know why my first kiss made me want to run.

"Hi, Mama." The only words I allow myself as I take the chair vacated by her nurse. I used to tell her about my day, about my life, but I stopped when I realized that it hurt too much to never get a response.

I touch her hand lightly, tentatively. Her skin is warm, as it always is. Soft and smooth. I rest my hand on it and wish for just about everything to be different.

I never stay long. I only stay as long as I can bear it, as long as my heart can beat through the sight of her lying still before me, grey hairs slowly mixing in with the auburn to show the passage of time. It is the only indication, because her face shows no lines. No laugh lines, no frown lines. No wrinkles to show that she has fully lived her life. She had only twenty-four years to live it. How could that possibly be the whole of it?

I lift my hand carefully from hers and stand to leave the room. I walk through the door without looking back. This time, it is my heart conspiring with my eyes, telling them to stare straight ahead. Conspiring with my neck to keep it from turning my head to look over my shoulder. Conspiring with itself, a stuttered conversation all its own, telling itself to hold tight to all of its pieces. Telling itself not to break.

My guards and I make a quiet processional back down the stairs, through the hallways to my bedroom. I try to shrug off the pensive silence, to reassure my heart that I will keep it whole. That I will keep myself whole.

"Have you ever been in love?" I ask abruptly.

My question does not eliminate the silence. It merely adds a layer of cautious tension to it.

Percius reacts first. He laughs and says, "None of your business." And then, belatedly, "My lady."

I glare up at him, and he offers me the full power of his smile in return. There is no chance that someone hasn't fallen in love with *him*.

"Come on, Perc. I'm sick unto death of thinking of my own love life."

"Well, don't turn your nose this way, my lady," Tiven drawls from behind me. "Impertinent though he is, Perc is right."

I grumble and kick at the ground a little as we continue on. "Some friends you are."

We walk on a little before Demes pipes up unexpectedly from the front.

"I've got a girl."

I perk up instantly, clasping my hands together. "Ooh, tell me about her, Dem!"

"He does not," Perc cuts in dryly. "Ignore him, my lady."

"I do so! Just because I haven't told you about her doesn't mean she's not real."

"Go on then," Percius says in magnanimous skepticism, eyebrows raised to the ends of his wayward curls and arms spread wide. "Do tell."

"She works down in the kitchens. Sneaks me cakes on baking days, sometimes two or three." Demes shoots a smug look over his shoulder at Perc.

"And?" I ask eagerly.

"And?" He looks puzzled.

I deflate, shoulders slumping as Percius guffaws beside me.

"Never mind, Dem. She sounds lovely."

"Oh, she is. I'm hoping to find another one, too, to sneak me berries."

Another one…Lord. I regret asking.

"There you have it," Tiven says, and even he can't keep the humor from his tone. "Dem's got a girl, and the rest of us are entirely focused on our jobs."

"I'm focused, too!" Dem swings around to face us, walking backward now. "The cakes aren't distracting me. They help me, really. Give me an energy boost."

"You realize you're using the girl for sweets, Dem," Perc says sardonically.

"And what do *you* use them for, Perc?" Demes shoots back.

I look up in time to see Percius' face shift into a ferocious, quelling glare. He sees me see it, though, and he quickly turns innocent. "I don't know what you're talking about."

"Even *I* know what he's talking about," I say, enjoying the way Perc's tanned cheeks redden. This is just what I needed today. This moment. This laughter.

"No, you don't," he mutters.

Tiven clears his throat.

"No, you don't, my lady," Percius revises.

I grin up at him. "Keep telling yourself that, Perc."

We reach the door of my room, but before entering, I pause and look up to my right, to the pillar of silence there. Jax is like a black hole swirling beside me, an absence of anything yet all the more noticeable because of it.

"Are you going to be angry with me much longer?" I can't help sounding utterly forlorn. I miss his gruff counsel, his contributions to the banter of the others. This is the longest he's ever been upset with me, and it weighs my already weighted shoulders down an extra inch or two.

Just when I'm sure he isn't going to answer, and that instead his silence will be my answer, he says, "Another day or two yet."

I sigh and nod down to my toes. "Goodnight, men."

"Goodnight, my lady," comes their chorus. It is one voice short, an incomplete harmony. I miss the notes of it, the bassline to the steadiest rhythm in my life, but I tell myself to be patient. Another day or two yet, he'd said, and I know that he won't be rushed. Stony silences and scorching glares, those are the penalties for betraying Jax's trust. I'd known the price, and now I will pay it in full.

～＊～

Guin has my nightgown laid out on my bed, waiting for me. I trail my fingers along it and wonder if any other nightgown in history has seen the things mine has. Bloodthirsty falcons, picked over bodies, a blue-eyed boy from another world. It is a garment made for sleep, but instead, it is my armor.

"Hello, my lady," Guin greets me from the side of the room where she hangs my freshly pressed dresses. "Did you have a good day?"

I think about it, my fingers still lightly moving across the nightgown. "I did," I decide. "Although it was also a strange day."

"Strange how?"

"Well, I went for a walk with the man I am to marry. He isn't at all who I had envisioned for myself. He makes me ill at ease, but at the same time he rather fascinates me. I don't know what to make of him."

"Do you think he will make a good husband?"

"No," I laugh. "No, I'm quite certain he will make a terrible husband."

Her face falls. "Will he be cruel to you?"

"No," I say slowly, shaking my head. "He will never be cruel, not in the way you mean, at least. He's trying to protect me from himself. Trying to warn me about the sort of husband he will be. He won't be cruel, but he's certain he won't ever love me. And that is a difficult thing for my heart to accept."

"Understandably, my lady. You have a heart made for love."

I smile and turn so that she can start on my buttons. "I always thought so. But perhaps it will be enough to have a life of adventure. I'm certain nothing will ever be dull in marriage to Lord Velasian."

"I hope so," she murmurs behind me. "I hope it will be enough."

There is the barest note of skepticism in her tone, and it resounds mightily within me. I am skeptical, myself. Love is the adventure I had most hoped for. Anything else, even wandering the gambling halls on Arden's arm, his voice warm in my ear, gleams a little paler in comparison.

"Well," I shrug a little helplessly. "Regardless, it is the future I have in store."

I step out of my dress and pull my nightgown over my head. Guin's fingers fly through my hair, braiding it in my usual nighttime style. For a moment, I wonder if I should wear something else. I had resolved not to wear my nightgown anymore, but none of my other gowns seem much better. I imagine sneaking through the streets in one of my day gowns and wrinkle my nose at the thought. No, what I should do is try to steal a shirt and trousers from Florien. And procure a sturdier pair of shoes. Something easy to move and run in.

"Whatever comes, I will be there with you. Me and your four men out there. The king has already seen to it that we are part of the marriage agreement."

I experience a moment of blinding relief before it fades away. "Oh, Guin. I'm happy to hear it, but I hate that you'll have to leave your mother. Your home."

She waves a dismissive hand through the air, swatting my worry aside. "I won't be too far. I can still visit my mother from time to time. Really, I'm glad to be coming with you."

I turn to touch her elbow lightly, fondly. "Thank you, Guin. It truly is a comfort to know that you'll be with me. All of you."

She bids me goodnight, leaving me to lie in bed and stare at my ceiling. I can't stop thinking about the story Arden had told me. I try to imagine the boy he was, so deep in love that he'd been willing to leave his whole life behind. Willing to live in the country and raise *sheep*. I feel a sudden swell of hatred and resentment toward the woman who had broken his heart. The woman who had convinced him that love was for fairy tales and fools.

I wonder if he's wrong, if there's hope of unearthing the boy he was. He's had years to build his walls, to instill cynicism and disbelief in his blood. Is it simply forever to be a part of him now? The kiss hadn't seemed to change anything.

For him.

For me…I don't know. All I know for sure is that it had made me want to run. There is a tangle of other emotions, of other instincts, but that one shines the brightest. It shouts the loudest. He had kissed me, and I had wanted to run.

I set the why of it aside to be explored another time, another day. The night calls for me, though I once again don't know what I will find there. Whether I will be welcome at Cecily's, with the way Bran and I left things. Dread unspools within my stomach as sleep pulls me under.

CHAPTER THIRTY

Bran isn't waiting for me this time. I sit up under an empty rope and sprint for the shadows, eyes scanning all around me but not finding him there. It makes sense, I tell myself. He'd known of the hanging yesterday and so had come to help me. Today, he would know that there had been no hanging. He would know that I could manage this on my own.

Or he does not want me to come. Perhaps it has all become too much for him, and the knowledge that I am the niece of a king, and engaged to be married, is the final straw. Perhaps he misses sleep.

So many possibilities. I stand in the shadows and sort through them all, wondering if I should just stay here, pressed against the building, letting the night pass me by. It's unlikely for the falcons to come here to the empty gallows, so long as nobody else makes their way through here.

At the same time, I experience a sharp, resounding longing for my bed of moss. It was my escape for so many nights, through so many years, and I miss it. Perhaps I will try for the wall. I know which path to take, how to distract the falcons and get over the wall. I did it once before—with some assistance from Bran. This time, I'm almost certain I could manage it myself.

But the bed of moss stopped being my escape when Bran first arrived there. *He* became my escape, my reprieve from this world. Even though he isn't here to meet me, and even though I'm filled with enough uncertainties to make my stomach swim, I decide to go to him. Once I decide, I realize that there wasn't really any other choice.

I start on my way, missing his presence beside me but confident in my path. I know these streets, and I know which ones he had taken. I can manage it just fine without him, and anyway, he shouldn't be risking himself so often for me.

I'm about halfway there when I hear the first crunch of gravel. I'm tucked into an alley, heading into a maze of them that will take me farther from the main streets, when it comes from behind me. It's loud. Reckless. Those are not cautious steps.

They are falcon-summoning steps.

I grit my teeth and tell myself to keep walking, but instead of listening to my own stern order, I turn the wrong way. I cannot seem to help leaning out a little bit to look at the street.

It is foolish of me. Utterly foolish. I look anyway.

The moon is waning, so I have to squint a bit to make out the shadow of a figure, walking square in the middle of the main street. It's a meandering walk, completely without urgency. Each step makes me flinch. I want to shout at whoever it is, to tell him or her that those footsteps mean death here. *Surely* they must know, though. Surely there is nobody here who does not know what it means to be caught out after sundown.

The approaching flap of wings does not surprise me, nor do the shrieks singing through my ears and my body, a song I have heard time and time again. A song that makes every muscle in my body clench, every hair on my arms stand at attention. It has been a few nights now since I heard it, but not nearly long enough. I know too well, too clearly, that the next note in the song will be the screams.

And there is nothing I can do. I have no weapon, little chance to survive them another time, especially with half a journey still between me and Cecily's home.

The possibility that it might be Bran walking there whispers through my mind, but it vanishes quickly. He would never be so careless. Whoever is out there seems to have no care for their own life. Even with the approaching flaps, the growing shrieks, he does not run.

The falcons appear overhead. I duck more deeply into the alley, pressing my back into the wall. I want to keep walking, to put as much distance between myself and what is to come as I can manage, but I don't trust my feet to be as completely silent as they would need to be with the falcons so close.

The shrieks silence abruptly. They don't lift and blend into a song, or taper off into thwarted squawks. They merely silence. I lean just the slightest bit forward and watch as they pass directly over the walking figure.

They let him go. There is no chance that they don't see him, and one even seems to dip a little over him, but then they continue on their way. They circle back in the direction from which they had come, and they leave the person to continue making his slow, meandering way down the middle of the street.

It makes no sense. I have never seen anything like it, in all of my years here. There was the one rescued woman, but other than that, all that I have ever witnessed when someone was caught out is quick and painful death. Skin torn from bone. Screams of agony. Nobody has ever been allowed to continue on their way.

Confusion clouds my mind as I walk the rest of the way to Cecily's. I flip through what I had seen over and over in my mind, searching for some explanation. I'm anxious to ask Bran about it, to find out if it sounds like something he's ever witnessed.

I let myself in quietly, the house echoing silence all around me. I wonder with the beginning of deflation whether they're all already in bed.

No, merely silent. Bran and Cecily are waiting for me when I turn away from the door. I open my mouth to tell them what I've seen, but Bran cuts my words off swiftly.

"Where were you?" His voice carries the same sharp edge, the same agitation it had when I had left him last night. It sets me on edge, enough of an edge that I do something reckless. I turn back toward the door and start to turn the knob.

He's there before I can even begin to pull it open, one hand shooting out to hold it closed.

"Are you out of your mind? You were going to go back out there?"

"It seems preferable, if you're going to continue snapping at me!"

He looks as though he has several ideas of what he would like to say, but I watch as he consciously swallows each one. He leans back against the door, effectively blocking that exit. I turn for the stairs, but that route is cut off by Cecily.

"I had a hell of a time keeping him from going out to look for you," she nearly snarls.

I fling my arms in the air and turn back to face Bran. He looks past me, to Cecily, and speaks in a softer tone than he'd used with me. "Can you give us a minute?"

I can only imagine the scowl he faces as she retreats up the stairs. I only imagine it, because I keep my eyes locked hard on him. I don't need to track the motion when he lifts his arm, when his hand lands on the back of his neck. He is ill at ease, still swallowing words in search of the right ones.

"I'm sorry," he says finally, evenly. "I was afraid something had happened to you. I didn't mean to snap."

The riot in me calms instantly at his apology. "I wasn't sure if I was welcome here," I admit.

"Always come here," he says with strength. "No matter how big of an ass I've been."

"Even though—"

"*Always.*"

I feel the rest of the tension bleed from my shoulders at the force in his tone. "I'm sorry I worried you."

"Scared the hell out of me," he mutters.

"Are you not mad at me anymore, then? For last night?"

"I never had any reason to be mad at you. I was just…caught off guard. I overreacted. I've been thinking on it all day, and…you were right. I was mad about you for not telling me who you are, but who's to say the title is who you are? Who's to say any of us are what we were born into?"

Bran says it to me, but I wonder if he's saying it more to himself. I want to jump in and tell him he's everything. I want to tell him he's the sun, the moon, and all of the stars, so unless he was born in the sky, he's more. To me, he'll always be more.

But he opens his mouth to continue, and so I swallow the words. I let him finish.

"So if you tell me you're Reeve, you're Reeve. I mean, Trouble, first and foremost, but Reeve. You don't have to have the title here if you don't want it. And as for the rest of it…well, I'm gonna follow your lead. I'm not pacing now, I'm standing still, right here, where you are. Forgive me?"

I start to smile, but I feel it waver in the wake of the relief washing over me. I let my strongest instinct take hold, the one that is always at the forefront when I'm with him. I throw myself into his arms.

"Ah, Trouble," he says into my hair. "I'm sorry."

"I'm glad I didn't try for the wall after all."

My words are muffled in his shirt, but there can be no doubt that he hears them. Mostly because he tries to push me away and practically shouts, "You were going to try for the wall?"

I lean back, my forehead creasing a little at his shout. "I only thought about it. I didn't actually do it."

"You are going to be the death of me." He sounds like he means it.

I smile fondly, my hands lacing together behind his back and feeling exceptionally at home there, wrapped around him. "Jax says the same thing all the time."

I feel the tension travel up his spine beneath my hands. He clears his throat. "Is Jax…your future husband?"

"No," I say quickly. "No, Jax is my guard. One of my guards."

"*One* of your guards?"

"Are you going to start pacing again?"

"No," he sighs. "I just need to get used to the idea of you being one step outside of royalty."

I shake my head dismissively. "I'd really rather you didn't. Just Reeve, right? Or, if you insist—" I smile "—Trouble."

He studies me for a moment, his face just a breath and a tilt from mine. I wish he'd take that breath. I wish he'd tilt. "Is it so heavy? That title of yours?"

I subtly roll onto the balls of my feet, closing a little of the gap between us. "Sometimes. I know that I am lucky in my life, and that there are so many wonderful pieces to it, but sometimes…I wish for a life in which I was always just Reeve."

There is only so much I can do to get nearer to him, and I have done it, so when he is suddenly a little nearer, I know that it must be his doing. I hold my breath and wait.

The moment is shattered by footsteps behind us. I unclasp my hands from behind his back and step away before Cecily and Nor reach the bottom of the stairs.

"You made it!" Nor exclaims. "Cec had a hell of a time keeping Bran from going out to find you."

"Language," his sister scolds.

He rolls his eyes at her, then dodges her swiping hand. She catches air instead of him, her annoyance softening into affection. Their easy relationship reminds me of how things used to be with Florien. I swallow the envy and push my brother behind the door. He might as well always stay there. He has as little to do with my waking world as he does with my dream world.

"Oh!" I say suddenly, remembering. "Part of the reason I was late was because I saw a man in the street."

The mood shifts abruptly, darkening several shades. Bran stays leaning against the door while the rest of us center ourselves around him.

"Was he caught?" Bran scuffs a foot at the ground in front of him as he asks it.

"No… no, he wasn't. It was so strange. He was walking down the middle of the main throughway, loudly and slowly, and of course, the falcons came. But…they let him go. They passed directly over him, and they let him continue on."

"That's not possible," Cecily counters quickly.

"Well, it's what happened." I jut my chin a little at her instant dismissal.

"Did he duck into a doorway?"

"No. He kept right on walking, down the very center of the street. There's no way they didn't see him."

I really wish she would stop shaking her head so contemptuously. "You must have seen wrong."

"There is no way I could have *seen* wrong," I bite out through gritted teeth. "I was close enough to see it all happen."

"The moon isn't as full," Bran says quietly. "Your eyes might have been playing tricks on you in the dark."

I do a poor job at hiding my feeling of betrayal as I turn on him. "The moon is barely waning, Bran. It was bright enough. I know what I saw."

"It's just that that's not something that happens," he says placatingly. "The falcons are hunters, and anyone caught out at night is their prey. They don't make exceptions."

"Maybe it was a guard? One of Rancore's men?"

Bran is already shaking his head, a less contemptuous mirror image of Cecily. "The guards don't leave the palace walls at night specifically because the falcons don't discriminate. Meat is meat to them, and all humans are meat."

I set my jaw. "Well, I know what I saw."

He sighs and rubs his chin. "All right, then. We can think on it."

I glance from him over to Cecily, to her humorless smirk. I let my eyes skitter away from it quickly, frustration roaring inside of me. They land on Nor, who at least looks thoughtful.

"There could be a reason. Just because we haven't heard of it happening, doesn't mean it isn't possible."

"Thank you, Nor," I say quietly, though his is not the support I had most counted on. "Anyway, I'm going to head upstairs. I'm sure you'll all need to get to sleep, too."

I only make it to the second step before Bran falls into place behind me. I chafe at the way he had sided with Cecily, but when I look back over my shoulder at him at the top of the stairs, he flicks his head to the left, to his bedroom door, a questioning look on his face, and I go into his room instead of mine.

He follows me in and closes the door.

"You're mad at me." He presents it as a statement of fact, not a question.

"Not mad, just…disappointed," I admit.

He sits down on his cot, and I sit beside him. There is no more thought given to keeping careful distances. The most natural thing is for my shoulder to touch his, for the side of my thigh to press against the side of his. It is natural, but fires still start there. My nerves still skip and thrill at every place his body touches mine.

"It just seems impossible," he says into the silence. "I've never heard of anything like it."

"As impossible as a girl from another world who visits yours in her dreams?"

His laugh is merely an exhale as he shifts to face me, one hand lifting to the back of his neck. "Yeah…you're right. I guess I should get used to things not always being like I thought they were."

I shift, too. The candlelight casts him in oranges and yellows, except for the places where the shadows drape him in greys. There is never enough light.

"Blue," I say musingly. He lifts an eyebrow. "Your eyes. What kind of blue?"

His lips tilt into their smile, warmer than the candles' glow. "My mother used to call them the very blue of the sky at dusk."

I smile a little wistfully. My favorite shade of blue. Of course. "My brother used to call mine the very brown of mud."

He laughs at that. "I've always liked mud."

Everything inside of me warms. "I've always liked the sky at dusk."

The moment sits on a precipice, and I think about reaching out to touch his face. To push the moment onto one side, the side where my hand can touch him and where the warmth inside of me becomes an inferno. But he exhales long and low and shifts away, pushing the moment the other way.

I stand on restless legs and go to crouch before his stack of books. There is another book of poetry at the top, a slim volume of short stories beneath it, two worn journals which look to have been handwritten beneath those.

"Do you like poetry?" I ask absentmindedly as I shuffle through the books. "I've been greatly enjoying the one you lent me."

"Hm," he says noncommittally, uncomfortably. I shoot him a questioning look, but he dodges it artfully. "I'm glad you're enjoying it."

I start to say something else, to ask another question, but whatever I'm about to say falls off the edge of my brain the second I see the last book in the stack.

My fingers trace the title, know to follow down, down, down the massive curl beneath the A. They know each curve, each line, each letter.

A History of Acarsaid: Centuries Before.

"I have this book," I whisper.

CHAPTER THIRTY-ONE

I turn to face him with the book still clutched in my hands. "Bran, how is it that you have this book?"

He shrugs, a wholly uncertain motion. He looks suddenly nauseous, like he would rather be anywhere but here. "It was my mother's."

"It says Acarsaid! You acted as though you didn't know it at all, when I told you where I was from."

One hand rubs at the back of his neck before the other one lifts to join it, to clasp together with the other and stay there. "I didn't know."

"How didn't you know? I don't understand, Bran."

My mind is in overdrive. To find something of my world here, something that links this world to my own, sends my heart into a flurry of beats. I am suddenly, sickeningly afraid that this truly is all inside of my head. That my subconscious has decided to drop hints, breadcrumbs, to cruelly taunt at the connection between here and there.

He drops his hands, and his face shifts away from uncertainty. He looks...defiant.

"I can't read," he says, the words a declaration, a dare. "I never learned, so I didn't know what the book was. I don't know anything of poetry."

My knees are starting to ache, frozen in my crouch. "Oh," is all I say at first. I feel the panic from the book melt away a little, pushed aside by the look on his face. I stand to go sit back beside him, bringing the book with me. "It isn't anything to be ashamed of."

"Yes, it is."

"It *isn't*. You live a different kind of life here. You train for war, you don't learn to read. That makes sense, now that you mention it."

"Nor can read." His tone is still defiance, though he seems to direct it inwardly now. "He taught himself. And Cecily can a little, more than I can anyways. My mother never could, and she wanted for me to try, to make something more of myself, but I've never managed it."

I put my hand on his, but he pulls instantly away. Only until he sees the fall of my face, though, and then he tucks his hand back under mine, soothes it by placing his other hand on top.

"But you can fight," I insist. "You fought off six falcons to save my life, to save Cecily's. And the way you fool the falcons…you get over the wall so cleverly. I've always marveled at it. Everyone has strengths, Bran, and everyone has weaknesses. Our weaknesses don't lessen who we are as people."

He shrugs, though it doesn't seem to come easily. It's stilted, measured. "I always wanted to, though. The way Nor sits there with his nose in a book, like he's somewhere else for a little while. Somewhere that isn't here. I wanted that. I *want* that. And the way you talked about that book of yours, that first night. Like they're real people you know. It gave you something, that story. Something to want for yourself that's more than what you've got."

I see longing, spelled out on his face. Longing to escape, longing to dream. Longing to *read*, for the same reasons I adore it. For the same reasons I treasure it. Now, I treasure it even more. I always took books and the ability to read for granted. Now, I can plainly see their value.

"I can teach you," I whisper. "Someday."

Someday.

I say it as though we have a someday.

Please, let us have a someday.

His hands are warm on mine, and I think we're back on the precipice. His eyes are on our hands, so I can't tell what lies within them, but I think we're back there. I think this might be another tipping point.

This time, I'm the one who tips us back to safety. I pull my hand gently free and trace the title of the book again. "It's so strange that this book is here," I say quietly.

"It is," he agrees, the rebellion gone from his voice. "What do you think it means?"

I don't tell him my greatest fear, that it means that he isn't real. That none of this is real. I shift as close as I can, my body pressed along the edge of his, to reassure myself that he cannot possibly be anything but real.

"I don't know. It's strange, though. It has to mean something, for a book from my world to have ended up in yours."

"My mother always told me to guard these books," he muses. "She couldn't read, either, so I always found it a little strange, but she was adamant that I keep them with me. That's why I couldn't leave them behind when I came here. It was a waste of carrying, but I couldn't shake it, her insistence."

"When did she die?" A cautious question, spoken in a cautious tone.

"Seven years ago. The winter before I turned thirteen."

"I'm sorry."

"So am I."

"What happened?"

He sighs, leaning back against the wall. I settle back beside him. "There's a lot we don't know about each other, huh?"

"There is," I agree. "But you don't have to tell me if you'd rather not."

Bran puts his hand face up on his knee, and I put mine inside of it. We stay like that, in the candlelight, with the book on my lap, as he tells me about his mother.

"She got sick. She tried to keep working through it, but it knocked the wind out of her 'til she could barely leave her bed. They cut her rations, since she wasn't contributing to the work. I tried to give her mine, but she wouldn't have it. She wanted me to keep my strength up, knowing I'd have to start training soon.

"Without food, it just got worse, faster. They came for her one day when I was at the kitchens, begging for an extra ration. There was one guard who wasn't all awful, and he took pity on me and gave me a little more, but by the time I got back…the door was hanging open. She was gone."

In a flash, I remember the first night he had seen me. The first time we had spoken. I had lied and said that I wasn't in training because I was caring for my sick father. I remember being caught off guard by the flatness in his tone when he had said, "If he's sick, they would have taken him." It matches the flatness in his tone as he speaks now, as he tells me his story. It knocks holes in the sides of my heart, turns it into a sieve, leaking tears that prick at my eyelids.

"I'm sorry," I whisper.

His shrug drags his shoulder up along mine. "It's been some years now."

"Yes," I agree. "But I know how it can still hurt, even after years."

I let my head fall to the side, onto his shoulder. "What did you do then?"

"I got by. I should've been sent to the orphanage, but Cec and Nor's mom took care of me. I didn't want to leave my home, but she made sure I had clothes and got my food rations. She got me by until I was thirteen and could start my training."

"What happened to her?" I'm afraid to ask.

"She died last year. An accident in the factory, they said, but she had a face on her, like Cec. A face on her, and a mouth on her, pretty much an older version of her daughter, and I think they got to her."

"What a cruel world." The weight of it keeps my voice low, barely even a whisper. To think, I had been complaining about the weight of my title. It is nothing, less than a feather, in the face of this world, in the face of what Bran has had to endure.

"It is that," he agrees. "But it's the only one I know."

I bury my nose into the side of his arm and breathe in the smell of him. He smells like soap and metal, like fire and life. He smells alive, and real, and he cannot possibly be anything but those things.

"Your father?"

"I have no father," he says instantly, his tone empty of everything. His arm stiffens under my nose, defiance finding its way back into him.

"Okay," I say quietly. When it's clear that I won't push the subject, he relaxes against me.

"What about you? What's your family like?"

I concentrate on opening the door, on bleeding the day into the night. I draw forth my father's face, my brother's. Carrick's and Everly's. My mother's.

"My father is busy. He was meant to have an heir and a spare, but he had my brother and then me. So he focuses on my brother, and I think he just kind of forgets about me. My brother used to be my closest friend, but now he is my father's miniature, and he forgets about me, too. I adore my aunt and uncle. They're busy running the country, but when I do get to see them, the visits are always happy ones. My mother…" My voice trails off, dipping into different shards than those that Arden had laid there. "My mother fell asleep when I was four years old and never woke up. I visit her now and then—I visited her today—but there's been no change in fourteen years. They don't expect anything to change."

I sense him turn his head to look down at me. Bran rests his lips briefly on my temple, the barest reassuring touch. It eases so much within me. The tangle loosens, the shards soften, I remember my mother's smile and don't feel as though the memory strangles me.

"What a pair we are," he says.

"Yes," I agree. "A mess of a pair."

He laughs a little, his lips still so close to my skin that I feel the whoosh of air behind his laughter. "Promise you won't try for the wall without me."

I lift my head to smile at him, my softest smile, the one that shows the most of who I am, mixes in the most of who I want to be. "I promise."

He smiles back, but he also yawns, a gaping and drawn out yawn that has me laughing and pushing away from him. "You should get to sleep. I hear you've been sloppy in training, you know."

A second yawn almost immediately follows the first, though he smiles through it and tugs me back toward him. "Don't believe a word of it. I'm never sloppy."

"Nonetheless." I pause. Consider. There are words that want to be said, fighting their way out. Words that I can't say. I step outside of myself and say them anyway. "Can I sleep here tonight?"

His eyebrows move infinitesimally upward. I feel awkward and unsure, stepping back inside of myself and wishing the words unsaid, or wishing them said better. Wishing for him to answer, and for his answer to be yes.

"Just to sleep," I amend in a rush. "Your cot is so much more comfortable than my cushions, and you have a window, and…" I trail off with a self-conscious shrug and half of a smile. "And the company is infinitely better."

Bran studies me a moment longer before sliding off the cot. I think for one mad second, one wretched heartbeat of a second, that he's going to go to the door, to show me out, but instead, he starts blowing out the candles. Once they're all little more than wisps of smoke and remembered flame, he comes back to the cot.

"Move a little," he murmurs through the darkness, the depth of his voice unending. It seems to have acquired a touch of shale, a spattering of gravel.

I shift toward the wall, making space for him to lie down. When he does so, I realize just how small the cot actually is. He takes up the majority of it, leaving only a small sliver of space for me. What was I thinking, asking to stay?

"Lay down, Trouble," he says, tugging lightly on my arm. I do so uneasily, my body pressed close to the seam between the cot and the wall. My forehead presses into the wooden wall, and I breathe it in for a moment before rolling my eyes at my absurdity. I allow myself to shift back a little, instantly running up against the length of his body.

"There you are," his voice comes from somewhere near the top of my head. "I was starting to wonder if you'd somehow pushed through the wall."

I shift back a little more, experimentally. There isn't a place on my body that doesn't touch a place on his. There isn't a place on my body that isn't alight, that isn't aware. All of the warmth flooding my veins seems to collect and pool deep in my stomach, simmering and tantalizing. I revel in the feel of it, so unfamiliar.

I am as near to him as I can get, but I want to be closer. I want… the very opposite of running.

"I'm not going to get any sleep at all if you don't stop moving like that," he whispers gruffly.

I freeze.

"You can breathe."

I let my breath out slowly, and the night is filled with his quiet laughter near my ear, with the feel of his body against me and around me, with the burning knowledge deep inside of me that if this isn't real, there isn't a thing in my life that is.

"Goodnight, Bran."

"Night, Trouble."

I hear the moment he falls asleep, the evening out of his breaths. I track all of the shifts of his body, of his arm settling across my waist, his face burying into my hair. It is the closest to sleep I've ever come in this world, the drowsy contentment of this night. When the sun starts to rise, I turn carefully in his arms to watch the warm light dance across the curl of his eyelashes. There is enough of it that I think maybe, just maybe, I will be able to see the dusk blue of his eyes.

I'm called home before he ever opens them.

CHAPTER THIRTY-TWO

The day passes slowly, interminably, my mind in Tenebris even as my body is in Acarsaid, wandering the informal gardens and staring blankly at book pages without absorbing their contents. I have lunch with Everly to discuss the engagement ball, but even then, my thoughts are barely present. When she comments on my distraction and hints that it's Arden's doing, I allow her to assume.

In reality, I keep Arden behind the door all day. I let Bran roam freely through my mind, memories of the night flitting smiles across my lips and unleashing sighs that make no sense to anyone else around me. They probably all attribute it to Arden.

It's a relief when the night comes, when I'm back outside of Cecily's door. My walk had been thankfully uneventful—the rope swinging empty once again, no shadowed men walking loudly through the streets. The moon is ever waning, but this route is becoming second nature to me now, as the one to the wall once had been. That one had led me to peace as this one now does.

The main room is empty when I arrive, empty of any sign of life but the dancing of the fire. The night is warm enough that I do not crave its heat, so I don't linger. Instead, I start for the stairs, anxious to see Bran. I'm nearly to the top step when I hear him, the low notes of his voice intertwining with Cecily's more dulcet timbre.

"…every night?" I catch the end of a question in the barest tone I've ever heard from her. There is no snarl there, nothing painted over it for my benefit. I think it must be her most natural voice, one she reserves only for Bran and her brother.

"I don't know, Cec." Bran sounds flustered, on the edge of annoyance. Still, it makes me smile just to hear his voice. "She has nowhere else to go."

My feet stop where they are, one step from the top. Three steps from Cecily's doorway. Frozen. No trace of my smile remains.

"This isn't a halfway house, Bran."

"She saved your life. Doesn't that count for enough to let her to stay here until we figure things out?"

"So you're letting her stay out of obligation then?"

A long pause. I hold my breath, leaning my head against the stairwell wall. I shouldn't be eavesdropping. Nothing good ever comes of it. I can't seem to unstick my feet, though.

"She has nowhere to go, Cecily," he says finally. "And she's ill-equipped to deal with our world. Hell, she's the niece of a *king*. What do you want me to do, throw her to the falcons and wish her luck?"

"Of course not. I'm just trying to understand…"

The rest of her words are muffled by approaching footsteps from the other end of the hallway. Before I have a chance to react, to process anything other than the words "obligation" and "ill-equipped" ringing loudly in my ears, Nor appears. He starts to turn toward Cecily's door but does a double-take when he sees me a few steps away.

"Oh, hey, Reeve. When'd you get here?"

I try for a smile, but when it won't come, I back up a step. When

Bran appears beside Nor, I back up a few more, swinging around to take the last few steps facing forward and hoping that the shadows of the stairwell were enough to hide my face from Bran. I hadn't had a chance to arrange it into anything but hurt.

Unfortunately, there's little chance he didn't see. He reaches the bottom of the stairs half a second after I do, grabbing my elbow lightly to swing me around.

"Reeve…"

I flinch at his use of my given name, at the apology behind it. It neither erases nor drowns out the word "obligation" still thundering in my ears, still swimming in my blood. I had thought he wanted me here.

I shake his hand from my arm and watch it fall limply back to his side. Perhaps that touch had only been obligation, as well.

"It's fine, Bran. You don't have to explain." Each word comes out a dead, flat thing. I am without emotion, or perhaps I have too many emotions and they have cancelled each other out entirely. Either way, my voice is a dead, flat thing, and I wonder if my heart might be, too.

"Hey." He is unrelenting, stepping closer so that I have to look up if I wish to see him. I do not wish to. Instead, I stare hard at his collarbone and miserably try to decide what to shove behind the door. All of last night? All of our nights? Was it all obligation?

"Look, I don't know what you overheard…"

"Nothing," I say hollowly. "I just got here."

"Liar."

My face collapses into a glare, and this, at least, can be directed to his face. He's right, of course, to call me a liar, but there is enough anger building in me that I don't care.

"I'm freeing you of your obligation. You have certainly paid anything you thought you owed me in full."

He looks at a loss for a second, but then he matches my glare with one of his own. The fire in the room may be dying, but our eyes locked on one another spark a new one to life. "I don't want to be freed of it."

I laugh, a charred sound, not anything like it's supposed to be. "You're not throwing me to the falcons, Bran. Even if I haven't been visible here for the past eighteen years, I've been a part of this world. I can navigate it without you."

"Hm," he says, his eyes glittering, his voice smooth and low. "That's all well and good. But what if *I* can't navigate it without *you*?"

I don't have any words with which to respond. He has stolen them all. He looks angry, tense, flustered. I don't think he likes that he asked the question. I don't think he likes what he means by it. What *does* he mean by it?

I find the words to ask him.

His laugh is also charred, also burned at the edges. The room is made of wood, and we are building an inferno. "I do feel obligated to you. That hasn't gone away. But that's not *all* I feel about you. I think I've made that clear."

I shake my head slowly. I think we're on another precipice, but this one does not sit upon a hill; it sits upon a mountain. It sits among the clouds. I'm not sure I would survive the fall this time if he tipped the moment the wrong way. I'm not sure which way is the wrong way.

"Not clear enough, then." The glittering in his eyes takes on a different shape as he decides something, as he grabs hold of my hand. I let him have it. I don't know what he's decided, but the precipice is so high up that the air is thready, my breaths are shallow.

He pulls me over to the door, only pausing briefly to look over his shoulder at me with kaleidoscope eyes—shifting, beautiful, the colors of the fire where it reflects within them. My own eyes are wide, my mind scattered and lost to that look in his eyes. He lifts a finger on the hand not tangled in mine and presses it to his lips, swinging the door open.

He takes me out into the night with him, hand in hand. We wind silently through the alleys, across the gravel streets, ever closer to the wall. I feel as though I'm in a dream within a dream, outside of myself, someone else.

But if this isn't real, my worries sing. *If this isn't real, what is?*

Bran is someone else, too. I look up at him in the moonlight as we walk, at the side of him I've never seen before. Perhaps this is the side that drove him to the lake so many nights. The side that risked death. The reckless side, with hellfire in his smile and in his eyes, sparking against something flammable inside of me. I have never seen him so free, have never been so free myself.

When we reach the wall, he grabs a careless handful of stones, weighs them in his hand for just a second before swinging around to fling the lot of them down the alley. The falcons flock after the skittering rocks as we push into the shadows. Once they've cleared, the air still swirling around us from their beating wings, he looks down at me.

"Go," he whispers.

I race for the wall. He's behind me, propelling me upward, while my eyes stay on the sky. We're over the top of it and collapsing onto the other side before I even take a proper breath. We are a heap of limbs on the crosshatched vines, tangled up in one another, breathless and scrambling and so alive, so alive, so alive.

We make it to the forest in one piece, through the forest somehow, out the other side. His hand is sweaty in mine, his hair plastered damply against his forehead while mine flies wild, free of its braid. The lake glistens, the sky both above it and within it. It looks like magic. It feels like home. I leave him behind and walk into the water, up to my ankles, letting it wash its magic over me.

I throw my arms wide and start spinning. I can hear Bran laughing, softly, and it is music. I swing to a halt, my hair streaming a second behind to land over one shoulder, and then I spin the opposite way. My circles are swaying, dizzying, the wind cascading through my fingers. I don't stop until the whole world is spinning with me, and then it keeps right on moving even as I stand still, even as he stands still before me. His face is lit from within, his tilted smile fully formed and all for me. The trees and the water and the very air swirl around me in swoops and shadows as I step toward him. My joy is a tangible thing, formed by his laughter and his smile and the way my hair tangles around my shoulders like a wild thing. *I* am a wild thing. I am uninhibited and free and his smile is all for me.

His hand meets mine in the middle before the rest of me reaches him. He tugs me the final step, closing that last little space between our bodies, pulling me into him, against him, around him. He tries to swipe my hair out of my face with his free hand, his fingers getting all wrapped up in it, and he laughs again. He releases my hand from his to carefully unwind the strands, so gently and reverently, my body curved into his as I look up at him. There are no more strands blocking my eyes when his fingers trail across my cheek. I see the way his eyes wander across the plains of my face. I feel the way his fingers follow. I'm holding my breath and hoping that he never stops. Never stops looking at me in that way or touching me in that way or setting everything I am on fire in that way.

His fingers stop their wandering down along my jaw, his thumb resting somewhere just below the corner of my lips, and then his eyes find mine again. They're closer now. If the sun was out, all I would be able to see is the color of his eyes, there in front of mine, surely making me forget that there are other colors in the world.

But there is only the colorless moon, and only the symphony of stars, and all I can see is the look in his eyes just before he kisses me.

And it's enough. Even without the sun, even without the color of his eyes there before me, that look is enough. It is more than enough. It is a living, breathing fire touching my heart and telling it as gently as fire can tell anything that nothing will ever be the same.

My hand is on his arm, and then it's somehow resting on his cheek, until I feel it in his hair. It does everything on its own accord because he is kissing me, and I am kissing him, and there is no room for any conscious thought.

Bran stops too soon, but it would always be too soon. He lifts his face away from where mine is still angled upward, the hand that isn't bunching the fabric at my hip re-tangled in my hair. The silence between us feels uncertain now, and stunned, until he tries to extricate his hand and we start laughing again. He makes me turn around so he can pull his hand free one more time, and then he spins me back around and pushes me lightly along the shoreline. I grab his hand in both of mine and tug him along with me, behind me as we walk along the water's edge.

I look up at the shadows on his face, at the night all around him, framing him. The sky is a riot of stars, and his smile is full of catastrophe. The night belongs to us. He belongs to me.

Chapter Thirty-Three

We soak in as much of the night air and freedom as we can before we return to the wall, making our way back to Cecily's with less of a fervor than we had left it. With his hand in mine and mine in his and magic still simmering in the air between us. When we get back to his room, I wrap the blanket tightly around myself as we climb onto the cot. He puts his arms around me, but there is a carefulness there. An acknowledgement that now we have kissed, and now we are more than we were the last time we shared this cot.

Hours later, we hear the screeches. They strip the magic away from the night instantly, sending him to the window and me two steps behind him. He blocks it, though, standing squarely in front of it as I stand on my tiptoes behind him.

"Bran…"

"Go back to bed." His voice is hard and emotionless, also stripped of its magic. I touch his back as I try to see around him, and I feel the tension there. I feel the reality of what this world is. The reminder that it is a nightmare first, a dream second.

A human scream—female, terrified—floats up to our ears. The tense line of his back ripples against his visceral reaction to it. My teeth start chattering, though I am far from cold.

"It sounds close. Surely we could…"

"No." He cuts me off firmly, leaving no space for pleas or arguments. "I mean it, Reeve, go back to bed. You don't want to see this."

I don't want to, of course I don't want to, but I can hear it. I can hear the screeches as though they are beside me, above me, surrounding me. We were out on that street just a few hours ago, winding our way back home after our trip over the wall. One careless step, and it might have been us, screaming. It might have been us, being torn to shreds.

I drop down onto the floor of his room and cover my ears as the screams come again, again, feeling the full weight of my fear, of my cowardice. I had been screaming, just like her, with the precise same note of terror, and Bran had saved me. It is so rare to be saved here. I should do something other than sit on the floor and cover my ears to block out the sounds of her fear. I should save her.

But the screeches have already overlapped each other. They have already merged, blended, become something other than wild monster shrieks. They are a song now, a haunting song, and there will be no saving her. It will be over soon.

And so I cover my ears. I squeeze my eyes shut, though they can't see what is happening. My pounding heartbeat does its own part to drown out the sounds outside, but it doesn't do enough. Suddenly, Bran is beside me. He pulls me onto his lap and pushes my head into his chest, adding his own hands over mine to cover my ears. I want to protest that it will leave his unprotected, but I am selfish. I am cowardly. I keep my head pressed there and listen to nothing but the pulsing of his heart.

When he finally uncovers my ears, the room is silent. He has spared me the severing of her screams, the victory song, the flaps fading away from whence they had come. He has spared me as much of it as he could.

I am surprised to discover that my cheeks are wet.

I wipe at them hastily, climbing off of his lap and walking to the window. There is nothing in the street to indicate that anything happened. It looks as peaceful as it had when we left it such a short time ago, the moon shining down upon it in what may be blissful ignorance, what may be silent judgment.

I turn back to where Bran still sits on the floor, his knees bent for his elbows to rest upon, a wretched look upon his face.

"There was nothing we could have done."

I nod stiffly and sit on the edge of the cot, using the hem of my nightgown to erase any lingering traces of my tears. This is not for me to cry over. This is not my loss. This is someone else's loss. The woman who lost her life on the street below. The family and friends left behind to mourn her. I wonder why she was out tonight. I wonder if it was worth it.

It could so easily have been us.

"This isn't right," I say finally, my voice as wretched as the expression on his face. I stare at my hands in my lap, at how useless they appear there. "None of this is right."

"I know."

I look up at him suddenly, fiercely. "People keep dying."

"I know."

"Stop saying that!"

He sighs and slashes an impatient hand across his face. "What do you want me to say, Reeve? You forget that I've lived here my whole life. This is the way the world is. There is no bright and happy place for me to return to when the sun comes up. This is my life, day and night."

My shoulders slump, the ferocity leaking from them. He's right, of course. I am a visitor to this world. I visit its horrors, and then I return to my palace, to my guards, to my protected gardens and forests. He lives it always, without escape.

"I wish I could take you with me," I whisper.

He slides over so that he is kneeling before me, his own frustration vanishing into the shadows of the room. He lifts my hands in his and bows his head over them, kissing the backs of them lightly, one at a time.

"I don't think of them as nightmares anymore," I continue. "Horrible things happen here. It's an awful, cruel world. But I can't bring myself to think of them as nightmares anymore. Not truly. Here, with you, they feel more like dreams."

"I didn't know," he says, his quiet tone at odds with the depth of it. It is a river, an ocean, the bottom so far from the surface that I'm not sure I'll ever reach it. "I didn't know how dark it was here until you came along and made it brighter. You're like…breathing in water all of your life and then suddenly discovering what it's like to breathe air."

I swallow hard and free one of my hands from his to swipe at his hair, to push it off of his brow and also to buy myself time to soften the lump that has formed in my throat. The room is nearly black, the house around us nearly silent but for the occasional creak against the wind, and he is kneeling before me, his heart in his eyes and in his words.

There is a woman dead who had been alive just an hour ago.

Maybe she was meeting a friend, a lover. Maybe she was experiencing joy, freedom, reminding herself of all of the reasons that life is worth living even in the darkest of worlds.

There are so many things of which I am unsure, but right now, he is kneeling before me, and I am sure of this. I am sure of him.

I lean forward to kiss his forehead, to trail my lips down along the line of his nose. I kiss Bran everywhere he had kissed me, in the forest, with my hair and my soul a wild thing. That had been joy, freedom.

The reasons that life is worth living even in the darkest of worlds.

CHAPTER THIRTY-FOUR

I stop storing away the nights. I carry them with me all of the next morning, lost in memories of spinning, of the sky through the hair in my eyes, of him. Mostly of him. We had spent the rest of the night lying face-to-face on his cot, his eyes battling sleep to stay locked on mine until the lids could not help falling closed. There had been no room for words, and perhaps a fear of them. There is an ocean of unsaid words between us, and if they are spoken, they may form a chasm where the water had been.

It is unsustainable, perhaps childish, certainly foolish, but we left them unsaid. For as long as we can, we'll leave them unsaid.

The weather looks threatening through the window, clouds gathering and lingering, washing away the sunlight. I eat breakfast slowly, regretting that the coming rain will not allow for my usual outdoor meandering.

Still, I can't draw out the meal forever. I wander from the dining room and start for the garden room to pick at my stitching. Something mindless so that my mind is free to roam where it wishes. I almost reach it when I hear the familiar thumping of a cane along the stone floor.

Thrall.

As usual, my spine straightens and my chin lifts, both of their own accord. I think about darting the last couple of steps into the room, but this might be an opportunity. Lately, I have been considering how to broach the topic of my dreams with Thrall. I wonder if he might provide insight, might know something of them. This might be my chance.

He rounds the corner and starts to barrel on by me, my guards sweeping low in their bows as he passes.

"Thrall!" I call out.

He'd really rather not stop. I see it in the next few faltering steps, when he attempts to keep walking on. I don't know what gets the better of him, perhaps some deeply buried measure of respect for my station, but slowly, with the clearest of reluctance, he grinds to a halt and turns around.

"My lady," he booms, his cane thumping resoundingly as he greets me with that small nod that is not nearly a bow, not nearly deferential, but as much as he ever offers.

I curtsy quickly, though still deeply. "I wondered if I might have a moment of your time. I have a question I've been wanting to ask you."

He wants to say no. I can see it in his huffed breath, in the twitch of his eyes away, down the hallway. But whatever encouraged him to stop before works its magic now, as well. He slowly steps into the sitting room with me and takes a seat on the regal armchair within.

I perch on the sofa opposite his chair and watch as he situates himself, settling deeply into the cushions and resting his hands atop his cane. His feet barely reach the floor, but his presence sucks up most of the air in the room. I've never had a conversation of any substance with the wizard. I wish I'd planned it out more, prepared more. I take a deep breath.

"I heard a name recently, and I wondered if it meant anything to you."

Silence. It isn't a question, requires no answer. He'll waste no words on it.

I continue on.

"The name is Rancore."

His cane falls to the floor. His hands remain hovering in the air where they had rested upon it as we both listen to the echo of the cane's thud pulsing through the room. Neither of us look at it. Thrall lowers his hands to his lap slowly, deliberately, but I don't think the quiver I see in them is deliberate.

"Where did you hear that name?"

This is where I must be cautious. Where I mustn't reveal too much. If my dreams do have some element of magic, it's possible he could cut it off. Once, I would have welcomed it. Now ... I would sooner he cut out my heart.

I'm beginning to fear that's what it would mean, anyway.

"I heard it in a dream," I say slowly.

The palace's grandfather clocks are far away, one in the foyer and one in the hallway near my bedchambers, but I swear I hear the tick of them in the silence here. Perhaps it's just my pounding heartbeat, counting the seconds as he watches me.

"Tell me about the dream."

His voice brokers no argument. He serves the royal family, technically, but in reality, I think we all serve him. He doesn't rule Acarsaid, but only because he does not wish it. If he did wish it…there would be no power on all of the island that could prevent him from doing so. And so, when he issues a command, I answer it.

"It's an old dream. One I've had many nights."

"How many nights?"

I swallow hard. "Every night."

"What do you do in this dream?"

"I walk, alone. Mostly, all I do is walk." A half-truth.

"Are you ever seen there?" Thrall leans forward a little, the tips of his toes on the ground propelling him forward. His question is urgent, more booming than all of the others.

"No," I lie baldly. "No, I'm never seen there."

I shouldn't lie.

I know I shouldn't lie. Not when he asks it so urgently, not when he leans forward the way he does and lets his eyes bore into mine.

But I'm afraid. My fear is buried deeply in my bones and shouting louder than any other thought, that to tell him the truth would be to lose the dream world.

To lose Bran.

He nods slowly, leaning forward to pick up his cane. He looks comforted, either by my answer or by the return of the cane beneath his hands. "Good. If you aren't seen there, you're safe."

"What does the name mean?"

"It meant something here once," he says slowly, his eyes drifting away from me toward somewhere else, some time else, some time like the past.

"Something bad?"

"Something evil."

He shakes himself out of the moment, back to the present. "Regardless, if you can't be seen there, you needn't worry yourself over it."

The caveat flutters through my mind uneasily as he pulls himself out of the chair. I don't dismiss him, but somehow, even though he's the one who leaves, he has dismissed me. His cane pounds more heartily than ever against the ground as he takes his leave. I am left with his words, with that uneasy caveat, shivering down my spine.

I slump back into the cushions on the couch. Should I have told him that I *am* visible? What would he have done with that knowledge? I don't think he would have left so easily then.

But the fact of the dreams themselves had not seemed to trouble him. He had accepted quite readily that I dream myself in the same place every night. It was only the confirmation of my invisibility there that had seemed important to him. And he knew Rancore's name. The world cannot exist solely in my head, built brick by brick by my subconscious, if he knows the name of the wizard within it.

I want to know more, what all of it means. I want to have all of the pieces of this puzzle. But the fear of losing it, of either losing my visibility or losing the dream world altogether, churns too strongly inside of me.

I'll try to find out more on my own, without bringing Thrall into it. Perhaps I'll explore the library, see if I can find a book of magic or of Acarsaid's past which mentions Rancore.

Not just now, though. A footman finds me there, still slumped deep within the sofa's cushions, and informs me that Lord Velasian is awaiting me in the formal sitting room.

Chapter Thirty-Five

I spend the walk there trying to quickly push the night world behind the door, yanking at the threads that connect to Arden to pull anything attached to him forth, instead. It leaves my thoughts in disarray, a tangled mess of memories, and unfortunately the one which lands at the forefront as I reach the sitting room is the one of him kissing me in the forest, the one where my instinct had been to run.

I halt in the doorway with that image set firmly behind my eyes, overlapping the one in front of my eyes: him standing at the window, watching the storm clouds, the first handful of raindrops running down the glass and forming shadows on his face.

My instinct is still to run.

I force myself to walk toward him instead, clenching my hands into the skirts of my dress as he turns to face me.

"There you are," he says, smirk in place, the green of his eyes in motion. "I thought you'd be halfway across the sea by now."

I pause in my approach and tilt my head quizzically.

"You ran away from me rather swiftly a couple days ago," he explains. Then he steps toward me, leans a little closer. "After I kissed you."

I take a faltering step backward even though a few feet still separate us. My guards are in the hallway to give us privacy, but the door remains open for propriety. It's silly for me to feel as though I'm trapped.

"I have a headache." I stumble over the words. "I'm not sure I'm fit company today."

"Still running, then?"

I stop backing away and lift my chin. "I'm not running. I merely have a headache."

"Liar," he taunts, and that draws forth a night memory. I don't have room for it right now. I push it away. "I never took you for a coward."

"I'm not a coward," I counter instantly, scowling up at him and forcing myself to recover a step forward.

"Then why do you keep running from me?"

I open my mouth to retort, to deny what is obviously the truth, and then I sigh. "I don't mean to."

"Are you scared of me, then?" He takes pains to ask it drolly, but I catch the note of sincere concern there.

"No," I muse. "Not really. I'm scared of a future with you. What it will mean for me." I smile a little sadly. "That was my first kiss."

"Ah," he says softly. "And it wasn't what you thought it would be."

I hurry forward to put a reassuring hand on his arm. "Oh, it was nice. Really, it was. I think I just had my expectations set too high."

He puts his hand over mine, holding it in place. "Ouch."

I huff out a sigh. "I truly meant that in a less insulting way."

He laughs a little. "I'm sure you did. In any case, I'm glad you told me. I'd rather you did so instead of running."

I smile up at him fondly. We could be friends, I realize. Even if he will not love me, we could be friends, and we could go on adventures,

and I could have half of the life I hoped to have. The other half...
perhaps I could find it in my nights.

Arden lets go of my hand to reach into his pocket. He pulls a
small box from its depths and flips it over in his hands once, twice.
His eyes are on me, his head tilted at that angle which can only
be deliberate, so that he watches me through his lashes. I look
meaningfully between him and the box and motion with my hand
for him to get on with it.

He laughs and tosses the box at me. I barely catch it, caught off
guard. I scowl at him, scowl down at the box, scowl back up at him.
I toss it back.

"Are you rejecting my gift?" He flips it over in his hands once more.

"You can't simply *toss* it at me. Honestly, Arden, how you've
successfully seduced so many women..."

"So many women...You mustn't believe *every* rumor you've heard
about me. I'm sure one or two of them are fictional."

"One or two." I roll my eyes. "Which means the other thousand
or so are based on fact."

He shrugs nonchalantly, his lips deepening in their curve. "One
must do something with one's time."

I shake my head sternly, even though my own lips threaten to
tilt. I wonder how it must feel to be in possession of this skill, the
ability to breathe charm and temptation. I almost can't blame him for
utilizing it to the extent he has. Almost.

I pointedly look back at the box.

He shoves one hand in his pocket and holds the box out to me
on the palm of his other hand.

"I have a gift for you," he says grandly.

I settle one hand on my hip and tuck the other patiently under my chin.

"It occurred to me that we have gone about this all a little strangely. A little backward. You said that you wished to be courted, and I thought you might also appreciate a ring."

He pulls his hand free of his pocket and uses it to open the box. Then, with just a slight pause, he drops to one knee before me.

"I thought you might also appreciate a proposal."

My heart climbs up to my throat and stays there.

He clears his throat, and though the charm stays there, I also see a hint of the other Arden, the one who had believed but was cured of it. I see the entanglement of the two sides of him laid out before me in the forest of his eyes, swaying more than dancing now. I think that I might say yes even if this wasn't already set, even if we weren't both of us ensnared on this path.

"Sweet girl," he murmurs. "I'm sorry that I'm not the knight in shining armor you had hoped for. I'm sorry that I'm more likely the dragon, the destroyer of innocence, the breather of fire. But if I am to be shackled to just one woman for the whole of my life, I'm glad that she has your eyes, and the way that you roll them at me, and the absurd way that you see the world through them. If it has to be anyone, I'm glad that it's you."

He proffers the ring up higher in his palm, an offering, the softest of his smirks set in place for me. "What do you say? Wife of a dragon, co-breather of fire?"

There is a curl to the word "wife." A lift to it. I feel it reverberate through me, feel it assign itself to me. I will be this man's wife. In a world where my options were Roneldon or Del or the man kneeling before me, even though Arden cannot, will not, love me, I will always choose him.

"Truly, dragon or not, you are probably the best of the options I had before me," I tell him.

His smile grows a little. "Waiting."

"Roneldon, can you imagine? More than my toes would have needed saving."

A dimple appears in his left cheek. I'm not sure I knew it was there. "Knee is getting tired, dear."

"And Delavar…honestly, a lifetime of conversations with the man would have left me hateful of colors and foods. He seemed to want to describe them to death."

His smile is a rose, a lily, a midnight blue orchid. It blooms. "Just answer the question."

"I suppose my answer is yes then." I let my own smile grow. "Rhetorical though it is, I can think of worse lots in life than being your wife."

He shakes his head up at me, and sure enough, I am not fully immune just yet. As with Percius, my heart forgets itself, skips over its next few beats. The rain batters loudly against the windows, and he will never love me, but right now, looking at him smiling up at me, I can't resent a drop of it. A drop of the rain, a drop of anything which led me to this moment.

He stands and pulls the ring from its casing, tossing the empty box over his shoulder with laughing eyes. He grabs hold of my hand and slides the ring onto my fourth finger. We study it critically as I hold it aloft in the air between us. It's a brilliant shade of red, a ruby tucked in diamonds. It forms a teardrop, a teardrop made of blood. It's rather startling there on my small finger.

"You probably shouldn't wear it swimming," he advises. "It'll take you straight to the bottom."

I laugh. "The crows will follow me endlessly on my walks now. It's exceptionally shiny."

Our eyes meet over it, our smiles matched sets. It's a moment of such camaraderie that I am flooded with immeasurable hope. Arden is still danger, still intrigue, still skipped heartbeats, but I think that somewhere in the past few days, I've already begun to think of him as a friend.

"Until the ball tomorrow?"

Lord, tomorrow. It had rather snuck up on me. "Until the ball."

He kisses my hand, only my hand, though the wicked curve of his lips tells me that he thought about kissing more than that. I try to hide my relief when he leaves without doing so.

~ ✳ ~

That night in bed, I twist my hand first one way, then the other. I let the narrow moonbeam sliding through my curtain catch the ring, and then I let it fall away.

It isn't as heavy as I had feared. I appreciate its ostentatious beauty as one would appreciate a painting in a gallery. It is lovely there, on display, and I can marvel over it from afar, but it would look altogether out of place in one's home.

My eyelids grow heavy, but I can't stop staring at it. Nor can I halt my churning thoughts.

I will not marry for love. The certainty of it resonates within me, but for the first time, I feel no despair. I feel a strange sense of gratitude, rather. If I could not marry for love, I can't think of a better outcome than friendship. Than those moments of companionship— the walk through the forest, the card game on the hilltop, his laughter as he'd looked up at me from the sitting room floor.

I turn my hand again to catch the moon.

I don't need to wonder why this acceptance has settled over me.

I will not marry for love, but I will know love. I think I know it already.

I turn my hand to let the moonlight fall. I'm anxious to see Bran now. My eyes close, and I am nearly gone before my hand drops.

CHAPTER THIRTY-SIX

He's waiting for me in the shadows. Though no body swings overhead, no falcons threatening to close in around me at any second, he's waiting. His smile curls up gently as I sprint over to him, flinging myself wholly into his arms this time instead of stopping short. His breath huffs out of him from some combination of surprise and amusement as he catches me.

I allow myself a moment to bury my face in the crook of his neck and simply breathe him in, to erase the city square and the gallows and everything around me that isn't him, and then I reluctantly pull back to look at him. The shadows are too thick and murky to make out the details of him, but the feel of his presence alone is enough to propel the day behind the door with no effort on my part.

Bran carefully untangles me from him and starts on our path home, walking only a few steps before pausing to reach his hand out for mine. He's free of the darkest shadows now, half of him draped in moonlight. My smile meets his as I reach my hand out.

As he clasps it and starts to draw me forward, our hands turn slightly, and with that turn, I see a glint.

The ring catches the moonlight.

It draws both of our eyes—mine, absentmindedly, distractedly, but his…his, it draws abruptly, freezes them. Our hands are suspended between us, the moonlight firmly caught by the bloody teardrop of my engagement ring, and his eyes cannot seem to leave it.

The temperature of his hand in mine has not changed, and yet somehow, it feels like ice. It loses its softness, and though it doesn't tighten, it loses its gentleness, as well.

I turn my hand to let the moonlight fall.

At the same time it drops away, so does my hand from his. He lets go as though burned, as though my hand was set on fire against the ice of his. I open my mouth to say something, anything, but he turns away. I follow him through the streets and the alleys, all the way to Cecily's house, and he does not once look back.

And so all I see is his rigid back. All I see is the set of his shoulders, the stark line of his jaw. He is a handful of steps ahead of me, but he is miles away and getting farther with every step. He is slipping away from me as surely as his hand had slipped away from mine, and I cannot stop it. The ring is right there, on my finger, and I cannot stop it.

By the time I close the door behind us, I should know what to say. I have had the whole of the walk, the whole miserable walk, to think of how to explain, how to apologize, what I should even be apologizing for. I should not have worn the ring here, of course. It was an oversight, utterly careless, and it had hurt him. The why of it does not matter.

Although I wonder. He'd known I was spoken for at home. I'd explained to him the circumstances. Why then had I felt such a strong sense of betrayal emanating from him in that frozen moment before I had let the moonlight fall?

He stalks to the fireplace, his back still rigid. There is no sign of

Cecily or Nor down here, and I wonder if they're already asleep. I am once more cowardly, wishing for their presence here to lessen the tension filling the air like smoke.

"What is it?" I ask quietly from behind him.

His shrug is stilted, the very opposite of nonchalant. It is not an answer, so I approach in search of one. I stop half a step away, to his right, just close enough to see his face.

"I'm sorry I wore it here. I forgot to take it off."

The side of his face I can see is expressionless, as expressionless as his voice when he says, "It's a nice ring. Bigger than any I've ever seen."

My right hand clasps my left tightly, covering the ring, shielding it from him or him from it. I wish I had a pocket to drop it in, but the damage is already done, anyway. He's seen it, and it's done something to him that feels irreversible in a way that scares me. His expressionless face, and his expressionless voice, terrify me.

"Bran, I...this doesn't change anything. I told you that I was spoken for at home."

"You did," he nods slowly, his lips twisting a bit. "You did tell me."

"But it doesn't change anything! It's a marriage of obligation. I don't love him. I..." I love *you*, I almost say, but I swallow the words unsaid.

"So what, then?" He swings to face me suddenly, ferociously. "You'll fall asleep in his bed each night and then spend the rest of it in mine?"

I take a stuttered step backward as though his words had been set aflame and catapulted at me. Each one strikes hard and true, shattering my disillusions and the door I had built in my mind.

There is no door. There is no Day Reeve, no Night Reeve. There is only Reeve, only me, and I am one person. One small person, a coward of a girl, who is to be married in my waking life. My real life. And while I judge my future husband for his faithlessness, while I chafe under his inability or unwillingness to wholly commit to me, I have been spending my nights falling a little more in love with the man who stands before me.

It isn't fair to either of them. I had been naïve to think that I could have them both.

He is still staring at me with a savage sort of desperation, with ice dripping behind his eyes.

"You're right," I try to say, though the snarl of emotions gets in the way. The words come out strangled and dismal. "You're right."

Bran looks a little like he doesn't want to be right. He lifts his hand to rub roughly at the back of his neck before seemingly deciding something and swinging away, toward the door.

"I've got to get out of here."

I lunge forward, my hands reaching out to grab him of their own volition before I order them to fall. He is not mine to touch.

"No. Stay," I plead.

"I need to think. I can't think here, with you."

"I'll go. I'll go to my room and stay there for the night." For every night? It doesn't bear thinking on just now, but there is no longer a door to shove the thought behind. There is nowhere to hide from my own misery.

He's still walking toward this door, the door that does still exist. "I'll be fine. I'll be back later." The fire and the ice are gone again, leaving him once more expressionless and blank.

"Bran…"

"I'll be fine," he says again. But then he pauses. He looks over his shoulder at me, and for a split second, the curtains flutter and I see what lies beneath the careful blankness. I see an internal war being waged behind his eyes as they bore into mine, direct, on fire. I see so far into them that I think I might fall. I think I might never stop falling, falling, falling into them. Clear down to the depths of him, clear down to his soul. He opens and closes his mouth twice before more words come. Before he says, "I thought that this...I thought that we..."

But if there are ends to those sentences, they don't come. He doesn't say them. He slams his mouth shut and shakes his head once, hard.

And then he's gone.

My hands still reach out as though to stop him, my whole body still leaning in the direction he had gone, my ears straining for whatever he had been about to say, but I don't move. I let him go.

He is not mine to stop.

When I look down, it is the firelight, this time, which catches the ring. I turn it this way and that, marveling abstractly at how red it looks in the flames. How much like the glint of blood.

Maybe he had a door in his mind, too. Maybe he had stored away the knowledge of my betrothal, kept it locked there and allowed himself to forget it, and the sight of my ring in the moonlight obliterated it. Turned the door to kindling, unleashed the full knowledge of the impossibility of our situation.

There is no way that I can blame him.

But I can blame myself. Lord, can I blame myself.

I make my way up the stairs heavily, as though there are weights strapped to my feet and resting on my shoulders and pounding against my head. I have felt the weight of this world so many times, but never so acutely. Never with such a certainty that there will be no more lightness in it.

I'm certain that I want to be alone, to hide in my cell until I'm called home, but somehow, I stop before Cecily's open door. I can hear the quiet timbre of her voice, and of Nor's voice, and it halts my steps. I think that perhaps being alone is the last thing I want.

They stop speaking when I step inside the doorway, both heads turning to face me. Nor greets me with his open smile, while the smile that had been on Cecily's face vanishes instantly. The contrast is marked, one beckoning me to stay while the other making me want to turn away.

"Hey, Reeve," Nor says with a small wave. "Where's Bran?"

His smile drops away in the face of whatever answer my expression gives. Cecily leans forward, eyes glittering. It's she who asks, "Where is he?"

"He left," I answer hollowly. "We argued…" I trail off. Can I even call it that? We had not so much argued as spilled the ocean of unsaid words, allowed the chasm I had dreaded to spread between us.

They stare at me, this time no contrast to their countenances. Both spell worry.

"Nor," Cecily says quietly. He's already halfway off the bed, as grim as I've seen him. "Be careful." He gives her a quick nod in response.

"Where are you going?" I ask even as I move out of his way.

"After him," he says, and then he, too, is gone.

I swing to face Cecily, my confusion apparent.

"He isn't always careful. Bran. If you fought, and he left, he might not be as careful as he needs to be out there. Nor will remind him."

I trudge over to her bed and perch on the edge of it without her invitation, filling the spot vacated by her brother. "And now they'll both be in danger."

"They'll be okay," she says, although I don't think it's to reassure me so much as it is to reassure herself. Then, she focuses wholly on me. "Why did you let him go?"

"I didn't want to," I say defensively. "He said he needed to get out of here, though, and who am I to stop him?"

"Who are you, indeed," she mutters with a sharp edge, her brow creased into a glare.

I match it with one of my own. "Look, I didn't ask to dream myself here every night, or to suddenly be visible. I certainly didn't do it as a personal affront to you."

"Maybe not, but you dragged him into it all. He's risked his life time and again for you, and now he's doing it again, just to get away from you. Whatever happens to him will be on *you*."

"Have you even *told* him you love him?" I growl, as fury joins the desolation and fear coursing through my veins. I suddenly want to hurt her as badly as I hurt, as badly as the truth in her words hurts. "Or is that my fault as well, the fact that he doesn't know?"

She reels back. "He's my *friend*."

"Oh, please. I see the way you look at him when he isn't looking, and the way you hide it away when he is."

Just the one small candle is lit in her room again, just that limited source of light, but it does enough to show me the flushing of her face. I imagine it to be a furious shade of red. I'm glad to see it, glad she's angry, too.

"I would have told him," she snaps. "Soon. But you came along with such novelty, a girl from another world, and you distracted him entirely."

"I saved your life!"

"*And* you ruined it!"

We are each breathing hard, glaring at each other as our mirrored fear unleashes a week's worth of pent-up words. Once they're out in the air, though, I can feel their potency leak away. Her words lose their ability to hurt me, because I am already hurt. The truth of them, which I had already known, already hurts.

She slumps a little, and I do, too.

We both spend some time searching for our next words, my eyes scanning the room for them while hers stay locked on her bedspread. She finds hers first.

"I was going to tell him that night. I was on my way to his house, not mine, the night I was attacked."

I am surprised to feel regret join the other emotions tangling inside of me. I wouldn't have thought there was room for more. "You should have told him the next night. The one after that. Any night since."

She starts shaking her head before I even finish. "It wouldn't have mattered. Any moment after the moment he met you was too late to say them."

I swallow hard and look down at my hands. "You are who he should be with, though. You're the one from his world, who understands him best, who knows when he won't be careful. I'm... I'm not for him."

"It's too late for that," she says quietly. She has stripped away everything with which she usually coats her words for me, all of the derision and disdain, presenting her words to me now in the same unvarnished way she does with Bran and Nor.

"You should tell him," I plead. "Tell him, and maybe he'll feel the same. Maybe he'll stop risking himself for me."

"I said it's too late for that."

"It isn't, though! Not until you've tried. You didn't see the look on his face before he left. He needs something good, someone good, who's here, who can give him a whole life instead of only ever half of one. I'll…I'll stop coming here. I'll find somewhere else to hide at night, and I'll leave you all alone, and—"

"*Reeve.*"

She has inserted her own plea into my name. It halts my streaming words.

"He'll follow you. Wherever you go, he'll follow. It's *too late.*"

"He left," I say miserably. "I asked him to stay, and he left."

"I'm guessing he saw that rock on your finger and it scared him." She practically snarls down at my hand where it rests on her bed, and for a split second, I see a wildness in her eyes. A rage. A sharp edge that tells me how much she hates that she has to say these words, how much she hates that they are true.

Are they true?

She stashes the look away, behind shutters, behind a defiant lift of her chin, when she sees that I see it.

I slap a hand over the ring, realize the futility, and let it slide away. "I'm engaged to be married at home."

She stares hard at me. "Why?"

I shake my head. "Why what?"

"Why are you getting married to someone else when you're over here making eyes at Bran like he hung the moon?"

I bite my lip hard enough to taste blood. "I am expected to marry. My family…it's expected of me, and I couldn't let them down."

"Do you feel about him the way you feel about Bran?"

I can see Arden laughing, Arden smirking, Arden who believed and was cured of it.

But then there is the urge to run. The relief when he does not try to kiss me.

I don't feel those things with Bran.

I shake my head slowly. I don't know how to differentiate my feelings for the two of them, these men from different worlds. I may not be split into Day Reeve and Night Reeve, but I feel as though I am a different person with each of them. Arden's Reeve and Bran's Reeve.

One is an upheaval, and the other puts all of my pieces back into place.

Cecily sighs long and low and frustrated. "He's halfway in love with you, Reeve. Maybe more than halfway. If you feel the same… figure it out. Talk to him when he gets back, once he's gotten his restlessness out of his system, and figure it out. Don't break him, though, you hear me? He's been through enough. He doesn't need you coming here and breaking him."

The words don't come easily for her. She is telling me to be with the man she loves. She is telling me that he is halfway in love with *me*.

Is he? I know that I am, more than halfway, but is *he*? It feels impossible, as impossible as everything else feels right now. Oh, to have a door to shove it behind. To build it back in place and store away all of the questions and fears and the feelings that threaten to strangle me.

Instead, I have to face it all head on.

I have to process the possibility that he loves me, and the knowledge that I will never be able to give him all of myself. None of this would ever be fair to him, to Arden…to me.

"Tomorrow," I whisper. I will need all of the night and all of the next day to sort through everything. All of the week, all of the year, all of my life. "I'll talk to him tomorrow."

I let myself out and finish my journey to my cell. I don't light my candle, instead lying on the cushions and losing myself to the thoughts that won't be pushed aside. I think about Arden, about his ability to make my heart skip beats and his certainty that he won't love me. I think about Bran, about the steadying look in his eyes and the way my hands know just what to do when he kisses me.

I think about the life I have ahead of me. Marriage to Arden, a life of the adventures I've always craved even if they will be lacking in love. Nights spent here, possibly visible, possibly not. If I remain visible, I will have to decide what to do. Will I continue coming here, if I can't be with Bran? What if he finds another woman, even if it isn't Cecily, who can give him both her nights *and* her days? I'd rather not know. I'd rather risk my way to the lake each night than wait for him to fall in love with somebody else. He'll have someone at home, someone he loves, and he'll stop coming to the lake. I can have it all to myself.

Alone, every night.

I am so lost in thought that I don't even realize at first. I don't realize that the sound I hear is the front door slamming open. I don't realize that the footsteps running down the hallway are Cecily's.

I don't realize that the screams are his.

Chapter Thirty-Seven

I'm out of my cell and halfway down the stairs before my mind catches up with my body's realization that it's Bran who is screaming. By the time I reach the bottom step, though, all of me knows, and all of me is frantic to reach him.

I freeze as I skid into the entry room, though. My feet root themselves where they land, my eyes locked on the scene in front of me.

On Nor, bloodied, crouched low. He is using the whole of his body to hold Bran in place.

On Cecily, her hands bloodied though it is not her own blood, also crouched low. She is working frantically over Bran, her hands dancing across his body and adding more blood to that which already coats her skin.

On Bran, oh, on Bran. He takes up the most room in my eyes, and in my ears. He bellows in pain as Cecily works, as Nor tries to hold him down. That shout reverberates through me, shudders its way through my heart and halts its next several beats. Time itself might stop, as my heart does. Time itself might stop, except it doesn't, because he is still screaming, and still losing blood, and I still cannot move.

"Reeve," Cecily snaps. "Bring me the alcohol and some cloths."

Yes, I will bring her alcohol and cloths, I agree as my eyes stay locked on him. Just as soon as I can move, just as soon as my heart starts beating again.

"Reeve, *now!*"

She shouts sharply enough and loudly enough to propel me forward, to unroot my feet and send me stumbling toward the stack of crates. I claw through them frantically, knocking several over in my haste, until I find the alcohol, a handful of clean white cloths. I dive over to her on the ground and set them beside her.

I don't want to look. I can't *not* look.

His wound is gaping. It spans diagonally across his abdomen, slashed and jagged, with smaller gashes on either side, all of them spilling more blood than he can possibly stand to lose. I feel hopelessness start to swell inside of me, a dawning horror that I will lose him in a far worse way than I had thought. I suddenly *want* for him to fall in love, I want to watch him fall in love, I want to watch him be alive. I can withstand anything so long as he is alive.

"Reeve, help Nor," Cecily orders, wiping at the blood to try to see the damage more clearly. Bran's renewed roar tells us all how that feels. It tells my heart that it is not yet time to resume its normal function. "Get him to stay still so I can work."

I crawl over to sit above Bran, at his head. Nor shifts down a little, leaving me the space. I set one hand on either side of Bran's face to still its thrashing.

"Bran," I say, but my strangled whisper is nothing, barely anything more than silence, drowned out entirely by his screams.

"Bran," I try again more loudly, leaning over him to catch his eyes with mine. What I see in them strangles my voice further, stutters my heart more erratically. Where there is usually an ocean of comfort and steadiness, there is now an ocean, a world, an endless depth of pain. He is swimming in it, drowning in it, and staring down at him, I am drowning too.

"Reeve!"

Cecily's voice propels me to the surface. He is still thrashing, still making her work difficult. I take a deep breath and tell myself that even without a door, even without the ability to shove aside the sight of that pain and the reflection of it in me, I must do this. I must focus.

"Bran," I say firmly. "Bran, look at me. *Look at me.* You're okay. I've got you. Do you hear me? I've got you."

I lower my face until it's inches from his, until all he can possibly see is me. His eyes are locked onto mine desperately, unblinking.

"Bran, you have to stay still. You have to let Cecily fix you."

He doesn't seem to hear me. Each touch of Cecily's hands sends him into another fit, another thrash. She's cursing freely now, and when I glance up, I see that Nor is sweating profusely, one arm bleeding from its own slash of a wound as he tries in vain to keep Bran still.

I lean all of my weight onto Bran's upper arms and lower my face back to his.

"Bran," I say, switching from a command to a plea. "Bran, look at me. *Please*, look at me. Bran, you have to stay still. Cecily has to fix you. You have to be okay."

I don't know if it's my weight on his shoulders or the entreaty in my words, but he quiets a little. He stops screaming, though his teeth grit against each other in a way that makes me wince. He looks at me as though *I* am the one to save him. As though I am his lifeline, the thing that will keep him from drowning in the ocean of pain.

"Cecily?" I ask quietly, not allowing my eyes to leave his for even a moment.

She knows what I'm asking. "Talons. They're deep, and they made a mess of things. A little deeper, and I'm not sure he would've even made it this far."

I want to close my eyes against the nearness of it, how close I was to losing him, but I force them to stay open, to stay on his. This isn't over. I may still lose him. I have to keep him still. It is all I can do right now.

"I'm trying to get the bleeding stopped," she mutters, more to herself than the rest of us. "He can't lose more blood."

No, he can't. My knees are drenched in it where I kneel, and Cecily's and Nor's hands are coated in it, and his stomach...his stomach is lost in it. It is still spilling warm and viscous from the wound, and he needs it to stay inside of him, to keep him alive and smiling at me and calling me Trouble in that way he has that unmoors my heart and unleashes fireflies in my stomach.

The dying fire behind me catches at my ring, reminds me of its presence. It reminds me of the red of it, of how I'd thought it looked like a bloody teardrop. I want to slide it off and fling it across the room.

All your fault, my conscience taunts. *If he dies, it's all your fault.*

I start to say something, perhaps to ask Cecily if the bleeding is slowing yet, perhaps to ask Nor what happened out there, but whatever question was about to come forth is chased away by the pull, deep inside my stomach.

A familiar pull. A tug, calling me home.

No.

I look frantically up at the window, and there is a slight lightening there. A slight give to the black of it, a slight warning that the sun is coming. It can't be time yet, though. The sky isn't even hinting at orange yet. I have minutes still, not many, but minutes.

Except I don't. The pull is insistent. I don't have time to warn them, or even to look back down at Bran's eyes one more time, before I am abruptly deposited back into my own bed, back into my own world, with bloodless hands and bloodless knees and the echo of his screams ringing in my ears.

CHAPTER THIRTY-EIGHT

I sit bolt upright in my bed, my hair in wild disarray across my eyes. I shove it aside frantically, just in time to see Guin turn away from opening my drapes. I was not wrong; the sun has not yet risen.

"Why did you wake me?" My voice is as wild as my hair, but more desperate. More rageful. I feel them both, both the desperation and the rage, billowing inside of me and taking on a life of their own.

The smile Guin had turned my way fades. "Queen Everly requested I fetch you. She requires your assistance in the ballroom."

"You are *never* to wake me before the sun rises." My words are whips, tipped in fire, covered in thorns, and I am not careful with them. "Do you hear me?"

It is still fairly dark in my room—*the sun has not risen*—so I have to rely on her response to know her reaction. It is tense and defensive, unapologetic but confused. "I work for the king and the queen, my lady. Their orders supersede yours."

I will have all day, I realize. The whole of the day to face, without knowing Bran's fate. Without knowing if he's alive, or bleeding to death on the floor. I left Nor to hold him down alone, left Cecily to stop his bleeding on her own. I left Bran's eyes frantic, awash with pain, without mine to lock on to.

All day. I'm not sure I can bear it, and yet, I have no choice. A touch of warmth is even now spreading across my cold stone floor, carrying with it the day for me to face. Even if I could somehow lie down and fall back asleep, I will not be able to return while the sun is up. There is nothing I can do until nightfall.

Guin has stiffly set about her work, drawing forth a gown from my dressing chamber and laying it at the foot of my bed. She radiates hurt and uncertainty, but I have no room for it just now. There is only Bran, only Bran's blood on my hands, only Bran's screams.

Lord, tonight is the *ball*. I will have to survive a ball without knowing if he's alive.

Not just any ball, either. My engagement ball.

I drop my face into my hands and force myself to breathe in once. Twice. A third time, long and slow, shaky.

I will have to rebuild the door. It is the only way I will be able to survive this day.

First, I gather up the desperation. I bottle it up, deep inside where it can't slip out as a wail if I open my mouth to speak. I seal it as tightly as possible, squeezing my eyes shut against the effort, because this desperation, this screaming, blazing desperation, would make today impossible.

There is nothing I can do.

Next, I set to work on the rage. It takes longer, as it extends in so many directions. It touches upon Guin, upon Bran and his recklessness, upon the falcons and their master, upon all of Tenebris. It touches most upon myself. I thrust it aside with all of the force it requires.

There is nothing I can do.

There is a lot of blood to set aside. It covers everything, including the inside of my eyelids. It takes a great deal of effort to sweep it behind the door. To forget the glint of it in the dying light of the fire. To forget the way it had flowed along the cracks in the wooden floor.

There is nothing I can do.

Lord, the screams. The pain in them. The agony. It is silent in my room, so silent that with my hands covering my face I'm not even sure if Guin is still here, and in that silence, all I hear is the screams.

I push them behind the door, too.

There is nothing I can do.

Bran. The way he smiles, the way he laughs, the way his hands feel on my skin. His eyes that are the precise color of the sky at dusk, but are only ever colorless to me, only ever steady except for the occasional catastrophe, only ever an ocean unto themselves.

He is the hardest to store away because he is not just an assault on my eyes, not just an assault on my ears. He is those, yes, but he is also an assault on my soul. An assault on my heart. He is too much, almost, but I force him back. To survive the day, I force him back.

There is nothing I can do, nothing I can do, nothing I can do.

When I lift my head from my hands, I feel nothing. Guin *is* still present, and I watch her blankly as she hovers near the gown she has laid out for me.

"Do you require assistance getting dressed?" Never so stilted with me, never so humorless. I should apologize.

Not today.

"No, thank you." I'm proud that my voice is empty of emotion. I'm proud of my door, of how strongly I have rebuilt it. "Please inform my aunt that I will be down shortly."

Once she is gone, I push my covers back and walk softly to my dressing table. I splash water across my face, cool and fresh. How different water is from blood. Cool instead of warm, reassuring instead of suffocating. Even though there is no longer any blood on my hands, I feel as though I am washing it away.

But that is a thought for behind the door.

I squeeze my eyes shut, count out my next breaths until they are no longer gasps, and then, I ready myself for the day.

～＊～

I find Everly in the ballroom, turning a slow circle in place. Around her, footmen and maids bustle this way and that, none empty-handed. Vase after vase of gardenias and roses are carried past me where I pause in the doorway, a moving garden. The gaping room is already filling with their light scent.

I use the moment before my presence is noted to watch Everly at work. Early as it is, she is put together flawlessly in an aquamarine day gown to match her eyes, her blonde hair swept up in a braided bun. She is the conductor, directing everyone around her with a light flick of her hand here, a gentle word there. Everyone moves to the beat she sets, eager to serve and strike just the right note. I wonder if they would smile so genuinely for any other conductor, or if it is Everly's lightness, her kindness, which makes them go about their work so readily.

"Ah, Reeve, there you are!"

No longer unnoticed, I step the rest of the way into the ballroom. My guards fall into place just inside the doorway, lining the walls on either side. I had said little to them on our walk to the ballroom, instead devoting those moments to reinforcing the door. Flashes of images and memories of sounds keep finding their way through, and I'm worried it isn't as strong as I had thought. I'm worried it won't last the day.

"You wanted to see me, Aunt Everly?"

"Yes, the maestro is around here somewhere…Oh, there he is! He wanted to go over tonight's repertoire with you, and allow you to select the song for your dance with Lord Velasian."

I follow her pointing finger to the far corner of the room, catching sight of the stout maestro behind an upright bass.

"He has to leave soon to prepare for the evening, he says, so he was rather insistent that I fetch you. Musicians…such a demanding lot."

I smile absentmindedly as I assign blame for my premature awakening to the little man with the quivering moustache and the blatantly false hairpiece. It takes a moment, a heartbeat, for me to make sure that the rage stays contained.

I turn my false smile to my aunt. "Of course. I'd be happy to go over the selections with him."

She tilts her head. "Are you all right, dear? You look like you're not entirely here."

I'm not. I'm in a small room, kneeling in a pool of his blood, my hands on either side of his face. I'm not here.

I keep these thoughts to myself. I tighten the lid on the desperation. What I say out loud is, "I'm fine. Still not fully awake, perhaps."

She laughs, the tinkle of it at odds with the screaming in my head. "Well, after you meet with the maestro, you can feel free to rest for the remainder of the day. All of the other details are taken care of. We need you alert and ready to dance the night away!"

Until the sun goes down, I promise myself. I will smile and say all the right things and dance until the sun is down, and then I will make my excuses. I will not waste a single moment that could be spent with him.

If he's alive, my inner voice chirps. *If there's even a him to return to.*

I add a second bolt to the door. A third, a fourth.

Nothing I can do, nothing I can do, nothing I can do.

"I'm looking forward to it!" I lie.

We go together to meet with the maestro. He may have requested my input on selections, but he clearly already has his own intentions for the evening, and I let him push me toward them. It takes no effort. I have nothing in myself that cares.

He does leave the decision of my first dance with Arden entirely to me. I select a slow, swaying piece, a romantic little melody centered around the cello. Although both he and Everly sigh and exclaim over how perfect it will be, I only choose it because of the ease. Because I know it, because it's one of my favorites. I don't spare any thoughts to the romance of it, to what it will be like to dance to while in Arden's arms.

Once the maestro has excused himself to begin whatever preparations he feels will take the remainder of the day, I start to leave the ballroom. I am halted by Everly, by her tentative hand on my arm.

"You're sure you're all right, dear?"

"I'm sure." I smile my reassurance, lifting my own hand mechanically to rest over hers.

"There's…something I wanted to tell you." She still seems uncertain, although there's something glowing behind the uncertainty. Something growing and blooming. It feels like a big moment is upon us, but I am somewhere else for it.

"I've wanted to tell you for weeks now, but I wanted to truly be sure. You may know that your uncle and I have fervently hoped for children. We have not yet been so blessed, but, well…" Everly smiles a little shyly, a little brilliantly. There is so much hope in her expression, so much cautious joy. "Come the winter, you will have a cousin."

I clasp my hands under my chin and feel an entirely unforced affection swell inside of me. I had known that they struggled to conceive, and I had known that it was one of the weights on my uncle's bowed shoulders. I can't think of any two people who deserve this joy more.

"Oh, Aunt Everly," I breathe. "I'm so happy for you. For both of you. You will be wonderful parents."

"Oh, Reeve, thank you," she whispers, and I think it has to fight its way through a lump in her throat. Her aqua eyes brim with tears, some of the caution leaking from her joy. "It means so much that you think so."

"I *know* so. You have been like a mother to me all of these years, and Carrick has been more of a father to me than my own has ever been. This little one is so lucky."

She throws her arms around my neck, and I wrap mine around her waist. A baby. Such a precious gift, so fittingly bestowed. I am so happy for her. So happy for Carrick. So happy in this moment.

But there is a screaming in my ears, a desolation in my heart, blood on my hands. I can hear them, can feel them from behind the door. They echo. They pierce the moment. When I pull away, I excuse myself quickly so that she won't see that my smile has withered upon my face, turned to ash, turned to stone.

CHAPTER THIRTY-NINE

I tell myself not to, but I glance at the grandfather clock in the foyer as I pass it. It tells me that this is only the beginning. That the day has hardly even begun, and that it has no intention of rushing itself. I stop by the dining room for breakfast, but when the first few bites turn to ash on my tongue, I put my fork down. I sit and stare at it for no purpose other than to pass a few more seconds, to get a little closer, and then I give up and shove my plate aside.

Once more than half of the day has been given to moping, to the pier, to the hilltop, to the meandering forest pathways and then the meandering palace hallways once the rain begins, I decide I need a new plan. I can hear the distant chimes of the clock, each one seemingly farther apart from the last, and I need more of a distraction.

I need to *do* something.

Nothing I can do, my mind reminds me, and that may be true. But it may also not be. Maybe I can do something from here, even if it's not the same, not enough. Anything would be better than *nothing*.

I find my way to the library. It's a beautiful room used far less than it should be, especially since our librarian had passed on early last year. The maids keep the books and the floor from gathering dust, but the room still has an air of disuse that makes me feel sorry for it. It's a room meant for use, meant to help, to educate, to escape.

It's meant for so much more.

I wish they had more novels. I would have kept coming, long after my studies ceased, if Miss Quaresma held any stock in novels. But what few I have are only thanks to my mother. She loved to read, I'm told.

I stand in the center and turn slowly in place, eyes scanning the rows and rows of books. The ceiling is domed in glass, and I remember that it lets in the most magnificent sunshine on days that are cheerier than today. As it is, the rain pelts down upon the glass in a light, dreary sort of pitter-patter, making the lamps set out around the room on various flat surfaces necessary. I start to walk around, sparking matches and lighting the lamps, and my guards join me until they are all ablaze, settling a warm, welcoming glow over the room.

"Okay," I declare, settling my hands upon my hips. "Let's see if we can find anything on magic, or history, or, ideally, a combination of the two."

I will be useful today. I cannot do anything about Bran, but I can try to learn as much about the dream world as I can. If Thrall knew Rancore, he should exist somewhere within our history books. Lord knows there are enough books on Thrall to fill several shelves.

I take a step toward one of the shelves, but I stop when I notice that none of my guards have moved.

"What?"

"We aren't librarians, my lady," Percius says with a shrug.

"Yes, I realize. Neither am I. But I'm certain we can find what I'm looking for if we all start scanning the shelves."

"I'm just as certain we won't," Tiven counters. "There are the shelves here, the shelves along the wall, the shelves up all the way by the ceiling."

"Well, Miss Quaresma must have kept some sort of order to them." I continue resolutely to the nearest shelf and scan my fingers along the titles. A book on moon cycles, beside a mystery novel, alongside an encyclopedia of native plants. My brow creases lower and lower the more I scan, the more I ascertain that there truly does not seem to be an order to them. "Blast."

"She was a bit loony there," Demes chimes from where he leans casually against one of the shelves. "Talkin' to the books and whatnot like they were people. She may have had an order, but who's to say it made any sort of sense?"

I want to argue the point, but I can't. My shoulders slump at this hitch in my plan. I had counted on this taking time, plenty of time to distract me until I could set about readying for the ball, but like this…It would take days, or even weeks, to scan through all the titles and find what I'm looking for.

"You need the help of someone who's used this room more often than any of us has," Tiv advises.

I nod slowly, agreeably, until I realize who that means.

There's a reason my visits here became so infrequent. A reason I stopped wandering down here to soak in the sunshine through the dome, to laze by the fireplace and flip through whichever book Miss Quaresma cheerfully shoved into my hands.

I sigh grimly.

"Dem? Please have a footman fetch my brother."

Chapter Forty

He arrives more quickly than I would have expected, although I suppose in actuality that it's been a while since I held any expectations where my brother was concerned. I hadn't even been sure he would come.

I'm still uselessly scanning over weathered spines and faded titles when he steps into the room and takes some of the warmth from the glow of it. I stand up straight and turn to greet him as my guards step tactfully outside of the room to wait in the hallway.

"Florien. Thank you for coming."

"What are you doing in here?"

"Looking for books."

He rolls his eyes. "Yes, I assumed as much, as this is a library."

Don't glare, I command myself. *You need his help, and so you must be nice.*

"I'm seeking books on magic and history, preferably where they overlap."

He tilts his head quizzically. "Why?"

"None of your concern." I forget my command to be nice.

He stares at me for a moment and then swings away toward the door. I'm tempted to let him keep going, to stubbornly do this on my own even if it takes ages, but I rush forward to block his way before he can reach the door.

"I'm sorry," I attempt sincerely through gritted teeth. "Will you please help me in my search? You've spent a great deal more time in here than I have in recent years."

He studies me long enough for me to engage in a sizeable inner argument about whether or not I can do this without him. Finally, he says quietly, "Yes, I have."

He starts toward the shelves in the far corner, and as I follow him over, I wonder how many days it would have taken me to reach that section. Two or three, perhaps. When he starts to climb the ladder toward the upper shelves, I add another day or two.

"Miss Quaresma did have her reasons," he calls down over his shoulder. "Although they aren't a lot of use to the rest of us. She grouped them by feeling, by how the books made her feel to read." He pauses in his climbing to point over his shoulder. "Starting over there are the ones that made her happiest. They kind of loop over and around from there, to the ones that made her sad, the ones that scared her, the ones that bored her to tears."

I throw my hands in the air. "Well, how am I ever to find anything, in that case? Who's to say that I would have the same feelings toward a book as she did?"

He laughs as he continues climbing, and lord, I don't remember the last time I heard my brother laugh. It makes me think abruptly of my mother, although his tone is lower, more resonant.

I realize suddenly that I have missed my brother, and I prod at the feeling uneasily, wishing it would not settle. It is tied by his laugh to missing my mother, and feeling either of those things today might be too much for me. Too much of too much.

"You picked this section fairly quickly. What feelings did magic and history evoke in dear Miss Quaresma?"

"Magic scared her. History..." He flicks his chin down across the library to another set of shelves. "History bored her to tears."

I laugh a little at the thought of a librarian bored by history, on a day when I would have thought laughter to be impossible. I have years of resentment in me, built high and steady on one of the hills of my heart, but I feel a little slide off. Just a little, not enough to make a real dent, but enough so that I feel it. He made me laugh, today of all days.

"There aren't too many here," he continues. "Thrall keeps the bulk of them, the more useful ones, in his private quarters."

I huff a sigh. "Those will be next to impossible to get my hands on, then."

"Yeah...I won't be any help with that undertaking. Thrall hates me."

"I think he hates us all, a little bit. Or at least has no patience for us."

He picks a book from the shelf and leans over to drop it into my waiting hands.

"Remember the time you accidentally stepped on his robes at Carrick's thirtieth birthday celebration?"

"Oh, lord," I groan. "I was terrified for weeks after that he would spell me in some way in revenge."

"Well, you did reveal the bony lower half of his legs to the bulk of the kingdom. You deserved at least a raincloud following you around for a month."

I laugh again, this time a little harder. "It would've been the perfect vengeance, ruining my walks."

He flinches a little at the mention of my walks, walks he used to join me on, and he falls silent. His silence in response to our abnormal, easy banter feels weighted. I remember myself and the tension between us abruptly in the echo of it. He leans down to drop another two books, avoiding my eyes as he does so. I wonder at what lies beneath the weight on his end.

He climbs back down the ladder and slides past me to go toward what is apparently the bored-to-tears section he had indicated earlier. These are lower to the ground, not requiring the use of the ladder. I go to stand beside him, keeping a careful distance, scanning titles as he runs his finger along the spines.

"This one?" he asks quietly.

"Yes, that one looks like it could be useful."

Gone is the ease. We are back to the us we have been these past few years, the stilted, strained us.

Once I have a sizeable stack of magic and history books in my arms and Florien has declared the appropriate stacks thoroughly searched, he shifts his weight from one foot to another and back again in an awkward silence.

"I assume you have no further need of me?"

He says it so properly, so like my father, that I respond coldly. "Thank you, no. I have no further need of you at all."

He can certainly hear the unmasked ice in my words, and he steps backward, toward the door, away from the cool blast of them. He starts to turn but swings abruptly back to face me.

"You're always so mad at me."

It isn't a question. I lift my chin.

"What did you expect?"

He shakes his head slowly. "You blame me even though I had no choice."

Today is not the day for this conversation. My mind is in shambles, my thoughts scattered to the wind. I cannot gather enough of them for this. I cannot push enough things aside to pull forth the years of resentment between Florien and I and study them properly.

Or maybe it's the perfect day for it. The perfect distraction.

"You had a choice to never visit. You had a choice to never speak to me. One day you were there, everywhere with me, and the next you were gone entirely."

I can see his swallow travel along his throat. "Father kept me busy."

"So busy you couldn't even be bothered to visit? To visit even *once*?"

I find the words so easily. They have been building in the back of my throat for years, waiting, and they crawl forth happily now, eager to finally be said.

"We used to do everything together! You were my best friend in the world, my *only* friend in the world who wasn't hired to be there, and then you left, and you didn't look back."

"I looked back," he shouts with startling force. "I looked back for a long time. I would sit poring over books and ledgers right there—" he turns to point at the window in the corner, beside a small table and chair, "—and I would watch you go on your walks. The same walks we used to take. I'd watch you laugh with your guards, and run up the hills. Your life didn't change, Reeve. You didn't have Father watching your every move. You didn't have his expectations, his pressure, his demands. You still got to be *free*."

"I got to be alone," I say quietly, thawed by the blazing heat of his words. I was wrong to think that today was the day for this. "You of all people should know that I never wanted to be *free* of Father's attention. I wanted—all I've ever wanted—was a piece of it. Just a sliver of it. But it belongs to you."

"I don't want it." He sounds as tired as I do, the fire gone from him as the ice is from me. "I don't want to be the pillar he rests his hopes upon."

I nod slowly in silent acknowledgement. Not in approval or understanding, because the depth and the breadth of the resentment in my heart is such that I don't have those in me to give, but I acknowledge his words. I acknowledge that he has been dealt cards that he does not wish to hold, same as I have.

The clock chimes somewhere in the hallway. It resonates enough times, finally, that I know I should go up and begin readying for the ball.

There are four years of silence between us. Four years to become strangers, to perhaps remember that we once whispered secrets to one another but no longer to remember what they were. Four years to build our respective hills of resentment strong and high within our hearts, so that they cannot be torn down easily. Not by one conversation, in a candlelit library, with the rain still sliding down all around us.

And so I smile a little, a shadow of my usual smile and say, "I should get ready for the ball. Thank you for your help, Florien."

His smile mirrors mine. Same shadows, same sadness. "You're welcome. Save me a dance?"

"Yes," I agree, though it is etiquette. I will dance with my uncle, with my father, with him. Still, he asked, so I answer as though it was not a given. "I'll save you a dance."

It isn't much, but maybe I'll see it as a beginning.

CHAPTER FORTY-ONE

I fiddle with my mother's necklace and listen to the muffled laughter coming from the ballroom. I pull out the practiced laughter easily, search harder for the real laughter. So many people, only a thin wall away from me, and I have never felt more alone.

Or more tired. I fight my body's urge to droop, commanding my spine to behave as though Thrall is about to walk in the room at any moment. The chances of this actually occurring are exceptionally slim, borderline nonexistent, but I try to trick my spine, anyway. Because the person who will walk in the room, at any moment, is Arden.

I presume, anyway. He's late. He should have been here fifteen minutes ago, and we should already have made our grand entrance. Instead, I sit in the small chamber off to the side of the ballroom, perched on the arm of a settee, attempting to fool parts of my body.

I smooth out my gown for the hundredth time, though it needs no smoothing. It's made of a silk that cascades rather than creases, gliding down along my body like water on a windless day. No waves to be found. There hadn't been time to solicit a new gown, so one of Everly's had been altered for my use. It's beautiful, and at my first fitting, I had been honored to wear it.

Today, all I can see is the color.

Red.

The deepest of reds.

It matches my engagement ring perfectly.

It matches his blood in my memory even more perfectly.

I smooth it out, again and again, but I don't look at it.

I'm exhausted from the effort of surviving this day. Of holding the door closed and pretending that Bran isn't somewhere dying, or dead, or at the very least in pain. People are laughing next door, and soon—whenever Arden sees fit to arrive—I will have to join them. It feels like an impossible task, but this whole day has felt impossible, and here I am anyway.

The door opens, allowing the laughter to bounce inside more raucously. I flinch against the sound as Arden slides silently inside. He closes the door behind him, muting the noise and encasing us in only the echoes of merriment.

He walks over to me like a memory, wearing the same black dress clothes he had worn on my birthday, the same glitter to his eyes. The smirk is there to complete the picture, and we're almost strangers again, almost about to be introduced for the first time, almost about to dance our first dance under a glow of possibility.

I take no care of the illusion. I shatter it.

"You're late."

He looks the complete opposite of chagrined. He looks buoyant, each step toward me floating six inches off the ground. He is always so full of life, always emitting it like sparks from his fingertips, from his eyes. Mostly from his eyes.

"And you were worth the wait."

I roll my eyes. "You weren't the one waiting."

"Wasn't I? I may have been the reason I had to wait, but I still had to wait."

He takes my hand warmly in his, bowing over it and pressing his lips to the back of it. He shoots me that practiced look of his, through the eyelashes, his lips still warm against my skin. I sigh and shake my head.

"Are you going to insist on showering charm upon me for the duration of our marriage?"

Arden lifts his head a little so I can see his slanted smile. Sparks from there, too. "You love it."

I scoff. "I do not."

"Do too."

"You are impossible!" I don't intend for it to come out a laugh, but it does. The sparks are hitting me, infusing me. I can't repel them all. "And we're only getting later the longer we stand here."

He shrugs indifferently. "Let them wait. I'm sure they'll think you're worth it, as well."

I stand from my perch and smooth out my gown yet again, still not letting my eyes wander down to the red of it. It isn't difficult, this time, because standing has brought me dangerously near to him. I clear my throat uncomfortably and attempt to step around him, but as usual, he allows me no quarter. He steps to the side in tandem with me and takes my chin lightly in his hand.

"Did you get into our betrothal papers?"

I wrinkle my brow. "What?"

"You look like you might fall asleep on your feet."

I pull my chin away and purposefully make a wide circle around him on my way to the door, glaring over my shoulder at him. "For such an accomplished flirt, you really ought to know better than to tell a woman she looks tired."

He catches up to me in two long strides, reaching for the door before I can do so. He opens it a crack and then holds it there while I tilt my head impatiently at him.

"Is it too heavy for you? Do you require assistance opening it?"

"Such sass," he murmurs, his eyes twinkling. "I require no assistance, thank you. I merely realized that I had been remiss."

"In saying I look tired? Certainly."

"In not kissing you."

I falter back a step, even though it takes me away from my destination. Either nobody is laughing in the ballroom anymore, or my senses have given themselves over entirely to him. I suspect it is the latter, and I try quickly to seek out sounds from the next room. Anything to distract me from the nearness of him, from what his words do to my insides. Anything, maybe. Anything, except I do not look back down at my dress. I do not look back down at the red of it. I need to be distracted from something else more than I need to be distracted from Arden.

"You kissed my hand," I stammer.

"Insufficient." His voice can be sandpaper, can be silk. Somehow, he makes that one word both.

"It really isn't necessary."

"I beg to differ." He clicks the door shut and leans back against it. "Are you going to run again?"

I realize that I have taken several more steps back and force my feet to hold their position.

"No."

"Are you going to make me come to you?"

I swallow hard. "Arden…"

This time he's the one who tilts his head, although he does so patiently. He waits.

"I'm tired," I say finally, quietly.

The sparkle in his eyes fades. The tilt of his lips flattens into a straight line, into enough of a straight line that I wonder if this, not his smirk, was once his default expression. He looks like the other Arden, the one who believed in love. The one who was cured of it.

"Come here."

It's a command, softly issued. Softly enough that I slump my shoulders and take a step forward.

"That's a start. One more, love."

I think the endearment alone propels me the next step. From there, he leans forward to take my hand and tug me nearer to him. To my surprise, he doesn't tug me directly into his lips. Instead, he pulls me into his body, all the way flush with it, my face in his chest and my hands gripping the lapels of his jacket. When he brings his arms up around me, I heave a great shuddering sigh and let myself sag against him.

"You really shouldn't have read them," he whispers into my hair. "I told you they were dreadfully boring. You should have taken my word for it."

My laugh gives half of itself over into a sob. "I didn't read the papers."

"You don't need to lie to me. I know this particular brand of exhaustion, and it screams of numbers and property drawings."

I lean back a little. "There were drawings?"

"Not good ones, either." He lifts one hand to touch my cheek. "Are you ready yet?"

"For you to kiss me?"

His smirk crawls back into place, and he is the memory of himself once more. "Nobody's ever ready for that particular brand of magic."

I roll my eyes and shove away from him. "Arrogance in spades."

"Don't speak of spades, sweet. I saw how you mangled them in twenty-one."

"I didn't *mangle* them. I merely requested more."

"And more, and more, and more. Greed will be your downfall."

I laugh, a real laugh. "Greed and arrogance, what a pair we make."

He leans around me to pull the door open, fully this time. "I'd say we're a twenty."

"What are you assigning us, then? A king and a queen?"

"No, no, I am but a jack to your queen."

I tuck my hand into his arm and let him lead me out into the hallway. "Lowering your rank? That isn't the arrogant Arden I know."

"Know and love?"

"Know and tolerate."

He throws back his head and laughs. "I'll bring that around to know and like, just you wait and see."

We listen as the footman announces our arrival. The doors open as though in slow motion, and the blazing candlelight within glints off of my ring. We both glance down at it where it rests on my hand, on his arm, and then, as though my eyes summon his or his summon mine, we find ourselves looking at each other.

"Know and like achieved, I think," I say softly. I don't feel alone right now. "But don't let it go to your head."

The first look the assembly in the ballroom get of us, of the newly engaged Lord Arden Velasian, Marques of Rynfall and future Duke of Baewar, and Lady Reeve Lennox, of the unexpected union of the kingdom's most desirable man and the king's favored niece, is of him leaning down to kiss me. Of me lifting up onto my toes to kiss him back.

CHAPTER FORTY-TWO

I get used to being on his arm. I get used to the feel of his muscles under my hand, to the exact tilt of my neck that is required for me to look up at him as he speaks to me, as he speaks to others, as he speaks to others about me. He tells a charming story of how taken he was with me at my birthday ball, how quickly I had swept him off his feet. The first time he tells it, he says, "She utterly entrapped me," and at my sharp look, he clears his throat and says, with his most wicked smile, "*Enthralled* me, pardon."

I smile serenely up at him, but I also swish my dress forward enough to surreptitiously stomp on his foot with the sharp heel of my shoe. He winces and sends me a wounded look before excusing us and limping to the nearest chair.

"Ouch," he complains as he leans down to study his foot. "I'm surprised you didn't puncture the shoe."

"Terribly sorry, dear," I say in a sickly sweet tone. "Entirely accidental."

"Liar." He lunges up out of his seat and sweeps me onto the dance floor in the same motion, leaving me struggling to catch my breath through my laughter and the fast-paced orchestra piece.

I start to feel as though I'm part of a team. Half of a whole. As though it's he and I against the whole of this ballroom, and we are spinning circles around them. We are laughing at our own private jokes, and his eyes are dancing only for me. He drinks his whiskey, and I try a glass of punch or two, and when the whole room starts to spin around me, I hold tighter to his arm.

I forget about doors and screams, talons and boys with blue eyes. I accept compliments on my dress and look down at it without thinking of anything but the fact that it *is* a beautiful shade of red, why thank you. I stuff silk and gravel into the holes inside of my heart and will them to stay in place. I will this to be all there is, this carefree jubilance, the sound of his laugh overlapping mine.

It's a silly wish. A silly will. When I return from a trip to the ladies room, I find him in a corner, his eyes on a woman who isn't me, his laugh intertwining with hers as though he's already forgotten the sound of mine.

I forget it, too.

In that instant, I forget it.

I am not the only one who sees them, and they all see me see them, as well. I back away from their pitying stares, from their mocking glances, stumbling out onto the terrace before he ever even notices that I'm there.

The terrace is a memory in itself. There is a shadow of him there, as I lean against the railing. A shadow of him reaching for me, a shadow of him touching my face. I turn away from his shadow, as I had that night. I was right to turn away. Whatever instinct it had been, it was the right one.

I take deep breaths to clear the clouds from my mind, inhaling the scent of recent rain. I let the silk slide out of the holes and feel the gravel drop away, remembering myself and remembering Bran and remembering that I had promised myself that I would leave as soon as the sun had set. The sun had set, and I had kept dancing.

In my eagerness to not be alone, to not feel so *tired* anymore, I had shut more than just Bran and the night behind the door. I had shut *myself* behind it. I had forgotten doors and screams, talons and boys with blue eyes, and I had forgotten myself. I add it to my ever-growing list of shames.

I tear the door to shreds. I tear down anything that separated me from him, anything that separated me from myself.

It's time to go.

I turn back toward the ballroom at the same time the terrace doors open.

For half a second, before the lanterns catch hold of him, I think it's Arden, come to find me. But as soon as he takes another step forward, I see that this figure is shorter, darker. His hair less artful, his eyes softer.

"Oh. Lord Delavar, hello."

"Good evening, Reeve. I hoped to catch you alone."

Something in the way he says "alone" makes his soft eyes look sharper. It makes me think abruptly of my guards. They were stationed around the perimeter with the other palace guards, scattered, but I'm sure they saw me come out here. I'm sure they saw Del follow.

When he steps forward, though, the lanterns catch his face and I shake off the sudden fear. It was only a phantom from the punch, from the stretching black shadows touching upon his face. There's no reason to fear Del.

"Well, you were successful. Was there something you wanted?"

When the terrace doors open again, I expect to see Jax come flying out with his sword drawn. Instead, Arden steps out to join us.

"There you are," he says, stepping around Del to stand beside me. He kisses the top of my head, although I suspect that it's more for Del's benefit than mine. He also settles a possessive arm around my waist, warm and heavy.

For my part, I keep my attention on Del, and even through the darkness, I can see him tense at Arden's arrival. There is enough light to see the tightening at the corners of his mouth, the corners of his eyes.

"Here I am," I say evenly. I'm grateful that someone else is out here now, too, but I wish it hadn't been this someone else. My memory is filled with other things now that the door is down, but there is still room for the one where his laugh overlaps hers. "Del, you were about to say something?"

His eyes flit between Arden and me. "I, uh, just wanted to say congratulations on the betrothal. To both of you."

Lord, *he* had proposed. And I had told him I wasn't ready to marry anyone quite yet. As soon as I remember, a river of pity flows through me. I want to reach out and touch his arm, to tell him that I'm sorry. That's likely what he had sought me out for, anyway, for an explanation if not an apology. I owe him both. As it is, with Arden holding me glued to his side, all I can do is offer him a smile which I hope holds some of the words I want to say as I tell him, "Thank you, Del. It's very much appreciated."

Arden says nothing. My smile turns into gritted teeth as Del shifts uncomfortably from one foot to another.

"Well, I'll leave you two alone then," he finally says.

"Okay," Arden says agreeably.

He's going to think my last stomp on his foot was a tickle, I think to myself grimly. But I keep my bared-teeth smile in place until

Del is fully back in the ballroom, the doors closed behind him. Only then do I shove away from Arden.

"I'm not sure how I feel about you meeting men on dark terraces. Other than me, of course."

"You could've been nicer to him," I ground out.

He shrugs. "I have no interest in being nice to him. He's an utterly dull sort. A little odd. Not someone I care to impress."

"You don't need to *impress* him. Just be nice."

He tilts his head down at me, the lantern glow catching just half of his face, just half of the lines and curves of it. Just half of the beauty of it. "Why are you angry with me?"

"I'm not *angry* with you," I growl.

"You're growling."

"I'm not *growling*." An echo of a memory, but it isn't of him.

Are you going to growl again? I hear in Bran's voice.

I push the memory aside.

"I suppose we'll have to agree to disagree there," Arden continues. "Anyway, I've been looking for you for some time now. How long were you out here with him?"

"You might have found me a little more quickly had you looked in places other than Lady Windemere's cleavage."

He jerks his head back an inch, out of its tilt. The half of his face I can see shows his surprise, but I think I also see a flash of guilt. "What are you talking about?"

"I'm talking about the fact that I am not *in* Lady Windemere's dress, and as that seemed to be the primary place you were searching, it's understandable that you did not find me."

The anger I feel toward myself is a lit match pinched between two fingers, the flame spreading further and further until I feel the sting of it on my skin. Instead of dropping it, I use it to light a second match. This one burns with my anger toward him. I should go, because the sun is set and the door is gone, but instead, I let the matches blaze hotter and brighter. I feel them sear my fingertips.

He's silent for several seconds following my outburst, and in that silence, adding kindling to my flames, I imagine him devising and discarding excuse after excuse. I wait to see which one he decides might fool me.

"I was merely talking to Lady Windemere—"

An unimpressive choice.

"Don't patronize me, Arden. I stood there for a full thirty seconds watching the two of you undress one another with your eyes, and the rest of the ballroom watched right along with me."

He runs a frustrated hand through his hair, shifting it away from a careful mess and closer to a savage one. "Look, I told you that I wouldn't make you promises I couldn't keep, and I made no promises."

"You didn't tell me that you would make a fool out of me."

His hand drops to his side. "That was not my intention."

"No, your intention was to flirt with Lady Windemere because you were already bored with me." My exhaustion is back, and it bleeds wholly into my tone. I'm tired of letting my fingertips burn. I turn toward the terrace doors. "I have a headache. I'm going to retire."

I'm not surprised when he blocks my escape. I sigh and keep my gaze level, which makes it even with his chest. I can see it rise and fall as he sighs, too.

"Reeve…" There is always something unexpected about his use of my given name. It lends him a sincerity that I can't help but believe is unpracticed. It makes my heart thump twice in one beat. It makes me look up at him. "I apologize."

His match flickers. I hadn't expected an apology.

"I promise you I'll be more discreet in the future."

It flickers fully out this time, but only because I drop it into the dirt. I am too tired to hold it, too tired to discuss his discretion, too tired to stand here when Bran is somewhere, within reach of my closed eyelids. I am too tired to hold his gaze.

"Goodnight, Arden."

He still won't let me go.

"I wasn't bored with you."

I wish he would move.

"Reeve."

He won't until I acknowledge him.

I look up.

"I'm sorry I hurt you. I'm sorry that I'm the dragon and not the knight."

"I like you as the dragon," I say quietly. "I just wish that I was enough, even if just for one night, for you to focus the whole of your fire on me."

He lets me step past him this time. I don't look back, even when I hear him speak again. His words follow me, though. They follow me back through the ballroom, through the goodnights and the thank yous, through the explanations of my headache, through the knowing looks from those who had seen him with Lady Windemere, all the way up the stairs and into my bed. This interminable day has finally passed, and I am just a close of my eyes away from seeing Bran.

Just before I allow them to slide shut, just before my dreams come to take me, I hear the echo of Arden's last words to me. I hear them in gravel, in silk. I hear them in fire.

I hear him saying, "Maybe you are."

Chapter Forty-Three

I arrive beneath the gallows still dressed in my red gown. There had been too many buttons I couldn't reach, and I hadn't had Guin to help. I had dismissed her for the night after she had helped me dress for the ball in near silence. The tension had been stifling, but I had stayed quiet. I had resolved to clear the air tomorrow, when my fingertips were less raw and I had seen Bran well and whole, when my mind was clear enough to come up with a lie of an explanation for my ill treatment of her.

And so, upon failing to reach the first few buttons, I had simply collapsed into bed in my gown. I had taken off my ring, though. I had caught the glint of it in time and tossed it onto my bedside table. I wonder if that ring will ever represent anything other than Bran's spilled blood to me again.

Bran's spilled blood and a tie to a man who says I am enough but breathes fire for women who are not me.

I'm beginning to hate that ring.

I roll to my feet as soon as I arrive, briefly tangling in the endless silk of my skirts. I grab them up in one hand and sprint to the shadows, listening to the easy swing of the rope. My hair is still pulled loosely over my shoulder in an avalanche of curls in the style Guin had fashioned for the ball. Strands pull free and fall across my vision as I run.

I slide into the alcoves on silent feet and scan my surroundings once slowly, then again more frantically, then one last time because a blind and stupid hope tells me to try again. To check the shadows more carefully. To make sure.

But of course he isn't here. Even if Bran survived, he would be in no condition to sneak through the streets to meet me.

Not *if* he survived, I amend. He's alive.

I hurry down the familiar path to Cecily's. I let the swishing of my silk skirts blend with the light rustle of the wind, darting down alleys and leaping across intersections. I am incautious, rushed, the word *if* still circling my mind like a falcon on razored wings. *If* he's alive, *if* he's alive.

He's alive, he's alive, he's alive.

I am about halfway there when I feel him grab my wrist. I experience a moment of knee-weakening relief at the confirmation that he *is* alive, of course he is, and he's *here*, before my skin tells me that it is not his hand.

This hand has no callouses. This hand encircles my wrist with bruising force, which Bran would never use. This hand is attached to someone who isn't him, someone who I swing around to face and can make no sense of in the moonlight.

Because I recognize him.

Because he should not be here.

"Good evening, Reeve. I hoped to catch you alone."

There is barely enough moonlight. In another night or two, the moon will be new, and there will be none at all. The stars do their best, though, and they show me that here, his eyes are not soft. Here, his smile does not curve gently. Here, everything about him is sharp and dangerous. Not Arden's kind of danger, but the kind that Jax guards against. The kind that pushes the bones of my wrist against one another until I have to bite back a cry of pain.

"Del...Del, what are you doing here?"

"Same as you, I'd imagine. Walking."

His tone is different, too. This tone would not belong in a ballroom, or out on a terrace, or in the king's court. It belongs here, to the night, to these dark streets. Jagged and sinister with an undertone of irreverence.

It is also loud.

It is careless.

We are standing in the middle of the street.

"We have to move." I try to tug my wrist from his grasp, and when that fails I grab hold of his arm and try to pull him along with me. My only focus is getting out of the street, out of the waning moonlight. "Del, it isn't safe here."

"I'll keep you safe," he says with a slow, curious tilt of his head. "Don't you trust me?"

"How are you here?" I continue to try to pull him, wincing again as my wrist bones grind together.

"Dreaming, of course."

I pause, looking away from his unmovable arm and back up at his face. "You dream this place, too?"

"Every night."

I stare slack-jawed up at him. "Are you...visible?"

"Oh yes."

He speaks with a strange sort of glee. It makes me realize that I am not on a terrace, my guards thirty feet and a shout away. Arden is not going to wander out and fasten me to his side. I am well and truly alone, and my instinct to fear Del is not faltering this time.

We are still in the middle of the street.

"We can discuss this more later, but for now, we really need to get out of the street," I say in a harsh whisper. "If you've come here every night, you know what it means to be caught out."

"Ah yes, the birds."

Then he throws his head back and laughs. It plunges my whole body into an icy pool of water. I start shaking uncontrollably as his laugh bounces off of the houses surrounding us, reverberating through the night. I start pulling in earnest now, my bare heels digging into the gravel until I feel them pierce the soles of my feet. I pull even harder.

"Please, stop," I beg. "They'll come."

He stops laughing as abruptly as he started and looks back down at me. "I said I'd protect you."

I think my wrist is breaking. The force of his hold and my frantic yanks counteract one another and send pain shooting up my arm. I don't let myself stop, though, even though we haven't moved an inch.

I'm about to open my mouth to plead again when I hear the beat of their wings.

I gasp and stumble, my feet sliding against the gravel until I nearly fall into him. He continues to stare down at me, seemingly oblivious to death approaching swiftly above us.

"They'll kill us. They'll tear us apart. Please, Del, we have to get inside."

"I'm beginning to get the impression that you don't trust me."

"I…"

Whatever I had been about to say dies in my throat as they appear above us. They are barely shadows, barely differentiable from the rest of the night, until they start to shriek. The sound is so familiar, so representative of my lifetime of nightmares in this place, so *close*. I have escaped once when they were this close, thanks to Bran's arrival and his fighting abilities. Here, with Del's eyes on me instead of above us, with his unwillingness to move a single step, I know that I won't be so lucky.

I begin to scream.

I scream for help. I scream for mercy. I scream for Bran.

Nobody comes.

The shrieks start to mingle with one another, and at the first harmonious note, the first indication that it has become a song, my screams break off into sobs.

"Ye of little faith," he says. Through my tears, I watch him pull a small object from his pocket. He holds it in the air above his head without ever taking his eyes from me, and as though pulled away by invisible threads tied to the sky, the falcons jerk upward, away. They break out of their formation, their song fading into nothing. When they fly away, they take even the echo of it with them.

We are left alone, still standing in the middle of the street, as I swipe my tears away with the back of my free hand and stare at him.

"How did you do that?"

"Magic." His smile grows, stretches from one ear to the other, but it is still lined with knives, freshly sharpened and gleaming with dark promises.

"It was you," I whisper. "I saw you one night, walking. I saw the falcons let you go."

"And you didn't say hello?" He shakes his head in mock sadness, at odds with the stretched smile. "I was going to tell you earlier that your dress is my favorite shade of red."

I look down at it stupidly. I do not understand how I am here with *Del*, my wrist half-broken, the falcons called off, still not knowing if Bran is alive or dead.

"I have to go," I whisper. "Please, Del. I have somewhere I have to be."

"So do I," he whispers back, although his whisper is clearly just for show. He makes it conspiratorial. "And you get to come with me."

"No." I lean away again, as far as I can get from him. "No, I have to go. I'll speak with you in the morning, in Acarsaid, and we can figure all of this out. You can speak with me alone there, I promise."

"No guards? No Velasian?"

"No guards, and no Velasian. I swear it."

He shrugs. "Well, perhaps we can do that, too. But for now, we have to do this."

He turns and starts the opposite direction of the one I had been headed. He pulls me inexorably behind him, even as I try to dig my feet more firmly into the pricking stones and dust.

"No! I can't!"

"You can," he calls over his shoulder. "Look, you're doing it."

I abruptly stop pulling and launch myself at him. My free hand is curved into a claw, a talon in its own right, and I use it to swipe wildly at his face. I have the benefit of catching him by surprise, so that even though I weigh little compared to him, I manage to tackle him to the ground. He lands with a sharp gasp beneath me, dropping his hold on my wrist. I shove myself off of him and take off down the nearest alley.

I hear the moment he starts to follow me. My footsteps are quiet here, but his are not. His are loud, skidding, careless. They are closer, and then they are closer, and then they are directly behind me. I duck and swerve, but it isn't enough. This time I am the one tackled to the ground, the one landing with a whoosh of expelled air, the one pressed into the street.

"There was an easy way, you know," he pants against my ear. "There was an easy way, and then there was this way, and you chose poorly."

He yanks me to my feet and spins me to face him. "Do you want to try the easy way one more time?"

My wrists are crossed in front of me, his hands holding them tightly together so that instead of just one set of bones protesting, I get two. I glare at him through the dark, taking some pleasure in the bloody scratches carved across his face. I can feel his blood under my fingernails. Blood drips down my own face from my sprawl across the gravel, and I feel it on my tongue, but I glare up at him through it.

And then I kick him in the groin.

He drops, just as Jax had said a man would if I kicked him there, but he doesn't let go of my wrists. He keeps them locked in place even as he doubles over, yanking me down with him. I thrash and fling my body every way it can go, ignoring the screaming pain of my fragile bones as they twist and gnash. His grip is iron, though, and when he finally rights himself, his eyes are steel.

Steel forged into a dagger.

"Don't say I didn't try."

The last thing I see is his hand, clenched tightly into a fist. His fist, coming closer to my face. Closer. Closer. I jerk my head to the side too late, too late, and the last thing I see is the brightest star, the one closest to the moon, the one I used to follow to the wall, before everything goes black.

Chapter Forty-Four

I rarely get peace from my rest because of the nightmares. On occasion, I will nap during the day, and I will be pulled into a deep, dreamless rest. My dream world has never come for me when the sun is up, and so those midday naps, either in the comfort of my bed or the glow of the hilltop, are my only respite. The only time I can shut off everything.

Except, apparently, for forced unconsciousness.

I'm not sure this counts as sleep, but I know I do not dream. I simmer in unrelenting blackness for a length of time, an entirely unknowable length of time which could be anywhere from a minute to an hour to the whole of the night, before I become aware that I am in it. And then, with my head throbbing to the same rhythm as my heart, I pull myself out of it.

When my eyes slit open, the first thing I see are the candles. There must be hundreds of them glaring down upon me, enough to cause my head to protest more insistently and my eyes to decide to close again. It takes several tries to open them.

I blink several times to adjust to the light. It is positively blinding, utterly excessive. The longer I glare up into it, the more I am able to differentiate one candle from another, from another, from another. The ceiling is covered in them. They hang upside down above me, suspended by something I cannot see.

The flame burns downward, too. It makes no logical sense, but the flames reach toward me, straight down, ignoring the demands of gravity.

Magic, I realize. The candles are held this way by magic.

As soon as I realize magic, I realize where I am.

I'm in the palace.

I look around to confirm. There is no furniture, but the walls are made of cinder. The floor is made of stone. There is a door breaking up one of the walls, but even it is made of stone. There is nothing of wood here. Nothing like any of the houses I have seen in my nightly meanderings through Tenebris. *This* is a cell. I erase the descriptor from my little room at Cecily's. That room was cozy and welcoming compared to this one.

The only place I have never been able to access here has been the palace grounds. The walls around it are twice as high as the walls around the city, the gates sealed shut against the night. I spent one whole night in my childhood standing in front of them, staring in at the palace, marveling at the dark beauty of it. The sharp turrets and the spiraling staircases leading up to the front and sides of it. It was all cinder, all stone.

I visited again a handful, a dozen times, but there was never any change to it. Never any way to enter, never a relenting of the shivers that drove up my spine at the sight of it. *Del* brought me to the palace.

That bastard hit me.

The memory of it comes rushing back, along with the throbbing of my head and of my wrists. I glance down at the latter and wince at the black and blue encasing them both. I can at least bend the left one, but the right one, which he had held the longest, refuses to move. The slightest flex of it shoots needles up my arm, and so I rest it carefully on my lap.

I look around again, but I see nothing more. Just the candles, just the walls, just the single door. I drag myself to my feet, still cradling my wrist, and cross the room to push carefully against the door. My feet sting with every step.

Unsurprisingly, the stone door does not budge. It does nothing at all to indicate that it is even a door, even capable of opening. There's no handle, on this side at least, which makes me believe I'm in a dungeon of sorts.

I wonder how long I've been in here.

I pray fervently that Guin will find a reason to wake me up early. That there will be some urgent need at the palace to awaken me, and she will not take my shouted reprimands of yesterday to heart, and I will be pulled back home with two undamaged wrists and four guards to sic on Del.

I can't believe he *hit* me.

I touch my temple lightly as I retreat back to the corner, as far away from the door as I can manage. My forehead is tender to the touch, and I suspect it sports a bruise to match my wrists. It will be gone in the morning, and I'll have a rather difficult time explaining to my guards that Lord Delavar attacked me in my dream—in a *real* sort of dream, I'll have to explain, not the usual sort they'll think I mean. But still, they'll listen. They'll believe me enough to go after him.

And then I'll knee him in the groin again.

And I'll punch *him* in the face.

A seething rage boils inside of me already, but it is nothing compared to the heights it reaches when I think of Bran.

The first note of an *if* starts to form itself in my mind, but I push it aside. I reform my thought around the certainty I want to feel. Bran's alive, and he must be worried about where I am. Even as we left things, I believe that he'll worry. I hope he didn't go out looking for me.

I should be there.

I have survived a whole day without knowing, without seeing him and confirming once and for all that the *if* in my head does not belong there. It was interminable. I had built fresh doors and put too much behind them. It had asked so much of me, too much of me, but I survived it. And now ...

There seems little chance of getting out of here the natural way, and so I must wait for the sun to rise.

When the sun rises, I will be free of this.

I will have to survive another day without knowing how he is.

But when the sun rises, I will be free of this.

I repeat it over and over again.

I am still repeating it when the door slides open.

I scramble to my feet and stand ramrod straight in the corner of the room, watchful and trying not to look as terrified as I feel. When I see that it's Del, I relax my stance and scowl.

"You bastard," I growl as I stalk forward. "I'm going to make you regret—"

Someone else enters the room behind him before I can finish my threat.

It is just one man, a lone man with quiet steps and a willowy figure, but his entry steals the words from my tongue. I try to figure out where they've gone, why they've dried up, what it is about this man, but I can't find it by looking at him.

He's dressed head to toe in black, his grey hair cropped close. A small smile plays at his lips, frozen. Engraved. I don't think it means happiness in any form. It is simply the way his face was formed.

Unremarkable as he is in appearance, he carries something remarkable. His presence is a push and a pull, a weight on my ankles dragging me miles below the water's surface. He resonates power.

He is the sort of man who makes razor-winged falcons into pets.

He needs no introduction, and he gives none. He merely tilts his head sideways and nods once slowly, considering. His smile does not move.

"Welcome, my lady."

His voice does not boom or resonate. It's nothing like Thrall's. All it has is a slight rasp to it to make it anything at all.

I manage to push just one word through my fear.

"Rancore."

CHAPTER FORTY-FIVE

The frozen smile deepens, but it doesn't reach his eyes. Nothing reaches his eyes. They are pale blue chips of ice. Flat, without dimension. They reveal nothing, they are nothing. I have a hard time holding his gaze.

"You know me?" He sounds curious, half-amused.

"I know *of* you." Of his cruelty. Of his darkness, of his pets, of his war.

"Ah, how wonderful. My reputation precedes me."

He had walked past Del to enter the room without acknowledging him, but he glances back at him now. I watch him study Del's face, the dried blood cross-hatching down his cheeks and over his nose. They may be little more than shallow scratches, but they mark him well.

I can still feel his blood caked under my nails. I take vicious satisfaction in it.

Rancore looks away without a word to the other man, only a shake of his head and a small sigh. He redirects his empty eyes my way, and my thoughts immediately re-tangle. I wish that he had found more to study on Del's face, that I had left more gashes.

"I'm pleased you could join me today." As though it was by choice.

As though he had not just studied the marks I had left on the man who brought me here against my will. "Lord Delavar tells me that you are a frequent visitor of our wonderful land."

"I'm not sure I would call it wonderful," I force out through my tense jaw, my gritted teeth. I feel as though I am a pawn in his game, in a game I never wanted to play and whose rules I do not know. I feel hopelessly behind, unsure how to catch up. If only I knew how long it was until sunrise. How long I must muddle through this.

"No? It has been some time since I have been outside the palace walls at night. Perhaps it is different than I remember."

"You might consider keeping your bloodthirsty pets caged up at night." I force my tone to match his—pleasant only on the surface. "It might improve the ambiance."

"Oh, they're harmless, really. Beautiful, don't you think? I was pleased at the shade of blue. Have you seen them up close?"

"I've seen them close enough, and from the experience, I would not call them harmless."

He waves a hand. "We'll have to debate the matter in depth later, when we have more time. For now, I'm afraid we're in a bit of a rush. I was not informed of your presence in a very swift manner, and you were asleep rather longer than we would have preferred."

"Apologies for my lengthened unconsciousness." Still pleasantness on top, but layers of rage beneath it. Layers upon layers. I want to direct it Del's way, but I also refuse to acknowledge his presence. He is beneath my notice.

"Yes, well," Rancore sighs. "Lord Delavar was a trifle heavy-handed in his techniques. I'm certain he feels the utmost contrition."

Out of the corner of my eye, I see Del open his mouth to speak. I also see Rancore tilt his head, just the slightest bit to the left. Del closes his mouth.

"I don't suppose you'll go about this civilly?"

I lift my chin and square my shoulders. I pretend I am in the presence of a different wizard. A diminutive one with a thundering voice and eyes that hold deep secrets. That Thrall would spark fear in me seems childish now, unwarranted. It is nothing compared to what this wizard inspires.

Rancore sighs as though disappointed.

The smile is still in place, still frozen. It is pleasant in curve, pleasant in depth, but so far from pleasant. So far from anything a smile is supposed to represent.

"I wish we had the time to approach this differently, but as I said…time is of the essence."

He knows that sunrise calls me home. He would know from Del, if nothing else. I wonder if it is soon, if it is the cause for his rush.

"Lord Delavar," he says, jerking his head in my direction. Del takes a step toward me. I take a step back. The wall is not far from my back, not far from my sides. There is nowhere to run. My mind considers and discards, considers and discards, and I am no closer to a solution when he takes another step toward me.

He moves slowly, warily. I wonder if his face still stings, if he feels the phantom drag of my fingernails piercing his skin. I slide one foot backward for balance, assuming a fighting stance hidden beneath the folds of my dress. My guards have drilled several self-defense techniques into my head over the years, but right now, I can pull no conscious plans forth. I work on pure instinct, a fierce desire to not let this man touch me again.

My fingernails bite into the palms of my hands.

I'm saved from his next step forward by the arrival of someone else in the small cell.

He steps through the door, just behind Rancore and Del. His quiet entrance escapes their notice, but it can't escape mine. There are so many candles, so much light, that I can see his face quite clearly.

He shaved his beard, I think stupidly to myself. I'd forgotten how lovely his jawline is, how young he looks clean-shaven.

I start to take an uncertain step forward, toward him, at the same time that my instincts scream at me to step back. I end up taking a little stumble of a step to the side, a faltering little side-step out of my equilibrium.

I swallow hard and relocate my voice.

"Carrick?"

CHAPTER FORTY-SIX

Even as I say it, it feels wrong. Everything about this feels wrong: his beardless face, his presence here, the storm brewing in his eyes. Carrick has never looked at me like that. His eyes carry weights, yes, and also worries, but they don't flash hatred like lightning, so quick and sudden that it might almost have been imagined. "Don't say that name," he bites out in my uncle's voice. Then, he seems to straighten himself. He rolls his shoulder, settles his jaw a little more firmly. When he speaks again, it's less of a bite. It's less of anything at all. "Rancore?"

He addresses the wizard, but his eyes stay locked on me. He prowls closer slowly, cautiously. Even his walk is different. He is my uncle, but fitted to my nightmares. Sharper at the edges, as Del is, raging beneath the surface with something barely leashed. The winds of his slate grey eyes carry so many things, too many to name, but amongst them, I think I see pain.

"Your Highness," Rancore says from behind him, and the title rears my head back. Yes. That is my uncle's title, assigned to my uncle's face, my uncle's eyes in color if not in contents. He said not to say the name, but it is his. "I'll gladly explain to you later—"

"Explain now."

It is the command of a king. I believe that if ever there was a time that Rancore's immovable smile would fade, it would be now. Even his deadened eyes cannot hide the flash of consternation spurred by the order.

But he has no choice.

"She was found wandering," he says slowly, ponderously. Each word is chosen with the utmost care. "Lord Delavar recognized her."

"A member of my brother's court, then," the king says in the same tone as before, emptied, stalking forward another slow, languorous step. I retreat until my back is to the wall, once again tucked into the corner. It doesn't make me feel any safer. "And she addresses him so familiarly."

"Your brother?" I shake my head, confused. "Carrick is your brother?"

The question falls out of my mouth before I have a chance to consider whether it's wise. It isn't, of course. He'd just told me not to say that name. He freezes mid-stride, directly in front of me, and turns to face me head-on. He's less than two feet away, just a lean and a reach from me.

"I said not to mention him."

The flash of hatred roars back to life behind his eyes. This time, it lingers for an extra heartbeat before flickering out. It leaves more pain behind than it had last time, a greater storm brewing. I wonder if any of us would survive if he freed it from its tether.

"What's your name?" I whisper.

"Your Highness—" Rancore attempts.

The king lifts one hand, and Rancore's words halt. He studies me for a long moment before dropping into a smart little bow. "King

Siber, at your service."

Of course. The king of this realm, Bran had told me. Their indifferent liege. King Siber of Tenebris.

But there is no of course about it. My uncle's brother? My uncle's *twin*? I can't stop shaking my head.

He smiles a little, his lips twitching upward just as Carrick's do. They form the same shape, the same curve. But there is nothing easy about this smile. It is as haunted as his eyes, as storm-tossed and volatile.

"No?"

I stop shaking my head. He steps closer, and there is nowhere for me to go. The toe of his shoe is on the hem of my gown. I feel its slight pull, but I don't look away from his eyes. I wonder how firmly he has battened down the hatches, how well he contains his storm.

"What's your name?" he purrs. His eyes flick up toward my temple, pounding harder than ever, and I think there's a dip in the rising gale. I think that there is pain, and hatred, but also a flash of pity now. He forgets his question before I can answer it and chooses another. "Who did this to you?"

I swallow hard. "Lord Delavar."

"Hm," he murmurs. "Rancore?"

The wizard seems to always know what the question is, even without Siber voicing it. He steps forward, drawing closer to us. "We believe that she will be able to provide some valuable information for our cause. Lord Delavar has assured me that her position is such that she will know a great deal about the palace's inner workings."

He's dancing carefully around the truth of who I am, to the kingdom and to Carrick in particular. Either Del has not told

Rancore, or Rancore is purposefully keeping it from Siber. Regardless of which, I see a sliver of opportunity. I turn pleading eyes to Siber, to the man who looks so much like the nearest thing I have to a true father.

"My name is Lady Reeve Lennox. King Carrick is my uncle."

Siber backs up as though my words were my hands, as though they pushed him backward. It isn't a simple storm, it's a hurricane. It is untethered, wild. I wonder frantically who it will strike first.

But I say the rest.

"If you are who you say you are—and I can't imagine how you wouldn't be, as you are his spitting image—I suppose that makes you my uncle as well."

"Rancore!" he roars, the sound of a wounded animal.

The wizard is beside him in an instant, a soothing hand lifted but stopping short of resting on Siber's arm. "Your Highness, I assure you, I will get this all straightened out. I will confirm her identity, and I will determine her usefulness. I will deal with it."

Siber is breathing hard. His eyes are wild, locked on me. He looks like he is at war, within himself perhaps, under attack though I have not moved from my corner. I'm torn between wanting to cower and wanting to reach out and place my hand on his arm. To shove aside Rancore's hovering hand and replace it with my own, to calm the raging storm.

Because it isn't all rage, though that is there. It isn't all hatred, though that is there as well. It is pain, and hurt, and waves of them overlapping each other, one after another after another, without ever breaking.

In the end, I neither cower nor reassure. I stand still, I wait, and I plead for the sun to rise. Short of that, I plead that the storm will land in my favor. That he will turn it on them, on Rancore's hovering hand and Del's fist. I plead that it will matter that I am his niece.

"We need to move swiftly, Your Highness. The sun will rise soon, and we'll lose our opportunity." The wizard speaks in a slow, placating tone. The tone of a parent attempting to calm a toddler on the verge of a fit.

Siber closes his eyes for a heartbeat longer than a normal blink, and when he opens them, the storm has abated. The grey of them is even, emptied. I realize then that he will not be the one to save me.

He stares at me for one more long moment before turning away.

"Please," I whisper. "I don't know anything that would help. I just want to go home."

His steps falter, and he turns his head the slightest bit my way, but in the end, he doesn't turn it fully. He doesn't look at me. He speaks in a flat tone to match his drained eyes. The storm has come and gone, and it has left nothing in its wake.

"You'll be all right. Rancore will see to it."

He continues on to the door. I want to follow him, to grab hold of his arm and beg him to stay. Rancore stands between us, though, tangling fear within my throat and halting any steps I might have taken.

Siber only stops once more before passing through the doorway. He studies Del's face before flicking an approving glance my way. "Well done, niece," he says in a quiet voice.

And then he is gone.

CHAPTER FORTY-SEVEN

"Lord Delavar," Rancore spits out as soon as the retreating footsteps in the hallway vanish. "Now."

There is no hesitation in Del's approach this time. He takes three long strides forward and grabs hold of my wrist. My poor, battered wrist. I can't stop a yelp of pain, my whole body flinching. His only concession is to shift his hold an inch higher, to the pale skin just above the black and the blue.

Rancore swirls toward the doorway to lead the way, and I have no choice but to be dragged behind in Del's firm grasp, my feet finding no traction on the stone floor. We leave the cell and round a corner, climbing up one set of stairs before encountering another hallway. As we turn to walk down it, a window comes into view at the far end of the hallway.

The darkness is relenting.

Rancore's curse ricochets back toward us as hope springs high within me.

"Hurry," he bites out, his cloak billowing out behind him as he strides swiftly ahead. Del does his best to keep up, but with the window in sight, I don't go easily.

We pass a long table in the hallway, laden with artful decorations. I frantically grab things as we pass it, throwing vase after vase, picture after picture, at the back of Del's head. He dodges some of them, but some hit him squarely, disorienting him and swaying his steps.

"Delavar!" Rancore's voice is no longer directed ahead of us. He's turned around. "She doesn't need to be conscious for this."

Del instantly rounds on me with retribution and fury in his eyes, along with that eerie brand of glee he'd sported earlier. I grab the last item from the table, a golden paperweight in the shape of a bird—*a falcon*—wings spread, beak open in what I can almost imagine is a song, the killing song. It's the size of my head and nearly too heavy to hold in just one hand. I use it wisely, though. I smash it into his face.

He bellows in pain, releasing his hold on my arm long enough for me to swing back the direction we'd come and start running. I hear shouts from behind me, and I think they're from more voices than just Rancore and Del. I wonder who else fills this palace, if any of them might help me. I doubt it, though. Right now, I think it's up to me to escape.

Me and the sun.

I race up the staircase we had taken to get to this floor, the silk of my dress clenched tightly in one hand to keep it from tangling in my feet. I sprint up and up, listening as first one set of footsteps follows, then a second, a third, a fourth, too many to count. A stampede of footsteps flooding the stairwell behind me.

And then I hear them above me, too.

I make a split-second decision and dart out into the next hallway I reach, careening headlong down it without pausing to inspect it. I hear what sounds like a tussle behind me as multiple bodies try to force their way through the stairwell door at the same time. I hope that it slows them down enough.

I try a door to my left, but I find it locked. I spin back toward the hallway and continue running, pausing only to try another door, this one on the right. Locked, as well. I'm losing precious seconds each time I veer off to rattle a doorknob, so I decide to keep running instead. I am running toward another window, again at the end of the hallway, and this one shows more than just relenting darkness. It shows a hint of orange.

I'm out of breath, gasping for air and fighting to keep the bubbling terror rising at the back of my throat from choking me. But there is orange in the sky. I have minutes, maybe less.

I reach the end of the hallway. There are no branching hallways to the left or to the right, no other doors to try. There is only the window behind me, with armored guards and bloodied, howling Del rushing closer and closer by the second.

My eyes dart left, right, up and down, but they find nothing. Nothing to save me. No tables, no vases, just the candles above and the threadbare carpet below.

They'll be upon me in seconds.

Swinging around, I smash the window with my fist. There is no pain at first, then a blinding pain, then no pain once again as the tinkling of the glass falling to the floor, and the muted sound of it falling outwards, down, overlaps the approaching footsteps. I grab a long shard of glass up off the ground and hold it clasped in both hands in front of me.

And then I wait.

Del shouts at the guards to slow, and they do so instantly. I wonder what power he holds here, over these guards for another kingdom, that they follow his commands.

His face drips blood. It covers the front of his white dress shirt. One eye is swollen nearly shut while the other still sports my scratches from earlier. He looks as though he's been in a fight, and not as the victor.

He uses one hand to swipe at his mouth, where I think I see fewer teeth than he possessed earlier. He looks down at his hand with mild curiosity before grinning up at me.

"Does my face match your dress?"

I clutch the glass so tightly that I feel it slice my hands. I force myself to loosen my hold a little, to not damage my hands so much that I can't use my makeshift weapon if I have to.

There is a soft glow behind me. The sun is rising, lifting, pulling itself up into the sky behind me.

It isn't a precise science, I hear myself say. *Sunrise or a couple minutes before, a couple minutes after.*

Please, I plead inside my head. *Please let me wake up.*

He takes another step closer.

I feel the breeze at my back, leaking in through the hole in the window. I wonder if I should jump. How high up am I?

If I die in a dream, do I die in real life?

Please let me wake up.

Another step, and he's within reach.

He leans forward slowly, tauntingly. He is still grinning through the blood.

"Grab her!" I hear from far behind him. Rancore has finally caught up. Del lunges for me, and I stab forward with both hands.

How many times have I heard the falcons at their feast? The distinctive sound of talons driving through skin, through muscle, through bone? There is no other sound like it. No other sound that haunts me so consistently.

The glass glides through easily. Through skin, through muscle. It halts at bone, but it doesn't matter.

I know that this sound will haunt me.

The gasp he makes, of pain, of surprise, will haunt me.

I feel the tug in my stomach.

Home, it promises. *Home*.

I pull the glass out a half second before I sit up in my bed.

CHAPTER FORTY-EIGHT

My face is wet.

Had I been crying in my dreams?

I'm having trouble stopping.

"My lady, are you all right?"

Guin is still uncertain, still undoubtedly angry with me, but she perches at the edge of my bed with a furrowed brow and leans toward me with concern in her eyes.

I want to fling myself into her arms, but instead, I use the edge of my comforter to wipe my face dry.

I slide out of bed in my red gown and run over to my dressing room.

"Guin, can you please request an audience with King Carrick and Thrall? It's urgent."

"King Carrick and…my lady, is everything all right?"

"No. No, it isn't. Please, Guin, hurry."

She resonates confusion, but she does as I ask, leaning out into the hallway to send Demes to the task. I am grateful to hear her stress the urgency. A second later, she's at my back, working on the buttons.

"My lady, you're scaring me. Can you tell me what it is?"

"I can't, not yet. I just…oh, please hurry, Guin. Rip the gown if you must."

She doesn't end up ripping me from my gown, but her fingers fly down the buttons at impressive speed. She has me stripped to my chemise and climbing into a lilac day gown within minutes.

"Thank you," I say over my shoulder as I start toward the door.

"My lady…"

I pause in the act of turning the handle just long enough to offer her what I hope is a reassuring smile. "It'll be all right, Guin. Promise."

It's a promise I have no business making.

～＊～

Jax, Tiven, and Percius are at full alert when I step out into the hallway. Demes hasn't returned yet, so I pace three steps forward, swing around to pace three steps back. When Demes still hasn't returned, I turn abruptly to the left and throw myself into Jax's arms.

"Hey now," he says, not faltering even a step back from my sudden attack. His gruff voice so near to my ear is a comfort, but it does not stop me from shaking. "What is it, my lady?"

"Stay close today, Jax? Tiv, Perc? Please?"

"Of course we will," I hear Tiven say from behind me. The concern in his voice is clear.

I push away from Jax and reach my trembling hand up to my hair, shoving it out of my face. I hadn't allowed Guin the time to fashion it properly, so it falls free and wild around my face and shoulders.

"What is it?" Jax asks again. His hand is on the hilt of his sword as though to protect me from something, anything.

His hand on his sword, the concern in Tiv's voice, the tilt and furrow of Perc's head, combine to unleash fresh tears. It flusters the three of them instantly.

"My lady—" Perc starts, reaching a hand out toward me.

"What is it?" Jax asks with more strength, his entire body tensed.

"Reeve," Tiven says. He has never slipped. Not once, in all of the years I have known him, has he dropped the title from my name. All three of our heads swing toward him, but he doesn't seem to notice. His eyes are still on me, his forehead covered in creases.

"His Highness and the wizard Thrall will see you in the king's study now," Demes' voice comes from behind me.

My breaths come as pants as the five of us practically sprint through the palace. My mind is still a wreck, a battered door and a shard of glass clenched tightly. The tears, at least, have dried. By the time we reach Carrick's study, I am halfway to composed.

My guards seem of a mind to follow me inside, and I'm of a mind to let them, but I regretfully tell them to wait outside.

"I'll be safe inside," I promise when Jax, Perc, and Tiv, at least, open their mouths to argue. Dem knows that something is amiss, sees it clearly on the faces of his comrades, but he waits readily enough. He tugs Perc back into position outside the door, and by some force of will, Tiv stops Jax.

I don't knock. I open the door silently, and then I shut it behind me.

Carrick is standing behind his desk, Thrall to the side of it. They're both braced, expectant.

I have a hard time tearing my gaze from my uncle. I take in the beard, the strong slope of his shoulders, the neat trim of his hair, but more than any of that, I take in his eyes.

They're not a storm. They're not a hurricane. I'm not worried that they'll destroy everyone in their path.

"Reeve, what is it?" He asks quietly, and that too is different. His tone doesn't rage or fall flat. It feels safe. It reminds me that even when I think the tears have dried up, more could easily be summoned.

"Carrick…" My voice cracks. I clear my throat as he pushes away from his desk and walks around it to come to me. He touches my chin with a gentle hand, tilts it up lightly.

"What is it?"

It's time to tell it.

"I was attacked last night, in my dreams. I was attacked by Lord Delavar."

His hand drops away. His whole face drops, slackens, loses its concern. It loses its expression entirely. He opens and closes his mouth as though at a loss for words, but Thrall has no such loss.

"You are visible there?" His voice is a lash. I flinch against it.

"Yes," I say quietly, stepping around Carrick to face him. My uncle still stands frozen in place. "As of my eighteenth birthday, I am visible."

"I asked you if you were visible," he booms. His hands rest on the head of his cane, and even from here, I can see that his knuckles are white. "I said that you were safe as long as you could not be seen. And you *lied?*"

Carrick swings around. "You knew she dreamt herself there?"

I turn to him. "You know that it's possible?"

The three of us stand facing one another, our unanswered questions floating in the air between us, tension-laced and fraught.

Carrick breaks the silence first. He walks slowly, heavily back to his desk. He sinks into his chair and puts both hands on top of his head for a second before placing them on the desk before him.

"Reeve. Have a seat. It seems we have much to discuss."

I do as he orders, sinking into my own chair as deeply as he had.

"We do, but first...Lord Delavar—"

He leans back in his chair to yank a bell pull. Instantly, the door swings open to admit a footman.

"Send a contingent of guards to the residence of Lord Delavar. Have him brought here and locked up until I can speak with him."

"Yes, Your Highness."

The door closes silently again, and I feel a little of the tension leak from my body.

"Now tell me. All of it."

He sounds more king than uncle now. Orders, not requests. I am ready, though, all the more so now that Del is about to be detained.

"I have dreamt the same place every night of my life, but until I turned eighteen, I was invisible there. Once I discovered that I could be seen, I found a safe place to hide at night. I met people there. I started to learn about the place, called Tenebris, and the lives of the people there. I was on my way there last night, to the safe house, when Lord Delavar accosted me and took me to the palace."

"You were at the palace?" Carrick asks, barely above a whisper. He lost all the color in his face when I began to speak, and now, in that nearly-whispered question, he is neither uncle nor king. He is something else, something different. Something scared.

"I was held by the wizard Rancore. They knew that I would be gone with the sunrise, so they were in a rush to get me somewhere. I don't know what they wanted to do with me, but they mentioned wanting information. They thought I might be of some use."

"Rancore," Thrall spits from behind the desk.

It is his only contribution. I look back at Carrick. His eyes are locked on me, almost desperate.

"Was there anyone else?"

I know then that he knows. He *knows*.

"Yes," I say slowly. "Yes, I met their king. I met King Siber."

I watch his throat move as he swallows. His next question fully commits to a whisper.

"How was he?"

CHAPTER FORTY-NINE

My head jerks backward, thudding into the back of the chair. I want to ask half a million questions, all colliding with each other for priority, but he looks like a shadow, my uncle, the king. He looks like a boy asking after his brother.

And so instead of asking questions, I answer.

"He seems…lost. He seems to carry a lot of pain, and a lot of hatred. He…he knew your name."

Carrick closes his eyes. "Yes. Yes, he'd know my name well."

"How is he your brother?" I ask, my questions unwilling to hold. "How is it possible? What *is* that place I dream?"

Carrick's eyes are still squeezed shut, and I wonder if he's fully here anymore. Thrall answers, instead.

"You dream Tenebris. Twenty-seven years ago, Rancore was banished. King Draegen took an interest in his particular brand of magic, in the power behind it, but then as it began shifting nearer and nearer to darkness, to black magic, he decided there was no room for it in this kingdom. He rededicated Acarsaid to the magic I practice, and Rancore was banished.

"He raged. He refused. He was deeply embroiled in the dark arts by then, and he used it to take out many of the king's men before he could be contained. The darkness comes at a price. It costs much, and he depleted his strength quickly. He was weakened, and so he faded off into the background, his threat seemingly neutralized, when really what he was doing was honing his skills and gathering his strength. What he did next..."

Thrall trails off, his eyes wandering past me, over my shoulder, into the past. "I should have anticipated. I should have seen in him that he would not go quietly."

I feel as though I'm with him in the past, watching it all play out. Carrick's eyes are still shut.

"He took the poor quarter. He threw up a wall, one that couldn't be breached, taking a piece of Acarsaid with him. A portion of our people. That wasn't all he took, though." At this, Thrall's eyes return from the past and find Carrick. Carrick opens his and turns to meet the wizard's gaze. Whatever they exchange, I don't exist through it. They are in a world unto their own. "He took the king's son. The younger of the twins. He took Siber."

I see the shudder run through Carrick's body. He looks down at his desk.

"He was fascinated with Rancore," my uncle says quietly. "Six years old and mesmerized by him, by his power, by his stature. He'd follow at his heels, peppering him with questions. Nobody saw the harm in it at first, not until the dark magic came out. The contact was severed then, but nobody took the time to explain, to either of us. We were not made to understand that he was evil. When my father found out that Siber had been taken..."

There is a pause, mid-sentence. It is not silent, though. It screams. It bellows. I can hear in it what will come next.

"He blamed himself the most. He blamed himself for allowing Siber to be so trusting. For not breaking him of it."

I try to imagine the man I met last night as a six-year-old boy. It isn't difficult.

"You couldn't break the wall and get him back?" I turn desperately to Thrall, even though, of course, I know the outcome. I know they did not get him back. "You're far older, far more powerful, I'd imagine. You must have been able to do *something*."

"My magic is pure," Thrall snaps. "It splinters off the darkness of that wall, shies away from it. He cannot be reached behind it."

"But how can I—"

"There's more to the story, Reeve," Carrick says gently. I wonder at the gentling of his tone. There had been bleakness there, and no small amount of pain, but now it has gentled. My stomach tenses, rattles a little inside of me. I suddenly don't want to hear what comes next.

"Aurelia," Thrall says. His voice is far from its normal booming. It's almost...soft. He has gentled to this part of the story, and that scares me even more. It especially scares me when combined with my mother's name. "Aurelia was eleven years old, and she would not let it go."

"She loved Siber most," Carrick says, though he says it fondly, not bitterly. "He was trouble, pure and simple, dragging me into scrape after scrape, but Aurelia would always swoop in and defend him fiercely against any threat of punishment. My parents used to call her his little mother."

My mother, I think dismally. My protective, kind mother.

"She would not leave me be," Thrall continues. "She was in my rooms every day, demanding I break the wall. Her mother grieved, and her father raged, but Aurelia did neither. She came every day and insisted I do something. She made it into a project of mine, something I prodded at obsessively. Eventually, over the course of many years, I managed to make a window of sorts. Not a hole, not fully, but a window. Your mother could pass through the wall, but only in her sleep, and never visible to the occupants."

Like me. My mother had wandered those same streets, night after night, like me.

"It made her miserable." Carrick pushes restlessly out of his chair and prowls to the window, his hands clasped tightly behind his back. "She'd come and tell me about the lies Rancore fed the people, and even worse, the lies he fed Siber. He told Siber that we hadn't wanted him anymore. That he was nothing but a spare, and that I was the only one of any value to our family. Aurelia would wake up sobbing, reaching out as though to touch him."

"And so she pushed me harder," Thrall murmurs, watching Carrick lean stiffly against the window frame. "She would not let up. She'd wake up each morning from watching Siber fall more and more into disillusionment, into the certainty that he had been unloved. And some years later, the year before King Draegen passed and Carrick assumed the throne…"

"You made her visible there," Carrick finishes. The words themselves are accusation, but the tone is not. The tone is empty. "And she never woke up."

The silence in the room is louder than the shrieks of Rancore's pets. I feel it building against my ears, pounding against my ribcage. Some years later, the year before King Draegen passed, the year before Carrick assumed the throne. The year I turned four.

She never woke up.

There are tears streaming down my cheeks, unchecked. Carrick stares out the window, but the sunlight reflects off of his, still checked, pooling in his eyes. He had lost his brother, then his mother to her subsequent grief. His sister, then his father. He had lost everything.

I stand on shaky legs and walk over to the window to stand beside him. I lean into the warmth of his body, the steadiness of the uncle who has been more father to me, more anything to me than anyone else in my family, and he lowers his arm around my shoulders.

"I'm sorry," he says quietly, for my ears only. For a second, we're alone in the room, alone in the world. Alone in our grief. "I'm sorry that I didn't stop her."

"She loved her brother," I whisper through the building, stretching, wailing lump in my throat. "She loved him enough that I doubt anyone could have stopped her."

She had made it her life's mission to reach her brother and to remind him that he *had* been loved, that she had loved him, that he was missed. I can't resent her for it, though I'm not sure I've ever missed her more than I do in this moment.

"They're planning a war," I say, lifting my voice to reach Thrall's ears, as well. I pull away from Carrick, and he turns from the window. "I think Lord Delavar must be helping them plan it."

"The fact that he was there…I wonder if Rancore has a hole of his own into our world. I threw a wall of my own magic into place, so that people can pass through from this side but not from his, but I wonder if he's found a way."

"We'll find out when we question Delavar," Carrick answers. He has steel back in his tone, the kingdom back in mind. I still see in him my uncle, but I see less of the brother. Less of the boy who lost his whole family.

"What will I do tonight?" I ask. "Rancore might come after me."

The two men exchange a look. Carrick imparts his steel on the wizard, inserts a command in his stare.

"I'll protect you," Thrall says finally. "I will make sure that you cannot be touched."

"How?" I ask.

But he turns away as though my question is of no consequence to him. As though he's finished with me.

"You needn't worry, Reeve," Carrick says quietly. "Nobody will be able to hurt you again." He strides back to his desk purposefully, sitting down and gesturing Thrall to the other side. "We'll inform you when we learn more from Delavar."

Thus dismissed, I retreat back into the hallway. My guards surround me instantly, worry still heavily painted upon their faces. I want to smile reassuringly at them, but my mind is too weighted by everything I have learned.

I start down the hallway with one destination in mind.

I lead them to a small staircase, set way in the back. It leads to only one door.

I startle the nurse again, and I apologize again for my lack of notice. Once she leaves, I lower myself heavily to her vacated chair.

"Hi, Mama."

CHAPTER FIFTY

I tuck my hand under hers and feel the steady beat of her pulse against my skin. I lower my forehead all the way until it rests on top of her hand.

I breathe in the smell of her. She still smells of the perfume I remember so well, the light, flowery scent that floats through my mind whenever I think of her. I allow myself to pull forth the old familiar melody she used to hum as she got ready for a ball, or as she lay stretched upon the hilltop while Florien and I ran circles around her. I let it play through my head uninterrupted by screeches, unmarred by screams.

There are no windows in this room, nothing to indicate the passage of time. I don't even feel it pass. I feel nothing but her hand against my cheek, my hand under hers, the melody in my head and her perfume in my nostrils.

The footman finds me there eventually, a note in his hand. It's written in my uncle's scrawl, hasty and distinctive.

Lord Delavar did not wake this morning. Doctors believe him to be in a coma. Guards stationed in his bedroom in case this condition changes. You needn't fear him.

I inhale slowly, but this time, my mother's perfume is not all I smell. I smell blood. I smell *his* blood, pouring down his face, pouring down my hand where I stab the glass through his stomach.

I glance down at my mother and realize.

I realize what happens when you die in your dreams.

I wonder if my mother even spoke with Siber. I wonder if she made it to the palace, through the gates, past the stone doors, and somehow managed to find him.

Or if the falcons got her before she even had a chance.

I crumple the note and let it fall to the ground, returning my cheek to her hand. I close my eyes and try to remember the notes of the song, but they won't come to me again. All there is, is the sound of talons tearing through skin. The sound of glass tearing through his stomach.

By the time I leave my mother's room, the sun has fully set. My guards allow for my silence as we retreat back to my room, not pushing it or me. Guin also sees something in my face that holds her questions. She helps me into my nightgown without a word, only a whispered goodnight before she lets herself out.

I lie in my bed and stare at the ceiling, trying to stop myself from picturing my mother running through the streets of Tenebris. Trying not to think of what her screams would sound like. Trying not to think of how easily the talons would separate her skin from her bones.

I don't have the energy to even try to build a door to store the images behind. When I can't fight them off, I let them play through, over and over again, until they've spent themselves.

Until they finally give themselves over to a blue-eyed boy made of star-shine and steadiness. Bran. Thrall had promised me protection tonight, and I trust him to see it through. If he is powerful enough to prod holes in the wall, he is powerful enough to send something through to shield me from Rancore.

I need not fear Del anymore, at least.

My thoughts threaten to stray to a shard of glass, to the feel of cascading blood, but when I close my eyes, I will be with Bran. I will be able to make sure he's okay—*he must be okay*—and I will tell him everything I've learned. Of the links between our worlds.

I focus on Bran.

I let my eyes close.

CHAPTER FIFTY-ONE

I wake up in the same place I always do, but instead of dread, I feel anticipation. My mind chants *if*, but I am sure. I am certain. He is alive, and I am going to him.

He's waiting for me.

I'm halfway to the shadows when I see him standing there, tucked deep into the murky darkness, only his shining eyes giving his presence away. I'm tempted to fling myself wholly at him, around him, into him, but he holds his midsection carefully. I skid to a halt a foot away from him, beaming a smile full of relief up at his dear face.

He keeps staring over my shoulder.

My smile falters. I look back to see what he sees, and I realize that there was a hanging today. The body is not yet picked over, which means the falcons will be here soon. There is worry all over Bran's face.

I reach out to touch him lightly on the arm, where I'm sure it won't hurt him.

"Let's go, before they get here," I whisper.

He doesn't look at me. His eyes stay locked on the square just beyond me.

"Bran," I say a little more fiercely. "Come on."

He still doesn't move. He still doesn't look at me.

Unease begins to spread inside of me. I step closer to him, lifting onto my tiptoes so that my eyes are level with his.

He continues staring straight ahead.

Not at me.

Through me.

"Bran," I say a little more loudly. I lift my hand to his cheek. *"Bran."*

His eyes stay locked on the city square.

Where I arrive every night.

I hear the first flap of razored wings. It's joined by a second, a third.

They're coming, they're coming, they're here.

I lower my hand to his chest. I place my other one there as well and use them both to push. He still doesn't falter.

I push with all of my might, and I say his name again. Again. Again.

I scream it.

But he cannot see me.

He cannot hear me.

I am invisible in this world.

To be continued in

DREAM
WITHIN A
DREAM

Acknowledgements

It is a surreal feeling to even have the opportunity to write these, and I have been so worried about doing them justice. About thanking everyone who played a role in this book being in your hands right now. There are so many!

Nothing to do but begin, so…deep breath, here we go.

This book would not exist without my sister Alexandra. We stood in her kitchen one cold February evening in 2014, and she told me about a dream she had about a girl who falls in love with a boy she meets in her dreams. And as you now know, if you're reading this after having read the book, that is the idea that lies at the very heart of *All That We See or Seem*. She was also the first to read this story, in all of its roughest forms, my official namer of characters, Arden's biggest fan.

My other four beta readers—Jenna for being the world's most wonderful writing partner and unofficial life coach, as well as the founding member of Team Brave; Angela for containing Reeve's dramatics and never giving me anything but her honest opinion; Natalie for her English teacher expertise and always asking the best questions for me to deep-dive into my characters; Megan for circling the word "shove" on far too many pages and highlighting her favorite lines. All of them, each one of them, for their endless support and encouragement.

My dad, for taking me to the library every weekend growing up. My love of reading is all thanks to him.

My mom, for bragging about my book to her friends.

Madcap Retreats, which gets the majority of the credit for why I believed this dream of mine could become a reality. All of the wonderful authors who were a part of it, but in particular: Maggie Stiefvater, who has always been my biggest writing inspiration and whose wisdom I will never tire of absorbing. Court Stevens, whose enthusiasm and kindness carried us all through five days of intense writing exercises. Natalie Parker, who organized the retreat and devoted so much of herself to helping a group of aspiring authors. Tessa Gratton, whose world-building lessons forever changed how I write books. All of the writing friends I made there—I never knew how much I needed writing friends until I had them, and now I can't imagine going through this journey without them.

Janeen Ippolito, Sophia Heotzler, and everyone else at UUP, who believed in this story and guided me through every step of transforming my words from a Microsoft Word document into a real and true book.

Jenny at Seedlings Design Studio for designing that beautiful cover. I could not have asked for a better face for my words.

Mia for laying on my lap for most of the writing of this book, Finn and Penny for insisting on walks at just the right moments, when I was stuck and needed a break from my laptop screen, and Rogue for...something, I'm sure.

My nephews, Evan, Declan, Chase, and Bram, for being constant sources of joy and laughter in my life and for letting me sing songs to them all the time.

Keith, for helping me figure out the rules of invisibility and searching for logic where I often forgot to put it.

Kim, for always, always listening, and, when I told her I was going on the retreat, telling me, "As my father-in-law always says, we all have fantasies, it's whether or not you make yours come true. Go make yours come true."

Everyone who has been excited about this book. It has positively *fueled* me. Coworkers in my numbers world, old friends from grade school, relatives in Germany, people here and there and everywhere who have supported me in my pursuit of this dream. I can never sufficiently describe how gratifying it has been.

And, last but very not least, you. If you are holding this book in your hands, you are playing a part in making my dreams come true. Thank *you*.

About the Author

Kristina Mahr devotes her days to numbers and her nights to words. She works full-time as an accountant in the suburbs of Chicago, where she lives with her two dogs and two cats, but her true passion is writing. In her spare time, she enjoys spending time with her family and friends, reading, and waking up at the crack of dawn every weekend to watch the Premier League.

OTHER BOOKS AVAILABLE THROUGH
UNCOMMON UNIVERSES PRESS

Halayda
by **Sarah Delena White**
A mortal alchemist. A faerie king. A bond that transcends death.

Coiled
by **H.L. Burke**
In the vein of Eros and Psyche, two cursed souls find each other on a forsaken isle and together must shed the darkness inflicted upon them—or else live as monsters forever.

Lawless
by Janeen Ippolito
A dragon felon, a forsaken prince, and a jaded airship captain walk into a city—and everything explodes.

Priceless
By Janeen Ippolito
A little ambition can turn into a lot of trouble—even for the city's wiliest double agent.

To keep up-to-date with our blog and newest releases, find us online.

UNCOMMONUNIVERSES.COM |

CPSIA information can be obtained
at www.ICGtesting.com
Printed in the USA
BVHW082025130120
569427BV00006BA/50/P